TIMELESS
DESIRE

GWYN
CREADY

sourcebooks
casablanca

Published by Sourcebooks Casablanca, an imprint of Sourcebooks,
Inc.
P.O. Box 4410, Naperville, Illinois 60567-4410
(630) 961-3900
Fax: (630) 961-2168
www.sourcebooks.com

Originally published in 2012 in the United States of America by
Astor + Blue Editions LLC.

Printed and bound in the United States of America.
RRD 10 9 8 7 6 5 4 3 2 1

This is for the devilish, determined, and deeply vexing boy who, as if by some otherworldly magic, grew into one of the most hardworking, steadfast, and honorable men I know. Wyatt, I couldn't be prouder.

One

"I THINK LIBRARIANS ARE THE GLUE THAT HELPS STICK a community together," Marie said, clasping a hand over her heart. "We're on the battle lines of community involvement."

"Really? That's what you think?" Panna gave her fellow librarian an amused look and handed the young patron standing before them his copy of *Animal Farm: The Graphic Novel*, now gum free. "Well, I don't know about battle lines, but sticky certainly seems to be a part of it."

Panna's eyes went automatically to the always dashing Colonel John Bridgewater, Viscount Adderly, or at least a marble facsimile of him, standing heroically astride the statue base, sword at his side, ready to charge into the Battle of Ramillies. It did seem rather odd to have a larger-than-life statue of an eighteenth-century British war hero in a small-town library in western Pennsylvania. One might expect Andrew Carnegie or, more likely, Mike Ditka or Honus Wagner, both of whom had been born in Carnegie and were more in keeping with Pittsburgh's sports-loving, blue-collar sensibilities. But one of Bridgewater's descendants had been a huge donor at the library's founding a hundred years earlier, and the statue had been his stipulation. Bridgewater, with chiseled profile, shoulder-length waves, and closely fitting breeks, had for Panna always called to mind a slightly more battle-tested d'Artagnan, that handsome, brave hero of Alexandre Dumas's *The Three Musketeers*, one of her favorite books. But there was something so magically lifelike about the man—as if he might jump off his pedestal at any moment and pull her roughly into his arms, damning the eyes of anyone who might object to a good-bye kiss in the middle of the periodical section. Suffice it to say, Bridgewater had loomed large over Panna's daydreams as well as her seat at the circulation desk, especially in the last two years.

Marie, who had caught the direction of her coworker's gaze, said, "Have you ever noticed that from just the right angle, it looks like he's carrying a stack of interlibrary loan requests in his pants?"

"*Marie!*"

"Oh, right. Tell me that isn't why you always pick this seat."

Marie was a petite brunette in the second year of a master's program in library science who still got misty-eyed at the idea of municipal services. Panna, on the other hand, had been working the stacks for eleven years—six as head librarian—and was able to boil her learning about librarianship into two golden rules:

First, in a world where your job is interacting with the public, you get back what you give. And second, avoid Friday-night shifts at all costs.

With a start, she looked around. "Oh boy. I don't see Mr. Albert anymore."

"Yikes!" Marie flipped up the counter on the circulation desk and tore off.

Mr. Albert read the *Pittsburgh Post-Gazette*, the *New York Times*, and the *Washington Post* at the library every day. He also liked to take pictures of women's feet.

Panna turned to the next patron in line, a lovely regular in her late seventies named Mrs. Olinsky, who'd been trying for months to set up Panna with her son, George.

Panna gave the older woman an inquisitive frown. "You don't seem to have any books to check out."

"My son's outside in his Mercedes and wonders if you could come out to give him a recommendation on a book. It's a new Mercedes."

"Mrs. Olinsky, we've talked about this before."

Mrs. Olinsky's shoulders sagged. "I know, I know. No dating yet. But don't wait too long. A nice young woman like you shouldn't be alone."

No, she probably shouldn't. Thirty-four was still young. But since Charlie's agonizing death two years earlier, she felt about as old as Mrs. Olinsky. Panna's heart had gone into a hibernation from which it felt like it would never awake. The world of dating seemed about as far away as the Battle of Ramillies and about as much fun, which was why she wasn't looking forward to the blind date Marie had set up for her that night.

Marie bounded up to the large, U-shaped circulation desk, waving a camera. "Found him. I told him we'd put this away until he was on his way out."

Mrs. Olinsky pointed to the window. "Oh, look! There's George now. Isn't he handsome?"

Panna gave her a firm look. "If he *really* needs a recommendation, you can tell him I'll be out in a minute."

Mrs. Olinsky cast her eyes downward. "I guess he'll be all right on his own."

When Mrs. Olinsky disappeared, Marie grinned. "Still working on you, isn't she?"

"Oh yes. But so far not succeeding."

"She doesn't have the determination I do. To scale the Panna Kennedy castle wall, one needs tenacity, innovation, and a carefully crafted—oh, Panna, what is it?"

A tear had welled in Panna's eye, and she swiped at it in irritation. "It's the dinner tonight. I just…I know I should do it. I *know* I should. And I will. It's just I feel like it's going to be awful and hard…and wrong. I'm sorry."

Marie put her arm around Panna's shoulders and squeezed. "Hey, it's fajitas with me and Kyle and Kyle's cousin, Steve, not forty-five minutes at the Quality Inn."

Panna snorted through her sadness. "I know. And I *want* to do it. I swear."

"Oh, yeah, I can tell." Marie gave her a gentle smile. "Charlie was a pretty great guy, huh?"

"The best." Their life had been perfect: They worked at jobs that made them happy, and read and cooked and traveled when they could afford it. They'd even been trying to conceive before his diagnosis. Her hand went to her stomach unconsciously, feeling the emptiness there. So many dreams she'd said good-bye to...

Widowhood sucked. There was no other word for it. During the first year, Panna felt like she'd been laid out on a rack and gutted. She had gone through the motions of living but could barely remember any of it. That time stood as a wrenching blur in her head that she hoped would never reemerge with any clarity.

In the last year, however, she'd begun to find some degree of normalcy, and she clung to her solitary routine like a nautilus to its shell, ready to withdraw into her nacreous walls at a moment's notice.

But what gnawed at her most, even more than the emptiness in her chest, were that words like "routine," "solitary," and "withdraw," which had never applied to the old Panna, were now part of her world. She and Charlie had always been risk takers—climbing rocks, trekking through Nepal, even skydiving on their honeymoon. But losing Charlie had made her lose her nerve, and she hated how she'd changed.

Panna's cell phone began to buzz. It was Jerry Sussman, the attorney for the town. She walked away from the desk. "Hey, Jerry. What's up?"

"Sorry to call so late. I just got word from my contact in the state budget office. Nineteen percent reduction in funding."

"*What?*" She hurried into the soaring entry hall and slouched against one of the curving stairways that bookended the space. "That's...that's twice what we were thinking for a worst-case scenario."

"It's bad."

"*Nineteen percent*. There are only six librarians here.

That means we cut evening hours and at least one position. Damn it." She kicked the ancient, little half-sized door on the storage room under the stairs and the knob rattled. This place was like a home to her, and the people who worked here were like family—especially now. She didn't know how she'd have survived without them. "Thanks, Jerry. I appreciate the heads-up."

"Sorry it wasn't better news."

She said good-bye and hung up, shaking with the rush of emotion. This place was a landmark, she thought, gazing at the tiled Greek key design in the floor, a memorial to a time when people revered places like libraries. She wiped a speck of dirt off the intricate wrought-iron banister with the elbow of her sweater.

She wondered if they'd soon be returning to the time before Andrew Carnegie had taught America that libraries were worth investing in, back when people had to pay subscriptions to belong to a library and only the well-to-do could afford to have access to them.

Oh, John Bridgewater, why can't you be at the forefront of this battle? We could use a little of your mighty sword. Or at the very least, why can't your descendant be around today to astonish us with his amazing generosity?

She stopped. His generosity… According to the town's history, the viscount's descendant had written a large check to the library's building fund back at the turn of the century. He'd also donated a bunch of books, most of which had either been lost to old age or sold. But he'd also donated some *objets d'art*—at least, that's what she thought the agreement said. She'd only looked at it once, and then not very carefully.

One donation, she knew, was a piece of pewter tableware called a nef that sat on the mantelpiece over the library's hearth, just under the dour portrait of Andrew Carnegie. The nef had been fashioned to resemble a three-masted sailing ship, with a conch shell as the ship's body and decks that held the salt, pepper, and whatever other spices people in the eighteenth century used to season their food. It was extraordinarily gaudy and preternaturally ugly, and it frequently caused young children to laugh out loud just at the sight of it. But what—and where— were the other *objets*?

She'd never seen them. Maybe they'd been sold along with the books that had been donated. The problem was that Panna had never had any dealing with the Bridgewater stuff, though she remembered Barb, the head librarian before her, making occasional reference to it. The agreement had been negotiated by Clementina Martindale, the first librarian in the place when it opened in 1901. Panna also remembered there'd been a rumor that Clementina had had a torrid affair with Bridgewater's wealthy descendent, and inasmuch as Panna felt that the moral rectitude of any one librarian reflected on all of them, she'd made it a point to push that rumor out of her head.

Panna combed her brain for anything else she could recall Barb telling her.

Last donated books sold or thrown away in the sixties. The statue repaired when a workman carrying a two-by-four on his shoulder accidentally damaged it. Newspaper clippings and other stuff related to the Bridgewater gift stowed safely in the storage room.

Stowed in the storage room?

Panna took a mental walk through the library, from the Grand Army of the Republic meeting room upstairs, through the director's office, around the stacks on the main floor, and even into the occasionally flooded basement. There was no nook or cranny she hadn't thoroughly examined during her tenure here. And "stowed" was such an unusual word. Not "stored." Barb had definitely said "stowed," which to Panna implied lowness, the sort of place where reaching it would require bending.

Her eyes lit on the half door under the stairs. It was triangular in shape and a little under five feet tall, with an ancient glass knob. She'd never opened the door. Had never even seen it open. In fact, the door had been painted so many times that there wasn't even a line separating it visually from the frame anymore.

Panna dug in her pocket and found her ring of keys. There were only three really old keys left. The rest of the locks had been replaced. She tried the first. No luck. The second wouldn't even go in. The third one, however, fit perfectly. She turned it, and the dead bolt slid open with a satisfying click.

She grabbed the knob and tugged, but the door was so tight, it wouldn't open. She pulled harder, anchoring her feet. Knowing her luck, the door would fly open and she'd be flung across the entry hall. Finally, she put her foot on the frame and jerked. The door came open and she managed to keep from falling. She crouched and looked. The space inside was pitch-black. Not just dark, but absolute nothingness—full light until the edge of the threshold, then a black plane that might have been a wall had she not known no wall was there. The hairs on her neck stood on end. Something bumped the door she held, and she fell forward into the space before catching her balance and backing out.

"I'm so sorry," said the patron, turning around. "I wasn't expecting that door to be open."

Panna could barely spare the man a response. What she had seen in that brief instant amazed her. It was the altar of a beautiful chapel with a vaulted ceiling and a carved wood altarpiece bathed in sunlight—a room far too large to fit in the space under the stairs.

She tried to make sense of it. How could a chapel occupy a space no larger than a powder room? How could a well-lit room be invisible through a pane of blackness?

No explanation came to her. None was possible.

She touched her forehead, wondering if the ibuprofen she'd taken earlier had been spiked. She'd never heard of the drug causing hallucinations, but *something* had to be making it happen.

Another patron walked by, and Panna looked at him as if to say, "Can you believe what you and I are seeing?" But the man only nodded pleasantly and kept walking. It was as if all the rules that applied in the physical world had been rewritten, and she was the only one who could see it.

Panna put her hand into the space again cautiously, watching it disappear through the plane of black, and experienced a rush of adrenaline she hadn't felt in a long time. She and Charlie used to spelunk. The darker the passageway, the more excited they'd gotten. She knew she should be scared and slam the door and report this to someone, though she had no idea what she'd say. But she also knew something in her was keeping her from fleeing. She closed the door and considered.

Librarians were born curious. If they weren't, they didn't make it in this field. Part of her was freaked out, no question. But another part—a more primitive part—was deeply interested. Her unconscious mind knew what she was going to do even if her conscious mind hadn't quite caught up. Tingles were running up and down her spine.

The hall had emptied, and she reopened the door. The void was blacker than anything she'd seen, blacker than black velvet. Teetering on the edge of a thrilling fear, she thrust her entire arm into the darkness.

Gone from sight. Just like that. Her upper arm looked like the Venus de Milo's where the demarcation between visible and invisible lay.

She bent and took a cautious step into the void.

The minute her eyes entered, she gasped. The chapel *was* beautiful. To the right of the altar stood a tomb, made entirely of marble, with the form of a prone woman holding lilies of the valley carved into the lid. Sconces and a tapestry hung on the wall behind the tomb.

Panna looked down and nearly jumped. On her feet were a pair of embroidered mules, and the blue silk of her summer sundress had descended into a floor-length wave of cerulean and lace. The discovery so surprised her that she jerked out of the chapel and back into the library's entry, slamming the door. The gown had reverted into the sundress.

For a long moment, Panna stood absolutely still, trying to process what she'd just witnessed. An empty chapel...just over the threshold of a long-forgotten storage closet in Carnegie, Pennsylvania.

Something about the scene niggled at her super-revved brain. Then it struck her. The sconces on the wall hadn't been sconces at all—at least, not as she knew them. They'd been unlit torches. There'd been no electricity. Long gowns and no electricity.

"Hey, Panna." Henry, one of the children's librarians, gave her a wave as he strode past.

"Hey."

She could lock the closet door and throw away the key. It would all be over as easy as that. That would be the responsible thing to do. Not to mention the smart thing.

But Panna had had enough of being smart and responsible since Charlie's death. She didn't want to feel smart. She wanted to feel alive.

She slipped back inside the door frame, pausing exactly at the center, moving back and forth between the long-gown world of the chapel and the sundress world of the Carnegie Library. She felt the same heart-fluttering giddiness she'd felt before leaping out of that plane.

"Let's do it, Charlie," she whispered.

Two

PANNA EMERGED IN THE CHAPEL, SKIRTS RUSTLING. THE chapel was tiny, with room for only a handful of people, and a door in the middle of the nave seemed to open into a carpeted hallway.

Her nerve endings quivered as she walked. The warm, pleasant air of the evening felt like a dream. Even the dust motes floating lazily in the rays of the setting sun seemed magical.

The burnished floors gleamed under her feet, and the lush green upholstery on the pews was embroidered with a large *B* in gold thread. No shy and retiring chapel owner here. No devotee of sacrifice, either.

She caught a glimpse of her reflection in a polished silver urn that stood next to the tomb. The dress, a jacquard the color of an afternoon sky, fell in gorgeous, soft ripples, and when she looked down, she could see the exceedingly low-cut neckline was trimmed in jet. She wasn't exactly sure what was under the dress, but she knew it wasn't enough, for her breasts felt unbound, and despite the flashes of muslin slip beneath the silk and the hose knotted tightly at her thighs, the evening air moved freely over her hips and belly as she walked.

Several tall candleholders, the height of a man, were arranged on the floor around the room, but only the candle in one—the one near the tomb—showed any sign of use.

She reached for the pencils she wore in her hair like she always did when she was thinking. Her hair was still up, but the pencils had been replaced with a French knot and several metal combs. In addition, several loose ringlets trailed past her collarbone to the neckline of her dress. With its deep décolleté, the dress felt just this side of wicked. Panna had the body for it, with full, high breasts and rounded hips, but not the mind-set. In fact, her usual work outfit was jeans and a silk blouse. Charlie hadn't been fooled. He had always made her own up to the full potential of her body when they were in bed. Oh yes, she thought with a heated stab of longing, that was something he had done very well.

Despite her nature, however, she found herself bowing to the power of her dress and throwing back her shoulders.

She heard steps at the rear of the chapel and sprinted into the adjacent hallway to hide. The steps grew closer, and Panna's heart thumped, but instead of coming toward the hall, they turned away and, she assumed, toward the tomb.

For several long moments she heard nothing. At last, her curiosity got the best of her. She tilted her head just far enough to view a narrow slice of the chapel. Seeing no sign of the person who had made the noise, she leaned in farther.

At last she saw boots, highly polished and black. The man who owned them was kneeling at the tomb, head bowed, hands resting on the railing surrounding the marble. The shoulders under his red coat were wide and proud, and his wheat-colored hair glinted with sparks of gold. While nothing on his face betrayed his emotions, Panna could feel the intensity of his devotion.

Perhaps sensing her presence, he angled his head toward the door.

Panna jerked out of view. But fear of discovery wasn't the only thing that had made her jump. She'd recognized that profile. She'd looked at it every day for the last ten years. That was John Bridgewater, Viscount Adderly.

Had he seen her? Would he speak to her? Would he be like the John Bridgewater of her rather fertile imagination? To have seen in the warm and exceedingly handsome flesh what she'd only glimpsed in lifeless marble was a shock.

Her palms started to dampen, and she nearly laughed out loud. *Good Lord, I've fallen into another world, in another time, and what I'm most unnerved by is meeting the man depicted by a statue.* This trip through the looking glass was growing stranger and stranger.

She braced herself for his arrival, but he must not have seen her, for no footsteps sounded.

She waited as long as her curiosity could bear and then ducked her head around the corner again.

He was still in his reverie, and Panna noticed for the first time that his hands were clasped not in prayer but in fists. He loosened one to swipe an eye with his thumb.

Her observation began to feel like an intrusion, and she pulled back. The hallway, long and elegantly appointed, ended in a pair of closed doors and a window at the other. She made for the doors.

But another entryway off the hall made her stop. The room was lined on one side with opulent oriel windows, each with its own cushioned window seat. The space was as big as an elementary school gym and just as tall, with a massive hearth at the far end flanked by carved Chinese foo dogs. But far more important, every inch of the other three walls was filled with books in glass cases.

She stepped through the open door, thrilled that the man she'd daydreamed about had such a regard for reading. She'd seen libraries like this before—the J.P. Morgan Library in New York was a shining example of a man elevating reverence for books to a new level—but never one belonging to a denizen of the eighteenth century.

In all other aspects, the room looked like the drawing room out of a costume drama. The rugs were thick, the furniture finely crafted, and the desk...

The corner of her mouth rose. The top of a desk offers such an intimate glimpse of its owner's personality. Her own desk held a heart-shaped stone she'd found on her first date with Charlie, half a dozen books she intended to read, a few snippets of upholstery fabric she was considering for a new chair, and a ball of thick red yarn, whose vivid color made her smile every time she looked at it even though she didn't knit.

This desk was not that of an ordinary gentleman. The ink-smeared blotter, account books, and loose ribbons could have belonged to any land-owning nobleman, she supposed, but the beetle fossil, halved nautilus shell, and shining, brass-mounted magnifying glass attested to a more curious intellect. The irony of the open nautilus shell was not lost on her.

The cry of a gull outside made her look up, and she was shocked to discover the room she was in was easily three stories above the ground, casting its shadow over a stout, crenellated wall. She was not in a country home. She was in a castle.

A wide stretch of river beyond the base of the castle wall divided the estate's unblemished parkland from fields of green and gold grain. On this side of the water, a small town hugged the shore, a church steeple rising from the center like the gnomon of a sundial above the buildings around it. Another town sat across the wide stretch of water on the opposite bank. Or perhaps it was all one town, divided by the waterway, but with no bridge connecting the two sides. The thing that caught her eye, running as it did along the water on the near shore, was a wide, sturdy stone wall that reached in each direction as far as the eye could see.

If she wasn't mistaken—and she didn't think she was—that was Hadrian's Wall, which could only mean she was somewhere near the border of England and Scotland.

She wondered what Colonel John Bridgewater, hero of the Battle of Ramillies, would be doing on the border of England and Scotland instead of out fighting one of England's enemies on the battlefields of Europe. She also wondered who the inhabitant of the tomb was. She thought of the scene in *The Three Musketeers* in which the handsome, brave d'Artagnan says a tearful good-bye to the woman he loves as she dies in his arms.

Panna heard steps and turned to hide, but it was too late. She found herself gazing into the surprised face of Viscount Adderly.

In the course of an instant, his surprise turned into anger, then an unreadable blankness. She could almost hear the mask snap into place.

He barely missed a step.

"If depositing a whore on my doorstep is the English army's idea of a peace offering," he said, drawing his appraising gaze across her as he passed, "you may consider yourself relieved of duty for the evening. Close the door as you go."

She was so shocked, it took her several beats to begin to form a response. She felt as if she'd just had her skin seared off by a fire-breathing dragon. Panna didn't take well to dragons.

"I am *not* a whore," she said, emphasizing each word with razor sharpness.

The man did not look back. It was as if she had been dismissed not only from the room but from England, the planet, and quite possibly all of existence as well.

He stopped at his desk, his eyes taking a careful inventory of his papers and belongings. Then he gave each drawer a firm tug. None budged.

He was checking to see if she'd taken something! Fury rumbled in Panna's veins. "Would you care to search me?"

"Would it be necessary in that dress?"

Her jaw dropped. She considered a response but decided she'd be wasting her breath. As her mother liked to say, "Never mud-wrestle a pig. You both get dirty, and the pig enjoys it." This pig could have his mud castle all to himself. She turned on her heel and stalked out, careful *not* to close the door, and rode her anger all the way back to the entrance hall of the Carnegie Library, where she happily slammed *that* door behind her.

Three

BRIDGEWATER WATCHED THE FLOUNCE OF THOSE proud shoulders. He'd expected a slam but instead got a cutting look of disdain—admittedly well deserved—as she made a deliberate path around the end of the open door.

He almost smiled.

Spies were not often so comely, especially the ones employed by the English army, nor so well suited to his tastes. If he hadn't been so surprised by the violation of his privacy and irritated by the depths to which his commanding officer would sink to wring information out of him, he might have invited her to stay. The fire in those green eyes had been attractive indeed.

He flopped into his chair, fingering one of the silk ribbons that were a vestige of his own information gathering, and considered the possibilities.

There were uses one could make of spies—feeding the enemy false information, for example—that sometimes made it worthwhile to further one's relationship with them. And if furthering his relationship with the woman happened to include drinking in the gardenia scent of her hair or partaking of those full lips or even something more, it would be a worthwhile risk. He knew exactly what he could and couldn't say, after all. His opinions were hardly secret, even among his fellow officers, having been voiced at countless dinners and councils. So long as he took care to keep his *actions* hidden from her, an evening with so handsome a spy might be just the diversion he needed. He was a solitary man, after all, and it had been such a long time since he'd talked of anything but the war.

Gazing at the hills in the distance, he considered the repercussions of the skirmish the rebels were planning tonight in Carlisle. He was willing to suffer the consequences, but he supposed willingness didn't enter into it. He had no choice. Not if he wanted to bring some semblance of peace to the borderlands. He'd have to live with the results of his actions, and so would the English army.

He lifted his nose, scenting gardenias again in the air, and turned, wondering if she'd changed her mind. But it must have been his imagination, and his disappointment must have shown on his face, for when the private entered, he said, "Is something amiss?"

"Nothing more than being kept under guard."

The man shrugged. "The colonel's ready to see you now."

Bridgewater sighed and stood. He wasn't looking forward to the conversation.

Four

D'ARTAGNAN? HA! BRIDGEWATER WOULD HAVE MADE a better Cardinal Richelieu, the musketeers' villainous nemesis. Panna was done with daydreams, especially ones involving time travel, and completely done with Colonel John Bridgewater.

She was still quaking with fury and the sheer shock of finding a storage room with a passageway to the past right in her own library. Jeez, no wonder no one liked cleaning those things.

Marie poked her head into the entryway. "Oh, there you are. For our 'Are they out of their minds?' question of the evening, we have the Teen Book Club wondering if they can do a *True Blood* costume party—hey, are you okay? You look a little, I don't know, weird."

Panna looked down. Blue sundress. That, at least, was in order. "No, no. Just, er, wondering about a good historical fiction recommendation. The one I just started stinks."

"Action or romance?"

"*Definitely* not romance. And, to be honest, I can do without the action as well."

"Hmmm." Marie considered. "That doesn't leave a lot. Maybe that new one by Tracy Chevalier?"

"Perfect. Thanks. Oh, and—"

"No on the *True Blood* party. Yeah, that's what I figured." Marie ran off.

‍✍︎

After a few more deep breaths, Panna brushed off her dress and made her way unsteadily to the circulation desk. She looked at the wall. *You have got to be kidding me.* The clock read 7:23. Her trip through the eighteenth century, *The Three Musketeers*, and pig wrestling had taken exactly eight minutes.

The shock of the experience was understandably hard to shake, and when she found herself looking up Howard Stern instead of Laurence Sterne for one very amused patron, she decided to reshelf books instead, something that was easy and relatively mindless. She gave the statue a carefully hidden finger as she passed.

What she had gone through was inexplicable. Unpleasant and inexplicable. Why would there be a time passage in a library? Why in *her* library? Were there others? Had anyone before her ever used it? Was the fact that it had carried her to John Bridgewater's time related to the fact that the library had a statue of said nobleman? It had to, didn't it? Did the time passage pose any sort of danger (other than to one's ego, of course)?

She grabbed a book at random from the cart. *Dear Nell: The Miraculous Story of Nell Gwynn's Rise from Street Urchin to the Bed of Charles II.* Now, *there* was a whore. Self-proclaimed, in fact. And why would

Bridgewater think that just because a woman wore a low-cut gown she was a whore? That seemed rather old-fashioned. Even more old-fashioned than the eighteenth century.

And what if she *had* been a whore? Would it have killed him to at least *consider* sleeping with her? Not that she would have done it, of course, but she happened to be quite a catch in that regard—not that John Bridgewater was ever going to find out.

What had he said? "If depositing a whore on my doorstep is the English army's idea of a peace offering, you may consider yourself relieved of duty for the evening."

What an imperious, sexist prick. Was it any wonder British noblemen these days were regarded as a bunch of chinless, toe-sucking scone eaters? And why would the English army be extending one of their colonels a peace offering, anyway? Some sort of sick fraternity gag?

The most important question, though, was should she tell anyone about what she'd discovered?

Marie appeared with an armload of books.

Panna tapped her foot. "Come here for a second. I want to show you something."

Marie followed her to the entryway. Panna stood behind the storage room door and pulled it open. "Take a gander in there."

"Seriously?"

"Yes. Tell me what you see."

Marie shrugged and looked in.

Panna said, "Do you think there's any way to leverage that into enough money to keep the library afloat?"

"Six cans of old paint, a broken stepladder, and a sign that says 'Quiet'?"

"What?" Panna bent and saw only the black void. "That's what you see?"

Marie frowned. "Are you sure you're all right? Maybe we *should* reschedule dinner."

"No, no. I'm..." What was she? "Fine" certainly didn't cover it. "...going to do it."

So Marie didn't see what Panna saw. Maybe no one did.

Marie gave her a concerned look and closed the door. "All right. I'm glad. Dinner with you is going to be the highlight of my weekend, you know." She started back toward the circulation desk with Panna close behind. "I work tomorrow, and Sunday I'll be spending the whole day working on my stupid group project for school. And the guy who's supposed to be doing the index says he's too busy to get it done, so I guess I'll be doing that too."

"What? No," Panna said. "Look, you've got to read him the riot act. First, if you don't give jerks like that a brushback, they'll just assume what they're doing is somehow okay. And second, you do not want to get a reputation for being a doormat. I mean, if you're going to end up with a reputation, it's much better being the bitch who wouldn't take someone's crap than—"

Panna stopped.

"Than what?" Marie said.

"Than someone with footprints on her back. Listen, I'm going to check something here. Are you going to be okay without me at the desk for a bit?"

Marie crossed her wrists, flashing the ever-present

rubber bands she kept there. "These may look like plain rubber bands, but in a library they have the power to deflect all manner of evil."

"Great Hera!"

"You've got it, sister."

Panna wondered if she, too, should strap on some rubber bands. She felt a satisfying super villain ass-kicking coming on.

Five

THE SECOND TIME THROUGH THE DOOR WAS AS EASY as the first, and Panna was not surprised to find herself back in the blue silk gown. *All the better to be wearing the tools of my trade when I stuff his accusations down his throat.* And while she had taken care not to close his door when she'd left earlier, she saw that he'd made an effort sometime in the last fifteen minutes to get off his imperious English buttocks and shut it himself.

The effort was probably good for him. Like listening to opera or taking cold showers. It built moral fortitude.

She knocked on the door.

He didn't answer.

She knocked again.

"Go away," he said huskily.

Damn it. She opened the door. He was seated at his desk, head in his hand, studying a paper closely.

"Please go away." The tone of his voice had changed completely from her earlier visit. It was flat and polite but on the edge of pleading.

The sleeve of his crimson coat had been rent,

exposing a narrow sliver of white. Then she saw the drop of blood fall from his chin to the paper on his desk.

"Bridgewater?"

"I don't know who you are, but 'tis best if you go. Your colleagues have done their job."

"I have no colleagues. Look at me, please."

He turned his head, and she took a step back. His lip was bleeding, as was his brow. There were contusions on his cheek and chin. And the way he hugged his side troubled her.

"As you can see," he said with a weak smile, "'tis not the ideal time to talk."

She looked around the room. A decanter filled with an amber liquid sat on a small table. She grabbed it and the runner on which it sat and went to him. She balled up the runner and poured the liquid into it.

"I'd prefer it in a glass."

There were two glasses on his desk. She pushed one toward him with the decanter and filled it. Then she held the cloth before his brow. "May I?"

"As you wish."

He hissed when the wetness came in contact with his skin. She did what she could to clean the blood away and poured more liquid on the cloth. He radiated a palpable intensity—like a caged panther.

"You do realize," he said, "that's a brandy de Jerez from the vineyards of Don Alfonso y Torres. It was a gift to me from Prince Eugene of Savoy."

"If you'd care to call for something else, I'm happy to wait."

He took a sip and waved her on.

"You haven't told me what happened."

"'Tis what happens when one plays with fire," he said. "I got my fingers burned."

"I wasn't gone more than fifteen minutes."

"I am a very quick study."

The gash ran an inch though his wide brow and was nearly half an inch deep. In her world, she'd have sent him to the hospital for stitches. She had no idea what to do here. She saw there was blood on his shirt.

"Is that yours or his?" she asked.

"Mine. I'm certain of it. I did not get off a single punch."

Bridgewater, the hero of the Battle of Ramillies, had not gotten off a single punch? Six foot two, broad chest, sizable hands, and arms long enough to outreach most opponents? He'd made the statement without a touch of shame, though she saw he was watching her for a reaction.

"You do not exactly recommend yourself as a fighter," she said.

He smiled—a smile that sent a surprising warmth through her. "Do you find yourself in need of one?"

"Thankfully for both of us, no."

He was handsome, there was no denying it. And whatever her feelings might be at present for the man before her, the attraction she'd felt for his marble likeness hadn't wavered.

He finished his brandy and poured himself another. He held the decanter over the empty glass. "May I pour one for you?"

She hesitated. Brandy was a big drink. She was more of a light beer sort of gal. Besides, between time travel, fistfights, and her uncertainty about Bridgewater, this seemed like a good time to stay clearheaded.

"Do not miss an opportunity to sample Don Alfonso's harvest," he said. "I promise you'll enjoy it."

"All right. A little, I guess."

He poured, obeying her wish.

When he finished, she held out the cloth. He poured another measure of brandy on it, sighing regretfully.

His lip had been split along the arch of his Cupid's bow. She daubed it clear of blood, admiring the pink fullness. Who would have savaged him like this? And why hadn't he fought back?

It dawned on her belatedly that her breasts were not only right at the level of his eyes but also dangerously close to falling out of her dress. However, his gaze had not strayed from her face. She flushed.

"I hope by now you've realized I'm not a prostitute."

"I'm not quite sure what you are." He said this without rancor, but still with an evident degree of suspicion. He took another sip.

Panna decided no response was necessary, which was just as well, since she didn't know what she would say in any case. He was having a different effect on her than she'd expected.

"You have an exhilarating view here," she said, tilting her head toward the windows. His lip was starting to swell, an eye was turning purple, and that brow was going to have a Frankenstein-like scar running through it, but she'd cleared away the dried blood and nothing was actively bleeding anymore.

"Exhilarating, aye." The tiniest hint of self-mocking hung in his voice. "And I've paid dearly for it."

"It *is* a castle, after all. I would think the price is dear for any castle."

He chuckled. "You're quite correct, though that's not the price I meant."

She tried to untangle his meaning, and he drank, watching the calculation on her face. His gaze was both appraising and faintly desirous. She felt the reverberations of it to her toes.

"I see the wall along the shore," she said quickly. "Borders can be places fraught with danger."

"They can, indeed. This one in particular. The Scots are edifying neighbors."

Then it *was* Hadrian's Wall, just as she'd thought. She tried to recollect what she knew of Scotland, England, and the early eighteenth century, but other than a romance novel that took place during the last Highlander uprising; the Sir Walter Scott stories she'd read in high school; Mary, Queen of Scots, who was too early; and the crime novels of Ian Rankin, which were far too late, her knowledge of Scottish history was rather limited. Clearly, she'd have to spend a little more time in Nonfiction the next time she was in the library. What she *did* know was that Scotland and England did *not* get along and, from the dozens of Regency romance novels she'd read in high school, that people didn't generally beat up a viscount.

"Come," he said, "you haven't tried your brandy." But when he reached for the glass to hand it to her, he winced and clutched his side.

She gave him a stern look, which he tried to ignore, but when she didn't relent, he stood with a groan and reluctantly untucked his shirt, lifting it high enough for her to see his side.

There was no bleeding, but bruises blossomed from his shoulder to his waist.

"I think you need some fighting lessons."

He laughed. The shirt went down, but not before Panna had taken in the broad, tan pectorals and finely cut abdomen. This was not a man of idle pursuits.

"And the only use Don Alfonso's brandy can be to my side," he said, gathering the sodden cloth from her hand, "is to baste it from within. Please." He gestured toward her glass. She picked it up, and he held up his. "To the transformative power of a quarter of an hour."

Did he mean the change to his appearance, or to the two of them? The way he looked at her made the answer clear. She lifted the brandy with a flush and drank. The liquor was smooth and full-bodied, with the faintest hint of oranges. "It's marvelous."

"The plains of Castilla-La Mancha. One can't do better for brandy. Or battle."

The boom of a nearby cannon pierced the quiet. Bridgewater didn't move, but Panna hurried to the closest window, one deeper and taller than the rest.

"There are troops in your courtyard," she said, noting the redcoats marching through the castle gate. More of them walked the castle ramparts, tending to fires in the large, black pots that dotted the perimeter.

"Aye. The English army has been sampling my hospitality since the beginning of March. I'm beginning to think I should be a little more circumspect in my invitations."

"But you're a soldier too, aren't you?"

He regarded her with an odd expression. "For now."

"You'd leave?" She supposed there would be nothing keeping a nobleman in the army. Certainly not a need to earn one's living. She wondered what it would be like to have the riches of a man like Bridgewater and the ability to feed and house several hundred guests—or build a two-story library.

"If that was the only way I could do what I needed to do," he said.

"The troops are hooking the cannons to wagons."

"Fools." He rose, wincing, from his seat and limped to her side. "They intend to form a line behind the wall, from Bowness halfway to Carlisle. And when it's dark, they will pelt the Scottish hills with cannon shot."

She gazed into the collection of houses across the river. "But there are so few homes. It hardly seems worth the trouble."

"There is one of some interest."

He turned her gently to the west. There, beyond the river, on a rise nearly as high as Bridgewater's castle, stood another castle. It had two towers and a rampart flying a yellow flag that flapped rhythmically against the purpling evening sky.

"Ah." Two castles, one English, one Scottish, situated so each owner could keep the other in his sights, preserved from violence only by the exigencies of the river and Hadrian's bucolic wall. She thought of the line from that Robert Frost poem. *Good fences make good neighbors.*

Bridgewater observed the gathering troops. The light from the firepots flickered in his hair. His profile was so like the one in her library. How had a sculptor in 1901 captured someone who'd been dead a hundred and fifty years with such accuracy?

"Will they destroy it?" She gestured to the Scottish castle.

Bridgewater laughed. "They might wish to, but it would be even harder to take that castle than this one. And destroying it would be damn near impossible. Instead, their cannon fire is meant to be a show of unity and strength. 'Tis a bloody waste of gunpowder, if you ask me."

It sounded as if no one had. "I take it you don't agree with the decision."

"A soldier always agrees with the decisions of his commanding officer," he said, his finger tracing the edge of the wound to his brow. "Especially when one's commanding officer also happens to be an earl."

"At some point do you intend to tell me what happened to you?"

He gave her a look. "I don't know. I haven't decided yet. Do you intend to tell me how you managed to get into a locked and guarded castle?"

She opened her mouth and tried to formulate some fabulous lie, but even after a frenzy of mental acrobatics, nothing materialized.

The corner of his mouth rose. "So I thought. 'Tis best if we stop asking questions, aye? Since neither of us seems very good at lying." He held out his glass.

She touched her glass to his and they drank. His lips curved into a full smile. "The evening is taking a turn for the better," he said.

"I'd say that was a compliment, but you had nowhere to go but up."

He laughed.

Don Alfonso's brandy was loosening her tongue. "Okay, personal questions are forbidden, but surely not every sort is? I have a number I'd like to ask."

"Good heavens. Shall I sit down?"

"Quite possibly. First, may I say I love your library?"

"You may, but it's not really a proper question."

She went to the bookcase beside the wide hearth. Her gaze ran excitedly over the titles, a number of which were in Latin or Greek. "History. Art. Medicine. Maps. A biography of Saint Peter. Oh my goodness! A copy of John Donne's poems!"

She pulled the handle of the case, but it didn't budge. She gave him a look. "Locked," she said sadly.

"Good Lord, the look on your face. 'Twould shame a saint." He made his way to her side and pulled a set of keys from his pocket. He found the one he needed and, with a quick turn, the door was open.

She pulled out a handful of books and placed them on a table at the edge of the hearth. A volume entitled *Animals of the Orient* was on top. She plucked it from the stack and sank to the floor. The illustrations had been hand-colored. The endpapers were trimmed in gold leaf. The crackle of the page sent happy shivers down her spine.

"Have I lost you?"

She realized she hadn't said anything in a full minute. "It's stunning." *And priceless.* The sale of a single book like this might save her library. Not that Panna was the type of woman to steal, of course. But, oh, if she were…

"I've seen a look like that once before," he said.

"'Twas on an adder—just as it was about to swallow a weasel whole."

She laughed. "I should like to swallow this whole—consume every last page of it. Look at that mongoose. Look at that peacock."

"I have a peacock, you know."

"You *do*?"

"Aye. He walks the castle's upper courtyard, and a more ill-natured fellow you have never met. But he is the color of snow. 'Tis very rare."

A white peacock? This place was magical! She felt like Dorothy in the Emerald City.

A voice sounded in the hallway, and the look of concern that came over Bridgewater's face made her freeze. He held a finger to his lips and pointed to a small alcove out of sight of the entryway. She complied at once, abandoning the book. In the alcove, she had a partial view of the door through a narrow gap between a column and a wall. Bridgewater returned to his desk and picked up a sheet of paper.

Someone knocked, and the door opened. Bridgewater's shoulders relaxed. The man appeared to be a servant and he carried a tray of food. "Please, if I may say, sir," the man said in a low voice, "this is an outrage. They are—"

"Reeves," Bridgewater said sharply, and the man stopped. Panna realized with a stab Reeves was about to say something Bridgewater didn't want her to hear.

"Leave the tray there." Bridgewater gestured to the table next to the hearth.

Reeves deposited the tray as directed. Then he raised the hanging leaf on the table and drew out a narrow gate leg to support it. As he did, Panna saw the back of a red-coated soldier come into view at the door. Bridgewater stiffened. Panna withdrew farther into the alcove to ensure she couldn't be seen by the soldier nor by Reeves, unless he turned.

"Make it quick, man," the soldier said to Reeves. When Reeves finished laying out the meal, he began to look around the room. It dawned on Panna that he must be looking for a chair upon which his master could sit to eat.

Then she spotted the cane-backed chair next to her. She inhaled. There was nowhere to go. She backed against the wall and said a small prayer.

Reeves reached the entrance to the alcove and did a stutter step when he saw her. He could see her but the soldier couldn't.

The soldier said, "What? What is it?"

For a brief instant there was silence, then Reeves said, "This is filthy. I'll flay the girl who cleaned this." He grabbed the chair and gave Panna an apologetic look.

"Nobody cleaned it, you fool," the soldier said. "No one's allowed in. Not until my orders change."

"Let us hope that is soon," Reeves said, sniffing. He set up the chair at the table. "Will this be enough for dinner?" Reeves asked Bridgewater carefully. "I can certainly bring more if you require it."

"He's not getting more," the soldier bellowed. "He's under arrest."

"Thank you, Reeves," Bridgewater said. "This will suffice."

"May I recommend the soup, sir? 'Tis most appetizing this evening."

Bridgewater's brow rose. "I look forward to it."

The man bowed and exited, followed, Panna assumed, by the soldier, for she heard the door close and Bridgewater appeared at the alcove's entry to wave her out.

"Are you being held here?" she demanded. "In your own house?"

He held up a hand, listening. "There," he said after a long pause. "You can talk. He just closed the door at the end of the hallway."

"And?"

"And what?"

"And you're being held?"

"Is that a question?"

She began to protest and then saw his smile.

"Aye." He offered her the chair at the table. "I am. The English army has accused me of collaborating with the Scots."

She declined the chair, too unsettled to sit. "Are you?"

He gave her a thoughtful look. "Of course not. I'm an English citizen. My grandfather is a Scot though, and that may have given them some pause."

A marriage of mixed nationality. Odd at the time. Odder still for a nobleman. She grabbed a hunk of cheese and a fig from the tray. "But surely they knew that when you joined the army."

"'Tis not illegal to have Scots blood running in one's veins. At least not yet." He inclined his head toward the food. "Do you mind if I…?"

"Not at all," she said, nibbling the fruit. "Please, go on."

He took a seat. "However, my grandfather is more

than just a Scot." He blew on the first spoonful of soup. "He's the chief of Clan MacIver."

She stopped chewing. Scots blood would be an awkward thing in the highly regimented caste system of English noblemen. But to have a clan chief in one's family—especially if one was a senior army officer—would have to be a social and political disaster. The clashes between the clans and the English army had long made the borderlands a bloody and dangerous place. Sir Walter Scott had made a name writing stories about it, and so had any number of other historical fiction authors.

"Good *Lord*. Are you saying your father married the daughter of a *clan chief*?"

Bridgewater put down his spoon. "Yes," he said carefully.

She flushed, realizing her rudeness. She'd asked the question as if she were examining the breeding history of a horse she was buying.

"I'm sorry. That was very impolite."

He bowed. Then he leaned back in his chair, considering her closely. "It's odd. You ask about things most people already know."

"Do I?" She struggled to keep her face under control.

"Aye. My grandfather. The peacock. The castle on the distant hill. Where is it you call home? That's not an English accent, nor even Welsh. There is something guttural and German to it to my ear, and yet it isn't German."

"No. I'm from—" She considered. "Penn's Wood. In the colonies."

His pupils widened. "Penn's Wood? The land of William Penn?"

She nodded, pleased he knew her home. "Do you know him?"

"I have been introduced, yes." A wry smile came over his face. "He's a bit of a frothing dog, don't you think?"

"William *Penn*?" She'd never thought of William Penn being anything except the figure on top of the Philadelphia City Hall and the face on the oatmeal box.

"I am not a religious man," he said, returning to his soup, "and religious men make me wary—anyone with fanatical leanings does."

Not a religious man? The man whom she'd first seen on his knees, praying? She thought his statement was a convenient untruth, though why he chose to tell it, she didn't know.

The cheese was marvelous—fresh and light with a grassy tang. She wondered if there were cows out on those darkening hills. Cows, peacocks, cannons, border intrigues—this was better than a novel, she thought. Then she remembered Bridgewater's bruised side and battered face and felt guilty for her blithe observation.

"And what brings you to Cumbria?" he asked, looking absently into his bowl as he scraped out the last bit of soup. He stopped for an instant, obviously startled, then broke his gaze and brought the soup to his mouth. "My apologies," he said. "We have an agreement. No more questions." He pushed the bowl away, tapping his fingers on the table. Whatever had come to him was still occupying his thoughts.

Then he stood. Affability restored, he carried the

decanter to the bookcase she'd opened, snagged her glass from the floor, and refilled it for her.

"Was that the man who beat you?"

"Who? The guard? No," he said amiably. "He and his companion held me while someone else did the punching."

His fingers brushed hers as she accepted the glass, leaving a warm tingle. She gazed at her hand as if she'd never seen it before.

"Is something wrong?"

She hid it, startled. "No. It's nothing."

He refilled his own glass and sat down again at the table. That look of smoky desire had returned to his face, and she felt a light giddiness spread through her, like the bubbles in champagne.

"Do you let the soldiers borrow your books while they're here?" she asked. "Or the townspeople?"

He looked at her in some surprise. "Of course not."

Panna's desire to keep her twenty-first-century self under wraps battled with her irrepressible evangelism on the topic of library access, and she knew which side would win. "Oh, but you should!"

"I've spent half a lifetime building this collection. You can hardly expect a man to let his books be scattered like seeds to the wind."

"But that's exactly the right analogy," she cried. "Think about how much knowledge you could sow by sharing your books with the people who live around here."

"Do you have a library like this in Penn's Woods?"

"I do."

Something like curiosity flickered in those gray-blue eyes. "Your husband's?"

"Oh, no," she said, the quickness of her reply surprising her. "I'm a widow. The library is just one I can use. In fact, I help take care of the books there."

"A library keeper?"

"Yes."

He studied her appraisingly. "How very interesting. I've heard of such a thing, though I admit I have never heard of a woman doing it. And this gentleman, the one who owns the library, he is wealthy?"

She could hardly blame him for assuming the library's owner was male. She imagined there weren't many women owners of anything in the eighteenth century. And Andrew Carnegie had been as rich as they come.

"He is."

"And how does my library compare?"

How like a man to ask such a thing. She looked around the vast room, her eyes trailing up the towers of wood and glass to take in the gleaming volumes. Her fingers tingled for the chance to hold them. Yet, what a thing to lavish on a single person. "For an individual, your collection is immense, and from the pieces I've seen, I think you have a very, very fine eye."

"Do I hear a 'but' in there?"

The rare man who listens to more than the words spoken. "Well, where I come from, a library is judged not just on its collection but upon the number of books it lends out. We call that its circulation. Your circulation, I am afraid to say, is exceedingly low—only the books one single person reads."

It dawned on her that she had no idea if his circulation

depended on the reading habits of one person or two. For all she knew, he had a wife who used it as well. His eyes twinkled clear blue. "And the man who owns your library? How large is his circulation?"

She searched his face for deeper meaning, but his features seemed pointedly unreadable. "Well, size is not the only thing that matters, of course."

"Is it not? I believe you just said it was."

"All right, yes, size is important. Very important, in fact," she added, walking the perimeter of the room to avoid looking into those eyes. "But there is range to be considered as well."

"The wider, the better, I suppose."

She gave him a look. He was alluding to something else. She could see the laughter in those warm eyes.

"Yes," she said carefully, "width is certainly a benefit."

"Though you would argue for distinguishing oneself with commanding depth in a few important areas too, I'm sure."

"Yes, as well as the sensitivity with which the collector—"

"Aye, the sensitivity. Always a concern. Then you would say his library exceeds mine in all important aspects."

The twinkle had turned to a kaleidoscopic glitter, and she flushed from her neck to the tips of her ears. "His collection *is* larger—"

Bridgewater put a hand over his heart. "Ooh. A crushing blow."

"—but as for the rest...I don't know. I would have to, well..."

"Sample it?"

His eyes met hers, only for an instant, but a seismic shock rattled her knees. Charming bastard. She downed a swig of brandy to moisten her throat. "Hmmm."

"That can be arranged, you know."

"Oh, I'm sure it could. Take heart, though. A man with a humble collection can still make an impact."

"Humble!"

"It's a matter of attitude, attentive execution, and something with which you may not be closely familiar—humility."

"Ouch. I withdraw to lick my wounds." Bridgewater stretched his long legs and grinned. "Well, I'm sorry to hear his collection exceeds mine. That is indeed discouraging. However, nothing inspires a man to greater achievement like another man's success."

"I think perhaps we should close the topic of libraries."

He chuckled. "As you wish. I remain open to a return to the topic, however, should it please you."

It had been a long time since Panna had flirted with a man. The flutter in her chest was like sunshine to someone emerging from a lingering illness. It left her feeling both exhilarated and a little light-headed.

She had come to an odd, high window seat. Unlike the other window seats, which were of normal size and depth, this one jutted out an extra two feet from the side of the building and stood a good twelve inches taller, which made Panna assume it offered the best view. However, she found it nearly impossible to get into it, given her gown and the glass in her hand—that is, until she spotted a swing-out step, about a foot off the floor, built into the wall.

She opened the step.

"Oh dear." Bridgewater cleared his throat.

"What?" She hopped on the wood. The step was quite steady.

"I—well, never mind." He shook his head.

"I've never seen anything like this."

"No, I, er, wouldn't think so."

Once she sat down, she noticed another odd feature. The seat angled slightly downward toward the half circle of windows in which it was located, which made sitting upright a sort of isometric exercise. In addition, about a foot before the seat reached the windows, the angle of the incline became even more acute.

"This is a very strange seat," she said.

His cheeks reddened. "It belonged to the man who built this place."

"Not you?"

"Oh, no. This castle was built in the fifteenth century and has changed hands a number of times in the never-ending tumult of the borderlands. Most of it was destroyed in a fire forty or so years ago—the same year as the plague. Only this wing remains."

"I see. And the seat?"

He shifted uncomfortably. "'Tis referred to as the surveying seat."

She took in the sweeping view of the ramparts, the river, and the seemingly endless hills beyond the towns. "I can see that. But the incline? And the odd height?"

"The story is told that the lord of the castle, apparently a roguish sort, designed it to give himself a standing view of all of his holdings—holdings that evidently were meant to include his lady…or, at least, whoever his lady was at the moment he decided to, er, take his survey."

"Oh," she said. "*Oh*."

The seat would accommodate a man standing, one foot on the swing-out step, and a woman, lying on her back, with her body angled downward and her head angled even more.

"Good God!" Panna exclaimed. "The view of his holdings would be directly between her—"

"Aye."

Seeing the world through rose-colored nipples. She didn't know how to respond. She suddenly wondered if Bridgewater had ever used it for such a purpose.

"As you said," he murmured, "a room with a view."

Panna scrabbled to remember the topic that had preceded the discovery of this amazing seat. The depth and breadth of his library's circulation had been almost as fraught with pitfalls. Determined to find a safer subject, she said, "There is one thing quite singular about your library, however."

"Oh?" He sat up, as relieved as she was at the change of subject.

"Yes, you have two stories of shelves, and no ladder to reach the upper story."

His face broke in a wide grin. "Do you know that you are the first person to notice? The army has been here three months and not a single officer has said a word."

She hopped off the seat and walked around the room, scanning titles as she went. Milton, Hobbes, Fletcher, Newton—even a Bible grand enough to make her wonder if it was a Gutenberg.

But she didn't stop to admire any of them, for while she was not exactly sure what shape the item she was looking for would take, she knew for certain the item did not come bound in leather.

She could feel the energy in the room shift as Bridgewater's gaze followed her, and she wondered if she might even use that to help her identify what she was looking for. She reached the table at which he was seated when the empty soup bowl caught her attention.

Scratched into the bottom of the bowl were the words "They know."

The pause in her step nearly gave her away, and he regarded her closely, but she managed to keep her attention on the bookcase in front of her.

"Your collection certainly reflects a wide range of interests," she said, pulling the first thing out of the air she could think of while wondering about the message in the bowl. *Who* knew? The army? And *what* did they know? Reeves was obviously a well-trained and loyal servant.

"Thank you," Bridgewater said. "I was lucky to have a very fine tutor."

She wondered if he *was* collaborating with the Scots, just as he'd been accused of doing. Of course, with the perspective of three hundred extra years, she knew the Scots would lose their independence to England and never gain it back completely, not even in her time. Were their struggles to remain free any less honorable than the struggles American colonists would be fighting three-quarters of a century from now? Of course, in the eyes of a ruling power, a group fighting for its freedom looks both traitorous and dangerous.

"Your father must be very proud," she said.

At the mention of his father, Bridgewater's expression changed. She could see him wrestling with a response. "My father and I are not close."

"Oh. I'm sorry to hear that."

"It's been a great loss for me. Perhaps not as much for him."

"Oh, I'm sure it *is* a great loss for him," she said, though the look on Bridgewater's face said otherwise. "Charlie's father—Charlie was my husband—wasn't an easy person to get along with. Charlie's older brother really resented him, and they were estranged. They ended up reconciling when Charlie's dad got sick, but by then there was so little time left. Charlie's father always said the thing he regretted most was not doing what he needed to do to have his son in his life."

Bridgewater shifted, and a hint of pain appeared in his eyes. "I think perhaps the situation with my father is different."

"Don't give up hope," she said. "There's always a chance people can mend their ways."

He bowed. "I'll do what I can."

She thought it best to let the subject drop and returned to her examination of the bookcases. A telltale flash of silver caught her eye.

The hinges were difficult to see—someone had attempted to camouflage them with brown paint—but a few scratches had exposed the metal beneath. She followed the vertical line separating metal and wood upward to where it met another line running horizontally the length of the bookcase. About four feet below where that line ended, she saw a slight impression. She slipped her fingers in and slowly swung the heavy, book-filled door open.

Bridgewater pressed the door closed with a soft but definitive *click*.

"I'm afraid I can't allow that."

He'd appeared at her side without a sound, and the pain in his eyes had been displaced by something chillier.

"Oh." The change in him unnerved her, and she found herself edging backward, clutching her brandy.

"I'd appreciate if you took care not to mention the door to anyone."

"Of course," she said.

He searched her eyes, evidently taking a measure of her trustworthiness. "If you cross me, you'll suffer for it."

"I won't. I told you I won't."

His coldness abated a degree. "I beg your pardon," he said after a long moment. "You've been most kind. But a man cannot trust everyone."

"Certainly. I understand." Though she wasn't quite sure she did.

He found the book she'd left on the floor and picked it up. "I'd like you to have this," he said. "'Twill double my circulation."

She felt odd taking it after his unsettling behavior. "I don't know."

"Please."

She accepted the book and tucked it under her arm. "Thank you."

"'Tis been a long time since anyone has tended to me," he said, touching his brow. "It made me quite content."

He took her hand and kissed it. His hand was soft and strong, and despite everything, she found herself lingering in his clasp.

A knock sounded at the door.

They froze. The alcove was half a room away. She began to run, but Bridgewater grabbed her arm, uttered a picturesque oath, and shoved her behind the door he had just forbidden her from entering.

Six

"GOOD EVENING, CAPTAIN."

"General." Bridgewater came to formal attention and waited. He'd hoped his sojourn as a sparring partner for his half brother's guards had been all the army time he'd have to serve today.

His visitor released him with a disgusted wave, the flawless queue of iron-gray hair flapping against his coat. "What happened to your face?"

"The colonel and I had a disagreement," Bridgewater said.

The general clucked his tongue. "Idiot."

Bridgewater said nothing. Anything he said would only make the man angrier. Instead, he considered the feel of the woman's hand against his lips. How his time with her had quenched the loneliness in him. Talking so openly perhaps had been foolish, but he hadn't said a thing she couldn't have learned from any inhabitant of the borderlands, if in fact she'd entered the room not knowing it already.

Take care, man. Falling in love with a spy is a sure bet on disaster.

Yet why had he thrust her into the one place he'd absolutely not wanted her to go unless, somewhere deep within him, he didn't believe she was a spy?

You don't want to believe it, that's why. That was her plan.

"I meant *you* were the idiot."

Bridgewater nodded. "I realize that, sir." *And perhaps I was.*

"Do you know why I'm in the borderlands, Captain? Do you know why Queen Anne sent her best general into this ungodly land of bloody-minded brutes?"

Given that the seat of the man's family had been in the north of England for the last three hundred years, albeit in the more "civilized" area south of Carlisle, Bridgewater took the "land" to which he referred to mean the parts of England close enough to Scotland to share in their brutishness.

"Because you're the most qualified man to lead this effort, sir." And it was true. Whatever disagreements Bridgewater had with the man before him—and there were many—he was the most canny, experienced, levelheaded leader the queen's army had ever produced. He'd earned every ribbon on that coat as well as the title he carried, even though he'd been born to that. His remarkable rise from a daring lieutenant to a distinguished general had been followed breathlessly by a youthful Bridgewater and had inspired him to take his own commission when he was old enough.

Which made the fact that Bridgewater intended to betray him all that much harder.

"Exactly," said the older man. "And when I say to you that the best way, the most efficient way, and the safest way to bring an end to the violence in the borderlands is to move our army over the Scottish border to Langholm, what is your reaction?"

"That you are correct, sir."

He grabbed Bridgewater by the lapels and jerked him hard. "Damn it, I know that's not what you think. I know from talking to the boy, Thomas. I know from the note we found on him. You are providing aid to the enemy. *Our* enemy. *England's* enemy." He flung him loose.

Bridgewater felt ill. Thomas had been captured? He prayed the boy hadn't been forced to endure the same two-fisted questioning he'd just experienced.

"Damn that bloody Scots grandfather of yours. Your mother wanted nothing to do with him, you know. What you're doing goes against everything she would have wanted."

"Don't talk to me about my mother," Bridgewater said through clenched teeth. "Ever. You are unworthy of uttering her name."

∽

Panna was afraid to move, afraid to breathe. But the savage edge in Bridgewater's voice so surprised her, she wanted to see his face.

She stood in a long, narrow space behind the bookshelves. She couldn't see the books—a number of closed wooden cabinet doors ran the length of the space, and the books stood on the other side of the doors. This meant the spines of the books faced the room in which Bridgewater stood, and that anyone who opened the wooden doors off this hallway would see only the opposite ends. As a librarian, this would have driven her crazy, except that someone—Bridgewater? His servant?—had written the name and author of every single book on a label in a fine copperplate hand and stuck the labels along the back of the shelf, an organizational arrangement she could see because the library's designer had thoughtfully put a small oval window at eye level in the center of every wooden door. This allowed her to see Bridgewater over the tops of the books, but given the low light and the small size of the windows, it would be considerably harder for someone in the main part of the room to see in. She ducked her head just enough to see.

Bridgewater vibrated with fury, and the general stared him down, as hard-eyed as a panther.

Whatever this was, it wasn't an army issue, for the general would have surely thrown Bridgewater in the brig, or whatever they called it in the eighteenth century, for that level of insubordination. This was something more personal, she thought. Why would Bridgewater object to the general talking about his mother? Had the general insulted her? Arrested her? Stolen her fortune?

And who was Thomas, the boy the general mentioned? Bridgewater's son? But no, the general would surely have known the boy then. The general talked as if he and Bridgewater shared a relationship beyond that of military connection. In fact, the way the general shouted at Bridgewater sounded almost exactly like the way her father used to shout at her brother—

Good God! She looked at the two men, nose-to-nose in profile. They shared the same leonine eyes, the same broad, slightly bent noses, the same clefts in their chins—why, even the way they stood with their fists balled at their sides was identical. She nearly laughed. The resemblance was impossible to deny. But it was the fury with which they confronted each other that, in Panna's mind, made her certain her guess was right.

Panna had two older brothers, one an insurance agent and one a Marine captain overseas, both great guys. Her father was gone now—both her parents were—but during her teen years, her brothers had tried their father's patience to the point that Panna had thought one, two, or all three of them would have to move out of the house. The anger and resentment in the eyes of these men had exactly the same look and feel.

Was Bridgewater, the future Earl of Bridgewater, staring down his father, the current earl? Panna would have been willing to bet her 401(k) on it.

The general brushed off his coat. "You look a fool, Captain. Pressing your suit to me like a common bounder—"

"I don't want your money," Bridgewater said with unrivaled anger. "I have my own. More than I could ever want."

The general looked around. "The ruins of a castle do not exactly spell grandeur. And the servants cannot feed themselves if their master is in prison."

"I make something," Bridgewater said. "Something that people can use. Something that comes from my own hands, my own mind. What have noblemen like you ever made?"

"Peace!" He slammed his fist against the wall, and a

nearby painting jiggled. "And war! When we choose! At our discretion! This is 1706, Captain. We're no longer mired in the dark ages of our ancestors, forced to endure what God sends our way. We fashion the world into something of our choosing. *That* is what noblemen do."

Bridgewater said nothing, but Panna could see he was regaining his composure. The men were slipping back into their professional relationship, though it appeared to be one that was almost as rocky as their private one, but one that Bridgewater could endure with some level of stoicism, at least.

She was fascinated. Why was it that being sucked into other people's family problems always seemed juicier and less harrowing than dealing with one's own? All she needed was a bowl of popcorn and a remote to feel like she was watching *The Real House Husbands of Northern England*. Then she remembered the pain in Bridgewater's eyes and felt a twinge of guilt.

"The note we found on the boy was in your hand-writing," the general said. "'Langholm, ten o'clock.' Do you deny it?"

"I do not. I told the colonel I do not. 'Tis not illegal to write the name of a Scottish town."

"Damn it, you know full well that's the time and place of the army's intended attack tonight!"

"How would I know that, General? You've never shared your battle plans with your men prior to a battle, and insofar as I know, you did not do so today."

"Then it's sheer coincidence that a note in your handwriting, detailing the time and place of tonight's attack, was found in the pocket of a street urchin with whom you've been known to consort?"

"He's not a street urchin. His father's a carpenter. And the note you found was given to him by me to remind him where and when to look to find the butcher's cleaver tonight."

The butcher's cleaver? A snippet of that creepy Lizzie Borden song played in Panna's head. Why would Bridgewater be telling a boy where to find such a thing?

"The butcher's cleaver?" the elder Bridgewater repeated, incredulous.

"Aye. In the direction of Langholm, sir. At ten o'clock."

The older man threw up his hands in disgust. He took two steps toward the door and returned, jabbing a finger in his son's chest. "If the army encounters a single armed Scot in Langholm tonight, you will be tried as a traitor and hanged."

Hanged? Any relationship to a television show vanished. And if they hanged the son of an earl, what would they do to a woman with an unrecognizable accent found in his room? Fear stirred in her gut. She needed to get back to the chapel and get out—and she needed to do it soon.

"I've tried to help," the general said. "But if the Scots have nosed out our surprise attack, there won't be a bloody goddamned thing I or anybody else can do to save you."

The face of the younger Bridgewater barely moved. "You've certainly done everything a commanding officer could do for an officer."

His father made a furious noise, turned sharply on his heel, and started walking directly toward Panna.

She was so surprised, she nearly stumbled. Panicked, she began to move farther down the hidden hallway, gathering her skirts to quiet them and keeping her head low enough to be hidden from the little windows.

The general reached the bookcase and turned, continuing in the same direction on the exterior glass side of the bookcases as Panna went on the interior wood side. He shook his head as if he were trying to sort out the difference between the man he thought he knew and the traitor who stood behind him. "You're a good officer," he said. "One of the best I've seen. Why would you throw it away to help the—"

The general narrowed his eyes. Had he seen her? Heard her? She reached the corner, turned down the hallway that ran parallel to the wall with the hearth and stopped, her heart pounding in her throat. She stretched her neck to peek from the nearest peephole.

Bridgewater was looking right at her, eyes flashing with irritation.

There was nothing I could do, she telegraphed back, equally irritated. Within this narrow hallway was a rickety staircase going up, and Panna realized that an identical hidden passageway must circle the second level of bookcases. She wondered if the stairs led anywhere else, offering a safe way to enter and exit when you didn't want the prying eyes of the castle upon you.

The general stopped right in front of her and made an interested grunt. Had he seen her? He was so close she could see the medals on his red coat. Sweat gathered between her shoulder blades.

"What's this?" the general demanded.

Every muscle vibrated with the desire to run, but Panna held herself still.

"What do you mean?" Bridgewater said carefully.

"Do you see this? Come here."

Bridgewater made his way to the bookcase.

"There."

"Sir?" Bridgewater bent to see what his father was pointing at. She could see the blond blur of his head and the dark pools of his eyes.

"Is that my copy of Caesar's *Gallic Wars*?"

Panna was so relieved she nearly moaned.

"Aye, I believe it is." Bridgewater unlocked the case and slid the book out. "I beg your pardon. I thought I'd returned it."

"Well...I do want you to have it. 'Tis something I would want all my officers to have."

Bridgewater bowed. "Thank you."

The general returned to his path around the room, and Panna realized with a start that if he continued in the same direction, he'd eventually come to the gate-leg table Reeves had set up—the same gate-leg table upon which the empty soup bowl sat. Panna didn't understand the tangle of loyalties and betrayals that had been revealed this evening, but she knew with utter certainty that no good could come of Bridgewater's father seeing the words etched on the bottom of that bowl.

She sorted through her limited options. She could scream, but drawing attention to herself would likely have serious repercussions for her as well as Bridgewater. Dropping a book on the general's head from an upper-level bookcase, even one the size of a

Gutenberg Bible, probably wouldn't knock him out unless she was very lucky. The only viable option seemed to be doing something with the table itself. But the general stood within sight of it.

Inhaling deeply, she squeezed past the back of the hearth, crushing her breasts as she rounded the corner. It was pitch-black, and she stumbled over something on the floor, slapping her palm against the bricks of the hearth to catch herself and sending a spray of detritus into the empty fireplace.

Panna held her breath so long that she thought she might faint.

"Good Lord," the general said at last. "It sounds as if the pigeons have taken roost in there."

In an instant, she was around the other corner of the hearth and behind the bookcase which had held *Animals of the Orient*. The little table where Bridgewater had eaten was directly in front of her. The front door of the bookcase was still ajar, and she reached for the handle of the wooden door near her. She was in luck. While Bridgewater had installed locks on the cabinet doors facing the room, he'd left the doors that faced the hidden passageway unsecured. She opened it slowly. The general crouched at the hearth, his back to her, gazing up the chimney with Bridgewater at his side. Bridgewater's eyes were on her, and his face was lined with strain.

With the Chinese foo dog statue blocking her from view, she slid her arm through the space left by the books that had been removed. Bridgewater became increasingly pale as he watched her.

The general grunted and made a move to stand.

"Do you suppose it's a matter of poor masonry?" Bridgewater asked suddenly, laying a staying hand on his father's arm.

"I hardly think so. 'Twas done by Matthew Francis himself. He was the best mason between here and York. No man would say otherwise."

She grabbed the lip of the table and flipped.

Crash.

The table hit the hearth and the bowl shattered. Panna jerked back into the darkness as fast as she could and closed the case with her foot.

"Damn it," Bridgewater said. "That happened a week ago, and Reeves said he'd had the leg repaired. No. Stay where you are. I'll take care of it."

Panna grinned. *Who says librarians aren't resourceful?*

Seven

WHEN THE GENERAL FINALLY EXITED AFTER A SECOND
round of frustrated fatherly exhortation, Panna pulled
herself to her feet and headed back in the direction she'd
come. She had barely covered half the distance when
she ran into Bridgewater, who was carrying a lit candle.

"I didn't know—"

"Quiet," he commanded.

He dragged her up the rickety stairs, around the
hearth and to the end of the upper passageway. He
leaned on the bricks there, and a door, completely
hidden from view, opened, revealing a small room.
Like the window seats, the space extended from the
side of the castle and had looming windows on three
sides. In fact, Panna could see into the bow windows of
the library. There were satchels heaped in the corner,
some empty crates, a telescope on a tripod, a small desk,
and a map on the wall from which ribbons holding
pencils hung. Bridgewater put the candle on the desk.

"What does 'They know' mean?" she demanded.
"Who are 'they'? Why was that written in the soup
bowl?"

"None of your business." He shoved her against the wall, looking hard into her eyes. The light from the sunset lit his hair a devil's red. "Who *are* you?"

"I can't tell you."

"A spy?"

"No," she said, offended. "I *helped* you."

"Who are you?"

"Panna Kennedy. My name is Panna Kennedy."

"And what are you doing in my castle?"

"I'm visiting."

"Visiting?" His fingers dug into her flesh. "From where?"

"I can't tell you."

"You'll tell me or you'll wish you had."

"From the future."

His face went blank. For a moment he said nothing. Then he laughed and let go. "That is the poorest lie I've ever heard. If you're a spy, you're a bloody awful one." He lifted her chin with a finger. "If you *are* a spy, however, I will find you when this is over, and you will live to regret it."

"I'm not a spy," she said hotly, flinging her chin free. "Would a spy have saved your sorry ass in there?"

He lifted a brow. "Perhaps your goal is to earn my trust."

"Perhaps my goal is to earn a thank-you."

He straightened, half-abashed. "Thank you."

"You're welcome."

There was something electric about being in such a small space with Bridgewater, and the hair on Panna's arm was standing on end. He could be both charming and dangerous, and she found herself unsure which incarnation of him was standing in the fading light with her.

"Panna?" His eyes continued their sharp appraisal. "What sort of a name is that?"

"My real name is Pandora."

He snorted. "Well, you've certainly been well named. This passageway is one of my most important secrets. You couldn't have picked a more inconvenient place to discover." He slipped off his officer's coat and loosened his stock, then withdrew a nondescript coat, knife, and pistol belt from one of the satchels.

"What are you doing?" she said. "Are you going to try to beat the army to Langholm?"

"Do you think that's where they're going, Mrs. Kennedy?" He pulled off his stained shirt, revealing a torso of well-hewn muscle.

"Your father said—"

"My *father*?"

Had she been mistaken? They looked so much alike. "He said the army would attack Langholm tonight."

"'Tis indeed what he said." Bridgewater slipped on a dark shirt and buttoned it. Then he drew the belt low around his hips.

"But you don't believe it?"

He didn't answer. She tried a different tack. "What about the boy?"

Bridgewater swayed slightly as he buckled the belt but otherwise ignored her question.

"Will they hurt him?"

The look he gave her through his one good eye was answer enough.

"A boy?" she said. "They'd hurt a little boy?"

He reached back into the satchel and pulled out a pistol.

An explosion shook the room, and for an instant Panna thought the gun had gone off. But a whistling beyond the window revealed the smoking trail of a cannonball in the reddening sky.

"They've begun the attack." She looked at the castle across the water.

"Demonstration," Bridgewater corrected as another cannon fired. He slipped the pistol into the belt. "They have not a flea's chance of taking the place." He unhooked a square panel of wood on the floor and lifted it. A narrow circular staircase came into view.

"Where are you going?"

"*We* are going."

"No, I can't." She thought of Marie waiting for her.

"I'm afraid you have no choice. I can hardly let you return to the people who employ you at this point." He gave her gown a disapproving look and muttered, "Though I could certainly wish for a less conspicuously clothed companion." He grabbed a pencil from the wall and began to fiddle with a sheet of paper on the desk.

"I'm not a spy. You have to believe me."

"The woman who just told me she came from the future? I don't think so. Tell me, if you come from the future, who is monarch after Queen Anne?"

She froze. Was it one of those Georges?

His mouth formed a thin line. "As I suspected."

"*No.* I'm telling the truth. I'm a librarian, not a historian. And the questions you're asking are from a *long* time ago. But I can tell you this much:

England conquers France. A hundred years from now, England is the world's first superpower. Your colonies stretch from one end of the globe to the other. You are ruled by a queen who sits on her throne for more than sixty years."

He gazed down the length of his noble nose at her. "A *queen*? A queen conquers the world?"

"Yes. Her name is Victoria. She's married to a prince named Albert. After he dies, she never recovers. She wears black the rest of her life." And Panna, who knew too well the abyss of grief, understood why.

"Queen *Victoria*?" he repeated, incredulous.

"Yes. And later she falls in love with a Scotsman, a man who takes care of her horses and—"

"A *groom*?"

"And Victoria and Albert's daughters—they had, like, ten kids—marry into practically every dynasty in Europe as a way to try to unify the countries, but it didn't really work. And in the end it didn't matter, because by the twenty-first century, the countries of Europe *are* united. Well, at least they share a parliament and courts and a common currency."

Bridgewater fell back a step, as if he'd taken a blow. "That's lunacy."

"It's not lunacy. It's what happens. I can tell you whatever you want to know. I'm not a spy. I came here by accident."

He regarded her closely, and she considered how hard it was to prove one was from another time. If she knew what happened an hour from now—or had a better handle on all those Georges—perhaps he'd believe her. Unfortunately, what she knew of the future sounded like the ravings of a madwoman, and that wasn't helping much.

He shook his head. "No. You're coming with me."

"Let me tell you about cell phones."

"What?"

"You no longer have to write letters. You can talk to anyone in the world anytime you want. Instantly."

His eyes darkened. He wasn't buying it—any of it.

"Gatorade," she cried. "Cheez Whiz. Reverse mortgages. QVC. Swipe right. Hot yoga. Lolcats. Sexting. Dijonnaise. Lady Gaga. Toaster Strudel. Kale cleanses. Selfies. Tofu turkey. Google Street View. Botox. Breakfast burritos. I can go on like this all day. Boca Burgers. Odor-Eaters. Krispy Kr—"

"*Stop!*" His face was a mixture of astonishment, confusion, and fear. He stared at her as if he were sizing up a flaming thunderbolt that had landed at his feet. "Never speak in such a manner again. You'll be hanged."

"Then you believe me?"

"How can anyone believe something like that?" He was angry now, and she knew that meant he was beginning to embrace the possibility.

"Do you at least believe I'm not a spy?"

"You want to convince me?" He folded the paper he'd been hunched over and dripped the candle's wax onto it. Then he pressed his thumb into the wax. "Take this to the home of my servant, Clare. The house is a mile past the inn, along the water, in the shadow of two large oaks."

She thought of the distance she'd be from the only portal back to her own world. She didn't know how to get out of the castle with the army guarding it, and she had no confidence that she'd be able to return to the chapel once she was out. This wasn't her life, her war, her country, or her time. And Marie and Steve were waiting. "I can't, Bridgewater. I can't. I have to return to my own time. Isn't there *anything* else I could do to prove it to you? Anything? You have to believe me. I'm not a spy."

He let out a long sigh, and the contentiousness seemed to drain out of him. "I can hardly accuse you of spying when you've turned down the perfect opportunity to read my note." He returned the paper to his pocket.

"Then you'll let me go?"

"I don't know what you are, Mrs. Kennedy. But if you tell anyone about this place or what I'm doing, my life will be forfeit. And if mine is, there's a good chance yours will be, too."

Had he meant the last as a threat or an entreaty to use caution? She couldn't untangle the emotion behind those hooded eyes. "I won't. I swear it."

He returned to the satchel, searching for something.

"Can you deliver it yourself?" she asked softly. "The note, I mean."

He withdrew a pair of dark, loose-fitting trousers. "I have less than an hour before the guard returns. I have something else to take care of."

"The boy?"

Bridgewater didn't answer. He pulled the trousers over his boots and britches and buttoned them. What was he involved in? Were the army's accusations true?

"Tell me, Mrs. Kennedy, how does one return to

the future? Is there a spell involved? Do you rise up like mists from a primeval lake and disappear into the sky?"

Was he mocking her? The look on his face revealed only polite and seemingly genuine curiosity.

"Get me back to the hallway," she said. "I can take care of it from there." It had struck her that revealing the location of the portal might not be wise for her or for Bridgewater.

She waited for him to ask more questions, but he didn't.

"The things you talked about..." His forehead creased.

"I could tell you more."

"Don't." He pointed to the stairs. "One flight down is the library, though there's no door there. Two more flights down after that is a door that leads out of the castle and across the ruins in the back. That's the door I'll be taking. But on the landing in-between is a door to a passage under the library that leads to another stairway. Take that stairway up a flight and you'll be at a door that leads into the hallway outside the library. The bolt is on the inside. There's a peephole. Make sure you don't open the door until the hall is empty."

As she was about to descend, he caught her arm.

"Not yet. There's a change of guard at a quarter past eight both outside and at the guard station at the end of the hallway beyond the library. While it should be a time of utmost attention, the soldiers use it as an opportunity to converse about the day's events." He turned the telescope toward the castle's drawbridge and gazed through the eyepiece. "Privates Swenson, Baker, Thorpe, and Coyne will walk into the courtyard soon. Swenson has white-blond hair, visible even on the darkest night. They will split into two groups of two." He pointed to a worn path in the distance. "Swenson and Baker will head to the gate to take the place of the men there. That's when I'll make my escape. Approximately three minutes later, Thorpe and Coyne will arrive at the guard station in the hallway outside the chapel to take the place of the men there. That's when you'll go down."

"How do you know all this?"

He released the telescope. "They were my men until this morning. I signed off on the duty roster."

What a change twelve hours had wrought. "And what time is it now?"

"It was almost eight o'clock when I entered the passageway."

She gasped. Eight was the time she had agreed to meet Marie's husband's cousin, Steve, at the library. Almost an hour had passed since she'd left Marie in the stacks. Time certainly moved at a terrifying speed here.

Bridgewater saw her face. "Another appointment?"

She flushed. "I—I—"

He looked away. "I see."

"No, you don't. I'm a widow, and my friend has arranged a dinner engagement for me with her husband's cousin, a man named Steve. It would be inconsiderate of me to abandon him."

Bridgewater fiddled with one of the ribboned pencils. "I will endeavor to ensure that you can keep your appointment," he said at last, lifting his eyes.

She wanted to say she had no desire to keep the appointment—that she'd rather linger here with him in the charged confines of this room, sharing the thrill of his covert plans—but when she opened her mouth to speak, nothing came out.

Eight or ten short minutes. That was the time she had left with him, and an hour in total was all they would ever share. It had been a fine hour—an amazing hour—and she found herself feeling quite sorry it would end.

"Count for me, will you?"

"Pardon?" she said.

"To three hundred. Slow and steady. That's the way we teach soldiers to mark time. Three hundred is about five minutes. I need to organize my pack."

There was something about the way he'd said "slow and steady" that made her heart skip a beat. She began. "One, two, three—"

"Slower."

He patted her wrist in the dark, measuring the beat. The light scent of spiced soap hung on him along with the sweeter notes of brandy. She inhaled. *Eleven, twelve, thirteen.*

Charlie had always had a joke: What's good in twenty minutes but even better in five?

Oh, Charlie.

She'd laughed every time he'd said it. Unsophisticated it might be, but there was something oh, so right about taking the express train home while you hung on to the overhead strap for dear life.

She looked at Bridgewater, intently rearranging his supplies. Did he like the express train? Or was he more of an Orient Express, make-the-journey-part-of-the-trip sort of guy? Not that there was anything wrong with a nice slow trip on the Orient Express, mind you, and Bridgewater looked as if he knew how to pass the time on a leisurely journey. But there was something about the way his eyes had lingered on her as they'd drunk their brandies that made her think he had a fiery five-minute express train in him as well.

God, where was she? *Let's say forty-eight, forty-nine, fifty…*

She looked down at the library's surveying seat, visible below them through the window, and a wicked tingle went through her. *No, I bet Bridgewater would have no trouble at all making good use of those five minutes.*

She imagined him freeing a handful of her hair and bringing it to his nose.

"Lilacs," he would say. "You have come to seek a donation, have you not?"

"Yes," she'd reply. "For my library."

Ah, if only real fund-raising were like this.

He would pour a brandy and hand it to her. Some of that impeccable Don Alfonso vintage that currently was making her head spin. His eyes would play an enigmatic game with hers.

"I'm willing to make the donation you seek."

"Excellent."

"And in exchange, I should very much like to bed you."

She would feel a peremptory shock. "That is outrageous, sir. Here?"

"Aye. Now."

"Are you not worried about your servants?" she would ask lightly, trying to quell her quaking nerves.

"Reeves has his orders for this evening."

A premeditated act. Yes, that would be Bridgewater.

Her legs would turn to jelly. "Have you considered simply seducing me?"

"I have. Though I doubt it would be simple."

He was right. It wouldn't be. Not with Charlie standing in the shadows. And that's what she liked about Bridgewater. He saw her complexity and wasn't put off by it.

He would take a deep draft of the brandy and gaze at her. "Sometimes a man just wants to feel he has purchased his pleasure."

"Sometimes," she would say, "a woman just wants to feel she's been purchased."

"Then it's settled?"

"Everything but the price."

God, this was better than the books she sneaked off to read in the back of the stacks.

He would reach for a pouch on his desk and open it. It would be filled with gold and silver coins, some large, some small. He would pick half a dozen and rattle them in his palm.

"I believe this is what you requested." He would slip his coin-filled hand into her bodice and cup her breast.

Oh, dear! The booms of the army's cannons outside...matched the pounding in her veins. *It must be the brandy. I would never...or would I?*

He would smile, and his thumb would trace the tender outline of her nipple.

"That was the price when you were making a gift," she would say. "Now you're making a purchase."

His brows would rise, and the light in those

sapphire eyes would sparkle approvingly. He would bring his mouth to her ear. "Double? Triple?"

She would point to the pouch on his desk and smile.

His hand would jerk away if he'd been burned. "Are you mad?"

"What would you call a woman who risks her reputation to bed a man in an unlocked room?"

His mouth would crook into a smile. "The mistress of her own library."

A happy charge ran all the way to Panna's toes, and she wiggled them inside her shoes, smiling.

"Did you finish?"

She jumped. The flesh-and-blood Bridgewater was looking at her curiously.

"Finish?" she repeated.

"Counting? Did you finish?"

"Er, yes. Two hundred ninety-eight, two hundred ninety-nine, three hundred," she said quickly.

He frowned. "That seemed a little fast."

"Did it? It seemed just right to me."

Of course, that's only how it happens in books—or in the minds of highly imaginative librarians. In her experience, there was usually a kernel of corn in someone's teeth, an uncooperative corselet of Spanx, a condom past its use-by date, or some other sort of humbling horror meant to remind the parties involved that nothing good ever comes from too much pleasure. But, oh, were it only so.

He fiddled with the telescope, checking the path below.

"Are they there?"

"Not yet," he said. "A few more minutes."

The evening had grown dark, save for the occasional booming punctuation of the cannons. Without the lights of the industrial world to compete with them, the stars in the Cumbrian night sparkled like a tray of million-dollar diamonds. She marveled at the number of them.

"Would you care to look?" he said.

"Pardon?"

"At the stars?" He swung the telescope's eyepiece toward her.

She'd never used a telescope before, and her lack of knowledge must have been apparent. He shoved a crate toward her with the toe of his boot and said, "It's exceedingly straightforward. Just put your eye there"—he pointed to the end—"and adjust here."

Standing on the crate made her a little too tall to look through the eyepiece comfortably, so she stooped, brushing a lock of hair out of her face. Against the deep blue black, she saw spots of light, some large, some small, some even appearing to her overexcited imagination to be the color of a robin's egg or a peach.

Bridgewater touched her cheek and she started.

"Open your eye," he said.

She'd shut the one she wasn't using.

"Your mind will let you see what you need with the one at the scope," he said. "In any case, a good soldier always wants to have an eye on what's going on around him."

The problem was there was too much going on around her. Her blood was still racing from her daydream and the brandy's delicious warmth seemed to have turned her arms and legs to rubber. Added to that, the brush of Bridgewater's coat against her arm was making her self-conscious almost to the point of light-headedness.

She moved a foot to better support herself on the crate and missed the edge. He caught her by the waist, steadying her easily, and when she straightened, she was looking directly into his eyes.

"What's that?"

The distant voice had come from the rampart outside—a guard speaking to his companion. The guard pointed to their window.

"Don't move," Bridgewater said.

"Do you see that?" the man said. "There, in that window. I thought I saw something move."

"It's my hair," she said, panicked. "They can see it."

"They cannot see beyond the reflections of the fire-pots on the glass." Bridgewater's chest was reassuringly solid under her fingertips.

"It's just the fire," the other guard said. "There's been nothing in that wing since the place burned in '86."

The men walked on, but Panna didn't move. Bridgewater's hands tightened on her waist, and his eyes sought in hers the answer to an unspoken question. He held her until the last echo of the soldiers' footsteps died away.

She clasped the rough wool of his lapels, intensely aware of the dampness of her palms and the beating of his heart. The answer she wished to give was such a complicated mixture of attraction, desire, and the pain of letting go of Charlie, she couldn't speak.

Bridgewater saw her disquiet and brought his

mouth to hers lightly, an offer she might accept or dismiss. She kissed him hungrily, reeling in the storm of emotion.

His lips were warm, and his mouth hungry. He brought his fingertips along the ridge of her spine, and though he handled her reverently, she could feel his desire like a harnessed panther, just under the skin. He was waiting for a sign.

But what sign could she give? He was opening a box she'd locked after Charlie's death. Her brain said, "Run!" but her body and her heart would have none of it. They had been denied too long.

Through desire or fear, she began to shake, and he pulled her into the glow of the candle so he could see her face more clearly.

"What is it?"

She shook her head, ashamed. "I think I'm afraid. It's been so long."

He pulled her close. "You need never be afraid with me. Ever."

Her mouth found his, and for a moment the world around them disappeared.

Panna would have happily said good-bye to the rest of the world forever, but she felt the cold length of the pistol between them. He had a mission and she had a home.

He let out a long sigh. "If I could make time stand still for us, I would," he whispered.

"I would too."

A distant bell rang. "A quarter past the hour," he said. He slipped from her arms, letting his hand trail slowly across her cheek, and then allowed himself one final kiss.

She clutched the wall for support, thinking of the library and Marie and the house that held everything that remained of Charlie. What was she doing here?

He aimed the telescope at the path. "Still not here." He *tsked*. "You're running late, soldiers."

She made her way to his side. The power of what they'd summoned thrummed between them like a guitar string. He squeezed her hand and swung the telescope upward, training it on a precise spot in the sky. "Here. Look at this."

She almost had to slip into his arms to reach the eyepiece. The lock of hair fell forward again.

"Come, come," he said. "We can't have this. Keep your eyes on the path." He pulled a pale green ribbon from the map. Then he removed the combs in her hair, letting the tresses fall across her shoulders.

"'Tis like a thousand rays of sunshine," he said gravely.

She gathered the hair to one side of her shoulder, and he fumbled twice before tying the ribbon in a neat bow around it.

"Thank you." Her voice was barely a whisper.

She bent to the eyepiece and he held up his hand. "Wait. See, the star there?" She tucked herself against him to follow his line of sight.

"Yes. It's part of the Big Dipper."

"The Big Dipper?" He examined the sky. "Oh, aye. I suppose so. In Cumbria, 'tis called the Butcher's Cleaver."

"So *that's* what you meant!"

He chuckled. "Aye. 'Tis an ugly name, I suppose, but it certainly fits the sensibilities of the borderlands. Look at the second star from the end. In the sky, not through the telescope."

She gazed where he pointed. "It's larger than the rest. It almost looks like it's pulsing."

"Now through the scope."

She looked again. "Oh! It's *two* stars! They're so close!"

"Like lovers circling one another in a dance. Slowly falling in love. And someday they'll be as one."

Their eyes met, and Panna thought he would kiss her again, but he busied himself with the adjustments self-consciously. "I'm eager to see them more clearly. My scope is good, but I hear in Leiden they are developing even more powerful lenses. Perhaps someday…"

He must have seen a movement in the courtyard, for he turned abruptly. "Private Swenson. 'Tis time."

Her heart lurched.

He grabbed the bag he'd prepared. "Now, remember: three minutes from the time Thorpe and Coyne break from Swenson and Baker. No more, no less. And remember to descend two flights."

"Two flights. Yes."

He slid the note back into her hands. "I don't know who you really are, Panna, but you say you're not a spy and I want to believe you. If you could take this to the home of my servant Clare, I would be very grateful. He can tell you the rest. I shouldn't ask you to risk yourself, I know. And, in truth, the things I strive for will survive whether you deliver it or not, but it would mean a great deal, and not just to me."

She shook her head and tried to give the note back, but he pressed it into her hand. Then he threw his arms around her and kissed her. "Come back to me,

Panna. Let us stop time together. I don't know when I've spent a more enjoyable evening."

He flew down the stairs.

She exhaled as his last steps died away. A long moment passed before she mastered her emotions. She looked down. Coyne and Thorpe were gone. How much time had gone by?

She tiptoed down the stairs, two flights as he'd instructed, though the staircase descended even farther, which is where Bridgewater said he would go. She ran through the passageway under the library and up the stairs on the other side. Since she'd lost track of time, she decided she'd count to sixty—this time without letting her mind wander—and slip out. According to Bridgewater, she'd be in the hall that ran between the chapel and the library.

By the count of thirty, she was quaking so much, she couldn't wait any longer. She opened the door. She was in the hallway she remembered from her arrival. Someone in the distance yelled, "You, there! Stop, I say!" followed by the *boom* of a pistol shot.

She sprinted into the chapel and through the short half door.

Her hands shook as she fumbled with the key, and it wasn't until she had safely locked the triangular door behind her back in Pittsburgh that she noticed the man standing with his back to her outside the darkened door of the Carnegie Library.

He waved when he saw her. Dazed, she went to the door, which had been locked in the time since she'd left, and slid the bolt. She wished she was anyplace on earth but here.

"You must be Kyle's cousin," she said, managing a weak smile. "I'm Panna. So sorry I'm late."

Eight

BRIDGEWATER FELT THE SHOT WHIZ BY HIS HEAD. HE dropped to the ground in the rubble of the castle's west side and rolled into a ball.

"There! Do you see him?"

Bridgewater recognized the distant voice as that of Private Able Kenworthy.

"That's a rock, you fool," said Kenworthy's duty mate, Bobby O'Hare. "There's nothing there *but* rocks."

"I saw it move."

Bridgewater was completely unprotected. If Kenworthy took another shot, even in the dark, Bridgewater would stand a better-than-even chance of getting hit.

"Which rock?" O'Hare asked.

"That one, I think."

Bridgewater braced himself. Shot by one of his own men. An ironic ending for an officer. If dying was to be his fate, he preferred that it be at the hands of his mysterious visitor, ideally after a long night of illicit lovemaking. At least he'd die happy instead of laid out like a practice target on the most uncomfortable stretch of Castle MacIver imaginable.

"*I* think it's a rock," O'Hare said. "But if you're so goddamned certain, haul your arse down there and find out."

"Aww. Bloody hell, I ain't going all the way down there."

In the unlikely event that he both survived and was restored to his command, Bridgewater made a mental note to have both men whipped for dereliction of duty.

Several moments went by without additional shots or discussion, and Bridgewater crawled over the heaped debris of the ancient wing until he reached the corner of two singed walls. This room was the only part of the wing that had remained intact after the fire, and since no one visited the ruins, it was a handy place to hide things you didn't want anyone to find.

She'd said she was from the future, but it was too foolish a cover for a spy. And yet, if she wasn't a spy and what she'd told him was true...

He shook his head, banishing the question from his present enterprise, and put his ear against the wall. Apart from the distant hiss of the firepots and the gurgling of the river, he heard nothing.

He leaned closer and made the sound of a nightingale's call.

He heard the scuffle of footsteps and an answering nightingale's call, clear and true.

Thomas.

The entrance to the room was directly opposite where he stood. That was where he supposed the guard would be situated. It would have helped to know which man it was—each, of course, had his own foibles. He was grateful to his judicious forebear who'd insisted that every room worth entering was worth exiting in at least two separate ways. Clare was the one who had pointed out the oddly placed chimney when they'd made their first inspection of the property before Bridgewater had bought it four years earlier and asked, "Why would there be a chimney in a powder shed?"

Why, indeed?

Bridgewater found a toehold in the rough stone and heaved himself quietly to the top. With a quick swing of his legs, he was inside the chimney and climbing down the carefully placed metal rungs. The last step ended a good eight feet above the hearth, and he dropped to the floor with a soft thud.

The boy stood before him, filthy, one ear covered in blood and eyes wide with terror. But it was the slim arm dangling limply at his side that darkened Bridgewater's vision.

Too bad I won't be able to offer you as fine a nursing as I had tonight.

Thomas knew enough not to speak, though Bridgewater could tell he was desperate to. Bridgewater thought guiltily of the boy's father and mother, who'd been so proud their son was aiding the rebels. Bridgewater would have to tell them how brave the boy had been. He wondered for a moment what it would be like to have such loving parents and to feel that sense of belonging. Though the disparity between their positions in the world was immense, Bridgewater had often felt Thomas was the luckier of the two of them.

Bridgewater whispered, "Can you climb with one arm?"

Thomas nodded and only gave a small groan as he was lifted to the rungs. When he found his footing and began to make his way, Bridgewater adjusted the satchel over his own shoulder, leaped, and climbed up after him.

When he reached the top, he heard a *click*.

Abel Kenworthy was pointing his pistol at Bridgewater.

"Good evening, sir." He held the boy by his bloody ear.

Bridgewater nodded. "Glad to see something of your training has stuck with you."

To his credit, Kenworthy chuckled. Which gave Bridgewater just the time he needed to withdraw his pistol from his belt.

Kenworthy paled.

"My incarceration will be over by morning—one way or another," Bridgewater said. "My bet is on me being your commander again. Each man has to choose which side of the line he'll stand on, Kenworthy. Now is your turn. You can be a hero tonight and spend the rest of your career walking the far side of Hadrian's Wall with sixty pounds of shot on your back. Or you can wave us on while I give you my word I'll be back in the library within a quarter hour, in which case you will enjoy the privilege of being one of the most favored privates in Her Majesty's army. Your choice."

Kenworthy's eyes went from Bridgewater's face to the tower where the colonel, an officer feared far more than the general, was housed.

"The third option being, of course, that I shoot you and run." Bridgewater cocked the pistol.

"I…"

"Don't take too long, Kenworthy. The guard on the other side of the powder shed may hear us, and only one of you can be the most favored."

"I have a right desire to see Galway again, sir. 'Tis my mother's home."

"A request for transfer, along with a highly complimentary letter of reference, will be sent by messenger to Colonel O'Donovan in Dublin tomorrow."

Kenworthy nodded but didn't lower his pistol. "Thank you, sir. But I'm afraid I must insist you say good-bye to the lad now and return to the castle while I watch. And you'd best hurry."

Bridgewater took Thomas by his good arm and hurried across the rocks. When they reached the next outcropping and were out of earshot, he crouched to look the boy in the eye. "I can't go with you."

Thomas nodded wordlessly.

"You'll be all right. Go to the surgeon's house in Longcroft. Tell him I sent you. He'll set your arm. Stay off the road. Walk along the river path. All right?"

"Aye." The boy's shoulders hitched and he started to cry. "I told them about Carlisle."

Bridgewater gave him a reassuring smile. "Any man in your place would have done the same. When your arm is set, borrow the surgeon's horse and go to Clare's as quickly as you can. The effort tonight must be abandoned."

Thomas nodded.

The note about Langholm had been a plant,

Bridgewater's attempt to divert the army's attention northward. The rebels' real target was Carlisle, to the west, where a raid was set to occur in just a few hours. Their objective was the destruction of a shipment of forty kegs of gunpowder coming from York. With surprise on their side, the rebels would likely be successful, and the loss of gunpowder would delay the English army's plans by several weeks. But with the rebels' real objective now known to Bridgewater's commanding officers, the rebels would be surprised and slaughtered, a warning to anyone who dared challenge the army's monopoly on power in the borderlands. Reeves's scrawled message "They know" had told Bridgewater the Carlisle plan had been uncovered, the outcome of Thomas's torture. He prayed Panna had changed her mind and was already on her way to Bowness to find Clare. By the time Thomas reached Bowness, it would likely be too late.

"They told me they'd find my mother and… and…" Thomas cried harder.

"They lied. They wouldn't." Even the colonel wouldn't do that. Nobility counts for something, he thought.

"It hurt so much."

Bridgewater sighed, thinking of his own interrogation. "You're no different than any man in that regard. I promise you."

Thomas rubbed a torn coat sleeve across his cheeks, eyes cast downward. "I don't make a very good soldier."

Bridgewater pulled him into his arms, careful not to jar the broken one. "No. 'Tis I. I do not make a very good captain."

Nine

"AGAIN, I'M SO SORRY." PANNA DROPPED ONTO Marie's couch and told herself to relax. She'd been babbling since the moment she'd gotten into Steve's car. Steve was a cop, and so far he'd treated her with the unfailing kindness cops reserve for lost children and stranded ducklings.

He waved away her concern. "Really, don't sweat it. Marie said she was sure you'd be back. You were. No problem."

As if on cue, Marie came through the door to the kitchen carrying a tray with two beers, corn chips, and a heaping bowl of guacamole. "Glad to see Steve was able to wrestle you to the ground." She laughed. "I told him you'd probably gone for a quick walk or something."

Yeah, to the eighteenth century.

"I-I-" Panna shook her head. "I'm an idiot. What can I say?"

Marie placed the tray on the coffee table. "Well, Kyle's charring the red peppers in there for the fajitas. I need to be standing by with a fire extinguisher. Back in a flash." She raised an eyebrow at Panna and ran out.

Steve grabbed the beers and handed one to Panna. "Hey, you know, I locked myself out of my car while it was running tonight. I'd forgotten to grab your cell phone number and went back inside to get it."

"Well, that *is* a good thing to have," she admitted.

"Yeah, too bad it was in my pocket the whole time." He clinked his bottle against hers. "To idiocy. The only difference, it looks much better on you."

She flushed and lifted the bottle to her mouth. She felt like she'd gone one too many rounds on the Tilt-A-Whirl. Steve was nice—nicer than she'd expected, with a wry smile and an unflappable approach to life that reminded her of Charlie—but she didn't want to be here. The sound of that distant gunshot was still ringing in her ear. They'd had to be shooting at Bridgewater. Had they hit him? She moved and the corner of Bridgewater's note jabbed her through her pocket.

She'd been very surprised to discover it still in her hand once she'd slammed and locked the triangular half door at the library. While her philosophy of time travel was by no means well formed yet, she'd assumed that, since the dress had disappeared both times she'd returned, the note would too.

The paper was folded tight and sealed with a plug of emerald-green wax that carried Bridgewater's coat of arms. What did it say? Why was it so important? Most important, what sort of danger was he in, and what would happen if she didn't deliver it to Clare?

If you tell anyone about this place or what I'm doing, my life will be forfeit.

She realized Steve was looking at her.

"Sorry. Did you ask me something?"

He gave her a considering look. "Sort of. I asked if you thought Marie would be mad if I dug into the guacamole, and you said 'My life will be forfeit.'"

"Oh."

"Needless to say, I put my chip down."

"Oh, Steve, I'm sorry. I'm a little frazzled tonight. Yes," she said, filling two chips with dip and handing him one, "let's have some. You're a cop, right? I can't think of anything more different from being a librarian—or, frankly, more interesting."

He laughed. "It has its moments."

"Let me ask you something. How accurate were guns in the early seventeen hundreds, I mean in shooting someone?"

The chip stopped halfway to his mouth. "Okay, *there's* a question I don't get asked very often."

"I'm sorry. I'm kind of distracted by this thing at the library."

His brows went up. "Involving a gun from the seventeen hundreds?"

"It's just…" She realized the worry wasn't going to stop, nor was the guilt. Had Bridgewater been shot? Who else would suffer without her intervention? "Steve, I'm really sorry, but I think I need to go back to the library."

❧

"Are you sure you don't want me to take you home?" Steve turned the wheel and eased the car onto Main. "I'm not a creep. I swear, I'll just let you off and say good night."

"I'm sorry," Panna said. "I know all I've done since

I met you tonight is apologize, but you really are a nice guy."

"Look, it's not easy losing a spouse. I know. My sister's a widow. Life stuck a pretty crappy fortune in your fortune cookie. You should have all the time you need to come to a place where you're comfortable with dating again, you know what I mean?"

The gilded domes of the Greek Orthodox church glided by. "I'm going to be honest. I didn't want to go out with you. I cried tonight at the library. But that's not what this is about. You're a lot nicer than I expected."

"I'm thinking about that for my epitaph, actually."

She laughed. "I know I'm not saying this very well. What I mean is, this isn't about you. It's about a friend who's in trouble. I might be able to help him is all."

He turned at PaPa J's and started up the long rise to the library. "That's a good instinct, Panna. There's one thing I've learned as a cop—you gotta follow your instincts." He pulled up to the columned entrance and opened his door.

"No, no. You don't need to let me out." She extended her hand. "I know it's been a crappy evening, but I really appreciate you understanding."

He held her hand for a moment. "Don't cry about me, okay, Panna? No one should have to cry. I'll call you again. If you don't want to go out, just tell me. No harm, no foul."

It had been a long time since a man had made her feel this at ease, and her eyes filled. "Thank you." She kissed him on the cheek and popped out, not daring to look back until she heard the car pull away.

Jesus, you're a mess.

She swiped at her eyes and, after she entered, walked in a wide arc to keep her distance from the door beneath the stairs, as if an arm from the past might shoot out, catch her by the foot, and drag her back. She flipped on the lights and felt her heart warm as the high ceiling, grand oval desk, and soaring hearth came into view. To Panna, there was something eternally comforting about this space. She did her best thinking here and had often come here in the late evenings during Charlie's last months, after he'd fallen asleep, to find the strength to carry on.

She dropped her purse on the desk and walked to the front of the statue. In the still marble, she looked for a reflection of the man and found it in the wide shoulders, the proud bearing, the aquiline nose. Only the eyes, with their dead stare, seemed unfamiliar to her.

"John Bridgewater, Viscount Adderly. Hero of the Battle of Ramillies."

She was embarrassed to say she didn't know the exact year of the Battle of Ramillies. She had looked it up once, to investigate the details of the man's exploits, but had failed to file that key fact away, more intent on Queen Anne's description of him as a "handsome man in the fullness of life."

That he was.

She sat down at the computer and pulled up Wikipedia. She'd been in 1706, probably late summer. There was a chance she'd discover the Battle of Ramillies had been in 1708 or 1709 or 1718 or some year that would prove he hadn't been hurt or killed by that shot she'd heard and that no harm had come to him because of the note that she hadn't delivered.

"The Battle of Ramillies, part of the War of Spanish Succession, was fought in Ramillies, present day Waloon-Brabant, Belgium, on May 23, 1706," she read, dejected. Scanning further, she found, "Decorated officers included Captain John Hay, Colonel Peter Brinfield (killed in action), and Colonel John Bridgewater."

There was nothing more on Bridgewater in the article, so she Googled "Colonel John Bridgewater" and came up with three references, the same three she'd found the first time she'd looked him up years ago. One was simply of a list of English officers under the Duke of Marlborough during the twenty years he'd masterminded England's military fortunes in Europe. There were three Bridgewaters, but only one with the asterisk indicating he had been decorated. One was a short account of Bridgewater's heroism in battle. He had made three separate runs through a line of French musket and cannon fire to bring back wounded soldiers from his company. The French had nicknamed him *le Fantôme Rouge*—the Red Ghost.

The last was an excerpt from a note Queen Anne had written at the time to one of her ladies-in-waiting. Panna had read it before. It talked of a whole range of things, and the historian who had excerpted it had described it as "effusive girl talk," which brought a scowl to Panna's face, but the part that had made Panna first fall in love with the hero Bridgewater—

Warmth rushed across her cheeks. It was one thing to say you'd fallen in love with a statue or an amorphous war hero from the pages of Google. It was quite another to say it about a living, breathing man you had met. She needed to watch herself.

Nonetheless, her fingers tingled as she read what Queen Anne had written to her correspondent so long ago.

> *I can understand why you couldn't stop smiling during our dinner last night, my dear. Viscount Adderly is a handsome man in the fullness of life. I do believe he has the finest calves I have ever seen displayed under my table. He is, of course, the heir to the Bridgewater title, and with that would come a good deal of gold as well as a good deal of responsibility. As you know, the lords Bridgewater have anchored the defense of the borderlands for several centuries. Could you live so far away from me, my dear, and forgo our friendship? Perhaps he is, as a wicked friend of ours might say, a better candidate for a more short-term "London marriage."*

Panna wasn't exactly sure what a London marriage was, but having met the man now, she thought she had a pretty good idea.

Then it struck her that Viscount Adderly was not a real nobleman's title—at least, not for him. Queen Anne's mention of the Bridgewater title reminded Panna that the oldest son of a noblemen used one of his father's other titles as a courtesy title until his father passed away and the official title came into his hands. Panna had read enough Regency-era literature to know Viscount Adderly was a courtesy title. The Earl of Bridgewater was the real title—his father's title.

She looked at the statue. "John Bridgewater, Viscount Adderly. Hero of the Battle of Ramillies." She rested her chin on her palm, trying to fight off the uneasiness that was coming over her. The Bridgewater descendant had commissioned this statue at the turn of the twentieth century, long after John Bridgewater had died. He would certainly have listed John Bridgewater's final title, wouldn't he?

Panna's heart began to pound. The only reason she could think of to explain why the Bridgewater descendent would list his forebear under a courtesy title rather than the official one was that John Bridgewater had died before his father had had a chance to pass the title of earl on to him.

Panna took the note from her pocket. How much danger was he in?

She didn't have a choice. She had to get the note to Clare.

Damn it, why did a kiss have to lead to such complications? Why did the rest of the eighteenth-century world have to intrude?

She felt no call to heroism and possessed no knowledge of spycraft or warfare except what she'd picked up in the novels of John le Carre or books like *Catch-22*, *The Red Badge of Courage*, and *Cold Mountain*. Bridgewater couldn't have chosen a less able co-conspirator. Hell, any video-game-playing teenager would have made a better ally.

Should she bring a gun? She didn't own one, and there certainly wasn't one at the library. She didn't have time to find one in any case. What *could* she bring? Was there anything here that would give her some advantage? She looked around at the carrels and bookshelves and scanners and jars of pens and pencils. There wasn't a lot here that would scare off an angry English soldier, although she had once broken up a fight in which one teenage girl plunged a sharpened pencil right into the hand of another.

Panna reached for the knot in her hair, to confirm that the pencils were properly sharpened, and was surprised to discover instead of her bun the ponytail Bridgewater had tied into place with a ribbon. She thought of the look on his face after he'd loosened her hair, and a frisson of pleasure went through her. Unwilling to undo this remnant of their time together, Panna grabbed a sharpened pencil and slipped it into her pocket instead.

Was that it? Was that the only weapon she could take on her mission?

Opening the desk drawer, she found a box cutter, which she put beside the pencil, and was just reaching for a small pair of scissors when the jangle of her cell phone made her jump.

She fished it out of her purse and looked at the display. It was Marie. *Shit.* She answered.

"Hey, are you okay?"

"Fine. I'm so sorry I spoiled the evening."

"My fault," Marie said. "I shouldn't have rushed you into a dinner with Steve. He's—"

"Actually he's great."

"Really?" Marie said, her voice filled with such joy, one would have thought Panna had told her they were splitting a winning lottery ticket. Panna was touched by how invested in her happiness Marie was.

"Really," Panna said. "A keeper. I just, um, have this other thing on my mind."

"Charlie?" The happiness receded.

"Actually, no, believe it or not." Panna realized she'd hardly thought of Charlie at all that night. She suspected Charlie would have found that a very good thing. "It has to do with another friend of mine who's in trouble."

"Oh. Something serious?"

"I think so. Say, if you were going to fight in a war in the borderlands of Scotland in the eighteenth century, what's the most important weapon you'd take with you?"

"Are you playing a video game?"

"No, this is something else. Sort of a what-if game? If you were going to travel through time to fight in a war in the borderlands of Scotland in 1706, what's one thing would you take with you?"

"Well, that's simple. A book on Scottish military history."

Panna blinked. Of course! Nothing would be more valuable! "You're a lifesaver."

"Great Hera!"

Panna laughed. "Thank you for understanding, Marie."

"Good luck with your friend."

Panna hung up and dove onto the keyboard. She hated to use Wikipedia, but she didn't have time to find and read every related book. She scanned the sections on Scottish military history and the reign of

Queen Anne. What she came away with was a clear sense that Scotland was doomed to be swallowed whole by England and a superficial understanding of the key battles that followed Ramillies—not to mention an affirmation that George I followed Anne in the English line of monarchs. She dared not print any of it out for fear it would fall into the wrong hands.

So there it was, she thought, laying out the items on the desktop. Her arsenal. A box cutter, a sharpened pencil, and about a dozen paragraphs from Wikipedia filed into her brain. Her version of a bell, book, and candle. Would the magic they evoked be as powerful?

She was just about to get up when a sentimental tug brought her fingers back. She typed "Big Dipper." The stars Bridgewater had pointed out, evidently called Mizar and Alcor, had been the first binary, or two-star, system ever discovered. But Bridgewater was wrong. The stars do not circle one another, slowly falling into one another's path. They are nearly six trillion miles apart and will never, ever get any closer.

The notion made her sad. Bridgewater had been so pleased by the idea of a paired star. And she had too—especially since he seemed to see the two of them as the stars. But there was nothing to be done about it, just as there was nothing to be done about the fact that no matter what her feelings for Bridgewater were, there would always be three centuries standing between them.

She tucked her purse under the desk, picked up

Bridgewater's note for Clare, grabbed her weapons, and headed toward the triangular door.

Ten

The Ruins Outside Castle MacIver, 1706

PANNA HAD BEEN PREPARED TO ESCAPE DOWN Bridgewater's secret stairway and across the ruins. What she hadn't been prepared for when she'd emerged again in the chapel was finding Bridgewater's library abandoned and wrecked. She gazed anxiously at mess. Several bookcases had been smashed, and books lay in heaps on the floor. The drawers of his desk had been opened and their contents scattered across the rug.

She hoped Bridgewater was safe. A lot had happened in the hour since she'd left—nothing good.

He'd said to follow the river for a mile after the inn, to a house in the shadow of two oaks, and she stood now on the bank of the river, its blue-black surface spangled with the light of the moon. Panna assumed the inn was in the little town to the west and set out in that direction.

The town was almost empty, it being so late, and the people who were out paid her little mind. The town ended as quickly as it had begun, and at the inn, a gable-roofed house at the edge of town called the Bowness Arms, Panna began to pace out a mile.

Halfway there, she noticed a man following her. She considered running, but leaving the path seemed like a bad idea. Clare's house lay ahead, but she was still a hundred yards away.

The man picked up his pace, and Panna's heart beat faster. She moved the note from her pocket to the inside of her bodice and walked faster. The next time she looked over her shoulder, the man had halved the distance between them.

Had he followed her from the castle? The inn? Did he know her connection to Bridgewater? And where was Bridgewater? Had he been captured? Killed? Would the delivery of the note make any difference now?

The man was nearly on her heels. Panna was a decent runner—every year she ran in Carnegie's 5K race in honor of fallen police and firemen—but she was also a woman who didn't like to be intimidated.

She dug her heels in—literally, pulled the box cutter from her pocket, and slid the blade into place. Then she turned around.

The man, barrel-chested and sporting a full black beard, didn't alter his pace. He approached her like a slow-moving freight train, moving in a direct line. "Put the knife away, lassie," he said as he passed her. "I'm Clare. If you've come from my master, you're safe with me."

She exhaled, relieved, and ran to catch up with him. "You're Clare. I thought—" The look on the man's face stopped her.

"You thought what?"

She shifted. "Where I come from, Clare is often"—*always*, she wanted to say—"a woman's name."

"There have been people who've said that to me." He gave her a grim smile. "But usually no more than once."

He started down the road again and she had to run to meet his pace. "You mentioned your master," she said. "Where is he? Is he safe?"

Clare stopped again and eyed her. "The man's a cat. He'll land safely. Which is not to say he doesn't lose a bit of tail now and then." Walking again, he said, "You're a new one."

"A new..."

"Whore."

"I—" Oh, what was the point? And how many whores did Bridgewater associate with, anyway?

"I'm Clare Jenkins. Who are you?"

"Panna. Panna Kennedy. I need to talk to you about—"

"Wait. We're almost there."

A small stone house with a thatched roof, trim shutters, and a stoop lay just off the path. A horse stood saddled under one of the oaks, and candlelight in the windows suggested inhabitants in addition to Clare. A black and white dog trotted out to say hello.

Clare rubbed the dog's ears and knocked on the door—three taps followed by a pause and another tap. "You're not from around here, then?"

Before Panna had a chance to answer, a curvy redhead of thirty or so, wearing a dressing gown and little else, opened the door. She looked at her guests and poked her head out to scan the path. Satisfied that no one was following them, she invited them in with a jerk of her head.

The main room was small, and three doors led off of it. There was a table and chairs, a couple of benches, and an impressive collection of pistols and long guns bolted to the wall. The dog sighed and stretched out in front of the hearth.

"This is Miss Kennedy," Clare said to the redhead. Almost immediately, one of the doors opened, and Panna found herself the object of interest of a blond and a brunette as well, each as attractive as the redhead and similarly clad.

She was pretty sure she'd figured out what sort of house this was.

"I'm Aphrodite," the redhead said. "And these are Athena and Artemis," she added, pointing first to her dark-haired companion and then the light-haired one.

Interesting theme, though I suppose it beats Scary, Posh, and Ginger. Panna shook hands with each.

Clare nodded at Aphrodite, who placed a jug and two cups on the table. "Would you care to sit?" he said to Panna.

She took a chair as Clare filled the mugs. She sipped tentatively. It was a crisp, woodsy ale. She felt the note in her bodice but wanted some answers before she handed it over. "I'm most concerned about your master. Are you aware he's being held?"

Clare nodded. Like Bridgewater, he appeared to be an expert at hiding his thoughts.

"When I saw him last, he'd been beaten up rather badly," Panna said.

This raised a small fire in those sable eyes. "Indeed."

"The army seems to think he betrayed England's interests."

"He does more for the people of the borderlands than Queen Anne or Marlborough and his bloody army," Athena said, flushing. "As far as they're concerned, we're as bad as the Scots."

Clare threw a warning look in her direction.

"I had the occasion an hour ago to be in the room where they'd been holding him," Panna said. Aphrodite and Artemis exchanged knowing smiles, and Panna felt her cheeks warm. "He was gone and the place had been ransacked."

Clare snorted. "No room in that castle would hold him long."

Panna gazed at the women, wondering if it was safe to mention the hidden passageways and exits. "I know what you mean," she said, "and he had, er, availed himself of the facilities—we left at the same time—but he told me he intended to be back within the hour. And he wasn't. Or if he'd made it back, he was gone again by the time I returned."

"Which officer beat him? Did he say?"

"The colonel and his men."

Clare's beefy fingers tightened around his mug. "Is that all?"

She thought about the message from Reeves, and about the visit from Bridgewater's father, and about Thomas, the boy who'd been captured and questioned, but she had no idea how much of that she should share. She hoped Bridgewater's note would provide all the information that needed to be shared.

"He sent me with a message for you." She pulled the note from her bodice and slid it across the table.

Much to Panna's surprise, Clare ignored the letter and reached for her ponytail, pulling the ribbon free. Drawing the fabric taut along the tabletop, he examined its length as if he were reading a ticker tape.

"Oh, Christ." He leaped up.

"What is it?" Panna frowned.

He held the ribbon before Aphrodite. She paled and handed it to Athena. "I'll take the horse."

"As fast as you can, lass."

Aphrodite threw on a coat and grabbed a pistol from the wall. A moment later she flew out the door, and the thunder of the horse's hooves filled the night.

Panna's surprise evaporated with the cold realization that she had served as an unwitting mule for Bridgewater. When had he written the words? She thought of the pencils hanging from ribbons on the map. It must have been then, while she'd bided her time imagining the possibilities of the surveying seat. Heat blossomed on her cheeks at the thought of the kiss they'd shared. She combed her memory for the sequence of events. The kiss had definitely come before Bridgewater tied the ribbon around her hair. Had the kiss only been a pretext to get her hair down so he could retie it?

The buzz of shame in Panna's ears was so loud now, she feared that everyone in the room could hear it.

"What about the note?" she said at last.

Clare's gaze fell to his boots. He'd watched the realization of Bridgewater's betrayal crawl across her face. He picked up the note, broke the seal, and unfolded the paper.

"I apologize," he said, his eyes lifting from the note. "The whore's ribbon is a trick we've used a number of times to great success."

"I'm *not* a whore. I am a friend of Bridgewater's—a library keeper from Penn's Woods."

"Oh." Clare's eyes softened. "I can see where it would be doubly hard for you then."

Yes, being seduced by a lord so that she might serve as a living, breathing envelope for his war correspondence was not her proudest moment.

"The note," she repeated sharply. "What exactly does it say?"

He sighed and pushed the paper toward her.

Nothing.

The paper was completely blank. Bridgewater hadn't trusted her. He'd needed to get a message to Clare, but he'd been careful not to put his faith in the crazed interloper who'd appeared out of nowhere, even after she'd made her feelings for him as clear as glass.

Embarrassed and angry, she said, "Why do I think you have a pretty good idea where Lord Bridgewater is?"

Clare's brow went up. "*Lord* Bridgewater?"

"Yes. Or Lord Adderly, or whatever this prodigal son is called."

"I do know his whereabouts."

"Take me to him."

Clare, not a man to be ordered into anything, looked at her, unmoved.

She stood. "Look, I made it here on my own. I can certainly make it back without your help."

He caught her arm. "I can't recommend it."

Had she been tricked not just into becoming a mule but into placing herself willingly in the arms of a man who intended to hold her against her will? Bridgewater would have a lot of explaining to do next time she saw him.

"Does he own this place?" she demanded, shaking her arm loose.

"What if he does?" Clare said.

"And I suppose he calls upon your services here from time to time?"

Clare's brows knitted. "Aye, he does."

"Of course he does. And Aphrodite, Athena, and Artemis are the women who have been carting his messages back and forth?"

"They are. And they've been doing it at great risk, I might add."

"I'm sure. Though surely there are *some* rewards for the whores of a man like Bridgewater, are there not?"

"*Whores?*"

Clare's face turned the color of eggplant, and Artemis and Athena burst into laughter.

"They're my sisters," he sputtered.

"Sisters?" Panna searched the faces of the four for signs of kinship.

The hair had thrown her—Aphrodite with her bright orange curls, Athena with raven hair, and Artemis with her thick moonbeam braid. Now that Panna looked, however, she could see Aphrodite's wide nose, slightly raised at the end, echoed almost exactly on the other women's faces and in a more masculine fashion on Clare's. But it was the intelligence mirrored in each of the four pairs of coffee-colored eyes that settled the question.

"We may pretend to be whores when necessary," Athena said kindly, inserting herself between Panna and Clare, who looked almost apoplectic, "However, 'tis only an affectation."

"I'm sorry," said a painfully embarrassed Panna. "I—well, I am not one, either."

For some reason, the plaintive afterthought struck everyone as humorous—well, everyone except for Clare, who was still trying to find his tongue. The women laughed again, and this time Panna joined in.

"Then you are Bridgewater's...accomplices?" she asked.

"We prefer 'colleagues.'" Artemis smiled.

Panna pointed to the ribbon. "Will you at least tell me what it said?"

Clare shook his head.

"Tell her," Artemis implored. "She risked her life coming here. She's part of it now too."

Panna wasn't certain she wanted to be part of anything, let alone an operation run by a man who would stoop to seducing people to get them to ferry his messages around town. Nonetheless, she was curious about the contents of the message.

Clare cleared his throat grudgingly. "There was a plan to attack tonight."

"Yes. Langholm."

"No, that was a ruse. The real target is Carlisle. Several tons of gunpowder are making their way to the English army via Carlisle tonight."

Panna cocked her head. "You're English, are you not? Cumbria, as I recall, is an English county. Wouldn't you and Bridgewater want to support the efforts of the English army to protect the borderlands?"

"We don't fight over borders. We fight to save lives. The gunpowder will be used to attack clans along the border."

"By your army—Bridgewater's army?"

He gave her a cool look. "Aye."

So Bridgewater was the head of a rebel group that was taking justice into its own hands. It was a very dangerous game to play, with the possibility of reprisals from either side if his work was discovered.

"And the ribbon?"

He nodded toward Artemis, who handed Panna the length of pale green satin. She pulled it taut. "Cancel C," he had written. *Carlisle*.

"Why cancel it?" she asked but knew the answer even as the question left her lips. Because "They know." The English army knew of the rebels' plans to attack the caravan of gunpowder. That's what Reeves had scratched into the bowl. That's why Bridgewater had needed her to deliver it.

"I'm not sure," Clare said, "but I suspect—"

"The army knows."

He looked at her, surprised at her guess. "Aye. I think you're right."

"I know I'm right. Bridgewater received a message like that earlier this evening."

"From whom?"

Despite their seemingly open conversation, she didn't want to betray Bridgewater's source unnecessarily. "Another colleague."

Clare's eyes lit briefly, acknowledging her caution, and he turned toward the window. She could see the worry in his eyes.

"What is it?" Panna said. "Aphrodite will be able to stop it, won't she?"

"If the army knows—" He stopped, unable to say the words. "There are fifty rebels there. More than enough to take the wagons with little struggle. But if the army sends a regiment..." Lines of worry appeared around his eyes. "If Aphrodite makes it in time, she can stop them. But Carlisle's three hours from here. Longer by night."

Panna cursed herself for her delay in coming. "What if she doesn't make it in time?"

"Let us pray she does."

Panna clapped a hand to her mouth. "Aphrodite doesn't know *why* Carlisle has to be canceled. She doesn't know the army knows." *Why did I have to be so damn scrupulous?*

A muscle in Clare's jaw flexed. "She's very capable. She knows the towns and forests between here and there as well as I do. She'll be prepared for anything. Three hours is a lot of time to ponder why the attack is being canceled."

Clare stared abstractedly into the night, his forehead furrowed. "You'll have saved him, you know," he said.

"Pardon?"

"You'll have saved Bridgewater's life. Suspicions about him have been increasing. There are men in the army who think he's a traitor, though they lack proof. But if they have somehow connected him to the planned attack in Carlisle..."

Panna thought of the note scratched into the soup bowl. The hairs on her neck rose. "What if they *have* connected Bridgewater to Carlisle? They know the rebels are planning to attack. How much harder would it be to figure out Bridgewater is at the bottom of it?"

"If they have, the attack will serve as proof of his treachery, and he'll be hanged at dawn."

Had her delay in the twenty-first century damned him to the gallows? Or would Aphrodite arrive in time? What if Panna hadn't come at all?

She felt a little dizzy and sat down again. "Why can't I go back to the castle?"

"The clans along the border have had enough of the English army setting up camp on their doorstep. The cannon displays are stirring the blood of the most violent factions, which I presume was the army's intent. Scottish raids are increasing. Three nights ago two men were found hanging upside down from a tree two miles from here. Their throats had been cut."

Panna closed her eyes, willing the image away. "But Aphrodite—"

"Aphrodite has a pistol and our best horse," he said, standing, "and she won't hesitate to use either of them. I can take you to Lord Bridgewater in the morning, if that's still your desire. Don't venture out there tonight. Not on foot. Not alone. You can stay in Aphrodite's bed."

She needed no further convincing.

He extinguished the candle and paused to gaze out the window. "I've lived side by side with the Scots all my life, and we've certainly had our disagreements. They're canny thieves and liars, though a man in my position almost admires that. But the army's appearance here has set the world on edge. The borderlands are a powder keg. A single spark will destroy us all."

Panna suddenly felt as if the world around was filled with flints and everyone was holding a striking tool.

Eleven

THE MORNING LIGHT DIDN'T LESSEN THE TENSION ON Clare's face, though he hid his worry in some rather engaging stories about Bowness, the town at the foot of Bridgewater's castle, and Annan, the Scottish town across the river, which, as it turned out was not a river at all, but a firth—the Solway Firth, to be exact, and the body of water along which Clare and Panna walked on their return to the castle.

Panna's sleep had been marred with dreams of explosions and mutilated corpses, and she found herself uncertain as to which side of Hadrian's Wall she stood, philosophically speaking. The rebels seemed to have carved out a third position, even more unenviable than the other two, like an unsteady barge in the middle of the water, waiting to be shelled by one side or the other.

Anxiety about Aphrodite and Bridgewater weighed heavily on her. Clare assured her that by asking a few discreet questions when they arrived in Bowness, he'd know what happened in Carlisle.

As they rounded a curve, both castles popped into

view—Bridgewater's on their side of the firth and the one in the Scottish hills on the other.

"Don't you think it's odd that two castles ended up so close together?" she asked.

Clare laughed. "You wouldn't if you knew the same man owned them."

"Bridgewater owns the other as well?" she said, shocked.

"No. His grandfather owns the one over the water. But his grandfather also owned Bridgewater's castle once. Back when this land belonged to Scotland."

"What?"

"Oh, aye, the land has passed into the hands of Scotland a number of times over the years. Sometimes the possession is so fleeting, the mapmakers don't even have time to record it."

She stared at the far castle, shocked. A Scottish clan chief in sight of his English nobleman grandson? This was the stuff of novels, she thought, entranced. "His grandfather, eh?"

"Oh, aye. Though Bridgewater and his grandfather are estranged."

"I'm not surprised. It must be terribly hard to be on different sides of a conflict."

He gave her an odd look. "I dinna think the conflict is all that separates them."

"Oh?"

"His grandfather disowned his mother when she fell in with his father."

Wow. Very Romeo and Juliet.

"Then his grandfather owns the castle on this side of the firth, too?" she asked, trying to untangle the family connections and property lines.

"No, Bridgewater owns this one. His grandfather lost it to the Crown thirty years ago. Forfeited it upon the loss of a battle. Oh, and an ugly battle it was. They set fire to the place. Bridgewater's grandfather barely made it out alive. Many didn't."

No wonder Bridgewater chafed at England's unflinching position on the Scots. "But how does a stone castle burn?"

"'Tis not the stone that burns, of course. 'Tis the wooden floors and rafters. And without the floors, which provide support, the walls collapse."

"Which explains the ruins around the tower and courtyard."

"Aye. Bridgewater was raised an Englishman. He purchased the ruins from the crown and restored them."

She was just about to ask about the crypt in the chapel when a horse roared up behind them. Aphrodite waved furiously, and Panna felt so overwhelmed with relief, she almost had to sit down.

"Canceled," the redhead said breathlessly when she'd pulled her horse to a stop. "Just in time. The men had already donned their masks. 'Twas a close thing."

"And the army didn't see the rebels?" Panna asked, thinking of Bridgewater.

"No. But I could smell them over the ridge, waiting to blindside us," Aphrodite spat.

"Have you heard from Bridgewater?"

She gave Panna a regretful look. "Not a word."

"Go home, lass," Clare said. "You're not dressed appropriately, and we wouldn't want anyone thinking you're a whore."

Panna laughed. "Thank you," she said to Aphrodite. "Truly."

The woman beamed.

"Get some sleep," Clare called, as the horse broke into a trot. "You did a bonny job." Then he saw the look on Panna's face. "Dinna worry about Bridgewater, lass. He knows how to take care of himself."

She thought of him facing down the earl. "He seems to have a rough time of it with his father."

Clare gave her a weak smile. "His family's been a source of great pain for Bridgewater. He doesn't share this with me, of course, but I've observed a deep sort of melancholy in him at times. After his mother died, I think he felt very alone."

Which helped explain his reluctance to trust others.

Two English soldiers joined Panna and Clare on the path, which meant the discussion as they completed the journey up the rise to the castle gate was limited to the history of Hadrian's Wall and the weather.

The gate was a looming affair, with a spiked portcullis and tiny guardhouses built into the stone on either side. Dozens of red-coated soldiers stood near the entrance, some engaged in marching drills, others peeling onions, and still others loading a small cannon onto the back of a wagon. Panna was particularly glad to see no one was building a gallows.

Clare pulled her discreetly away from the path. "This is as far as I'm going to go, lass," he said. "I'm not a popular figure with the army. 'Tis best I keep my distance. Are you certain you want to see his lordship?"

In truth, she was divided on the matter. She knew she wouldn't rest until she was sure he was safe.

However, discovering that the kiss she'd so enjoyed had been the means to an end had been a serious blow to her ego.

"I am," she said.

"I won't ask why, but I will advise you to take care. His lordship is not quite as smart as he thinks he is, but he's still a very smart and sometimes brutal man. If he smells deception on you, he'll find a way to make you pay."

Brutal? Had ten years of marriage and two of widowhood destroyed her ability to judge a man? There'd been no brutality in that kiss, only gentleness and longing. But then again, she hadn't sensed the deception in it, either.

"Where will I find him, do you think? In the library?"

"Hardly. He's right there." Clare pointed toward a knot of officers standing under the portcullis.

"Where?" She didn't recognize him, though some of the men were wearing tricornes.

"He's on the left. He's found on most mornings in the castle courtyard, presiding over the soldiers' punishments."

"Thank you, Clare. I appreciate everything you and you sisters have done for me."

He bowed. "I thank you for delivering the note, even if you didn't quite realize how you were doing it. It took a braw lass to attempt it."

With a brief wave he was off, and she made her way uncertainly to the gate. Despite Clare's assurance, Bridgewater wasn't among the officers, and she was a trifle nervous about navigating her way through half the English army in a low-cut dress. She kept a firm grip on the box cutter in her pocket.

A few of the soldiers stopped their work to stare as she passed. None, it seemed, was stupid enough to make a comment or catcall with officers standing by, for which she was grateful.

She strode across the short bridge that led to the castle's portcullis, remembering the advice of a friend who scouted locations in the film industry: "You can get in almost anywhere if you walk in like you own the place."

"You there."

Her heart thudded and she turned. The handsomest officer stepped away from the group.

"Where are you going?" he asked warily.

"I am looking for Viscount Adderly."

His face broke into a pleasant smile. "You've found him."

Twelve

"I BEG YOUR PARDON?" PANNA SAID, MIND REELING.

The other officers laughed then one of them said, "Perhaps if you'd bothered to shave, Colonel."

Colonel? Was this the colonel who had beaten Bridgewater? "I—I—"

The man before her was blue-eyed, with thick, straight golden hair pulled into a queue. Was he Bridgewater's brother? The mouths were the same, she realized, and the noses. But the colonel was several inches shorter and more classically handsome than the rugged Bridgewater—a peacock to Bridgewater's hawk. They were enough alike, however, that the sculpture in her library could have been of either of them.

"I do hope you'll forgive my whiskers," he said, bowing. "The regiments were out most of the night. I haven't had a chance to go to my quarters."

"I—that's fine." She hardly knew what to say. "And you're Lord Adderly, son of the Earl of Bridgewater?"

"I am."

"I think I may be looking for your brother."

"That would be a trick," he said, still smiling, "as I do not have one."

Had Bridgewater misled her on this too? Or had she misunderstood? Hadn't he said he was Lord Adderly? She reviewed their conversation in her head. He hadn't introduced himself, but she'd called him Bridgewater and he'd responded.

"No brother?" She scrambled to collect herself. "I'm sorry. I'd been led to believe you were someone else. Er, rather, that someone else was Lord Adderly."

His eyes, a rich turquoise blue, twinkled.

"This is your castle, then?" she said, uncertain.

The officers laughed again.

"Ignore them, milady. They don't have the manners they were born with. No, this is the home of Captain James Bridgewater."

"He's your cousin?"

"No. No relation, though we have been colleagues in the army these past ten years. Is it perhaps him you seek?"

"No." She'd been served a seven-layer salad of lies and subterfuge, and until she figured it out, she wouldn't commit to knowing anyone or anything.

"Then is it I you seek?" he said.

"Er, yes. Yes, it is."

He nodded, satisfied. "And why? If I may ask?"

Why, indeed? Panna wracked her brain for a credible reason.

"I'm seeking support for my library." It was the first thing that popped into her head as well as the only lie she thought she might be able to carry off successfully.

He held up a hand to the men and they immediately

stopped chuckling. "A library, is it? Well then, may we talk about it over breakfast?"

Panna's stomach growled enthusiastically, and she realized she hadn't eaten anything except some figs and a chip's worth of guacamole in the last twenty-four hours.

"Thank you, Lord Adderly. I'd like that."

"Adderly, please." He clasped his hands behind his back and walked with her through the gate and into the inner courtyard. "I'm afraid you have the advantage. I don't know your name."

"Oh. I'm—" Did she dare use her own name? What traps had Bridgewater lain? "—Mrs. Andrew Carnegie."

"Ah, a Scot." He bent to kiss her hand. His lips were soft and warm.

"Well, my husband is. I'm not, as you can tell by my accent. I'm a widow."

"I'm so sorry. I hope you are not much troubled by the conflict?"

She supposed what he was asking was whether she was a Scot at heart. "As with most people, my hope is for a swift resolution and a return to peace."

He chuckled. "Pardon my amusement. You're obviously not a native of the borderlands. There hasn't been peace here in four hundred years."

"My people are from Penn's Woods," she said. "Across the Atlantic. I have only lately lived in Cumbria."

"Oh? Where?"

Um. "Carlisle."

He was almost as schooled at deception as his colleague, Bridgewater, for though a spark of wariness appeared in his eye, his face remained open and smiling.

"And is that where your library is?"

"Yes. Though it hasn't yet been built," she added quickly, in case he did more in Carlisle than lie in wait for the rebels. "I'm seeking the help of a number of benefactors."

"I'm most intrigued. Tell me more."

Despite a restless night, Panna knew she looked good, especially in the blue gown. She had edged the neckline with a short length of diaphanous taffeta from Artemis's scrap bag to reduce the number of times she'd have to explain that she wasn't a whore, but it was still very eye-catching, and it—and she—were certainly catching the eye of this particular lord. She had never seen a man quite so obviously attracted.

They entered the castle and passed through a long, slate-floored entrance hall whose ancient stone walls had been hung with paintings of landscapes and battle scenes. She was surprised at the lack of portraits, which, at least in the movies, seemed to make up the majority of paintings in noblemen's homes.

But Bridgewater isn't a nobleman, she reminded herself. *He's a captain in the army who's apparently no relation to Adderly or the Earl of Bridgewater.*

Then she remembered the earl. She'd witnessed the scene in the library between Bridgewater and his general, assuming the entire time that the general was his father.

She looked at the distinguished profile of her escort. Was *he* the son of the general? Was the general even the earl? Too many questions and not enough answers. She felt as if she'd gone back to the start of some really interesting audio book on her iPhone and accidentally hit "Shuffle." Nothing made sense anymore.

"This way." Adderly touched her elbow.

Her plan was to ferret out some sort of confirmation that Bridgewater was alive during breakfast, then excuse herself to use the privy, hightail it into the chapel, and disappear. Nonetheless, she felt a small pang of regret. Here, she felt alive—alive and terrified, admittedly, but at least alive and feeling *something*.

She thought of the twinkle in Bridgewater's eyes as he'd watched her page through *Animals of the Orient* and the thumping of her heart as they'd raced through the secret passages. But most of all she thought of what it felt like to bring her lips to his and feel once again that force that binds lovers together, more powerful than a cannon shot and more inebriating than all the brandy in Spain.

Damn him for reminding her what that spark felt like and then extinguishing it when it had barely flickered to life.

An hour earlier, embarrassed at her foolishness, she'd begged Artemis for the return of the ribbon and then traced the hastily scribbled words with her finger, looking for some sense of the man who'd written them. She'd come up with nothing that would help her understand whether their time together had been just an interesting sojourn or a necessary step in fighting his war. She'd tied it at her wrist, a double loop to remind her of its double purpose.

Adderly paused before the carved oak entrance to the dining hall. The footmen pulled the doors open and Adderly offered Panna his arm.

The hall was long and grand, with a table half the length of her library, at which sat a dozen army officers eating or deep in conversation. Two servants manned a sideboard groaning with silver platters. The platters were piled high with cakes, breads, and a selection of fruit fit for a sultan, as well as a half-dozen chafing dishes warmed by candles, an ornate urn, and an array of bottles and pitchers. Another servant turned a pig on a spit over the fire, and the air was filled with its smoky, meaty scent. A third carried a tray so overflowing with sausages it would have made her heart leap with joy had not the man currently helping himself to a half a dozen been Captain James Bridgewater.

The talking ceased upon her entry, and the men jumped to their feet.

"Forgive my tardiness, gentlemen," Adderly said. "We have the good fortune to be graced this morning with a guest. May I present to you Mrs. Carnegie of Penn's Woods and Carlisle. I am delighted she's agreed to join us this morning."

The men made welcoming noises, and two places were readied for the late arrivals—directly across from Captain Bridgewater.

Bridgewater's eye was a dark shade of purple, his lip swollen and red, and he lowered himself to his chair as if several blades had been left in his side. When he was introduced to Panna, not only did he make no special acknowledgment of their previous acquaintance; he made barely any acknowledgment at all save for a polite but detached nod.

Heat climbed from her toes to her ears.

Adderly alerted her to the servant standing at her side. "Sausage, madam?"

"I beg your pardon. Yes, thank you."

One after another, servants loaded her plate with everything from a poached egg in a tiny porcelain bowl shaped like a rabbit to a slice of ham, a small dish of pears in syrup, and a cold mousse of parsnips and potatoes.

"Do you care for figs?" Adderly asked, pushing a plate toward her. "Captain Bridgewater imports the finest I've ever tasted."

She lifted her eyes to the captain, wondering if he remembered her enthusiasm for them the night before, but his gaze passed over her as if she were a stick of furniture.

"Yours are as fine as mine, John."

She'd had just about enough. "Captain Bridgewater," she said sharply enough to make the captain pause in the middle of a bite, "are you not related to the Earl of Bridgewater?" Hell, if she were a newbie to this party, she might as well make the best of her ignorance. And if it meant putting James Bridgewater in a tough spot, so be it. She forked a sausage violently and gave him a smile.

The men quieted, and Bridgewater wiped his mouth with his napkin.

"The family names are the same," Adderly said. "Though we are not related. 'Tis an unusual coincidence, to be sure."

"Extremely unusual," Bridgewater added, placing his napkin beside his plate.

"I can't help but notice your eye, Captain. Did someone get the better of you?"

"Until this morning, I was being held under suspicion of treason," Bridgewater said equably. "I'm afraid my jailers did not take a sympathetic view of the matter."

The other officers seemed to turn their attention to their plates. Several coughed.

"I'm glad all turned out well," she said.

"Thank you, milady. My incarceration was not as bad as my face might lead you to believe. Moments of it were quite satisfactory."

Her breath caught. Damn him. Well, at least she knew he was safe. She'd seen him with her own eyes. Though what constituted safety, she supposed, was a matter of some debate, given the varied and changing alliances here.

After a long conversation with Adderly about the charms of the history of England he was reading and the relative merits of leather versus vellum when covering books—during which time Bridgewater kept his eyes fixed determinedly on his food—Adderly pushed his plate away.

"Mrs. Carnegie has come to talk to me about a library," he said to Bridgewater.

"Carnegie," Bridgewater repeated. "I thought that was what you'd said. I wasn't sure I'd heard the name properly. Why you?"

"She is seeking my patronage." Adderly gave Panna a kind smile.

"I'm sure your support would mean a great deal to her."

Panna flushed. Bridgewater had uttered the words "your support" as if they held a distinctly unflattering meaning.

"Tell me, Mrs. Carnegie," Bridgewater continued, "have you seen the library here at MacIver Castle?"

Heat throbbed in her cheeks. "I have not."

"I've been told I have a very fine eye."

She wished she could kick him under the table or fling the rabbit-shaped egg cup into his lap.

"I'd offer to show you the place myself," he added, "but I'm afraid there's been a bit of a mishap there."

"A mishap?"

"Aye," Adderly said. "It seems someone with a grudge went through Captain Bridgewater's belongings with something less than care. I believe the room's been cleaned up, Captain. I assigned a soldier to do it this morning. And I shall have a guard set up so that it doesn't happen again."

"How kind of you."

"I have to say a few words to the general," Adderly said to Bridgewater. "If you would take our guest up to the library and show her around, I'm sure I'll be there in a quarter of an hour. Would you mind, Mrs. Carnegie? The collection may give you some ideas."

Bridgewater made a small, indeterminate noise.

She had to get to the chapel in any case, but the look of warning in Bridgewater's eyes made her hesitate. "Y-yes. Of course."

"Captain?"

"Certainly." He shoved his chair from the table and stood.

Thirteen

ADDERLY ENTERED HIS FATHER'S MAKESHIFT OFFICE AND closed the door. He fought the urge to chew the inside of his mouth, his mother's words ringing in his ear: "'Tis a sign of weakness, Addy. I shall not have it in any son of mine." Instead he grabbed a handful of hazelnuts from the bowl on the desk and popped one in his mouth.

"I think we have a problem."

The earl gazed at his son over his spectacles. "Aren't having the Scots at our backs, a rebel faction in our midst, and my best officer suspected of treason problems enough? I was just handed a message from the queen, demanding an immediate quelling of the unrest. Which do you suppose I should answer first, hers or the one signed by six of the clan chiefs, refusing to accept our terms?"

Adderly fought to keep his face still. "Do you recall the woman I told you about a few months ago? The, er—" He would not use "sorceress." The first time he had done so, his father had laughed. "The woman who claimed to be from the future?"

"The one who revealed the English would triumph at Ramillies?"

"Aye."

His father snorted. "I do."

In truth, Clementina had not traveled to Adderly's time. The exchange of information had occurred in a very different way, though he dared not tell his father anything about that.

"I think there's another."

"*Two* time travelers?" His father gave him a withering look. "And why do you think that?"

"A woman arrived at the castle this morning. Very handsome."

His father laughed. "Oh, Adderly, to you all handsome women are sorceresses. If you do not take care, you shall have more bastards running around than old King Charles."

Adderly gritted his teeth. "She says she's looking for support for a library."

"How much?" His father's face turned wary.

"That's not the point."

"It *is* the point. Don't you understand? When handsome women come calling for money, 'tis usually a sign of trouble. I have no doubt she'd say she was from the future, the Bay of Bengal, or the North Star if she thought it might induce you to hand over a bag of gold."

Adderly abandoned the effort. If he told his father the woman also happened to have the same name as the library from which his sorceress had come, he'd be berated for his stupidity.

But Adderly knew better. The woman spoke in that

same flat accent as Clementina. If she'd come with the intention of confronting him about what he'd done or even blackmailing him, she'd soon wish she hadn't.

On the other hand…

He considered what the information from Clementina had done for him. The battle had played out just as she'd described. It had been an easy matter for him to order the regiments to the fields using precisely the strategy history had recorded and watch it unfold like a chess game from his post in the rear.

He'd been a fool to not have extracted more from her when he'd had the chance, especially now that the means to do so had been taken away from him.

Mrs. Carnegie, or whatever her real name was, represented both an opportunity and a threat. If she had access to the same sort of information as Clementina, he had the tools to ensure that she gave it to him willingly. If she'd come to expose him, to call into question his reputation as a military hero or, worse, to offer her information to another officer or, worse yet, the Scots, he'd destroy her. Either way, the best start would be gaining her trust.

"Has the queen given us permission to attack?" Adderly turned his attention to the army's problems for a moment. He'd dearly love to receive another promotion from all of this.

"She has not." His father picked up the queen's note, its red seal catching the morning light. "According to my orders, we're to enter into a fight only if 'a reasonably injurious attack is made on the people of Cumbria or Northumberland.'"

"'Reasonably'?"

"Defendable. The queen will have to justify it to Parliament, and they are in no mood for another war."

Adderly groaned. He hated the Scots. Hated their thieving, lying ways. The sooner England could put the bridle in Scotland's mouth, the better. But clan chiefs like Bridgewater's grandfather, Hector MacIver, refused to bend. And MacIver controlled enough of the other clans to keep a surrender from ever happening.

"They killed two men near Bowness three days ago," Adderly said.

"*Someone* killed them. It could have been the Scots, the rebels here, Clan MacIver, or your great-aunt Joan. We have no proof."

Adderly looked at the castle in the distance. "Do you suppose Bridgewater is in league with his grandfather?"

His father leaned back in the chair. "I doubt it. There's only one person Bridgewater hates more than me, and that's his grandfather."

"Of course, with his grandfather the hatred at least has some basis," Adderly said. "The man banished Bridgewater's mother from his home, though I might have done the same thing myself in similar circumstances."

The older man shifted.

"Why do you insist on keeping him in our regiments?" Adderly asked. "It's an embarrassment to the family. The way he fawns over that crypt... Do you suppose he built it and had her moved there just to stick a thumb in the eye of his grandfather?"

"Bridgewater's an excellent soldier."

"As well as a traitor."

His father pushed away the queen's note. "Bridgewater doesn't support England's policies in the borderlands, but so long as a man in my army keeps his mouth shut and executes his orders, I can't fault him for his beliefs. And Bridgewater is the most capable officer I've ever seen on a battlefield."

Adderly tossed the remaining hazelnuts in his mouth, gave his father a deep bow, and left.

Fourteen

BRIDGEWATER CLOSED THE DOORS OF HIS LIBRARY AND tore into Panna. "What game are you at?" he demanded fiercely. "Do you know who you are playing with?"

"I thought I did," she said, equally as angry.

"I don't mean me. Though if I find you've crossed me, you will regret it."

"Adderly seems kind. Polite and kind."

"You realize, of course, he's the man who put this on my face." He gestured to his purpled eye.

"Perhaps you deserved it."

"Perhaps it's time for you to tell me exactly who you are."

"I told you, but you didn't believe me! I'm from the future. I came in through your stupid chapel. I saw you there, praying. But it looked like you were"—she paused, remembering his pained face—"busy. So I ran to the first doorway and found myself in your library. Which is when you marched in and insulted me."

"I don't believe you."

"But you do. Admit it. I don't talk like anyone

you've ever met. I probably don't look like anyone you've ever met."

His eyes flicked over her like a geologist assessing a rock formation.

"I could tell you what happened in 1812 or 1941 or 2001," she said, "and you'd be shocked. But it wouldn't matter because you wouldn't know if I was telling you the truth or not."

"I told you to be careful, lass. 'Twas not too many years ago you'd be burned at the stake for such a claim."

"I'm telling *you*, damn it. It's the truth. I have no interest in being here. And you have certainly done all you can to make me feel unwelcome."

A guilty twitch told Panna the remark had hit home.

"'All' is an exaggeration," he said after a moment. "At least, I hope it is. There were moments I tried to make you feel very welcome."

"And I saved you twice," she said hotly, refusing to be softened. "How much more proof of my loyalty do you need? Does anyone *ever* earn your trust? Or are you a man totally unto himself, with no need for others? That's a pretty sorry way to go through life, if you ask me."

Panna could see the reverberations of her words in his face.

"My circumstances have not encouraged me to be trusting."

"Your *circumstances*!" she cried. "You live in a castle—with a library fit for a king!"

He said nothing, though she could see the battle of emotions on his face. "You said you saved me twice. I know about the soup bowl. What else did you mean?"

"What do you think? I delivered a blank note to Clare."

"That was *you*?" A look of such intense relief passed over his face, she thought he might weep, and he swept her into his arms. "I know the rebels dispersed from Carlisle before the army saw them, but I didn't know why or how. You saved many men's lives," he whispered. "You saved *me*."

A tremble passed through him and she held him as tight as she dared. "I'm glad you're well—and free," she said when they broke apart. "What happened last night?"

"As I said, I had an errand to run."

"The boy? Thomas?"

"Aye."

"Is he all right?"

"He will be," Bridgewater said. "He was beaten. They broke his arm. 'Tis my fault."

She touched his hand. *What a burden to carry.* "What happened to you?"

"Once I freed him, I returned here. My absence hadn't been discovered. This morning I was told I was free to return to my post. Reeves told me that by the time the soldiers arrived in Carlisle, the rebels were gone. Which meant the grounds under which I was being held were no longer valid."

"They thought you had tipped the Scots off to an attack in Langholm."

"Believe me, if Scots had attacked an Englishman anywhere between London and the Shetland Islands last night, I would have been hanged for it."

"Well, I'm glad I arrived in time. I got to Clare's

house late last night. I wasn't sure." She gave him a look. "Clare's an odd name for a man."

The tiniest glint appeared in Bridgewater's eye. "Best not to mention that to him."

"I got that impression."

"'Twas in honor of an Uncle Clarence, I believe."

"In any case, once he got your message, he sent Aphrodite to warn the rebels."

She pulled the ribbon on her wrist free and dropped it into his hand.

He gazed at the length of satin, eyes downcast. "I apologize. 'Twas ungentlemanly to use you in such a way. Sometimes I...I don't know who to trust."

"Whom *do* you trust?" She was intensely aware that Adderly would be arriving shortly. "It would help me to know."

"Clare," he said. "Completely. Reeves. A few men among the rebels."

"Any in the army?"

He thought for a moment and then shook his head.

Servants and a few colleagues? "Surely you have some family."

"None."

"No brothers or sisters?"

"No. My mother is dead. She died before I even knew her."

"And your father?" She would make no more assumptions.

The blood beat in the hollow of his throat. "My parents never married. My father doesn't acknowledge me."

Bridgewater was a *bastard*! Worse yet, he was an

unacknowledged bastard. She opened her mouth to offer her sympathy, but those proud, wounded eyes told her it would be a mistake.

"He's an industrious man whose work is important to the country and at which he is much skilled," Bridgewater said, adding sadly, "but he is also weak and vain."

The conflict on Bridgewater's face as he uttered these two very different sentiments was heart-wrenching.

"The general *is* your father then?"

Bridgewater straightened, struggling not to give in to the shame of the situation. "Aye."

Which explained the general's behavior toward Bridgewater as well as Bridgewater's behavior in return. What a horrible situation—to spend your life in constant contact with a man who denies his fundamental tie to you.

"How can he not acknowledge you?" she said. "For God's sake, you look so much like him."

Bridgewater sighed. "Men choose what they wish to see. He chooses not to see it."

"But the other officers? The people of the town?" If *she* could see it, surely everyone else could too.

"I know there are men among the officers who believe he's my father. I can see it in their eyes when they look at me, the mixture of pity and jealousy, though how they might be jealous of this empty life, I don't know. But what good would it do them to gainsay a general? He's their commanding officer. And as for the people of the town..." He gave her a look. "You're on your way to convincing me you're not of this time for only a person who hadn't lived in eighteenth-century England would wonder at the falsehoods one will pretend to swallow from a wealthy nobleman."

"Then Viscount Adderly…?"

"My half brother. Not that he acknowledges it." Bridgewater shook his head sorrowfully. "Though in his case, I do not fault it. I truly think he doesn't believe it. 'Twould be impossible in his world for a man such as me to be related to him."

"Yet you carry your father's surname."

A wry smile lifted the corners of his mouth. "My mother was an optimist, I suppose. It has not served me as she had hoped. The people of Cumbria find my use of it rather foolish, and the officers…well, let's say 'foolish' would be a kind word for their thoughts on it."

Panna gazed at their opulent surroundings, which had, as Adderly indicated, been put almost to right, except for the missing panes of glass in several of the bookcase doors. This was a rich man's home, and yet Bridgewater was not the acknowledged heir of a rich man—that is, unless the money that had purchased this place had come through his mother from his grandfather. "Your mother had her own means?"

Bridgewater laughed bitterly. "Hardly. My grandfather disowned her when she found herself carrying the young earl's child. They never exchanged another word. She was but sixteen."

Panna blew out a long puff of air. Sixteen, pregnant, and abandoned. Panna wouldn't have survived.

"So she had you…where?"

"A priest in a village outside Carlisle took pity on

her. He allowed her to earn her living by cleaning the church—but not to take the sacrament," Bridgewater added with evident shame. "She died a few weeks after I was born—some sort of fever. He put me in the church's orphanage and served as a sort of father to me."

From orphan to army officer in possession of a small castle. An amazing rise in circumstances. It was impolite to ask, but she couldn't help herself. "How did you find yourself here?"

"In the castle? Or the army?"

"Either. Both."

"The army was easy. I enlisted as soon as I was able and earned my way to captain with exemplary service."

She thought of Adderly, the man whose likeness stood in her library. Both brothers had served their countries, but of course only the son of the earl would earn the lasting tribute of a statue.

"You enlisted in your father's regiment?"

Bridgewater made a self-conscious shrug. "As I said, he's an excellent officer, and I couldn't have chosen a better man to serve under. 'Twill do us no good for you to refer to him as my father. He was most angry the one time I rather foolishly approached him about it."

Panna thought it very likely Bridgewater was drawn to the earl's regiment for reasons that went much deeper than his admiration of the man's achievements. Every man longs for validation from his father, even if the only way to gain it is through success in one's own career. But what could drive a father to deny his child?

"Is it possible the general didn't know your mother carried his child?"

"I have the letters he wrote to my mother while they were…courting, I suppose one would call it." His jaw muscle flexed. "She believed they were engaged to marry. However, his family fortunes took a turn for the worse after some bad investments. He needed an infusion of gold to save the family estates. Instead of marrying my mother, he married a woman of means."

"You could show him the letters."

"To what end? They don't prove he's my father."

"They prove your mother and he had an intimate relationship."

Bridgewater shook his head. "My mother suffered enough. She died sick and alone. Having her most private thoughts held up to the light would be obscene. Besides," he added in a voice thick with anger, "I'm afraid I might kill him if he were to claim her letters were lies."

"Is that your mother in the chapel crypt?" Panna asked softly.

"Aye. Sorcha MacIver. May she rest in peace."

"You built that for her?"

"I did not. Though the question has been asked of me before," he said. "You see, this castle was once my Scottish grandfather's, before I was born."

"Clare told me."

"But it was nearly destroyed in a battle fire years ago."

"Then ceded to the English crown."

His eyebrows rose, as if he wondered what else Clare had shared with her about his family's past.

"Aye, it was," he said. "But not at first. Though

my grandfather wasn't welcome on English land after the battle, he still owned the place. He had the chapel rebuilt and had the remains of my mother—his daughter—removed from the pauper's grave in which she lay and buried her here. 'Twas done quietly. No man bore witness to his shame. He'd already built his new castle on the hill there, across the water, in Scotland. He called it *Nunquam Obliviscar*. 'Tis the motto of Clan MacIver: 'I will never forget.' Well, I'll never forget, either."

"Why did he move her here and not there, to his new castle?"

"This is where she grew up—when it was a part of Scotland. He'd behaved despicably toward her in life, so he tried to make up for it in her death. At least, that's my belief."

"You bought the castle in which your mother was already buried?"

"It had been my lifelong wish."

How sad to have lost a daughter, especially in such circumstances. "Your grandfather must've deeply regretted what he'd done."

Bridgewater snorted. "He couldn't bear the guilt, more like. So now he can look at the chapel spire along my ramparts and think he's redeemed himself. But he shall burn in hellfire for what he did. I may not walk with God, but I know enough to know what God would think of my grandfather."

She chose not to comment on the obvious contrast between the man she had seen fervently praying and the man who claimed he didn't walk with God. But none of what he'd said explained how he had come to live in such surroundings. "You're a wealthy man, Bridgewater. Career soldiers are rarely wealthy."

"Water pumps," he said. "I invested in Thomas Savery's device. I knew very little about the science when the opportunity came to me, but I knew there's no end to the amount of water men want to have moved. My investment made me rich. This"—he made a sweeping gesture around the room—"is the result."

"Water pumps?"

"Aye, and we're working together to make improvements to it as well. 'Tis more satisfying than you can imagine to wield a compass instead of a sword. Perhaps someday no one will need a sword."

She didn't have the heart to tell him that men would continue to turn to swords and things far worse in the future. "So you've made a very respectable fortune, and yet you still serve in the army?"

"One does not throw off one's training easily, Panna. Panna *is* your name, is it not?"

She flushed. "Yes."

"And might I still retain the use of it? Despite misleading you with the note, I mean."

The velvet of his eyes made her look down. "Yes, I suppose."

"Thank you. I apologize for my behavior. You're quite correct. To assume every man—or woman— has the potential to harm you *is* a sorry way to go through life."

"And I'd agree it would've been very hard not to be shaped by your particular circumstances."

He bowed his head, appreciative of her

understanding. "Though it is your circumstances that are perhaps the more worthy of comment."

His scrutiny brought a warmth to her face. She felt as if she were a butterfly in a bell jar.

"I have heard stories about time travelers—though of course one hears all manner of stories in the borderlands. I admit I never believed them. And if I'm honest, I'm not entirely certain I do now."

"I can understand why you'd be skeptical."

She considered trotting out a fact about England's immediate future, but something made her wary—not of him but of sharing the future with someone from the past. She felt a sort of paternalistic caution about offering information that could be so potentially dangerous, like a parent keeping knives out of the reach of a toddler.

"Let's assume for a moment that what you tell me is true—"

"Which is only fitting, given that I have twice earned your trust." She smiled dryly.

He coughed. "Indeed. Let me restate my thought. Since what you've told me is unerringly true, I am prompted to ask a few questions. First, from where did you come?"

"Penn's Woods—Pennsylvania. As I told you."

"And from when?"

"The twenty-first century."

His eyes widened. She knew what was going through his head now—three centuries of questions. How did people live? What had changed? Were there still wars? Carriages? Guns? Ships? Swords? She waited for the barrage.

None came.

He shook his head in wonder. "You're in very great danger."

Goose bumps rose on her flesh. "Why would you say that?"

"Do not tell anyone what you've told me, do you understand?"

"I won't, but—"

"You have not fought in a war. There are men who will do brutal things, stop at nothing to gain an advantage. If what you say is true—and I chose to believe it—you are the most powerful weapon a man could wield. Swear to me you won't tell anyone."

The agitation in his eyes frightened her. "I swear."

"I'm afraid..." His face hardened, but there was a look of gentle regret in his eyes. "I'm afraid you must leave as soon as you can. I don't wish it—Lord, I don't wish it—but it must be."

She felt a stab of sadness. "I don't wish it, either, Bridgewater."

"Our stars are crossed. 'Tis what a playwright once said."

"I know him."

Bridgewater held out his hand and she extended her own until their fingertips met. An exquisite pleasure radiated through her. She never wanted to let go. But she knew she would have to. They both would.

"Then you'll go?" He gazed at her, face lined with sorrow.

"Yes."

"Now?"

"Yes."

His arm fell to his side. "I don't know what to say. You came into my life like some sort of mythical creature less than a day ago, and now you must go. I owe you a debt I shall never be able to repay."

He took her hand and brought it to his mouth, but when those blue eyes came to rest on hers, she couldn't bear it. She threw her arms around his neck and kissed him. She felt as if she were losing herself inside him, his mouth, his arms, savoring the sweetly turbulent storm for as long as she dared.

Voices sounded in the hall, and they flew apart. Bridgewater took a step toward the window, arms at his side, his face flushed in the morning sun.

Adderly was giving an aide instructions as they strode in. Both men bowed to Panna. Adderly smiled.

"Has Captain Bridgewater been a companionable host?" he asked.

"He has," she said, flustered.

"Bridgewater, the general wishes to see you."

"Shall I accompany the two of you as far as the rose garden?" he said. "I believe Mrs. Carnegie would enjoy seeing it."

"Thank you," Adderly said, "but I believe we will stay here for a bit."

Seeing no other way to prolong his time with her, Bridgewater met her eyes with a careful gaze.

"Might I give you a memento of my library, Mrs. Carnegie?"

She nodded, afraid to speak.

Bridgewater strode to the bookcase nearest the hearth. It happened to be one whose doors were missing their glass. He slipped a hand through the opening and drew out a familiar volume. It was *Animals of the Orient.* Panna smiled.

He handed the book to her. "With my compliments."

"Thank you. Your library is exemplary. I've enjoyed my time here very much."

"You're most welcome." He took her hand and kissed it.

Panna was intently aware that this moment was the last she'd spend in his company. She withdrew her hand reluctantly, clutching the book's smooth leather. She wished she could tell him how much her time with him had meant.

"Bridgewater—" she began.

"Bridgewater," Adderly interrupted, "when you finish with the general, would you let Lieutenant Harrison know I wish to speak with him?"

Bridgewater nodded. He caught Panna's eye, his face asking the question he dared not ask aloud: Was there something more she wanted to say?

But the moment had passed. She relaxed her grasp and shook her head.

He bowed again and exited. Adderly's officer followed.

Adderly said, "Has the captain impressed you with his collection, milady? I'm told he has an account of the Battle of Stirling Bridge written in William Wallace's own hand."

"My goodness!" She thought of how much she'd been moved by *Braveheart.* "Have you read it?"

"I am not inclined to review the observations of a traitor to the Crown, milady. He came to a rather inglorious end, as I'm sure you know. Hanged until he was nearly dead, then disemboweled and cut into quarters."

"Surely, one can profit from reading the accounts of every side of a question—even the accounts of men with whom one disagrees?"

"You sound like the captain now," Adderly said, smiling. "He hurts his chances for advancement with the opinions he holds. He circles the edge of a fire I fear will consume him."

"Do you think so?" she said innocently. "I thought the charges had been dropped."

Adderly gazed at her through the blackest of lashes. "'Tis true we have no firm evidence against him, but I cannot deny my instincts. If you thought you had any sway with him…"

"What? Me? No, I do not." Why would Adderly think she would have sway over a man she'd supposedly met only fifteen minutes earlier?

"A shame." He nodded philosophically. "Shall we sit? I should very much like to hear more about your library."

She knew she ought to excuse herself, but her curiosity about the private upheavals in the two Bridgewater families got the better of her. Besides, what difference would a few more minutes make? "I heard from someone in town that Captain Bridgewater has made a claim against your family. That must be very awkward."

Adderly shook his head. "Aye. I'm afraid his mother planted in his head that he is the son of my father. Of course, the idea's ridiculous. My father would hardly have consorted with a Scot. 'Tis not unusual for men to make such claims. I am afraid greed or jealousy is often at the root of it."

"But he's quite wealthy, is he not?"

"That's debatable. He's not of noble birth, however, and that may be his motivation, though I do not pretend to know what is in any man's head but my own."

"And yet..." She gazed at that slightly bent nose and those catlike features. She was so tempted to ask if Adderly had ever considered, even briefly, that the claim might be true.

"'And yet'?"

"And yet that is hardly why I've come. I apologize. I'm certain talking of these things is unpleasant for you."

"One bears it as one can. Please, sit." He gestured to the chairs by the window.

She was glad he hadn't chosen the window seat. He had the eager-to-please look of a yellow Lab. She suspected that if she tossed him a ball, they could have played all afternoon. Given Adderly's general affability, she wondered for a brief moment if she might actually finagle a contribution from him.

"Actually," she said, "I wonder if you might direct me to the privy."

"'Tis just down the hall and around the corner. Come." He held out his elbow for her.

Though she wanted no escort, she could hardly say as much. She accepted his arm reluctantly.

He led Panna back into the hallway. What she saw there made her wish she hadn't been quite so determined to return to the past last night.

An armed soldier stood guard in front of the chapel door.

Fifteen

As the afternoon sun began its gentle descent, Bridgewater reviewed the last of the regimental drills, a task usually reserved for a colonel, but Adderly had disappeared and Colonel Van Allen had spent the day overseeing the stowage of the new delivery of gunpowder from the south, a task Bridgewater would normally have handled.

The men marching by did their best not to let their gazes linger on his battered face. His eye was fully purple now and his lip throbbed. He observed his men with a distant, disengaged part of his mind. His more active thoughts busied themselves with Panna Kennedy.

He could still taste the sweetness of her mouth and feel the thick, silky tresses as he'd removed those combs. How he would have liked their time together to have been unencumbered by the demands of war. He would have happily led her to his bedchamber and loosened the ties on that gown. She'd said she was a widow. He wondered if it was true. Whoever had schooled her in the pleasures of the flesh, however, had done his job well. A fire burned in her that had never been damped by coldness, cruelty, or clumsiness. He could almost feel her legs around him and the strength in her hips as she moved. She might be from the future, but there were some pleasures that hadn't changed in a thousand years, nor would they in the next thousand.

The future.

As he'd told her, he had heard stories, usually of a traveler who'd gone to the future and returned, only to be destroyed by greed or some stolen and misused knowledge. The stories were the stuff of nursemaid tales, meant to be instructive to children and keep them focused on their lessons.

But he couldn't deny that there was a sound to Panna's voice he'd never heard, not even on the ship of his sea captain friend, Hugh, whose crew came from all four corners of the earth. And as pleasing to look at as she was, there was a sense about her that was unusual. He couldn't say if it was the glow of her skin or the confidence in her gait or the uninhibited way she'd found a seat on the floor and opened the book. Little wonder he'd mistaken her for a spy.

He had no belief in the stories of fairies or selkie or the folk of the woods that people around here held dear. He may have grown up in the cold, unwelcoming atmosphere of an orphanage, but Father Giles had never let the children be fed the misguided tales of the borderlands. Father Giles had been a man of science, and under him, the children had learned math and astronomy and the names of the plants and animals of England.

So why did Bridgewater believe her?

He gave the lieutenant a minute nod, releasing the men from their exercise. He was to meet Robbie, one of the rebels, tonight in Drumburgh, but only if he could shake the man Adderly had put in place to track him. Bridgewater's eyes cut to the man, supposedly a tinker plying his pots and pans to the supply master. He'd been to the camp in various forms—a tinker today, a brewer the day before that—always lurking at the fringes of activity, waiting for Bridgewater to leave.

He caught Private Kenworthy's eye and made a surreptitious motion toward the space behind the tents. The man hadn't flinched, which probably meant he'd kept Bridgewater's confidence regarding the run-in outside the powder house with Thomas the night before.

Bridgewater walked toward the gate then ducked the a path to the tents. He found Kenworthy approaching Kingfisher, the peacock, with some sort of treat. The peacock reared back and leap, talons first, at Kenworthy's legs.

"Kingfisher," Bridgewater called. "At ease."

Kingfisher abandoned his attack and began to peck at the corn Kenworthy had dropped in his surprise.

"Canny bird, that one," Kenworthy said, wiping the dust from his trousers.

"If only all my recruits were as crafty. I wanted to let you know I've written to Colonel O'Donovan in Dublin. I expect an answer within a week."

"Thank you, sir."

"Kenworthy, I should like your help on another matter."

"If I can, sir." The man hitched his sword belt higher on his waist.

"Do you see the man showing the cauldron to Sergeant Pfeiffer near the gate?"

Kenworthy nodded, his mouth tightening into a knot at one corner. "When I was growing up, the tinker always polished his pots first."

"I would like you to purchase half a dozen pots for your betrothed."

"I don't have a betrothed, sir."

"Fortunately, the tinker doesn't know that. You only want the finest copper, but you know very little about pots, so he'll need to explain what to look for when choosing and how to properly care for each one. Whatever you do, just make sure he doesn't climb on his horse to go, even if it means you have to jump into the saddle yourself. I shall pay you for the pots tomorrow and I hope you will consider it a gift to your mother in Dublin."

"Thank you very much, sir."

Kenworthy went one way and Bridgewater went the other. He ducked into the overgrown rose garden and jogged to the other side, where he let out a sigh, thinking what it might have been like to walk Panna through these fragrant paths and steal a kiss against the sun-dappled stone wall. Then he slipped among a group of soldiers walking down the long hill toward his stables.

❧

Bridgewater had reached the crossroads and without thinking slowed Romulus to a trot. Drumburgh was only a quarter hour ahead, and he had planned to dine at the inn there before his meeting, but something was pulling him in the other direction.

The horse, unused to any sort of hesitancy under Bridgewater's hand, looked back questioningly.

"I hope you don't mind putting your supper off for a bit," Bridgewater said, "but if it makes you feel better, I'll be skipping mine entirely." The horse's ears went up, but he obeyed the tug on his bridle and turned in the other direction.

❧

The woman looked at Bridgewater appraisingly, and he wondered if she was glad to see her childhood acquaintance. It had been a long time since he'd crossed her threshold.

"Have you come to prepare yourself for battle?" She threw back her shoulders to remind Bridgewater there were men superstitious enough to believe bedding a naiad would bring them luck on the fields of war.

"No, I'm afraid not."

Undine tossed her head and returned to her turnips. A river nymph peeling vegetables. He supposed even fairies needed to eat.

"Have you seen Father Giles of late?" he asked, taking a seat at her small table.

"He doesn't approve of how I live."

As a whore, a spell-caster, and a fortune-teller? No, I suppose not. "He's well. He sends his regards."

"What have you come for, Jamie? I doubt it's to reminisce about our childhood."

"No. I want to ask you about time."

She stopped her peeling. "Time?"

"Aye. Is it possible, do you think, to travel from one time to another?"

She laughed. "Are you thinking of a new way to subdue France? Or is it Scotland this time?"

"Neither. I just want to know if it's possible and if anyone has done it."

She leaned against the turf of the cottage wall and gave him a curious look. He didn't believe she was a fairy, though she'd been telling the same story since he'd first met her. Mother a naiad, father unknown. Whether he believed her or not, however, he'd seen her read many a man's future, and a good deal of the things she'd said had come to be.

"It has been done, Jamie. Though not by many."

"It has?"

"There are people who can do it. The powers are not open to all. And you must find a passageway first. They are as rare as narwhals. There's one in the Highlands, near Pennan, I hear. Another near Langholm. And there are ways one can create one, if you have the power."

"What about Cumbria?"

She paused before answering, and he could see something flicker across her features. "I've not seen it."

He gave her a look. She was avoiding the question.

"Fine. Aye. I've heard there's one here," she said finally.

"Where?"

"Do not attempt it. Time travel can change a man. It finds a weakness and magnifies it. A greedy man becomes feverish for gold. A man with a taste for whiskey becomes a drunkard. An angry man becomes a killer."

"What sin of mine are you afraid of magnifying?"

She gazed at him as if she were doing an inventory of his character, but she didn't answer. Instead she said, "Why do you insist on staying in that man's army? He shall never love you as a father should."

The question was like a blow, and the hurt must have been apparent on his face, for she lowered her head. "I'm sorry, Jamie."

"'Tis foolish to wish for such things, I know, but I just think if I can earn his respect—"

"I know what you think," she said gently. "A son could think nothing else. I know he's proud of you. I've heard him say it."

Every officer comes to her, he thought. *I shouldn't be surprised.*

"Do you ever think what it would be like if he had married your mother?" She had asked the question in a way that suggested such an outcome might have brought him something other than joy.

"For one thing, I'd be his heir."

"You would. Though I don't think that's why you wish it."

Unblinking, his eyes held hers. "I'd be his son."

"And he'd be the better man for it. Jamie, you've never asked me to read your future, but I can tell you this: someday your pain will lessen."

He snorted. "And how might that be?"

"You must let go of your longing for your father. 'Tis the only way to cut the pain—well, that or become a father yourself."

What would it be like having a child with Panna Kennedy, feeling the life in her belly, putting the life into her belly? The blood prickled up his neck. And Undine's gaze caught every nuance of his thoughts.

She patted his arm. "You are a decent man, Jamie Bridgewater. Which is why I don't want you to try to find the passageway. Promise me."

So she didn't intend to tell him where it was or how to create one. He didn't mind. Panna had told him what he'd needed to know.

"'Tis not for me," he said.

"I'm glad." She wiped her hands on a towel and looked at him. "You don't imagine yourself as a man of the future, then?"

He considered this for a moment. "Let's say, there are reasons I *might* someday attempt it, but the reasons have nothing to do with money or knowledge."

She smiled. "I know. And I'm glad."

His cheeks began to burn again, and he turned to the window. "How do the time passageways work? Assuming one finds one, of course."

"The passageways are direct connections to specific times. Like a tunnel through a mountain. Some passageways are like triangles or squares, connecting three or four times, which can have unintended consequences. I heard of a man who went to the past to steal jewels from his mother, before she'd lost her fortune. But when he sent his brother to do the same thing, the man ended up tied to a post, facing Torquemada's torch in the Inquisition. The passageways are not something to play with."

"I'll abide by your warning. Is it possible I know anyone who's traveled this way?"

She resumed her chopping. "'Tis time for you to go, Jamie. I'm expecting a visitor."

He stood and put several coins on the table.

Undine gave him an amused look. "For that much I could cancel him."

Bridgewater clasped her shoulders and kissed her lightly on the forehead. "Take care of yourself, Undine."

She followed him out into the yard, watching as he mounted his horse. He was just about to gee Romulus forward when she jogged toward him.

"There's one more thing, Jamie. There's a limit to the number of times most men can go. The third time one returns to one's own time, the passageway is closed to that person forever."

"And that is the sum of what you know?"

She dropped her gaze. "Aye. That's all."

He turned Romulus and set out for Drumburgh, tipping his hat politely to a man on a bay horse smoking a pipe who was just turning in toward Undine's gate. She hadn't told him the whole truth, but what she'd told him he believed to be true.

Cumbria's time passageway was very likely to be found in his own castle. What else could explain the ease with which Panna had come and gone? He supposed he should've asked her, but he had a strong belief that the things God had chosen to make unknown to men should remain unknown. Was it not enough that she'd appeared when he'd been so deep in self-doubt, when he'd been praying for his mother to send him a sign that the path he'd chosen to follow with the rebels was a worthy one?

He'd believed the beating at Adderly's hands had

been the sign, and Bridgewater had lain with his head in his hands at his desk, battered and alone, when Panna had come back to him. He could still feel the gentleness of those hands on his face. Was that what time travelers were? Angels to comfort the afflicted?

Afflicted? He shook his head.

He was hardly afflicted. He was wealthy. He'd earned a name for himself in the army and in business, even if he could never earn the one name he desired most.

Well, angel or charlatan, it hardly mattered. She was gone now, and he knew letting her go was the only possible path he could have chosen.

Romulus paused, bringing Bridgewater out of his thoughts. They were at the crossroads they had turned at half an hour ago, and Romulus was waiting for a signal. It came, but not in the form either was expecting.

Hoofbeats sounded on the other side of the rise to the west. Clare's head appeared, and he reined in his horse when he reached Bridgewater.

"Do you know?" Clare said. "Is that why you're on your way to Carlisle?"

"Do I know what?"

"It may be nothing, sir, but I thought it best to let you know. I overheard a soldier at the stables saying he'd been asked to prepare the general's best riding horse for him, as Adderly and the library keeper had already taken off in the general's carriage for Bridgewater Castle."

Sixteen

Drawing Room, Bridgewater Castle, Carlisle, Cumbria

TWO CASTLES IN ONE DAY. PANNA SHOULD HAVE BEEN excited. Instead, she felt a strong uneasiness about Lord Adderly and his motives.

"Do you not like the wine?" Adderly gestured to her still-full glass.

"No, no, it's quite good. I…I am just so tired from our travel. I'm afraid if I drink anything, I'll be asleep in my seat." Or drugged, which was one of her worries.

He smiled. "Do not concern yourself. I have had a chamber prepared for you upstairs. Is there anyone we should get a message to?"

She could hardly say Bridgewater. She'd have no explanation for needing to notify a man she hardly knew. And Clare wasn't a possibility, either. "No. I live alone. My servant is visiting her mother in York."

"I hope you don't mind my bringing you here. As I said, I wanted to show you my home. And I believe the men attending the dinner here tonight could be additional sources of patronage for your library. 'Twill be a great opportunity for you to talk about your plans. An additional fifteen miles hardly signifies."

The carriage ride through the summer fields of Cumbria had been beautiful, but Panna would have enjoyed it more if each minute hadn't drawn her farther from the chapel in MacIver Castle. She was still uncertain how the guard came to be in front of the chapel door. Adderly's behavior toward her had not changed; if anything, he'd become more gracious and solicitous. Nonetheless, he'd been quite insistent on showing her his home, which sat in a wide park surrounded by thick forests of oak. It was easily four times the size of MacIver Castle, though, having been built several centuries later, it lacked the battlements of a true castle.

Adderly had clung to her side throughout the tour of the grounds and house, during which she'd determined her best route of escape. There she would change her clothes and disappear into the woods. The path to Bridgewater Castle had not been complicated—only two turns off the main road, and she could certainly walk fifteen miles or so back to Bowness, though it would take her much of the night. The best time to make her escape, she thought, would be as soon as she was released from his company to tidy up for dinner, which, given that it was nearly seven, ought to be soon.

"When is dinner?"

"We eat at half past eight, milady. I believe I hear some of the guests arriving now."

"Would you mind if I took a few moments to gather myself? I'm afraid the journey has left me a bit of a mess."

"Of course. Where are my manners?" He led her up the curving staircase, past portraits of august ancestors, each with the same distinctive bent nose and piercing eyes. She wondered if he planned on assuming the role of her lady's maid, but he finally released her at the entrance to a room not far from the servants' staircase and gave her hand a courtly kiss.

She closed the door, counted to two hundred, and exited. She was halfway to the stairs when a glimpse of an adjoining bedroom made her stop in her tracks.

It was several times larger than the one she'd been in, which had been quite spacious on its own. A thick Turkish carpet covered the floor, and a spectacular carved bed stood at the far end of the room, opposite an equally ornate hearth. The top of the mattress had to be five feet off the ground, and it included a set of wooden steps at the side that reminded Panna of a slightly larger version of the little staircase her aunt Elaine kept next to the bed for her toy poodle.

But it was neither the carpet nor the bed that had caught Panna's eye. It was a set of pewter candlesticks, fashioned in the shape of conch shells, that sat on the hearth. If she wasn't mistaken, they were in exactly the same style and of the same craftsmanship as a certain pewter nef with which she was intimately familiar.

The hallway was silent. There didn't appear to be a soul anywhere. She stepped into the room, intent on examining the candlesticks more closely.

On the floor were a pair of newly shined riding boots. Two *Army Gazettes* lay on the desk, and a gleaming red coat with colonel strips on it hung in an open wardrobe. This had to be Adderly's room. So the nef given by the Bridgewater descendent could perhaps trace its provenance to this very place.

She was nearly at the hearth when the faintest whisper of a voice made her freeze.

"...an attack? By the Scots? I hardly think..."

Panna recognized the speaker. It was the earl, who'd evidently arrived while she and Adderly were in the drawing room. But she hadn't made out the rest of what he'd said.

Panicked, she whirled around, trying to determine where his voice coming from. Was there a room attached to this one? She didn't see a door.

"We've gotten no signs, and there are scouts everywhere," the earl went on. "No, I am afraid they're waiting for us, and as you know, our orders from the queen are to not attack unless we are provoked."

The voice appeared to be coming from the hearth. She got as close as she could. The chimney had to be the same one that served the room below. She found that she could hear the conversation almost perfectly if she held her breath and bent her ear toward the grate.

"I shall be most relieved if the Scots do attack," said the other man. "This cursed waiting is hard on the men."

"If nothing happens by the first of August," the earl said, "my instructions from the queen are to pull the men out. Send them to General Marlborough in Europe."

"Are you serious?" the other man said, outraged. "That's four days from now! I've ordered every

division north of Oxford to join us here. Three
arrive tomorrow and four more the next day. That's
half the English army. Do you know how much it
will cost us to bring them here and send them away?
And what fools we'll appear for having done it?"

"Not only will we appear to be fools," the earl said,
"but if nothing happens, the queen will cut off funds
for any further efforts. We'll be down to the bones as
far as men and supplies are concerned. A fine assign-
ment for men of our experience."

For a long moment neither man said a word. Panna
could imagine them drowning their unhappiness in
their whiskey.

"I have an idea," the other man said, "though I
wouldn't like to sign my name to it."

"What is it?"

"Well, the way I see it, we need to find a way to—"
Suddenly the men stopped talking.

"Save it," the earl said hurriedly. "There's someone
at the door. Tell me after we eat. I'll make an excuse
for us to adjourn here."

Whoever it was entered, but Panna heard no
more than "Good evening, your lordship...General
Williston" before something made her aware she was
being watched. The hair on her neck stood up. She
turned to find Adderly in the door.

"Are you in need of something, milady?" Though
his voice was solicitous, there was something cold in
his eyes that shook her almost to silence.

"I beg your pardon for intruding." Her mind raced
for a reason that might explain her presence. "This is
your room, is it not?"

"Aye, it is." He smiled, but the coldness grew.

"I was leaving a note."

One eyebrow rose slightly. "I see. Would you care to tell me your message in person?"

He took a step closer, and she felt tiny prickles of panic race up her spine.

"I beg your pardon. I shouldn't have come in without your permission, but I found myself quite drawn to the beautiful candlesticks."

Adderly's eyes went completely dead for an instant, and Panna swore she saw him sway.

"I cannot disagree," he said. "Have you ever seen anything like them?"

Perspiration began to dampen her neck. "No. Never."

He gazed at her for a long time. "I had them made for me by a whitesmith in Spain."

"Lovely."

He took a step toward her. She said, "Would you mind having a bath prepared for me? I find myself in need of some hot water." Without another word, she hurried past him and headed back, feeling his gaze on her until she was safe in her own room, door closed behind her.

It took a good five minutes before her breathing slowed. What was it about Adderly that made the warning sirens in her head go off? To a dispassionate observer, his behavior could be described as nothing but thoughtful. Nonetheless, she would be glad when she'd put Bridgewater Castle behind her.

She tiptoed down the nearby stairway and, after a careful look in each direction at the bottom, flew out the door to the kitchen garden outside. The twilight sky had thrown the rows of late summer squash and beans into a purple darkness, and she hid herself as quickly as she could behind a long, vine-covered fence. At the end, she found a smokehouse from which the scent of cooking meat rose, though she was too nervous to be hungry. The distance from the smokehouse to the brewhouse, where she'd spotted a shirt and a pair of breeks hanging from nails during her tour of the grounds, was only a dozen paces, but Panna would be in the open. She could hear voices in the distance, coming from the kitchen, but saw no one close by.

She lowered her head and ran. The instant she closed the door to the brewery, she began to scrabble at her laces. She had just dropped her gown at her feet when a hand went around her mouth.

Her muffled scream died in her throat.

"It's me," Bridgewater whispered.

He released her, and she collapsed with relief against the stuccoed wall. He had changed from his officer's coat into a plain dark one similar to the one he'd had stowed away in the secret room of his castle.

"How did you find me?" She realized too late that only a thin layer of muslin covered her, and the undergarment was so loose that one sleeve draped dangerously over her shoulder.

"Clare," he said, keeping his eyes on her face. "Do you wish to be taken from here?"

It suddenly struck her that her behavior and the state of her dress might suggest she had come to the brewhouse for an assignation.

"Oh God, yes."

His shoulders relaxed. "Good. Then hurry."

"I was going to…" She cut her gaze to the clothes on the peg.

"Oh, aye. Very wise."

She grabbed the breeks and slipped them on under her shift, relieved to discover the brewer was a slender man. Then she reached for the shirt. She eyed Bridgewater, who seemed to be admiring her ankles, and he flushed.

"Oh, of course." He turned. "Will this do?"

"Well enough, I suppose." Panna was not one for false modesty. Nonetheless, she trembled as she pulled the fabric over her head and it fell free. The night breeze was warm on her breasts.

"Clare saw you being escorted into Adderly's carriage. He didn't like the idea. He followed you here and found me in Drumburgh."

She wondered if Clare thought she was being taken against her will or suspected that she was in cahoots with Adderly. Either way, she was glad he'd decided to inform Bridgewater. "I'd been planning to leave your castle, just as I'd told you," she said. "First I told Adderly I needed to use the privy, but he insisted on escorting me there. Then, when we stepped into the hall, there was a guard in front of the chapel door."

"A *guard*?"

"I take it you didn't put him there." She poked her arms through the sleeves. The brewer must be quite thin, for the fabric clung tightly to her curves.

"I? No," Bridgewater said. "Is there no other place from which you can…"

"Travel?" Did he still not believe her? "Not as far as I know. I always land there."

"'Always'?"

"Well, yes. The first time when we met, I'd just discovered the, er, well, portal, I suppose, in the library where I work. Then I came through again when I decided I wasn't going to put up with you calling me a whore." She eyed him over her shoulder.

"It could have been worse. You were either a whore or a spy. Of the two, I chose the least offensive."

She gave him a look.

A length of rope landed on the ground at her feet. She picked it up and began to loop it around her breeks. "Then, of course, the second time, after you'd shown me the double star and we'd said good-bye. And every time I've landed in the chapel."

"You returned to your own time then? After the double star?"

The note of hurt in his question made her squirm, and she gave him a regretful look. "I did. I told you, there were people expecting me."

"Steve," he said.

Bridgewater hadn't forgotten. She felt a small thrill pass through her, which she reluctantly put aside. There would be thrills enough just trying to get off the castle grounds without throwing desire in the mix too. They could explore that later—hopefully in a place far removed from Bridgewater Castle. "Yes. But I knew I'd failed you—or at least I would if I didn't deliver the note as you'd asked. And Steve was kind enough to take me back to the library."

"Someday I must thank him."

"You'd like him."

"If I'm honest," he said softly, "I don't think I would."

"Ready!" She turned to face him, and his eyes widened.

"Not good?" she asked, reaching for the brewer's cap.

"Well, it depends on one's point of view. If we want to draw the attention of every man between here and my castle, 'tis very good."

She looked down and saw the pink-tinged outlines of her nipples through the white. "Oh."

Clare stuck his head in. "Sir?"

"*Out*," Bridgewater commanded, and Clare disappeared.

He searched the space for something to cover her with while she tucked up her hair. In a moment, he returned with an apron, which he handed her.

She put it on and tied it behind her. "Better?"

He cleared his throat rather than answering, grabbed her gown off the floor, and led her by the elbow out the door.

Clare stood at the corner of the structure, hidden from the house, and scanned the grounds. "The horses are hidden behind the copse there," he whispered, pointing to a thick growth of oaks toward the middle of the park. "We can head over the rise there and then ride in among the trees."

By the time they reached the copse, two carriages were coming up the long drive. Bridgewater peered at them from the shelter of one of the oak trunks.

"That's General Cabot's carriage," Bridgewater said, frowning. "What could he be doing here?" He laced his fingers to provide a foothold for Panna to mount the horse.

Panna put her foot in his hand. "General Williston is there as well."

He lifted her up and into the saddle. "Williston? His men are in Lincoln, and Cabot's are north of Cambridge. What would they be doing here in Cumbria?"

"Williston gave the orders for all divisions north of Oxford to come to Cumbria. They'll be arriving in the course of the next two days."

A look of horror passed between Bridgewater and Clare.

"Oh, no," she added hurriedly. "Don't worry. It's very unlikely they'll attack."

Bridgewater gave a disdainful laugh. "With three divisions? Hell, they could take almost take Spain with that many men, let alone half a dozen angry clans."

"No, what I mean is, I heard them talking, the earl and Williston. The earl was very clear that their hands are tied. The queen has said they cannot attack unprovoked. And if nothing happens by Wednesday, all the troops are to return to the south."

"How did you hear this?"

"That's the best part. There's a fireplace above where the men were meeting. I could hear their voices through the opening quite clearly."

Bridgewater gazed at the house, considering. "Where was that?"

"I was..." It dawned on her she'd rather not say, and her pause prompted Bridgewater to turn.

"Where?"

"I was in Adderly's bedchamber."

An invisible curtain dropped over Bridgewater's features. He untied the lead. "I see."

"No, you don't see. I was in the process of trying to sneak out. His bedroom door was open, and I could hear voices from the floor below coming through the hearth when I walked by. It was the earl and Williston talking. I stood there as long as I could, until Adderly discovered me."

Bridgewater looked at Clare. "If what she heard is true—"

"It *is* what I heard. I heard it quite clearly."

He bowed in acceptance. "If it's true...good Lord, by Wednesday, the crisis will have passed."

The relief on both their faces was so evident, Panna hated to add, "But there's more."

"*More?*"

"Yes. Williston felt that having to return with no victory in hand would be highly embarrassing for the generals involved."

"It would be," Bridgewater said. "And rightly so."

"Which is why he has a plan."

"A plan? What sort of plan?"

"Well, I don't know. That's when Adderly found me."

Clare chewed his lip. "I wish I knew what the generals were thinking. For that matter, I wish I knew what the clans have in mind."

Bridgewater said to Panna, "There are some borderland clan chiefs who seek to avoid more fighting. Unfortunately, that contingent has lost power in the last year. There are others who want to bring the fervor to a head no matter the cost in human lives."

"Your grandfather?" she asked.

Bridgewater's eyes turned automatically toward the north, as if he could still see that yellow flag flapping against the Scottish sky. "I don't know for certain. I've never spoken to my grandfather—not once—in my entire life. So I only know what I've heard. And what I've heard suggests he bides his time in the middle, waiting to see which way the wind will blow. His clan is the largest around here, however, and were he to come down on one side or the other, his word would carry. Still, we've heard nothing to suggest the clans are planning an attack in the short term."

Clare's horse pawed the ground, and Clare scratched the creature's ears. "Nor have we heard they intend to hold off." He put a foot in the stirrup and pulled himself into the saddle. "So, do we wait, and hope the clans sit on their hands long enough for this to blow over?"

Bridgewater slouched against the closest tree and stared abstractedly at his father's castle.

"You need to know what the generals are planning," Panna said. "Any move you make without that knowledge could make things worse."

"There may be a way to find out," Bridgewater said. "I know a captain in one of Cabot's regiments. If he arrives tomorrow—"

"Tomorrow may be too late," Clare said.

"I don't see that we have much of a choice."

"You do," Panna said. "Me."

"Pardon?"

"Me. I can go back. I'll say I took a walk. I can find out what they talk about after dinner. The earl told Williston that that's when they'd pick up the conversation."

"You're kind to offer," Bridgewater said, "but they're hardly going to invite a woman into their confidence."

"She doesn't mean joining their conversation, Jamie. She means listening from Adderly's room."

A flush of anger lit Bridgewater's cheeks. "*No.*"

The horse fidgeted at the sharpness of Bridgewater's tone, and Panna clutched the edge of the saddle. "No?"

"No," he repeated. "I told you I don't trust Adderly."

"I don't, either. But I know I can get back into his room again."

Bridgewater's flush grew brighter.

"I don't mean like that." The thought of it sent a chill through her. She hoped Adderly would join in the generals' conversation. That seemed the only way to be sure he wouldn't corner her again.

"Let me try it, at least," she said. "If I don't succeed, I can always steal away, just as I did now."

"Absolutely not. Why do you suppose I came after you? And why Clare had to find me? Adderly has a damned ugly streak of brutality. Is my face not evidence enough for you?"

"Look," she said, "I accept that Adderly is a danger. Nonetheless, your father will be there. Do you honestly think your father would let anything happen to a woman in his own home? I haven't heard you say anything about your father that would make me believe you wouldn't trust him with me." She almost said "your life," but then, a man who'd had his paternity denied might argue his life *had* been taken from him.

Bridgewater bridled. The look in his eyes made his distaste for the idea evident. He looked at Clare.

Clare shrugged. "'Tis two more hours at most. We'd be here the whole time."

Bridgewater turned back to her. "You'd be in his *bedchamber*."

She wanted to say that she knew how to handle herself in a man's bedchamber, but she dared not—not with the cold fire in his eyes. "I'll be careful, I swear. And he'll join the other men after dinner, don't you think?"

After a long moment, Bridgewater held out his hand to help her from the horse. "I don't like it."

"I know. But I'm glad you're willing to let me try."

He made a dubious noise, as if he were already regretting his decision, and handed her the gown. "There's a sizable copper beech over there. Let us hope none of the generals have chosen this hour for a walk about the park."

Seventeen

Dining Hall, Bridgewater Castle, Carlisle, Cumbria

ADDERLY FILLED HIS GOBLET, THEN TOPPED OFF PANNA'S. "You've hardly drunk anything. This is Alsatian, you know. Dry, floral, with a dash of spice. Not unlike you, milady."

She smiled despite the nerves she was feeling. He had drunk more than enough for both of them and a few generals in addition, but other than a slight pinkness around the edges of his eyes and a taste for overblown similes, he had shown few signs of inebriation, which surprised her.

"You're too kind."

Adderly leaned closer. "My servant said you forwent your bath. I hope you were not unwell."

Panna felt a sudden, more dangerous vibe. Was he wondering where she'd been? She searched his face, but there appeared to be no accusation in his words, just the solicitousness of a tongue loosened by alcohol.

"As I said, the day looked so beautiful I decided to

walk in the park instead. I owe your servant an apology. I know setting up a bath is not an easy matter. I'm sorry I missed it."

Adderly waved away her concern.

The dinner, which had consisted of fish soup, the smoked ham she'd smelled, a large roast beef, geese stuffed with quail, and eel pie, was coming slowly to an end. The men at the table were arguing the pros and cons of Marlborough's latest strategy with the French.

The earl had appeared behind them, goblet in hand. "Adderly, might I have the honor of a few moments with our guest? You've been keeping her to yourself this whole night, and ladies are at a premium."

Only three women were seated at the table, and the other two were Adderly's seventeen-year-old cousin and her elderly traveling companion.

Adderly stood and bowed, giving Panna a good-natured wink before strolling to his father's seat.

"Did you like the park, Mrs. Carnegie? I am told Adderly took you on a tour."

He looked like Sean Connery in his sixties, with his neatly trimmed beard, piercing green eyes, and, of course, that slightly bent nose. But despite his conviviality, Panna's defenses were up.

"Aye. 'Tis lovely."

"We don't spend much time here, no more than a month or two each year, though this year, of course, the unpleasantness with the Scots has extended our stay considerably."

Panna could only imagine the expense of keeping an estate of this size to use a fraction of the year.

"What about the gardens? Did Adderly take you there as well?"

"He did. I've never seen anything quite so skill-fully laid out. He says the mermaids on the fountain spin and spray water from their shells when the water is running."

"My wife designed it."

Panna wondered about the woman who had taken Sorcha's place in the earl's heart. "I'm sorry I haven't had a chance to meet her. I take it she's elsewhere this evening?"

"Did my son not tell you? His mother passed away four years ago."

"Oh, I'm so sorry. I can see a lot of you in Adderly. Does he also take after your wife?"

The earl looked at her carefully. "Aye. They share the same fine sense of taste and love of art. I'm entirely lacking in what the world would call that sort of refinement."

"I don't think that can be true, sir. Your house is beautiful."

"Thank you. It has been in the Bridgewater family for nearly a century."

She paused, considering. "Bridgewater is, I think, a common name in these parts, is it not?"

"Not particularly. Why?"

"I was introduced to another officer named Bridgewater this morning, a captain. He's in one of your regiments, I think." She watched the earl's face for a sign, but he kept his expression even.

He shook his head. "I'm am afraid he's no relation."

She took a large gulp of wine. Dare she? "He looks

a bit like your son: the aquiline nose, the deep-set eyes. They could easily be cousins."

"They are not." He reached for the carafe of wine and filled his glass. "If you've heard he once claimed a relationship, may I just say that I believe he was misled by a desperate and destitute mother. 'Tis quite sad."

"Indeed it is."

"My son is rather taken with you."

"I'm most honored," she said, flustered. The earl obviously didn't believe in beating around the bush.

"He intends to become a patron of your library."

"I'm glad. He would be helping many people."

"Where, exactly, is your library to be built, Mrs. Carnegie? I've made a few inquiries on my way into town and have found no one who is aware of your efforts."

Panna's palms began to tingle. "My efforts have just begun. Opening a library that everyone can borrow from is a dream of mine. I've been a library keeper for a long time in Penn's Woods. If you'd like a reference from the man whose library I administer, I'd be happy to write for one."

The earl looked at her over the rim of his glass. "I don't think that will be necessary." He reached into the pocket of his frock coat and withdrew a folded note. "This is for you."

She opened it carefully and saw it was a bank draft for fifty pounds—an enormous sum in these days, she thought, considering that a century from now Lizzy Bennett's annual dowry income in *Pride and Prejudice* would be forty pounds. "Thank you very much."

He nodded. "I'm reminded of the time the archbishop of York pressed me for the sponsorship of his home for the insane. I said to him as I wrote the check, 'Do you know the difference between an archbishop and a whore?' When he declared he did not, I said, 'Two naughts on the bank draft.'"

Panna felt a wave of heat rise up her neck.

"I'm afraid he didn't laugh either," the earl went on. "Not even when I added, ''Tis little wonder both do their best work on their knees.'" He took a deep drink of wine. "Shall we agree this will end your, er, solicitation of my son?"

She placed the draft on the table and pushed it toward him. "You may keep your money, sir. I'll find the funding I require, and if it means I must scrape my knees on the carpet of every gentleman in Cumbria, I will do so at my pleasure—beginning with your son."

For a long moment, the earl said nothing, and Panna wondered if she'd be thrown out of the castle. Then the earl barked a laugh so hearty, nearly everyone at the table turned, including Adderly.

"I like your spirit, milady," the earl said. "You remind me of a woman I had the pleasure of knowing a very long time ago. And I don't doubt you'll raise the funds you need. Please accept this with my sincerest desire for your success. You have painted a picture that will be with me for some many years hence. Adderly," he called, rising, "you may return to your rightful place. I hope you're willing to support our guest's cause. I think you'll find the position of supporter quite satisfying."

Panna slipped the draft into her pocket as Adderly returned to his seat.

"You've certainly won my father's favor," he said.

"He's a most interesting man."

Adderly's eyes gleamed mischief. "I've been thinking about your bath, milady."

Oh, dear.

"I have a thought."

"Oh?" She picked up her glass. Dinner was ending, and in a moment, the men would be adjourning to wherever they went. Panna hoped wherever that happened to be would be the same place the earl and Williston had been this afternoon.

Adderly leaned closer. "What if I called for a bath in *my* room? You'd have the benefit of hot water without the embarrassment of having to ask a second time."

The only thing about the offer that surprised Panna was how many goblets of wine it had taken to prompt it.

"It seems a rather dangerous thing to attempt, if you ask me." She smiled.

"Does it?" He traced the outline of her neckline with his eyes.

"For example, where would *you* be during such an undertaking?"

He made a throaty chuckle and took another gulp of his drink. "Well, I could hardly ask for the bath if I wasn't in the bedchamber myself."

"Uh-huh. You understand my concern, then?"

"What if I were to tell you the bath had already been drawn?"

"I'd say someone has been counting his winnings in advance of the last hand of cards. 'Tis never advisable."

He laughed again. "What if I were to give you time to play the last hand?"

"How do you mean?"

"I mean this." He leaned close enough not only to tickle her ear with his breath but also to see nearly to her navel. "I have in mind to make a very large contribution to your library. However, I should like there to be a bit of sport in it. I am going into the drawing room with the officers for our usual brandies and talk of war. However, I cannot guarantee how long our discussion might last. If, knowing that, you're daring enough to take your bath in my room, you shall find a draft for thirty pounds in the pocket of your gown tomorrow."

Not quite as generous as his father. "And how will you know I've done it? If I'm wise, and I am—very—I shall be in and out of there as fast as I can manage it."

"Oh, I've already considered that possibility. I'm afraid you shall have to leave your gown in my room as proof. And your shift."

"Leaving me nothing but a towel?"

"Leaving you nothing," he said. "There are two towels next to the bath. Both will have to stay."

"I see." She took another long sip of wine, considering the challenge. "That's a rather long walk in nothing but my slippers, don't you think?"

"I find the notion exceedingly intriguing. I warrant it's the only thing that will get me through my colleagues' long-winded discussion."

"Let us pray it *is* long-winded."

"Aye, to that end, I can say this: I will stay until my father finishes his second brandy. You have my word as a gentleman on it. But one can never tell if this will be the night he sips and enjoys or the night he toasts and swallows."

The officers were rising from their chairs, and

Panna considered how much time it would take for the men to begin discussing how they intended to get around Queen Anne's restrictions once they got their brandies. Of course, she hadn't the slightest intention of taking a bath. As much as she'd enjoy collapsing in tub of steamy water after this long day, the benefits in this case definitely didn't seem worth the risk. However, the satisfied smile that spread across Adderly's face made it clear he'd taken her silence for assent.

She played with the napkin on her lap. "And what would you say if I were to tell you the library I'm imagining will cost considerably more than thirty pounds?"

The earl stood. "Adderly, would you lead our guests into the drawing room?"

Adderly caught Panna's napkin and dropped it on the table next to her plate, carefully brushing a breast with his arm. He said under his breath, "I would say plan on taking a very long bath."

Eighteen

PANNA STEPPED CAREFULLY AROUND THE STEAMING tub. Pink and white rose petals floated on the water, and a decanter of wine and two glasses stood on a small table within arm's reach. A book was there too. *The London Spy* by Ned Ward. She almost laughed. Adderly certainly seemed to be offering her every inducement to lose track of time. She'd brought the brewer's clothes with her when she'd left Bridgewater and Clare and stuffed them in a closet she'd found on the service stairway. Her plan was to meet her companions no later than ten o'clock at the same place in the park. The clock had just struck a quarter past nine.

The wind had picked up slightly, and even the light sough of it against the windows was enough to make Panna have to strain to hear the conversation below.

"Miss Cavendish handled dinner tonight with great aplomb," Williston said.

Miss Cavendish was Adderly's young cousin.

"Thank you," the earl said. "I shall pass along your praise to my sister."

"She is a fine girl," Williston said. "Very fine. I

hope you won't be offended, however, when I tell you I found myself wishing to have been seated next to the other lady at the table."

"Miss Cavendish's chaperone?" a third man said. "I'm sure we can arrange a late-night rendezvous. Let us hope she's kept her teeth in."

"I think Williston rather hopes she has her teeth out," Adderly said, and the room dissolved in laughter.

Panna rolled her eyes.

"I meant Mrs. Carnegie," Williston said, irritated.

The earl laughed. "I'm afraid my son has set that pudding aside for himself."

"She's a handsome woman, Adderly. How did you meet her?"

"At MacIver Castle," he said. "She arrived this morning."

"Aye, she pressed him into a donation for a lending library she wishes to start," the earl added.

"I hope she will press me as well," another officer said, and the men laughed.

"A lending library?" someone repeated. "For whom?"

"The people of the borderlands," the earl said.

"What on earth would the rabble there do with a library?"

"Nonetheless, that is her wish," the earl said. "And she's raising funds to make it so."

"Ridiculous. She'll never succeed."

"I think she might," the earl said. "She has great powers of persuasion."

Still another man said, "'Tis an effort I would be glad to have a hand in."

The laughter rose again.

"Aye," O'Donovan said. "I wonder what sort of lending privileges come with it."

Williston said, "Depends how big your donation is."

The men whooped. Panna shook her head. They were wasting precious brandy time on frat-boy idiocy. *What are your plans, fellas? Wednesday's just around the corner. Let's get on with it, shall we?*

"We need to talk about the situation with the Scots."

Williston. Finally, a voice of reason.

"Adderly will you pass me the decanter," the earl said. "I'm afraid this will require a second round, and you've been holding it rather close this last quarter hour."

Second round? C'mon, people!

"I am in no mood to preside over the borderlands with no more than half a dozen swivel guns and my broadsword," Williston said. "Let us pray for a battle."

"'Pray for a battle'?" Adderly said. "For God's sake, let us use the brains and balls we were born with, shall we? It's time for us to forget what the queen wants and do what we think is right."

"Such as?"

"Such as provoke a battle with the clans."

"Don't be absurd," the earl said.

"I'm not. There are ways to do it which would leave no trail to our doorstep."

"He has a point," Williston said.

"It's worth considering."

"No, it is *not*," the earl said, his disgust apparent in his voice. "Let's hope we have not fallen so low."

Chastened, the group fell silent. Then Adderly

said in a low, agitated tone, "You're wrong. This is a war, and the Scots wouldn't hesitate to use any sort of deceit if they thought it would give them some advantage. They're filth. Were it up to me—"

"'Tis not up to you, Colonel," the earl said sharply. "And I'll thank you to remember that."

For a full minute no one said anything. The silence went on so long that Panna thought for a moment the men had been dismissed, but then Williston said, "I suppose what you say is true..."

"You 'suppose'?" the earl said. "Holy Mother of God, if we cannot win this battle without resorting to such base tactics, we shouldn't be soldiers."

A noise made her spin in a half circle. Adderly was leaning against the door of his room, a drunken grin on his face. He stepped inside and closed the door.

Had he heard the voices? Did he know she'd been eavesdropping?

He walked to her slowly, weaving as he went, his eyes bright as embers. Her heart hammered in her chest.

She moved away from the hearth, hoping to keep him from the knowledge of what she'd been doing, and when their paths intersected he took her in his arms and kissed her.

"I can feel your heart pounding," he said.

Can you feel the scream that's in there too?

His kiss had been disconcertingly similar to Bridgewater's: the same warm mouth, the same stubbled cheek. But Bridgewater's had sent shock waves through her body and Adderly's only dread.

"You came," he said. "I wasn't sure you would."

Panna relaxed minutely. It appeared the future earl was not aware she'd been listening in on the officers' conversation. If she could get him to lie down and relax, he'd probably fall asleep.

A faint echo of Williston's voice floated through the hearth, and Adderly cocked his head, instantly aware.

She laid her palms over his ears and kissed him.

"And I waited," she said when they parted.

"I see that. I don't mind that you didn't bathe." He began pulling her toward the bed, though he nearly fell with the effort. "I shall enjoy you unbathed, too."

"Wait."

"I think not, milady. You have me too much in your thrall."

She was not going to sacrifice her honor for the people of the borderlands, no matter how deserving they might be. Besides, there was more to be learned from the officers.

"I think waiting will be worth your while."

At this he stopped, cocking an interested brow. She could see the effort it took for him to keep her in focus.

"I think you've had too much to drink."

"I think I have had just enough. I am still waiting to hear how waiting could be worth my while."

She swallowed hard. "I am planning to take that bath."

His eyes widened at the possibility of such a tableau. "Indeed?"

"Aye."

His grip relaxed a degree, and it was all she could do not to jerk herself free.

"There are few things that would induce me to delay the pleasure of joining with you," he said, "but I do believe *that* might be one of them." He lifted her chin with his finger. "You have promised to make waiting worth my while. Take care you do it."

He might barely have been able to stand upright, but the threat was apparent enough.

"Lie down," she directed, managing with effort to keep the quaver from her voice.

He released her arm and made his way to the door unsteadily. For an instant her heart soared. If he were to leave, even for a moment, she would disappear. But instead he closed the door and threw the bolt. The click sent a jolt of terror down her spine.

She willed herself to calmness, giving him a seductive smile. He stumbled toward the bed. Letting out a long breath, she returned to the tub, eyeing him over her shoulder as she moved. The men were still talking downstairs. She drew a hand across the petal-covered water. She could feel his eyes on her.

"*...you been in touch with our contact in Edinburgh?*" Williston asked. Adderly made no sign of hearing anything.

She reached for the ribbons at her bodice and loosened them. Adderly practically vibrated with anticipation. If she stretched this out long enough, he might fall asleep. "You must lie down, sir. I can hardly do this with you looking as if you are about to leap upon me like a bear in the woods."

With a chuckle, he flopped on his back on the mattress and gave her a prurient smile.

The earl's voice drifted out of the hearth. *"Do not refer to him as our contact, you fool."*

She slipped the shoulders of the gown free and let it fall.

Adderly was absolutely rapt now. *As well he should be*, she thought.

She took a deep breath and let the shift fall as well.

He let out a long, slow sigh. She felt like Daniel in the den of lions.

She stepped into the tub and lowered herself into the still-warm water.

"You have a gorgeous cunt."

Prince Charming.

She grabbed the ball of soap, dipped it in the water, and drew it slowly down the length of her arm and in a slippery trail around each breast.

"Oh, *aye*."

She tried to listen to the snippets of conversation from the hearth but, unsurprisingly, was having a hard time concentrating. Especially after Adderly jumped suddenly from the bed.

"What are you doing?"

"Keeping to the terms of our bet." He snagged the dress and shift, wove his way to the wardrobe and tossed them inside. Then he pulled a key from his pocket and locked the wardrobe door.

Oh shit.

But he didn't stop there. He skinned off his coat and shirt, then with considerable comic effort his boots and socks, hopping in an exaggerated circle. When he reached for the buttons of his breeks, she said, *"Adderly."*

"Aye?"

"I said to lie down."

But instead he made his way toward the tub, unbuttoning as he walked.

She kept her eyes on his face, deafened by the roar of blood in her ears. He raked his gaze over her, desire apparent on his face and in the straining of flesh against the front of his breeks.

"I'm bathing," she said, hoping he didn't hear the tremor in her voice. "Go. Lie. Down."

He trailed a finger from her collarbone to her nipple, which he twisted roughly. Then he stumbled toward the bed, pausing only to drop his breeks before stretching out unself-consciously on the bed.

She let out a silent sigh of relief.

The broad chest and tight stomach were clearly a Bridgewater trait, but she hoped the less-than-imperious family standard rising between Adderly's legs was a legacy of the countess's side of the family, not the earl's.

"I have no intention of asking him to consider such a thing," the earl said.

The lapping of the water as she washed made hearing the officers' conversation tricky, and when she finally finished, the voices had stopped. Adderly's breathing, however, had grown slow and steady.

Thataboy.

She dared not look, afraid that catching his eye would only rouse him. She sponged her back and sides until the water was so cold that it gave her gooseflesh. At last she heard a gentle snore.

Thank God.

She slipped slowly out of the water and padded to

where Adderly had dropped his coat. No key in the pockets there. She tried his breeks next, but those didn't even have a pocket. Where could he have put the key to the wardrobe? Without her dress, she'd be faced with running to the service stairway naked.

He stirred and her breath caught, but he only rolled onto his stomach, adjusting his erection, and let out a small fart. Then she saw the key. It was clutched in the fist under his cheek.

There was no way she was going to be able to fish it loose. Instead, she grabbed his shirt and slipped it on, then flew to the door, unbolted it, and ran.

Nineteen

"I TOLD YOU," PANNA SAID, TIRED OF ANSWERING. "There was no concrete plan, just Adderly's suggestion that the army do something the queen wouldn't approve of to provoke the Scots—and the whole notion was instantly rejected by your father."

Bridgewater finished buttoning her into the new gown and growled.

They'd been over this half a dozen times. She was glad darkness had fallen. The look that had come over Bridgewater's face as she'd approached the copse in Adderly's shirt would be burned into her mind forever. After she'd explained what had happened and why she'd had to do what she'd done, Bridgewater's demeanor changed from shock to a cool, businesslike formality. He'd handed her his coat stiffly and begun asking questions as if he were cross-examining an uncooperative witness at a hearing.

Even Clare had been embarrassed for her. After the second time Bridgewater had gone through his litany of questions, Clare asked if his own time might not be better spent scavenging new clothes for Panna, and Bridgewater had released him.

In less than an hour, Clare had reappeared, toting not only a clean shift but a gown of crisp, rose linen printed with tiny flowers.

And Clare's powers of conjuring were not limited to clothes. He had also found a wedge of cheese, several slices of roast beef, and a small jug of ale.

So while Panna tried to work her way into the slightly small gown behind her old friend the copper beech, the men ate. When she emerged, she saw Bridgewater had taken only a few bites.

"We'll need another horse," Clare said, "though I suppose she can ride with one of us."

Panna was surprised he didn't have an extra horse in his pack.

"No, we won't. She can have mine." Bridgewater flung the rind of his cheese into the woods. "I have an appointment, and I'll walk. It's in Drumburgh," he added by way of explanation when Clare cocked his head.

Whatever having an appointment in Drumburgh meant, it lit up a lightbulb for Clare. The question evaporated from his face and he busied himself with the cork on the jug.

"Return her to MacIver Castle," Bridgewater added.

"'Return her'? What am I, an overdue library book?"

"And tell Reeves to put her someplace where she won't be disturbed...the chapel."

Though Bridgewater had his back to her, she knew the pause had been for her benefit. He'd refused to meet her eyes since she'd appeared in Adderly's shirt. She wondered if they would part, never to see each other again, with him offering her nothing more than an anger-laden grunt. She was deeply disappointed in failing to learn more from the officers—and in realizing that Bridgewater was not going to be sweeping her into his arms and carrying her off to the nearest inn—and she just wished he'd do something to show his affection for her hadn't changed.

She puffed out her chest against the tightness of the bodice, wondering if she could pop a button into his forehead.

Clare said, "Didn't you say Adderly's guard was in front of the chapel? If so, not even Reeves may be allowed to pass."

Bridgewater let out a quiet oath. "You're right. I'll take her. They'll not deny me. You can take my place at Drumburgh."

"In case anyone cares," Panna said, "I am not a bag of horse feed. I'm perfectly capable of determining where I should go and when." This despite the fact that she felt like a bag of horse feed that had grown too big for its burlap.

Clare, sensing trouble, jumped to his feet and brushed off his breeks. "Then I'll head out." He waved and set off on foot, disappearing quickly into the thick forest.

Bridgewater picked up the loose gear, attached it to one saddle or the other, and began to make the small adjustments necessary to change the tack on Clare's horse to something more appropriate for a rider with legs a foot shorter.

"How far is Drumburgh?" she asked at last.

"Eight miles."

"Poor man. He should have a horse."

He tightened the stirrup with a jerk. "Unfortunately, we can't spare one."

"Look, I'm sorry if my presence here has been an inconvenience. Lord knows it's been no great pleasure for me, either. But I'll be out of your hair soon. I was only trying to help."

"'Help'?"

He turned on her so sharply that she took a step backward.

"That's what you call help?" A spark of fury flashed in his eyes. "Do you have any idea what I've been going through these last two hours, twiddling my thumbs while I waited to hear if you'd been found out or taken prisoner or attacked?" His voice grew husky. "Do you not understand you're a *weapon*? That he'd want what you know? And that if he found you out, you'd be at his mercy? Did you not see what he did to me? And I have the protection of a commanding officer. Do you think he would scruple to seize you or move you or hide you in a place I couldn't find you? He wouldn't. And I'd spend the rest of my days tearing the borderlands apart piece by piece to find you."

He pressed his palms to his temples, overcome with emotion and then flung them away.

"I—I'm sorry," she said, pounded by waves of regret. "I didn't mean to worry you."

"And then you stumble in, in his shirt, as if you *had* been attacked. Oh Christ!" He turned back to the horses.

Panna knew what it was to care so much about a person that their safety was more important than your own. With Charlie, that feeling had a come a little piece at a time. They'd dated for many months before she could honestly say she'd fallen in love with him. But with Bridgewater it had happened in a matter of hours. She supposed in a world where each day brings life or death to your doorstep, the rules were different.

She took a hesitant step. "Bridgewater, I'm sorry— very sorry. You're right: I *don't* know what's danger- ous here. I thought I could handle it, but I should've listened. We have a phrase where I come from for what I was feeling: 'scared shitless.'"

His shoulders relaxed and shook slightly, and she knew she'd made him laugh. He turned, giving her a small smile. "'Tis very apt." But then the smile was replaced with a look of quiet dread. "Tell me, *did* he hurt you? I was afraid Clare's presence or even mine may have kept you from being honest."

She wished she didn't have to tell him what had transpired, but she also knew she owed him the truth. "He didn't hurt me. He'd had far too much to drink and believed we were going to make love. He touched my breast in the bath, and it scared me in the way a woman can be scared when a man is drunk and determined, but he had no designs on me other than to get me into bed."

Bridgewater took a deep breath and released it. "Well, I suppose we can hardly blame him for that," he said grumpily. She smiled.

"Come." He bent by Clare's horse and laced his fingers once more, offering her a foothold. She felt as light as a ballerina when he lifted her, and she wondered briefly what it would be like to feel those hands on her knees or shoulders or cupping her breasts.

He'd called her a weapon. While it was no great compliment, she understood what he'd meant. But his words had a second meaning, one more important. He *believed* she came from the future. For some reason, that made everything else easier.

"Are you comfortable?" he asked.

"Yes." Comfortable enough, though she was not much of a rider, and she was sitting bare-bottomed on the blanket he'd put on the saddle. Fifteen miles is a long way, and tomorrow morning, wherever she woke, she knew she'd be blistered and aching. She hoped it might not be just from the saddle.

Tomorrow. Sunday. Her regular routine—hazelnut coffee, the *New York Times*, whole wheat toast, and a slice of bacon—seemed so remote to her now. It was as if it had happened in a whole different universe.

He swung gracefully into his own saddle. "Are you sure?"

She realized she was clutching the saddle with both hands and let go. "Yes."

He geed the horses to a trot, and Clare's mount fell in obediently behind Bridgewater's. Ducking his head to avoid a branch, Bridgewater led her onto a narrow path through the trees. "It's a half mile to the road and then a straight shot to my castle. This time, I'm determined to make sure you can get back to where you belong."

She was beginning to wonder if she knew precisely where that was.

Twenty

Bridgewater Castle, Carlisle, Cumbria

THE LIBRARY KEEPER ROCKED ON TOP OF HIM, AS practiced as a courtesan, her ripe breasts swaying as she moved. He brushed the hair from her face, watching the candlelight turn the tresses from gold to bronze and back again. His cock tingled with a pleasure so pure, it felt beatific.

She leaned forward, lifting her bottom, and he thrust deeper.

"More, Adderly," she whispered, gripping his shoulders. "More."

"I'll fill you to your throat."

"Sir?"

The woman began to slip away, like fog at dawn, and he grasped for her arms to hold her there.

"*Sir*."

"What?" He opened his eyes. The blond was gone, replaced by a short, ugly man with a vein-splotched nose, holding a candle and shaking him awake. His servant, Ellsworth. "Christ, what is it?" Adderly's head felt like a mortar had gone off inside it. The room was pitch-black. It was still the middle of the night.

"There's a man here to see you."

"Tell him to fuck off." Then he remembered the girl. It hadn't been just a dream. He sat up—too fast, for another mortar blast filled his head—and looked around. Empty tub, no woman.

"Where is she?" Adderly demanded.

"Where is who, sir?"

Good Christ, what was her name? "Carmichael... no, Carnegie. The library keeper." He flopped back on the pillows.

"In her room, I assume," Ellsworth said.

In her room? With her dress locked in his wardrobe? "Check on her."

"My lord, it's the middle of the night."

"*Check on her.*"

"What about the man in the hallway? He said you'd want to see him. He said it's about your 'prey.'"

The muzziness lifted in a clap of thunder. Why would the fool have said that to Ellsworth? "Send him in and check on the woman; then let me know. Oh, and bring me some brandy."

"Do you want, er..." Ellsworth gestured vaguely in the direction of his master's loins.

"What is it, man? Spit it out."

"Do you wish to cover yourself, sir?"

Adderly realized he was naked on the covers and had a throbbing cockstand. While he'd never minded being unclothed around women, who he believed had a very narrow experience of such things, he had an uncomfortable sense that men were better informed as to the range of acceptable size in this area.

"Get me my things," Adderly said, waving at the pile of clothes on the floor.

Ellsworth put down the candle and picked up the jacket and breeks. "There's no shirt here, sir."

No shirt? Adderly didn't like this. "Then a clean one."

Ellsworth tried the wardrobe. "Locked, sir."

For the love of Christ.

"Throw me my breeks then. Then let the man in and check on the girl. Hurry."

"Aye, sir." Ellsworth handed his master the breeks and hurried out.

Adderly lumbered to his feet and pulled them on. Had he fucked her or not? He certainly had in his dream. Surely, he'd remember if he'd done the same thing while awake. Goddamn it, what had happened?

Ellsworth reappeared in the doorway and cleared his throat. "Lord Adderly, your visitor." He bowed, waited for the man to enter, and slipped back into the hall.

Mathias Gentry was a tracker. According to the story he'd told Adderly, he'd begun as a child in the Yorkshire hills, finding fox and deer for wealthy men in hunting parties before graduating to cannier prey for wealthy men with more dangerous amusements.

"What are you doing here?" Adderly demanded. "This is my *home*."

Gentry chewed on a clay pipe and looked at the petals floating in the abandoned water. "It would appear you are in need of my services, my lord." The corner of his mouth curled in amusement.

Adderly picked the coat off the floor and threw it on a nearby chair. "Thank you. I am perfectly capable of deciding when and if I need to hire you. And as far as I recall, I don't owe you money, so why are you here?"

"I happened to run into Jamie Bridgewater on his way to Drumburgh earlier this evening."

Adderly paused. He'd assigned one his new recruits to follow Jamie Bridgewater and report any unusual movements, which would certainly include travel to Drumburgh, known to be the center of rebel activity. But Adderly had received no messages since morning. He should have known the recruit would muck it up.

"Oh?" Adderly said it with as much casualness as he could muster. Gentry usually demanded a pretty penny for his information, and the price only went up if you showed interest.

"I'd have been happy to follow him if I'd known you were interested."

"Who says I am?"

"One of your soldiers. I ran into him at the inn in Drumburgh. Seems the man slipped through his fingers. Thinks you'll be angry with him." Gentry moved the pipe from one side of his mouth to the other. "It never pays to try to save money, Adderly. If the English army knew anything about tracking, the borderlands wouldn't be in the state they are now."

Adderly wanted to grab the man and shake him. He felt certain Gentry knew enough not only to put Bridgewater in a noose but to find and stamp out the rebel faction and quite possibly the Scots as well. If only he could crack open that ugly head and get at the information.

"Where is he, then?" Adderly said.

"Your brother, do you mean? Or the soldier? I have a feeling *he* will be drinking away his Sunday at the inn."

"He's not my brother. Would you like me to have you thrown out of here?"

"I think your father would be quite interested to hear about the money you've spent trying to discredit your fellow officers—were I forced to tell him, of course. Did he really think the colonel who held your office before you were promoted was *accidentally* discovered stealing gold from the army strongbox?"

Adderly's vision darkened. The cockstand was gone, replaced by a burning anger.

Gentry shrugged. "If the matter is of no interest to you, I'll be happy to see myself out—"

"No. What's your price?"

"For you, my lord, a few crowns. Ten, to be exact."

"Jesus, I could buy the inn for that much."

"Unfortunately," Gentry said, "that's not where you will find your man."

"Where, then?"

Gentry waited. With a growl, Adderly went to his coat, withdrew a handful of coins and dropped them in Gentry's palm.

"Do you know the white-haired witch?"

"The witch?"

"Witch, fairy, mermaid—whatever you borderlanders call her. The one who claims she can see the future."

An odd tingle went down Adderly's spine. "Undine?"

"Aye."

Undine was the one who'd explained to him the magic that time holes hold and the limitations on their use. Of course, she hadn't known then that he'd already discovered one in Jamie Bridgewater's chapel. Once he'd told her what he'd found, her willingness to talk had vanished. "What about her?"

"All I can say is a ride betwixt her thighs is a magical thing, and clearly that's what Bridgewater thinks as well. I saw him leaving her cottage as I was coming in."

Adderly felt dizzy. Bridgewater was no whoremonger. As near as Adderly could tell, Bridgewater confined his carnal appetites to the occasional willing officer's wife and, if rumors were to be believed, to a woman over the border in Coldstream. No, if Jamie Bridgewater had been visiting Undine, it hadn't been to blunt his lance. It had been for something else. What were the odds that a woman with the same name as a library in the future would arrive at Bridgewater's castle and Bridgewater would go to see Undine, all in a matter of hours? Mrs. Carnegie must have told Bridgewater about the time hole. Perhaps he'd even found her coming through it?

Adderly's anxiety rose. The last thing he needed was Jamie meddling in his affairs. If Jamie were to find out that Adderly had simply made Clementina tell him how the Ramillies battle would be won, Jamie would undoubtedly tell the other officers, and the accolades that had come to Adderly for his bravery that day would be gone.

Mrs. Carnegie was a threat, no matter how one looked at it. Adderly needed to find out what Jamie had learned, and then he had to ensure that Mrs. Carnegie kept her mouth shut—forever.

"What time was Captain Bridgewater at Undine's?" Adderly asked.

"Five o'clock."

"How long was he there?"

"As I said, I saw Bridgewater as he was leaving Undine's cottage."

"Where'd he go after that?"

"I don't know," Gentry said. "But I do have a few thoughts on that topic."

"Aye?" Adderly felt the price of their conversation rising.

"Well, I don't know for sure—and probably won't until tomorrow—but knowing how generous your lordship is when you get information you find useful, I sent a half dozen of my best men in different directions to keep an eye out."

"Good. Let me know when you find out something."

Ellsworth reappeared in the doorway. "She's not in her room, sir. Shall I—"

"That'll be all." Flames of fury scorched Adderly's cheeks.

Ellsworth bowed and exited.

Gentry gave a small chuckle, then deposited the coins in his pocket. "First the captain," he said, walking to the door, "then the girl. You're not having a very good evening, are you?"

Adderly made no reply. Gentry tipped his hat and left.

Damn it, somebody would pay. Adderly was going to drop by the cottage of his old friend Undine, and then he was going to find the library keeper.

Twenty-one

Main Road to Bowness-on-Solway, Cumbria

BRIDGEWATER WATCHED PANNA RIDE. EVEN WITH HER gown rucked up like a milkmaid and some very questionable riding skills, she cut a handsome figure: straight spine, slim waist, loose tendrils of gold falling down her back. By the time they reached MacIver Castle, half the night would be gone. He let his mind drift, wondering what it might be like to salvage the other half—his wide, soft bed; the warm evening breeze on their skin; the taste of her honey-kissed mouth—but he knew that for her safety, he must see her home as soon as he could, even if it meant saying good-bye. He would be like Charon ferrying his passenger across the river Styx.

He thought of the line from the *Aeneid*:

There Charon stands who rules the dreary coast...

Aye, he was the Charon of the borderlands. He thought of the ferry that crossed to Annan, the town divided from Bowness by a mile of water and a millennium of bloody warfare, and the number of times he'd crossed, trying to find a place of compromise where these warring nations could rest.

Would there ever be peace? He'd seen so many unnecessary deaths. According to what Panna had overheard, there was a chance peace could settle over the borderlands by Wednesday. If the Scots didn't attack. If the English didn't provoke them. He dared not let his hope rise. It had been struck down so many times before.

Two starlings wheeled across the sky, and Panna's laughter lifted him out of his thoughts. He gazed at her, trying to memorize the graceful bend of her arm, the gleam of her skin, the way her collarbone spread like an angel's wings across her chest. What was the other line he remembered about Charon?

His Eyes like hollow furnaces of fire…

His eyes *were* like furnaces when he watched her. He burned for her in a way he'd never burned for any woman. But there was nothing to be done. She needed to leave his time. Even now, he listened in the night for the sounds of his half brother's horse or the horses of his brother's guards. If what Undine said was true, when Panna left this time, she would not be able to return. Three times, three opportunities. They'd exhausted their chances without even knowing it.

The quiet was interrupted by the distant sound of hoofbeats.

"Ride into the woods," he said, "and don't come

out unless I give the word, no matter what you hear. If anything happens, follow this road to the water; then take the path there to Clare's cottage. He'll get you to the chapel."

She obeyed reluctantly, and Bridgewater waited until she'd disappeared before pulling out his pistol and laying it across his lap. Then he turned his horse and galloped toward the sound.

When he'd topped the rise, he pulled Romulus to a stop and waited. The other horse was thundering toward him. He knew he'd kill Adderly if it came to that. He hoped it didn't.

The rider's head appeared, and a different fear came over Bridgewater. The rider was Clare.

"What on earth...?"

Clare pulled the creature to a halt. "The Scots, sir," he said, panting. "I ran into my cousin outside the inn at Drumburgh. She's married to a Scot from Galloway, and his sister works for your grandfather. According to my cousin, the clan chiefs have been called to a council of war."

"*What?* Where?"

"Nunquam."

His grandfather's castle. "When?"

"It starts at sun-up."

Twenty-two

Ferry Dock, Bowness-on-Solway

THE SLIVERED MOON SHONE ON THE WATER OF THE firth, the only thing visible in the darkness of the night. The breeze picked up, and Panna moved closer to the windbreak provided by Bridgewater's body. Even though they weren't touching, she felt his warmth.

"Promise me you'll go to Clare's house as soon as the ferry leaves," Bridgewater said, removing his coat and putting it around her shoulders.

"I will. I promise."

The ferryman, who had been roused from his bed, made room on the vessel for Bridgewater and his clearly jittery horse.

"I shouldn't have let you come here," Bridgewater said, pulling her close. "I should have insisted that you go directly to Clare's. But I can see his house from here, and I'll watch until I know you are safe."

"I hate to break it to you, my friend, but you didn't *let me* do anything. It would have taken more than you and Clare to stop me from seeing you off."

He narrowed his eyes. "More than me *and* Clare?"

"Okay, okay. You I could have finagled. Clare doesn't look like he finagles very easily."

"I'm uncertain of the exact meaning, but I'm sure Clare is entirely unfinagleable."

She laughed. Despite the upheavals of the last twenty-four hours, she did not want to leave him. The smoky scent of his coat filled her head, a souvenir to keep his memory alive. The only thing that made leaving bearable was knowing she could return.

"Clare will get you to Reeves," he said. "Between the two of them, they'll get you into the chapel, I promise."

"Thank you. I can't believe you're going to your grandfather's."

"I've been left little choice. If a council of war has been called, I must speak to him. 'Tis the only chance I have to prevent an attack."

"Will he even recognize you?"

"We've never met, 'tis true, but I have no doubt he knows me, just as I know him."

She glanced over his shoulder at the yellow flapping flag, visible under the moon's light. "What will your father think?"

"Let us pray he never discovers what I'm doing. The shadow of treason already hangs over me."

His words sent a chill through her. "But this isn't treason."

"Entering an enemy's stronghold during a time of war while in possession of secret intelligence about the plans of my own country?"

"Well, when you say it like that…"

He gave her a weak smile, and she couldn't bear it anymore. "Don't go," she said. "It's too big a risk."

"Ready, sir," the ferryman called. Bridgewater's horse flattened its ears.

"I haven't a choice." He tucked her head against his neck. "I don't wish to say good-bye, Panna, but I must."

"I'll come back," she said. "I'll come back if you wish it."

He turned his gaze across the water.

"What? What is it?" She tried to see into those sapphire eyes, but the night was so dark.

"I do wish it, Panna. I do. I want you to know that. No matter what happens, I want you to know it."

She fell into his arms and rested her head against him. He gave her a long, sad kiss.

The ferryman cleared his throat.

Bridgewater loosened his arms and took hold of her hand. "Good-bye."

"Wait." She pulled him closer to the shore. "There are things I can tell you. Things about Scotland and England. I can—"

"No." Bridgewater shook his head. "Don't."

"Why? They may help you. They may help you today with your grandfather. What's the point of me being here otherwise?"

"There are things a man shouldn't know."

"But surely the knowledge—"

"That sort of knowledge is the devil's work, Panna. I'm sorry. I know you want to help, but I must fight with everything I have regardless of the outcome. Fighting with everything I have is the only way I can live with myself."

"But what if I told you that—"

"That we'd win? I don't even know what 'winning'

would mean anymore." He brought her fingers to his lips and kissed them. "And if you told me we'd lose, where would I be? I'll do what I think is right until I can't anymore. That's all I'm capable of."

She squeezed his hand.

"Good-bye, Panna."

"Good-bye, Bridgewater. Until the next time."

"Aye. Until then."

He let her go.

She fought the urge to cry. "I have your coat," she called.

"Keep it." He led the horse into the boat and the ferryman began to row.

The wind whipped the shirt tightly around Bridgewater's chest and shoulders. Tendrils of hair flapped across his face, and he raised his arm in a sorrowful farewell as the ferry moved down the long length of the dock.

She didn't recognize the sharp noise as a shot. But Bridgewater did, and he turned immediately in the direction of the sound.

"Get down!" he cried, and his horse whinnied in fear.

She fell to her knees, heart pounding, and crawled behind one of the dock's wooden posts. How many shots could a gun fire in the eighteenth century? Of course, one successful shot was all it would take. Bridgewater had drawn his pistol and was scanning the river bank behind her.

Panna felt exposed on every side. She had no idea where the shot had come from or if another would follow. She heard footfalls in the grass behind her.

Two men with guns, cap brims low over their faces, jogged toward her.

Another shot rang out, and the men ducked. Bridgewater had fired. "Panna! Come!"

She ran toward the end of the dock.

"*Row!*" Bridgewater yelled to the ferryman.

The oars were massive and the boat was moving faster than she was running. The men were back on their feet, pelting toward her. Bridgewater held out his arms, and she leapt, catching him by the neck and knocking him into the horse. They both fell.

He rolled to the side. "Stay down."

The ferryman was rowing for all he was worth, putting ten feet between them and the dock with every pull.

Bridgewater grabbed a second pistol from his saddle-bag and crouched in the stern, gaze fixed on the dock. The men had reached the end of it and were reloading.

"Get down!" she cried. He'd be an easy shot.

"Who are they?" he wondered aloud.

They raised their guns. Bridgewater fired, and his shot illuminated the men's faces for an instant. One man jerked but didn't fall. The other man shot. Bridgewater's horse rose on his hind legs and nearly swamped the boat.

"Steady, Romulus."

The men onshore began to reload, but it was clear the boat would be too far across the Firth for them to reach it.

Bridgewater helped Panna onto a seat. "Are you all right?" he asked the ferryman, who made a gruff noise of agreement. Then he gently ran his hands along

Romulus's withers and flanks, not only feeling for a wound but also to calm him. "You did well, my friend."

"Who *were* they?" Panna said.

"I don't know. I've never seen them before."

They weren't in uniform, but that didn't mean anything; Bridgewater wasn't in uniform, either. Nor had she been able to tell if they were English or Scots. The men lifted their guns, and two more bursts of fire lit the night. The balls skittered over the water, landing twenty feet behind the boat and kicking up a fan of spray.

"If you think I'm doing this for fifteen pence, you're a goddamned fool," the ferryman said.

Bridgewater chuckled. "You shall have a crown, sir, to thank you for your braw rowing."

Panna, whose pounding heart was just starting to slow, said to Bridgewater, "I'd ask if there's anyone you know who wants to shoot you, but I'm pretty sure I know the answer."

"I wish…" He stopped.

"You wish what?"

"I wish I could be sure that I'm the target."

Could *she* be the target? She didn't even know how to respond.

"I'll make it two crowns," Bridgewater said to the ferryman, "if you can get us to Annan in under three-quarters of an hour. We're in a bit of a hurry."

Twenty-three

The Road to Nunquam Castle, Annan, Scotland

"DO YOU REALLY THINK THOSE MEN MIGHT HAVE BEEN after *me*?"

Hector MacIver's home stood at the end of a long rise, and Romulus was making his way up the road as if he'd traveled it a thousand times. Panna sat before Bridgewater in the saddle, self-consciously tucked against his lap.

"I don't know," he said. "If someone has found out where you come from, it's possible. But I don't want you to worry, Panna. No one will hurt you. Not as long as I draw breath."

The road turned, and to their right, the outline of the Cumbrian hills was visible across the water. She could see the tiny dots of watch fires burning along the ramparts of MacIver Castle.

Bridgewater gazed abstractedly up the road. She wondered if he was thinking of the first words he'd say to the man for whom he'd carried such anger for so long.

"You've never been here?" she said.

"Never."

"But surely you've been to Annan?" Her bottom was already throbbing from her short time in the saddle, and her inner thighs were beginning to tingle. In another world, those effects might have come with a postcoital bliss that would have made anything tolerable. She had to admit leaning against Bridgewater's chest was nearly as nice. He smelled lightly of soap and sweat, and when he talked, the words rumbled through her hair, sending pleasant shivers down her spine.

"Annan, aye," he said. "Many times. But I've never been to my grandfather's home."

"Will he be glad to see you?"

Bridgewater's hands tightened around the reins. "I don't think so. Not with the request I'll be delivering. And in any case I'm an outlander here. So are you."

"An 'outlander'?"

"The borderlands are neatly divided. You've seen the wall. Either you're a Scot or you're not, and if you're not, you're an outlander, not to be trusted. Though, to be fair, the same is true for the English. Neither side sees any shades of gray. *That* is the essential problem."

"But you *are* a Scot. Half Scot."

He snorted. "I might as well be half Turk. If you cannot swear your allegiance, free and whole, and especially if you won't also disavow the other half of your blood, you're worse than an outlander. You're an abomination. I'm an abomination in both my countries."

And in both his families. "I'm so sorry."

He shrugged. "I hope that someday the things that make us different will not be as important as the things that make us the same."

"You said your grandfather won't care for your request. I know it's hard for anyone to change their mind, but once he hears—"

"Asking the clans to put down their weapons will be a personal embarrassment for him."

"Why?"

"He considers himself to be a man who makes decisions with great care. If the clans have come together under his banner to attack Cumbria, reversing his orders will make him appear weak and erratic. And I'm sure if he's made the decision to attack, he's only done so after praying on the matter for many hours."

There was an unexpected sharpness in Bridgewater's words. "He's a devout man?"

"'Tis his breath and blood. He wears his devotion like a courtesan wears her jewels, both as proof of his worthiness and an indication of what a rut with him will cost. I once saw him bring the charge of an English regiment to a full stop by ordering his clansman to fall into a circle and pray."

"I should think you'd approve."

"I might," he said with a growl, "if the same impulse hadn't inspired him to tell my mother in the last letter he sent her that she'd brought untold shame upon her family and that her child was a disgrace."

Panna winced. What would it be like for a ten- or fifteen-year-old boy to find such a letter among his mother's possessions? She wanted to wrap her arms around him, tell him that he'd been a worthy child and had grown into an even worthier man, but she could tell by the rigidity of his posture that he would not appreciate her sympathy.

Instead, she laid her hands on his. "You lost so much. I can't imagine how you survived it."

For a moment, she was afraid even those words had offended him. But he squeezed her fingers and said in a voice thick with emotion, "You know what that means as much as anyone, I think."

And she did. While she had the benefit of the support of her family, the loss of Charlie had devastated her.

The press of his palm sent a warmth through her. She didn't want him to let go. "One goes on because one has to. There's no other choice."

"Oh, there's always a choice," he said, with more than a hint of sadness.

Panna thought of her brothers and nieces and nephews and of Marie, how she would worry. "It's easier when you have people you can count on, who look out for you."

"As I'm discovering."

A bubble of happiness rose in Panna's chest. He relaxed his grip but left his hand on hers.

For several moments, neither said a word, but in the silence Panna could feel him wrestling with something.

"I've come to think of it as a campaign," he said, and she knew without asking he meant more than the conflict with the Scots. "And I don't mean in the sense of driving for a victory. Losing a husband as you have is a rushing, horrifying battle in which you witness the destruction of all hope as you slash vainly at a superior enemy. My life has been a campaign, I think. A campaign against the grinding sorrow and loneliness. 'Tis little in comparison to the blood you've seen spilled, but 'tis a wound that seems never to heal."

He flicked the reins and made a clucking noise to the horse, evidently embarrassed at his admission.

"It's not little. Your life's been torn apart as much as mine, if not more. We have a great saying in my time for what we've gone through: 'It sucks.'"

He laughed. "Now *that* is a saying we do not have. I must admit it's very descriptive."

"And there's another one: 'Life is what's ahead.' I didn't know your mother, but I knew Charlie too well to think he wants anything for me but complete and utter happiness. That, I think, is the only gift that's worthy to give those we've lost."

Panna blinked. She'd heard it before many times over but had never found herself believing it—until now.

"Are all library keepers as wise as you?"

"There's a famous movie about a library keeper—it doesn't matter what movies are. Just think of them as books with pictures that move. It's my absolute favorite. And in this movie a library keeper is in love with a man, but the idea scares her because she's always been too busy doing the right thing to do the things that might make her happy. He tells her that if she keeps piling up tomorrows, all she'll end up with is a lot of empty yesterdays."

"Tell me, Panna, is that fable meant for me or you?"

She didn't have a chance to answer, for they rounded the next curve and Nunquam Castle—what could be seen of it in the dark—loomed before them. It was

Elizabethan in style, with gables and bay widows, and the main part of the house was anchored on each side by ornate chimneys. It wasn't truly a castle, lacking as it did ramparts, turrets, and towers. Nonetheless, it was of ample size to carry the name without question. The gatehouse that protected it was round and wide, like a face of a dog with its teeth bared. Gooseflesh ran across her arms. "Are you certain this is a good idea?"

"I'm fairly certain it's *not* a good idea. The clan chiefs are unlikely to be open to the arguments of an English army captain, especially one not speaking under the authority of his commanding officers. They may think it's a trick. I wouldn't blame them. But they *have* to change their minds. They'll be sending a thousand men to their deaths if they don't. If I can convince my grandfather, the rest will follow."

"And if you can't?" Panna wondered exactly how amenable Bridgewater's grandfather would be to the pleas of a child he once called "an abomination."

"Then I'll have to create a division in their ranks. Convince one or two. Get them to delay. If I can't convince them, or if they doubt my intentions, they'll either hang me themselves or turn me over to the English army, which will come to the same thing in the end."

"It's not too late to turn around," she said. "No one will have ever known you were here."

"Stop where you are," a guard called from the gatehouse.

"So much for that idea," Bridgewater said.

The guard and his companion lifted guns to their shoulders.

Panna drew in closer to Bridgewater. "Not very welcoming, are they?" she said under her breath.

"We'll be fine so long as we don't alarm them."

"I suppose that means refraining from mentioning I come from the future?"

"If you would." He brought Romulus to a halt and let himself off, then caught her arm. Even in the dark, she could see the steely glint in his eye. "If anything happens to me, you are to tell them you're the earl's niece and demand to be taken to him. Do you understand? He'll be furious, but they won't hurt you for fear of bringing the full power of the English army down on them."

"I will, I promise, but please, let's not have it come to that."

He offered her his hand. Dismounting, she discovered, was a tricky thing, especially when one was straddling a saddle sans underpants. He caught her by the waist and set her on the ground.

Then he approached the guards with his hands in the air. "I'm James Bridgewater," he called. "I'm here to see my grandfather. 'Tis a personal matter."

The men looked at one another. The larger of the two said, "No weapons."

Bridgewater looked at his shirt and breeks. "I left my pistols on the horse."

"What about her?"

Panna's heel had caught in the cobbles, and she was hopping in a circle to try to loosen it.

"I think you can see she poses little threat."

"*Hey.*"

The larger man nodded and took Romulus's

lead. The other escorted Bridgewater and Panna at gunpoint through the gatehouse to the massive door of the house. Panna's legs felt as if they were made of rubber, and she shook the dust and leaves off her skirt, hoping to make a decent first impression. It was still the middle of the night, and she had no idea what proper castle etiquette might be for such a late arrival.

The man with the raised gun stepped back.

Bridgewater lifted the boar's-head knocker, and the sound of brass thumping against brass rang out three times.

He gave her a forced smile. "Let's hope the guards' hospitality was not a just a trick to allow them to shoot us while we wait here."

After what seemed like forever, a tiny eye-level panel in the door opened. It immediately shut, and for an instant, Panna thought Bridgewater had been rejected yet again. But then the door swung open, revealing a stout woman in her seventies in a dressing gown and cap, holding a candle.

"Master Jamie!" She laid a hand over her heart and instantly started to cry.

Bridgewater gave Panna a confused look.

The woman shook her head, repeating, "I canna believe it. I canna believe it."

Eventually, the confusion on Bridgewater's face dissolved into compassion if not recognition. He patted the woman's arm tentatively, and she fell against his shoulder.

"I didn't think I'd ever see you again," she said, shoulders hitching. "Certainly not here. Oh, I wish your mother had lived to see this."

Bridgewater extracted a handkerchief from his breeks and handed it to her. He looked at Panna and shrugged.

The woman took the handkerchief, wiped her eyes, and blew her nose. "I'm sure you don't remember me, Master Jamie. But I remember you. I'm Mrs. Brownlow, your mother's nurse. Oh dear," she said, touching his cheek. "What happened to your eye? In a bit of a stramash, perhaps? Come in, come in. Your grand-da's not due back till the morn—" She stopped. "You *have* come to see him, have you not?"

Bridgewater nodded.

"Come, then," she said, urging them to enter. "Let me find you a place to lay your head. The castle's quite full—one of your grand-da's councils, you know—but there's still a bed or two to be had. Is this your wife?" She gave Panna a welcoming smile.

"Oh, no," Panna said quickly. "I'm an acquaintance of Captain Bridgewater from Penn's Woods—Panna Kennedy. It's very nice to meet you, Mrs. Brownlow."

Mrs. Brownlow gave her a dainty curtsy. "Welcome, Miss Kennedy."

She led them up a flight of stairs and down a long hall. At the end, where the hallway formed a T, two well-armed men stood guard in the corridor to the right.

"The clan chiefs are down there," Mrs. Brownlow explained. "No one's allowed in."

"Who's here for the council?" Bridgewater asked casually.

"*Och*, the usual. All the chiefs except McCann. He's taken to his bed, and his son attends for him, though what good that wee snip might do, I dinna know.

MacDowell, of course. Maxwell, MacClelland, Little, Beattie, Moffatt, Johnstone. A handful more."

The names meant little to Panna, but she could see the muscles tighten on Bridgewater's face. She felt as if a month had passed since she'd awakened that morning at Clare's house. She'd be asleep before her head hit the pillow. Fortunately for all concerned, she'd already had her bath.

Mrs. Brownlow led them past an alcove where a large crucifix hung. The woman crossed herself and mouthed a prayer as they passed.

When they reached the end of the hallway, Mrs. Brownlow lifted a ring of keys from her pocket and unlocked the door. "I shouldn't let you down here, Master Jamie. 'Tis the woman's wing. But I suppose no one will be fashed so long as I'm with you."

She led Panna into a small, clean room with a four-poster bed, two desks and chairs, a basket full of dolls, and a shelf which held a few slim volumes, an ark, and a carved set of animals. "This is the nursery. MacIver's grandnieces stay here when they visit. 'Twas your mother's room too, Master Jamie. The ark was hers."

Jamie looked as if the actual ark had been placed before him. He took an unsteady step toward the shelf and picked up a wooden elephant. One of the tusks was broken and the grain, smooth with age, gleamed in the candlelight.

"This was my mother's?"

"Aye. She called the elephant a clobber because your grandfather told her that an elephant could use its trunk to hit people."

He murmured, "Clobber," and shook his head with an amazed smile.

"Now, let's get you settled," Mrs. Brownlow said to him. "I'm afraid I'm going to have to put you in the servants' wing. There's an open bed there. I hope you don't mind. Miss Kennedy, the kneeler's there for your prayers. I shall have a pitcher and ewer brought to you, and I'll lock the door at the end of the hall so you may rest easy. My room's right there if you need anything. Will you be wantin' a lady's maid?" She opened a drawer, withdrew a candle, which she lit from the one she carried, and placed it in a holder.

Panna tried to shake the fatigue away, but it hung on her like a heavy coat. "No, I won't need a lady's maid, nor a pitcher and ewer. I'll be going right to bed."

She looked at Bridgewater, who had reluctantly returned the elephant to the shelf. "Good night," she said. She didn't know what the morning would bring or what his plans were. She wished somehow he could stay by her side. She felt safer with him at hand, but there didn't seem to be any way for that to happen.

He gave her a reassuring look. "I'll see you in the morning."

Bridgewater and Mrs. Brownlow left, and the door closed with a *click*.

Panna undid the ties of her bodice, slipped out of the silk, and crawled gratefully into the bed in her shift. In the distance, a cannon went off. Another of the English army's warning blasts. It was in the early hours of Sunday morning. Her shift at the library began at noon. Somehow, she doubted she was going to make it on time.

Twenty-four

Undine's Cottage, off the Road to Drumburgh

ADDERLY TIED HIS HORSE IN FRONT OF THE SMALL structure, cursing his pounding head. Even in the predawn darkness, without a single candle burning, he could tell Undine was there. A certain strangeness seemed to ooze from the windows whenever she was within. Gentry, the tracker, said Bridgewater had bedded the woman. Adderly doubted it. The men who visited Undine wanted to know their fates, and they paid dearly for it. He supposed it sat easier on a man's pride to say he needed a whore than to say he needed a woman to tell him how to cling to the path of luck and success or return to it if he'd gone astray.

What had Jamie Bridgewater come here for? Did the answer have anything to do with a woman from the future arriving at his castle the same day?

Adderly stepped up to the low door and lifted his hand, but before he could knock, Undine said, "Come in, Lord Adderly."

Adderly ducked to enter. "Light a candle, if you would," he said. "I can't see you in the dark."

"Do you need to see me?"

Her voice seemed to be coming from the right side of the room, but when she had spoken before, it had seemed to be coming from the other. "Aye."

A flame hissed to life, though Adderly had heard no flint and seen no other candle. The glow painted the room in pale yellow. She gazed at him with her cat eyes.

"I thought the time passageway was closed to you now, Adderly. Or have you found another?"

He winced. He'd wasted an opportunity to vanquish his enemies and enjoy untold wealth by dallying too often with Clementina. He could still smell the scent of roses in her raven hair and feel the gentle pop of her maidenhead as he'd taken her.

"Had I known there was a limit on the number times I could visit," he said with irritation, "I might have done things differently."

"'Tis not for man to know the secrets of time."

"No, but since I paid you, I rather expected you to tell me."

"You paid me to tell you your future. I told you the resolution of the crossroads you faced would be found in the chapel at MacIver Castle."

"Which is where I found the time passageway."

She shrugged opaquely and gave him a smile. "I trust you found your time in the future advantageous."

When he'd returned after his first brief but alarming visit to the future, he'd gone to Undine to beg her to tell him whether what he'd done was dangerous and whether he could do it again. Undine had urged him to abandon his desire. She'd told him the future is a dangerous place for a man ill-prepared for its marvels. Since, as a nobleman, he considered himself fully prepared for any situation, and because she gave him no specific threat to fear, he'd ignored her petitions and returned, finding himself instantly smitten with the doe-eyed library keeper.

What a heady time that had been, finding Clementina and that odd, amazing library. She'd been so scared of him at the beginning—and desperate to fill her newly built library with books. He'd made it a personal challenge to win her trust and seduce her. Gold had made both those things easy. Gold made so many things easy. He could still see the conflict on Clementina's face, torn between a man she thought she loved and her fear of being "ruined." He'd been amused by her reluctance. As if learning to pleasure a man did anything but raise a girl in a man's estimation.

"Aye, my time there was quite advantageous," he replied.

In truth, he'd realized almost immediately what gifts the future could provide. And he would have acted upon them immediately if he'd known his visits would be limited. Instead, he'd lost himself in pursuit of the girl. After several weeks he'd gone back, determined to see Clementina's library honor him; but after his third return, he found the space behind the door in the chapel in Bridgewater's castle transformed into nothing more than a storage space for candles and a broom.

Undine gave him a gentle smile. "Advantageous

enough that the Bridgewaters are still the richest and most admired men in northern England."

He didn't like the way she'd said it, as if it were a question. Nor did he like the way she'd said "Bridgewaters," as if she'd meant to include Jamie.

"You know as well as I do that I discovered a few things," he said, his pique rising.

"You did indeed. That the English would one day control Scotland."

"One day soon," he added emphatically.

"Though I suppose knowing that doesn't provide a man with the sort of advantage he might have hoped for. 'Tis not as if you know the outcome of a specific battle, or the place in Yorkshire where a vein of silver will be discovered, or the name of the sea captain who will succeed in finding a shorter way to the Orient. Perhaps you could send a trusted confidant to retrace your steps, someone who hasn't exhausted the limit of three visits."

As if Adderly had a confidant he trusted that much. He'd rather die than allow any other man the chance to learn the future's secrets.

His thoughts must have shown on his face, for the fairy woman said, "The idea is not to your way of thinking?" She tucked a strand of hair behind her ear. "I understand. Why have you come, Adderly?"

He squared his shoulders. He hated the way she made him feel beholden to her.

"I have heard Captain Bridgewater was here."

Undine regarded him coolly. "And if he was? There are many men who visit me, Adderly, each more desperate than the last." She gave him a meaningful look.

Bloody witch. "There's a woman here who I believe came from the future—the same future I visited."

"Indeed?" Undine's brow arched. "Perhaps she was so taken with the statue you erected to yourself, she couldn't help herself."

In his third and—unbeknownst to him at the time—final trip to the future, Adderly had undertaken to have a statue of himself made. It seemed only fitting, given that his gold had purchased most of the library's contents, and Andrew Carnegie, that prideful man, had already seen fit to seize the honor of the library's name. Adderly had overseen every detail of the design of the statue, choosing the artist, approving the materials, and even laying out the unusual design of the base—though of course that last had been for reasons other than artistic.

However, he'd never told anyone in the eighteenth century about the statue, except for the locksmith he'd consulted. Certainly not Undine, who'd greeted each of his visitations with stronger exhortations to stop. Had the locksmith spoken to Undine? Perhaps he'd come to her cottage for a reading. He supposed locksmiths were as curious about their futures as any other men. Undine had a way of finding out whatever a man knew.

"Perhaps she was." Adderly gritted his teeth, thinking of Mrs. Carnegie's disappearance from his bedchamber. "I'm more concerned, however, with the alliance I believe she's formed with Captain Bridgewater and what that might mean."

"Mean? To you, do you mean?"

"Aye, to me," he said sharply. "I'd like to know

why Captain Bridgewater came here last evening." He tossed a coin onto the table next to the candle.

"I don't answer questions regarding my customers, Lord Adderly. What would an hour with me be worth if a man thought his deepest secrets would be spilled for the pleasure of other men?"

He tossed two more coins on the table, his blood boiling. He expected his requests to be fulfilled.

"You may keep your money." There was an edge in her voice now. "I'm willing to answer whatever questions you may have about your own future, but I can't entertain inquiries about other men."

"Damn you," he said, furious. "I've paid you and paid you well. If this new library keeper possesses the future's secrets and has provided them to Captain Bridgewater, I demand to know about it."

"You won't know about it from me," Undine said, eyes flashing. "Your money can't buy my honor. Please take your gold and leave."

"A whore talking to me about honor." He laughed. "You were happy to take my money when it suited you."

"Get out."

"You say you're not willing to spill other men's secrets?" He picked up the candlestick. "Well, something's going to be spilled here, and whether it's Bridgewater's secrets or something else depends very much on what you do next."

He pinched out the flame and lifted the brass candlestick.

Twenty-five

Nunquam Castle

BRIDGEWATER'S KISSES FELT AS LIGHT AS BUTTERFLY wings, Panna thought dreamily, skimming her collarbone and the valley between her breasts. He brought his mouth to her nipple and suckled, pasting the thin linen against her flesh. The cool made her shiver, and her flesh hardened. He caught the other nipple and twisted, releasing a wave of wetness between her legs.

They were in her bed, though how they'd gotten here she couldn't say.

"I'll serve you," he said. "And then you'll serve me, aye?"

His hand slid under the cover, caressing a knee. Her belly contracted so hard, she bit back a moan.

"Your skin's like warm silk."

His hand traveled down her thigh until he reached her mound. He palmed her slowly, as if he kneading dough. Her hips rose automatically. She felt the damp heat. It had been so long.

"You like to be frigged?" He whisked the tips of his finger over her bud.

"Yes," she said, the word a puff of exhaled breath.

He stroked her more directly, kindling the flames. "Aye, you do. And do you like to do it yourself as well?"

She closed her eyes, unwilling to have him see the answer.

"Do you try to hide the truth?" He tugged her nipple and her legs strained open. "There's no hiding the truth in carnal embrace. Your body betrays you."

"Just as yours betrays you." His blood pulsed in the hardened flesh at her side.

She bit her lip to try to endure the exquisite movement of his thumb.

"Touch yourself," he said. "I want to watch."

She slipped an arm beneath the covers. The warmth rose on her face, and he observed, his eyes glowing in the darkness.

The familiar first touch sent a charge through her, and the second and third spread the warmth like reverberations in a smooth pond.

"Oh, aye, you *are* practiced."

She closed her eyes, used to summoning the images that would serve her, but changed her mind and opened them.

"Take off your clothes," she said.

He chuckled, but his eyes turned a clear emerald. He stood and slipped off his coat. His shoulders were wide and his waist narrow, and as the shirt slipped free of his breeks, she could see the lean muscles of his back.

His chest was lightly furred, and the curls of sparkling sable and gold ran in a thin line down his belly, disappearing into his breeks.

Powerful waves of desire rocked her, spurred by the sight of that chest and the tightly clinging fabric.

She beckoned him with a finger and he stepped toward her. Four brass buttons, each within arm's reach. She slipped one through its buttonhole, then its twin on the other side. The fabric loosened enough to reveal the edge of a thick patch of curls. She slipped her fingers into the silky mass. His belly was flat and hard.

The third button strained over the tip of the thick length it covered. She laid her palm over the end and pressed gently.

"*Ooh*. Wench."

She grinned. "Undo your knee buttons."

She could have done them herself but wanted to see the outline of his hips as he bent. The flexing divot of muscle sent a shiver through her.

"Shall I take off my boots?" he asked.

"Absolutely not."

She undid the third button, taking care to tease the flesh as she did it. The top of the breeks were sagging now, held in place only by a feat of marvelous physiological engineering. She tugged the last buttonhole over the brass. The breeks fell to the floor.

Unlike his brother, whose plumage would have underwhelmed a sparrow, Bridgewater's peacockery riveted her attention and stoked her desire.

"Don't move," she said.

"There are certain parts over which I am not fully sovereign at this moment."

She laughed a low, throaty laugh that reached all the way to her belly. She was like a pot of simmering water, and her fingers stirred the roiling liquid higher and higher. He watched her eyes, and she could see her desire reflected in his own.

He was right about the sovereignty, and she rolled the inebriating image of his twitching flesh in her mind like a piece of candy on her tongue, riding the waves higher and higher.

He sank onto the bed. She wanted desperately to grasp that warm steel and taste the salty proof of his desire. He pressed her against the pillows, running a finger over her lips. She parted them automatically and he smiled. But instead of bringing that part of him to her mouth, he lay alongside her and turned her toward him. Pressed between them, her hand worked its sweet rhythm, and he kissed her—a long, slow, searching kiss that she returned with equal hunger. He laid a hand on her cheek, and she pressed hers over it.

"Panna."

She didn't want to let go.

"Panna," he said louder, and she jerked to alertness.

She wasn't in her bed at home. She was still in the little room at Nunquam, and Bridgewater was stooped over her bed, completely clothed. The jagged gray light of dawn was spilling over the bed.

She jerked her hand from the covers. "What is it?"

"I've been shot."

Twenty-six

Undine's Cottage, off the Road to Drumburgh

THE PAIN IN UNDINE'S BODY WAS INESCAPABLE, LIKE A prison made of flesh and bone. And behind her closed eyes, more danger floated menacingly at the edges of her hazy consciousness.

"I thought I might find you here," she heard a man say.

Of course he'd find me here. It was her home, was it not? But the man was not speaking to her, for another voice answered—a voice that unleashed the return of cold fear.

"Bloody witch. Tried to stab me while my back was turned, no doubt to steal my purse."

She recognized the voice as Adderly's.

"Greed is a nasty thing, my lord. Is she dead?"

"Aye. Leave her."

Was she dead? There was pain—sharp, suffocating pain that felt like a flame held to every limb. And she knew she mustn't move. But it didn't feel like death.

"Where's the knife?" the other man asked. "I don't see it. Perhaps we should—"

"I said leave her, Gentry."

"As you wish."

Gentry. A greedy, mean-spirited man. She heard the splashing of water at her table. His lordship was washing her blood from his hands with the water meant for her coffee.

"Why are you here?" Adderly snapped. "I thought you were going to find Bridgewater. Or did he elude you as well?"

"Elude *me*, your lordship? Hardly. I have eyes over three counties. As I suspected, he boarded the Solway ferry some few hours ago."

"*Scotland?* He went to *Scotland* with the borderlands on the brink of war?"

"Perhaps he doesn't see the situation as you do," Gentry said.

She heard a muffled rubbing near the door. Adderly must have been drying his hands on her coat. Through the fiery pain, she felt the tingle of anger.

"What the bloody hell does that mean?" Adderly said.

"We're aware of his ties to Hector MacIver."

"To whom he hasn't spoken in his entire life."

"Until today," Gentry said.

"*What?*"

"He was tracked almost to the entry of Nunquam Castle. My men couldn't tell if he was visiting or spying. They rather hope spying, I think, for they'd earn a handsome reward for shooting him and dropping him at MacIver's feet. However, neither he nor the blond he was with seemed particularly concerned with concealing their presence."

The woman. That's why Jamie Bridgewater came here. Oh, gods of heaven and earth, what have I told Adderly that I shouldn't have?

"A woman?"

Adderly said this with such forced indifference, Undine thought, even Gentry could not have failed to miss the significance.

"Aye. Blond. Full lips. High bosom. Sharing Bridgewater's saddle with him. She was, shall we say, showing no signs of being ill at ease in his arms. Do you know her?"

"No."

Adderly was lying. Undine had told Adderly about her. The memories were slipping back. She'd said far too much, but what choice had she had? A bludgeon opens mouths. She'd told him that Jamie had asked about the woman, whom he seemed to know had come from the future. Undine shuddered as she recalled Adderly's viselike hands. She had to get up, find Jamie, warn him—though how she would climb over these walls of pain, she didn't know. Jamie was in danger and so was the woman. He had to be alerted to what his brother had discovered.

"What do you want my men to do with him?" Gentry asked. "Kill him?"

"No. Don't kill him. Bring him back to MacIver Castle. My father must see the man for the traitor he is."

"And the blond?"

"Her?" Adderly said with forced casualness. "Er,

why don't you bring her to me? There are things I should like ask her."

"As you wish, my lord. And for my troubles?"

"Damn you and your troubles. You may take whatever you find here. The witch keeps her money in a box under her bed, I think. But be quick about it. I need to put out a warrant for Jamie Bridgewater's arrest."

Twenty-seven

Nunquam Castle

"HOW IN GOD'S NAME..." BRIDGEWATER WAS UPRIGHT and talking, but Panna's heart was going a mile a minute. He'd been *shot*? What sort of place was this? She looked at the pattern of holes up one side of the back of his shirt. Perhaps half a dozen. She touched one of the spots near his ribs, and he hissed.

"I was visiting one of the clan chiefs," he said. "The chief of Clan Kerr is an acquaintance."

"The guards let you in there?"

"No. I scaled the vines outside. Went in an upper window. I wanted to present my case. Find out what was being planned if I could."

"And he shot you?"

Bridgewater hesitated. "No. That part was uneventful. But when I was going back down, I heard footsteps in the courtyard. I dropped and started to run. The man yelled 'Stop!' and then a gun went off."

"Did the person who shot you see you? Does he know that the person he shot is you?"

"I don't know. I don't think so. It was dark. I could barely see my hands in front of my face. I ran down the hillside and hid in the underbrush. I heard the man looking for me. They didn't find me."

"Take off your shirt. Are you bleeding?"

He stripped it off. Five shots had penetrated the skin of his back, but there was almost no blood.

"How did you get back into the castle?" she asked.

He gave her a lopsided grin. "Brewer's wagon. I saw it coming up the hill and managed to throw myself into the back, though it damn near killed me."

"Elegant. And how did you get in here? I thought the passageway to the women's area was locked."

"That was trickier. I'm afraid I had to boot the door in."

"Rather less elegant. What are we going to do?" She had once driven a neighbor who'd fallen down the stairs of his back deck to the hospital, but that was about the extent of her experience with emergency medical assistance. Charlie's decline had been an endless progression of IVs, shunts, and radiation, but no emergencies.

Bridgewater pulled a knife out of a sheath in his boot and put it in her hand.

"What do you want me to do with this?" she asked, horrified.

"Cut them out."

Her vision started to swim. "Are you *serious*?"

"They have to come out. If they don't, the wounds will get infected. Don't worry. I've suffered worse."

The blade was four inches of burnished steel. The hilt felt slippery in her hand. "I don't think I can."

"No one can until they try."

"I'll hurt you," she said.

"I'll abide. Just take the knife, make a quick cut, then flip it out with the point." He took the blade from her hand and found a ball in his side with a finger. Then he jabbed the point of the blade into the space just underneath.

Panna felt her stomach rise as a rivulet of blood ran down his skin and stained his breeks. Face contorted in pain, Bridgewater wriggled the blade point back and forth for an instant, then made a flicking motion. She heard metallic sounds as the ball bounced off the floor.

Bridgewater's shoulders relaxed, though she could see the sweat on his brow.

"There," he said, handing her the knife again. "Do you want me to lie on the bed or stand here by the window?"

She thought of her dream and flushed. Fortunately, the real Bridgewater, with his black eye, treasonous acts, and back full of buckshot, was doing his roguish best to keep her grounded in the reality of the moment. "Er, the bed will be fine."

Yet again she was wearing nothing but her shift. Bridgewater seemed to have a sixth sense about finding her in an unclothed state. Her gown was still on the floor. Bridgewater stepped around it and laid himself carefully on the mattress, settling on his good side with his back toward the lightening sky.

She went to the desk by the windows to look for something she could use to absorb the blood but found nothing. "I wish the light here were stronger."

He turned to look and the corners of his mouth rose slightly. "It seems more than adequate."

She looked down and saw dawn's glow had made her shift translucent, showing every curve of her leg clearly. She crossed her arms, and he lowered his head again.

"I'm sorry this is what it took to get me into your bed," he said.

With his back to her, she couldn't tell whether he was joking, but her heart did a flip.

Bridgewater's back was warm but hard as iron under her touch. The dark, puckered holes in his skin looked like some horrifying constellation. She examined the bloody blade and wished they had access to some modern medical care. "I need some alcohol."

He chuckled. "Come, now. I'm the one who must endure the pain."

"Not for courage. For disinfecting."

"Disinfecting?"

"Killing the—" She realized he wouldn't know what germs were. "Killing the stuff that makes infections. We kind of cracked that nut a hundred years ago."

His eyes widened. "No infections?"

"Well, not *no* infections, but certainly fewer."

He reached into his boot and withdrew a metal flask.

"Good Lord, what else do you have in there?"

"It's quite convenient when one is riding."

She pulled the cork and dribbled the liquid over the blade. "Is this from the vineyards of Don Alfonso as well?"

"No. Just good Lowland whiskey, straight from the barrel."

She tipped the flask to her lips and took a long, surreptitious draught. Then she poured the whiskey over his back. He gasped, clenching the sheet in his fists until the sting wore off.

"Disinfection sucks," he said.

She laughed. "Yes, it does." Thinking distraction was the about the only form of anesthesia she could offer, she scanned the wounds to choose her first hole and said, "So, what happened between you and the clan chief?"

"What do you mean?" he asked, instantly alert.

She drove the knife into his flesh and he jerked.

"I mean, what did you learn?" She could feel the metal shot under the skin, like a little ball bearing.

"'Twas not much help," he said through gritted teeth. "The council is committed to going to war."

"What reason did you give him for coming here?" There was no avoiding what came next: she popped the point of the blade upward, and the shot broke through the flesh. His shoulders relaxed.

"Hector MacIver is my grandfather, after all. I shouldn't think I need more reason than that."

She'd left a hole about twice as big as the original. Blood dripped down his back and onto the sheets. She jumped off the bed and ran to the wardrobe. There had to be something there. She found an old blanket and tucked it under his back.

"This wasn't exactly covered in my librarian training," she said, half in apology.

"You're doing well. I take it you really are a library keeper?"

"Of course I am. I work at the Carnegie Library in Carnegie—part of Penn's Woods."

His back tensed. "Adderly introduced you as Mrs. Carnegie. You have a husband, then?"

"No, I don't. Andrew Carnegie was a wealthy industrialist—"

"Industrialist?"

"Man of industry. Like you. Only his industry was steel." She aimed her blade at the second ball and pierced his skin. "He made a lot of money. More than almost any other man on earth at the time, which was the end of the nineteenth century. And after he did, he decided to devote himself to making others' lives better. He built more than two thousand libraries." The second ball popped loose.

"Two *thousand* libraries?"

"Some even nicer than yours, if you can imagine. He offered a library to any town willing to promise to maintain it into the future. The town I'm from was really once two towns, Mansfield and Chartiers. They wrote to Carnegie and said they'd be willing to merge and call the new town 'Carnegie,' hoping he would be swayed to give them a library."

"And was he?"

"Yes, he was." She began on the third hole. "While there were a few free libraries before Andrew Carnegie and his efforts, he's the person responsible for making people in my time feel that they have a right to free access to books." The third shot dropped onto the bed. She caught the edge of the blanket and wiped away the blood.

"A right to free access to books." Bridgewater shook his head, amazed. "What an astonishing development—and a very generous gift."

"Yes, but I'm not one to stand in awe of wealthy men."

"I've noticed."

She laughed. "But he did at least try to atone for his sins," she said, starting on the fourth extraction. "He gave away almost all his money before he died. He said, 'The man who dies rich dies disgraced.'"

Bridgewater turned so he could see her. "You speak of a time that sounds so different than mine—a time when rich men give away their money, and access to books is considered a right. Is it also a time of great peace?"

She shook her head with a sigh. "No. The same issues that provoke men now provoke them in the future. I'm afraid there'll always be a need for men like you, Bridgewater."

He turned back to his side. "I wonder…" he began, and stopped.

"You wonder what?"

"I wonder if you would call me 'Jamie'? Other than Clare and Undine, a friend I should like you to meet someday, there's no one who does."

She felt her eyes prickle. A man with so few to call him by his given name? "I'd be honored."

He caught her hand and squeezed it. "Thank you, Panna."

She squeezed back.

"C'mon now," she said, slipping free and dabbing at her eyes. "Let me finish. Lord only knows when Mrs. Brownlow is going to wheel in here. I've read enough stories of Gretna Green to know…well, to know that's probably not a good idea."

"Stories of Gretna?" He looked at her again. "You know stories of Gretna? 'Tis only a few miles from here."

"Well, yes. It's quite a popular theme in novels," she said, extracting the fourth shot. "In one of my favorites, the wayward younger sister of the heroine is lured into abandoning her virtue with the promise of a forthcoming elopement to Gretna." Panna found her cheeks warming as she told him. The world was a different place here, after all. "That would've been bad enough. However, the promise was a false one."

Bridgewater snorted. "They often are. I hope the blackguard got his due."

She smiled. "The hero of the story forces the man to marry the girl, thus saving the heroine and her family from shame. It's very romantic."

Jamie look at her, his green-gray eyes sparkling. "It sounds as if some things about the world do *not* change: the pull of war, the pull of lust, and the pull of love."

"You're right." She eased the blade into the last hole, and the fifth and last ball dropped into her hand. She poured whiskey over the puckered and bleeding holes.

"*Christ!*" he cried. "I can stand the blade, but getting disinfected is worse than getting shot."

"Here." She handed him the flask. "Drink up. We're done."

His face changed from an expression of complaint to the look of a three-year-old hiding the broken pieces of his mother's favorite porcelain figurine behind his back.

"What?" she demanded. "We *are* done, aren't we?" She looked again at his back, scanning the skin. Then she saw them. More tiny holes in his dark breeks. Ten or more.

He sat up, his face contorted in pain. "Those can wait until I return to Bowness."

"Is your ass somehow less prone to infection than the rest of you? I mean, I think the quote is 'War is hardest on those left behind,' not those left *in* the behind."

"I am *not* going to take off my breeks before you." He struck an upstanding pose—or at least as upstanding as he could make, given that he was bare chested, bleeding profusely, and sitting on a woman's bed. "'Twould not be gentlemanly."

"Oh, is 'gentlemanly' our guiding principle here? Well, I'm not completely dressed, as you pointed out in so gentlemanly a manner, so I see no problem in stripping you of your clothes as well." He flushed— rightfully, she considered. "Off."

He made a long, reluctant growl and stood up, back to her. He lowered the fabric carefully to his knees, then lowered himself even more carefully onto the bed.

Her dream had not done him justice. His flesh was the rosy color of peaches, his muscles were taut, and the arrow-straight line of his spine bisected the dimples of his lower back before disappearing into the shadowy place between perfect mounds of flesh. His buttocks were dusted with the same sparkling gold hairs that ran down his powerful thighs. Only the dark spots of the entry wounds marred the godlike perfection.

She let out a quiet exhale.

"Is it bad?"

She shook her head firmly before realizing she was responding to a different question. "Not too bad. You'll be fine."

She'd work from the shots highest on his buttocks to the ones more alarmingly placed.

"Hand me the whiskey, if you would," she said.

"No."

"Infection."

"I don't care."

"Surely, a big, grown-up soldier like you is not afraid of a little discomfort." She snatched the bottle from his hand and dribbled more onto the knife, letting it run over his wounds.

"*Bloody hell.*"

She took another fortifying sip and then positioned the tip of the blade over the first hole. Her hands were shaking less, but she found it much harder to concentrate on extracting this group of balls for some reason. She laid her hand on his hip to steady her work surface. His skin was warm and alive in her grasp.

"How long are you going to prepare for the next jab?" he said. "I'm not comfortable under this sort of gaze."

"And yet, this can hardly be the first time a woman's eyes have been upon you."

He made an imperious *harrumph.*

"I thought so."

"'Tis not a fair comparison."

"Isn't it? Trousers down, bottom warmed, all attention focused on the prick to come?"

She jabbed the knife in and flicked the first ball free in a single, easy movement. Damn, she was getting good at this.

He lifted his shoulder. "You have a very lurid imagination."

"Too many books. I knew a hunter once who told me—oh, I probably shouldn't say it."

"I'm afraid the bounds of propriety have been irretrievably broken at this point. There is no need to be reticent."

"He told me firing his gun gave him an erection."

Bridgewater let out a soft chuckle. "I believe I can do you one better. I knew a woman who kept a wooden paddle by her bed into which the outline of a bee had been cut. The strokes would leave a picturesque welt."

Panna giggled. "On you?"

"Now, why would you assume I had anything to do with this?"

"Bees, huh?"

"She referred to it as the sting of love."

The second and third balls were just as easy. Panna was starting to like the feel of the blade in her hand. She was also starting to like the feel of his ass there. She made the move to cut the flesh on the fifth ball when something she saw out of the corner of her eye sent the blade tip skittering for several inches across his flesh.

"*Ow!*" he cried.

"Sorry."

She hadn't entirely closed the wardrobe, and over the course of the last few minutes, its mirror-covered door had yawned open, putting a most remarkable reflection of the front of Bridgewater's body directly in her line of sight.

She lowered her eyes to the bedcover instantly, but the damage, if one could call it that, had been done.

The view of his front had been even more engaging

than the one of his back. Broad chest, carved belly, and a small mass of brown curls from which a sizable penis, as long as the knife in her hand, hung. Small explosive charges seemed to be going off all over her skin. She felt slightly drunk and very wicked.

"What is it?"

"Er, nothing." She tried to wipe the image from her mind, but her mind seemed quite intent on holding on to it. He was uncircumcised, which didn't surprise her, given the era, but Charlie and her other boyfriends had been circumcised, and the alternate style seemed more alluring and more dangerous.

I won't look again. Looking again would be wrong.

She inserted the tip of the blade into the fifth hole.

I'll only look if the ball comes out smoothly.

The ball rolled down his buttock and into the fold of the towel. He didn't even make a noise.

She stole a glance. Bridgewater looked like something one would see in a museum—a discus thrower or the Colossus of Rhodes—only in the living flesh.

Well, I've certainly seen what I needed to see. Definitely won't look again.

The sixth ball came out just as smoothly as the fifth.

She looked again. There was something utterly fascinating about that scant swaying weight. It was... well...hypnotic.

"Panna?"

She was so startled she nearly dropped the knife. She lowered her gaze instantly to the relative neutrality of his buttocks. "What?"

"Is something wrong? You haven't moved in a full minute."

"What? No."

She vowed she'd do better, and she'd taken out four more balls of lead before she found her eyes drawn inexorably once more to the mirror.

"You know," he said, turning, "if you wanted this to be fair, you'd remove your shift."

Oh God, had she been found out? But the look on his face was playful, not accusatory.

"Fortunately, that desire eludes me." She positioned the blade to remove the next ball.

"Surely a big, grown-up library keeper like you isn't afraid of a little discomfort."

"Why don't you just imagine I've removed my shift?"

"Too late for that."

She poked him with her finger and he yelped. He was getting a little too cocky for a guy with buckshot in his ass and a penis the size of a baby eggplant on display.

"I have a thought," he said.

"Oh, I'm certain of it."

"How many pieces of shot remain?"

She counted. "Five."

"I have been inspired by your story about Andrew Carnegie. I should like to build a free library for the people of Cumbria."

"You *would*?"

"And I shall fill it with one hundred books for each piece of shot you remove in the absence of your shift."

Her heart did a drumroll. When she felt she could control her voice again, she said, "How about this instead? You shall provide one hundred books for each piece of shot that does not require extensive knife-twisting to remove."

"Oh." His shoulders sagged. "'Tis another option, I suppose."

"Think of it as my way of saving you from dying disgraced."

"You are kind to protect me."

The last five pieces of lead came out without a hitch. She collected the tiny balls and then washed her hands and the knife with the whiskey. Then she washed his back and buttocks one more time. The bleeding had stopped, but he was going to be exceedingly sore for a while. She turned while he redid his breeks. He lay down again gingerly. The wool was dark, so the bloodstains didn't show. With his jacket over it, the holes would be invisible as well.

She hid the bloody blanket and the lead shot behind the wardrobe. Her shift was a little bloody, as were the sheets, but that could easily be explained by her period.

By the time she'd finished, Jamie was breathing steadily and she knew he'd fallen asleep. Little wonder. She gazed at the set of his mouth as he slept and the way his hand had curled into a ball under his chin. It was the same way Charlie'd slept. Bridgewater looked so peaceful. She suspected it was the first time he'd slept since she'd arrived.

So far, Bridgewater's arrival at Nunquam had inspired joyous tears and a barrage of gunfire, and they hadn't even met his grandfather yet. Not a propitious sign. Bridgewater had been blasted with birdshot, which meant the shooter probably hadn't been one of the guards, whose guns would shoot a single, larger and more deadly ball. Had it been someone out hunting who'd happened to stumble upon an intruder? Bridgewater said he hadn't been spotted until he was on the ground, which probably meant the shooter hadn't realized the man he'd shot had already been *in* the clan chiefs' wing rather than attempting to get into it. But the question that most concerned her was whether the shooter would be able to identify Bridgewater as the person he'd fired at.

Unfortunately, none of the questions were ones she or he could answer.

She sat on the bed and thought about her own world, so far away. It was Sunday morning. The staff at the library would soon figure out she was missing her shift. Marie would try calling, but if Panna didn't answer, Marie would probably assume she was ill and asleep. Monday was Panna's day off. Marie wouldn't get really worried until Tuesday.

The realization that no one would miss her for days made her a bit sad. She and Bridgewater were two of the same sort, she thought. Not lonely, but alone. She, at least, still had her brothers and their families. But that was different from having someone who tended to your wounds, worried about you when you were gone, and carried you constantly in his thoughts.

The morning light had intensified, and the gold strands in Bridgewater's hair gleamed. She slid next to him, smelling the peaty scent that permeated his skin now. The bed was narrow, and she stretched out, eliciting a satisfied "mmmm" from him. She knew she should wake him so that he could move to his own bed, but the pillows were so soft and her thoughts kept slipping back to that first kiss.

~

Panna was so deep in her dreams, she mistook the knock for the distant boom of a cannon, and it wasn't until she heard Mrs. Brownlow's whispered "Miss Kennedy?" that she woke and, still muzzy from sleep, ran to the door and opened it.

Mrs. Brownlow was accompanied by a stooped man with a cane and a pistol.

"There's been an intruder," Mrs. Brownlow said.

"Oh dear." Panna held the door open only a few inches and blocked as much of the view of her room as she could with her body.

"Has anyone bothered you?"

"No."

"Have you seen anyone?"

"No."

"The lock on the door at the end of the hall was broken."

The bed behind her squeaked, and the stooped man frowned. He lifted his cane and shoved the door open with a bang. Jamie had stood, and the bloodied sheet was clearly visible on the bed behind him.

"This is how you come to me?" the man said, his brimstone eyes focused in fury on Jamie. "Despoiling a god-fearing woman in my house?"

Despoiling? Then Panna saw the blood on the sheets. Jamie's mouth fell open.

"Did he rape you, lass?" The man, who Panna realized must be Hector MacIver, stared at her with concern.

"*Rape?* No, I—"

"Nothing happened," Jamie said hotly, pulling his shirt over his head.

"Who's your father?" MacIver demanded of Panna. MacIver was nearly as tall as Jamie and, despite his infirmity, looked just as capable of violence.

"I—I—don't have one. He's dead."

The man gave Jamie a disgusted look. "A fatherless woman?"

"You are mistaken, sir," Jamie said in a voice of cold steel.

"Mistaken?" the man cried. "Mistaken about what? Finding you in her room? The blood of her maidenhead on the sheets? You're a rutting English blackguard just like your father. Go back to him, where you belong, and leave my castle in peace." He swung around to face Mrs. Brownlow. "Aye, your Jamie has returned. Is he everything you expected?" Then he turned clumsily, his bad leg so twisted beneath him that he nearly fell, and hobbled out the door, slamming the cane against the wall as he left.

Mrs. Brownlow burst into tears.

Twenty-eight

DEEPLY IRRITATED BY HIS GRANDFATHER AND WORRIED for Panna, Bridgewater strode up Nunquam's imposing staircase. He was followed by his companion of the last few moments, a man with pistol drawn who had met him at the entrance to the women's wing and followed him wordlessly as he made his way through the maze of hallways, offering no suggestions on which way to go.

"I assume this is the way to see MacIver," Bridgewater said. The man didn't answer. "Rather shy when it comes to conversation, are you?"

Bridgewater had donned his coat and straightened his clothes before leaving Panna to settle Mrs. Brownlow, who'd wailed, "Your mother's heart will be breaking."

Why he'd expected a polite welcome from his grandfather, he didn't know. Clearly the man was as bitter now as the day his daughter had told him she was with child by an English nobleman.

He reached the top of the stairs and turned to the right, following the path of a servant carrying a tray.

"I assume you'll let me know—or shoot me—if I am proceeding in the wrong direction."

"Shoot you more's the likely," the man with the pistol said.

Bridgewater's back and buttocks were on fire, and it was all he could do to keep from limping. He'd been shocked by his grandfather's appearance. The last time he'd seen him, perhaps two years ago, the man had been as straight in his saddle as a ship's mast. An apoplexy or worse had stolen his vitality, but it seemed he'd hold his venom to the last.

You're a rutting English blackguard just like your father.

The only good thing about the incident in Panna's room was that the explanation for the presence of the blood his grandfather had seized upon meant the real explanation had not crossed his mind. For that reason alone, Bridgewater wouldn't correct him.

He wondered what it might have been like to take Panna's maidenhead, and the thought sent a raw tingle through him. He felt a stab of jealousy for the man who'd been lucky enough to serve her in that way.

Ah, but she wasn't a maiden. She'd buried a husband. The weight of that loss showed in her eyes and in her bearing. She was a woman in the fullest sense of the word.

The servant he'd been following entered a room and then did an about-face, nearly running into Bridgewater, who managed to keep the tray from falling.

"Steady, now."

The man hurried away.

Bridgewater looked into the room and saw what had caused the servant's retreat. His grandfather was seated before a cross, head bowed. The room was not a chapel—at least, not the sort Bridgewater could recognize. Other than a plain oak table and chairs, the only furnishings were a few shelves of books. Bridgewater stood quietly, waiting for his grandfather to finish. He could hear the old man's labored breathing.

"Not quite the ostentation of the library in MacIver Castle, is it?" his grandfather said after a long moment, head still bowed.

Bridgewater flushed. Criticized for ostentation by a man who'd built not one but two castles? He bit his tongue.

"Why are you still here?"

"I told you," Bridgewater said, "I have a matter of importance to speak to you about."

The man was nearly prostrate on the ground. How with a cane and a crippled leg he'd managed to get down to his knees, Bridgewater couldn't imagine. His grandfather turned to his side and, with evident effort, lifted himself onto a stool.

"There are many who wish to speak with me, including a dozen men under my roof right now whose wishes are more important than yours. What makes you think I'd waste my time with you?"

"It concerns what may happen between the clans and the English army in the next three days."

The chief of Clan MacIver's eyes widened. "You're aware an intruder was shot attempting to scale the castle wall?"

Bridgewater froze. "I heard there was an intruder."

"'Tis a dangerous time in the borderlands. I dinna

think even an English spy would be brazen enough to try that. He'd be risking certain death."

"If an English spy had tried it, he'd have succeeded, and you would never have known." *If a well-trained one had, in any case.*

His grandfather snorted. "If we find the man, I promise you, his death will dissuade anyone from attempting the same thing again."

Bridgewater shifted. The last spy who'd tried to infiltrate the clans had been a lieutenant in a Northumberland regiment whose head still sat on a spike on a bridge over the river in Dumfries.

"Where's your uniform, Captain?"

"I am not here on behalf of the army."

"Are you telling me your father is unaware of your appearance here?"

His choice of "your father" instead of "commanding officer" or even "the earl" was like a parry at the start of a swordfight, designed to provoke his opponent. It took all of Bridgewater's fortitude, whose levels of that helpful quality were already perilously low, to hold his tongue. "No."

"I see. And what would happen were he to learn of your ill-timed appearance here?"

It was a barely veiled threat, though Bridgewater had understood what he would be risking before he came. "I'd prefer he didn't find out."

His grandfather gave a little chuckle and dragged his leg up under him. "I doubt he'd be quite so concerned about your defilement of the girl, though. 'Tis rather a tradition in your family, is it not?"

Bridgewater's ears started to buzz. "Let's not

venture down that road, MacIver. His treatment of my
mother was hardly worse than yours."

The old man's eyes blazed. "Your mother abandoned the teachings of her god—"

"*You* abandoned the teachings of her god,"
Bridgewater said. "My father broke her heart, but you
killed her. Slash the blossom from the stem and it dies.
When you threw her out of your heart and home,
you destroyed her—just as surely as if you'd wrung
her neck."

"Your mother…" MacIver shook his head and
pressed his lips together, his eyes shut tight. "Your
mother broke *my* heart," he said, his face unexpectedly
streaked with tears. He rocked forward with a furious
growl, planted his cane on the floor, and dragged
himself to a standing position. He jabbed the gnarled
stick at his grandson. "Dinna speak your mother's
name to me. Ever."

Bridgewater vibrated with fury. He wanted to take
the man by the neck and fling him onto the floor. But
he knew he could no more take those fragile bones
into his hands than he could a child's. It was heart-
breakingly cruel that his first meeting with the man
had to come when it was too late to kill him.

"I'll never share any part of my mother with you,"
Bridgewater said. "Of that you can be certain. But that
doesn't change the reason I've come. Let's get to it, shall
we, and bring this ill-conceived reunion to an end."

MacIver's eyes bored a hole in him. "Speak."

"Does your word still carry the force of law with
the clan chiefs here?"

MacIver's face betrayed nothing. "One man, one

vote has always been the way of the borderlands, Captain. Surely your father told you that."

"I want your word that what I tell you will remain between you and me."

The old man shook his head. "You have my word—but only if I believe what you say. So I'd suggest employing your strongest powers of persuasion. The chiefs here would take great satisfaction in making an example of you."

"The English army has been given the order to prepare for a battle."

"Bloody bastards!" MacIver hobbled quickly toward the door. "I'll have my scouts confirm this. If the army thinks we shan't meet them blow for blow—"

"Wait." Bridgewater stepped in front of him. "Let me finish."

The servant with the tray reappeared and made his way toward the table.

"Leave us," MacIver said sharply.

The man bowed and exited.

MacIver eyed his grandson with the intensity of a jungle cat. "We've been prepared for this. The time's come to bring this matter to a head. The clans of Scotland willna endure an army at our doorstep."

"I want you to convince the clans not to respond."

MacIver's brows flew up. "Are you insane?"

"You'll lose. You must believe me."

Bridgewater knew he'd already committed treason by revealing the army's plans. The line he'd drawn for his own conscience, however, was that he wouldn't reveal the number of soldiers or the fact that the queen's orders gave the army only until

Wednesday to wait for a battle before they were to return south.

"You'd like that, wouldn't you?" MacIver said. "To take your victory without a struggle."

"'Twill be no victory for anyone if your men and the army come to blows."

MacIver stepped closer to his grandson, close enough that Bridgewater could feel the man's sour breath on his face. "You're saying to me that you want the clans to throw down their arms and allow the English army free rein to cross the border?"

"I'm saying I want you to keep the clans from attacking. You don't need to throw down your weapons. But you must keep them from mounting an offense." Bridgewater could see the machinations in his grandfather's eyes as he considered what it might take to reverse that plan.

"You ascribe too high a power to me, Captain. The clans will do as they wish. They always do."

"You must stop them. If your men attack, they'll be slaughtered. I'm not a Scot, but I don't wish to see that any more than you."

The flames in MacIver's eyes were fire now. "Not a Scot? Not a *Scot*? You're half Scot, you maneuvering English bastard. Would you deny your mother's blood?"

"*You* did!"

MacIver grabbed him by the coat with his good arm and shoved him into the wall. A whiplash of pain flew up Bridgewater's buttock and back.

"You've given me no reason to believe you," MacIver said. "None. You're asking me to betray my men. To snatch a battle from their teeth. You have no idea what you're asking."

"I know what I'm asking. But you must. You must keep them from attacking."

MacIver held the head of his cane aloft as if he would bring it down upon his grandson's head given the slightest provocation.

"If you wish me to trust you, you'll learn what it is to carry MacIver blood in you," the man said. "If you wish me to act on your words, you'll take the clan oath before the men here and claim your rightful Scots heritage."

Bridgewater would be throwing his lot in with Scotland. He'd be stripped of his commission, if not hanged.

"I can't," he said. "You of all people know what it means to have risen to a place where you command men. If the army discovers I've taken such an oath, I'll be removed."

His grandfather's grip slackened.

"Fine. You'll take the oath before me. And you'll marry the girl—here, now, before you leave. Show me you're not just a by-blow of that English black-guard. Show me you have enough MacIver blood in you for me to trust." He released his hold.

Marry her? Bridgewater's mind raced. "But she's not mine to command."

"One hour," MacIver said. "Appear before me ready to meet my demands, or I shall let the clan chiefs know we have an English agent in our midst."

Twenty-nine

PANNA OPENED THE DOOR AND LOOKED BRIDGEWATER over. "Hey, whaddya know? No new injuries. That's got to be a good sign, right?"

Jamie didn't laugh, though Mrs. Brownlow smiled from her chair beside the bed. In fact, Jamie had the same look on his face that Panna remembered her brother had on his when he found out his wife was having twins.

"What is it, Jamie?"

He summoned a small half smile at her use of his Christian name, and a sprig of joy blossomed in her heart. But the sprig wilted when he closed the door and said, "Panna, we need to talk."

The last time someone had said that, it had been Charlie after a routine checkup two weeks before their seventh wedding anniversary. Her throat dried. She knew she was being was ridiculous—Jamie could hardly have contracted a terminal illness in the last twenty minutes—but it was hard not to run down the same road.

He bowed to Mrs. Brownlow, whose tears had been calmed in his absence. "Would you be willing to give us a few minutes?"

"Hector wouldna want me to leave her alone," she said apologetically. "Not now."

Not after taking Panna's virginity, she meant. Jamie's cheeks flushed. Panna had assured Mrs. Brownlow that Jamie hadn't hurt her or drawn her into anything against her will but had stopped short of detailing any more clearly what had gone on between them. Even in the eighteenth century, Panna clung to her right to at least some privacy.

Jamie cleared his throat, and the flush grew redder. "Please? A few moments. I promise nothing will happen."

Mrs. Brownlow rose from the chair uncertainly, as if she were leaving a bottle of gin at an AA meeting. "I'll be right outside."

When the door closed again, Panna found herself feeling the sort of awkward, charged current between them as if Jamie *had* seduced her, especially with the regret that lingered in his eyes.

"I'm most sorry to have embarrassed you," he said. "'Twas thoughtless of me to come to your room."

She waved away his concern. "What were you going to do? You'd been shot, for God's sake. Please don't worry about it. I can deal with a little scrutiny. What happened with your grandfather? Will there be a battle?"

The regret in his eyes turned to worry, and his gaze turned toward the hills in the distance. "I don't know."

"What do you mean, you don't know? Jamie, what happened?"

He sighed. "I must ask you for a favor, though 'favor' is hardly the word to describe it."

"Certainly. Anything I can do. What?"

"I don't think you'll find it so easy to agree once I tell you. My grandfather was already quite angry, as you know. Then we fought about my mother."

"Oh, Jamie." Panna had held out a slim hope that once Hector MacIver got past his initial fury, the two men would reconcile.

"By the time I began to encourage him to cancel the attack, he was not inclined to put a lot of credence in what I had to say."

"But surely to protect his men—"

"Protecting his men is just as likely to depend on *not* listening to me. Panna, he has no reason to believe what a captain from Her Majesty's army says to him. The army's lied to the Scots too many times before."

"But you're his grandson. You're blood."

He gave her an amused look, his eyes as clear as the morning sky. "You sound like him. He'd be pleased." He stepped to the window, his hands clasped behind his back. "And blood"—his eyes flicked over the sheets, still streaked with crimson—"is the bargain he's offered me."

An uneasy feeling went through Panna. "*Blood?*"

"Mine—and yours. MacIver has agreed to try to convince the other chiefs to cancel the attack if I swear my oath to the clan—and you and I marry."

"*What?*" Panna felt dizzy.

"'Tis the vengeance he exacts for my ravishment of you. He finds the sins of the Earl of Bridgewater too richly inscribed upon my character."

She shook her head, unable to speak. She'd hardly considered another marriage, so absorbed had she been in simply trying to outrun the pain the last two years. She was very fond of Jamie, but fondness did not equate to marriage, not in her world. Besides, did he think—did either of them think—a marriage here would commit her to this time? "Oh, Jamie, I—"

"'Twould not be a real marriage," he said quickly. "I know you don't love me in that way."

She didn't know what to say. They'd known each other a day and a half. Despite a confusing maelstrom of attraction, desire, and admiration, she could hardly contradict him.

"And I myself have no high opinion of such a covenant," he added.

"You don't believe in marriage?"

His gaze fell. "I had no example from which to learn, save my father and his wife, and to me their marriage seemed only a wall built to protect their riches and keep out those who attempted to attack it, like my mother and me. I have no interest in such a thing."

"So you're saying we would marry with no thought of upholding the vows."

"Panna, I'm quite sensible of the fact that you're an unwilling visitor here—"

"Unexpected," she said softly. "Not unwilling."

"—and that I must deliver you to the chapel and back into the hands of those you've left."

She thought of Charlie and that empty bed.

"Even if I believed in the covenant of marriage," he said in a careful voice, "I couldn't have it with you. So, aye, if you are willing to accept the vow for the day or so it may take me to return you to the chapel, traversing the space of three centuries will put an end to it."

As if time or space could erase such a vow.

Panna was not a deeply religious person, though the things she did believe she carried deep in her heart. She knew one thing for certain, however. If she stood at an altar and pledged her troth to Jamie, it would be a pledge she carried with her for the rest of her life.

"Jamie, think about what you're asking."

"I know what I'm asking. And I know it's not fair. But there are people whose lives will depend on it. Clare's father died in a clash with the clans. So did his brother. Reeves's sister was left a widow with four children. He supports his own family and hers. In a battle of any size, there are at least a dozen men who die. In the battle the army and the clans will undertake, it could be ten times that. I don't have the right to ask you, but I won't shield you from the truth, either."

She thought of her brother fighting in Afghanistan and how she'd prayed each night for his safety. What would it be like to lose him? What would it be like to know that there was a woman somewhere who could've saved men in her brother's division from certain death but hadn't done it? Panna would be furious—beyond furious. Who wouldn't trade a mere wedding promise for the life of a man? Panna would've given anything—anything, including her own life—to save Charlie. How could she refuse the same succor to another wife or sister?

Jamie looked at her, his face as grave as she had ever seen it.

"And you say this vow will mean no more to you than it does to me?"

A muscle moved at the edge of his jaw. "No."

She nodded. "I'll do it, Jamie." Even if it meant one more vow life would keep her from upholding.

His shoulders relaxed and he threw his arms around her. "Thank you."

Panna squeezed him back, and when their eyes met, she found it impossible not to lift her mouth to his.

For a long moment the world stood still—no earl, no chiefs, no war, just her and Jamie in the morning sun.

"Ooh," she whispered when they parted.

In response, he pressed his fingers along her ribs and made a tiny noise of agreement deep inside his chest.

An unpleasant thought struck her, and she lifted her head. "Oh, Jamie, I just realized you said you had to swear an oath. What does that mean?"

She could feel the beat of his pulse under her palms. "It means I accept my place in the MacIver clan. *That* I can do. Hector MacIver is my grandfather, and there's nothing I can do to change it. Unfortunately, taking an oath also means I put the needs of the clan above anything else."

She knew enough from what she'd read of blood oaths to know that they were not taken lightly—not by those taking them, nor by those administering them. "But the army…?"

"Aye, the army and England. I've already taken oaths. I can't swear to anything that would displace those."

Here she was, worrying about the promise she'd make to a man she'd likely never see again when he was struggling with something much harder. "Then how can you do it, Jamie?"

"Making a blood oath to the MacIvers will save hundreds of men, if not thousands, Panna—Scots and Englishmen alike. For that alone, I'd swear my allegiance to the devil, let alone Hector MacIver. But I don't think such an oath violates my duty to England. For years, I've circled treason and looked into its ferocious jaws. I do what I do because I love my country, just as I love the kinsmen of my mother. I can navigate the murky waters of these loyalties just as long as I keep myself pointed in the direction of peace, which represents the best outcome for everyone."

She looked at him, a man who decried the church, standing before her with a black eye, a swollen lip, a body savaged by wounds from battles present and past. This man held peace before all else and was willing to sacrifice his soul to help deliver it.

"Oh, Jamie."

He pulled her to him again, and she lost herself in his kiss. She would gladly make a vow to him, thrilled to be in his orbit if only for a few more hours.

The door opened. Mrs. Brownlow's face fell. "Jamie Bridgewater—"

He held up his hand. "No more reproofs. Now is the time for congratulations. Panna has agreed to marry me."

Mrs. Brownlow cupped a hand over her mouth, happiness bursting from her round face. Having already foreseen what was coming, Panna reached for the handkerchief and handed it to her.

"*Och*, Jamie," the older woman cried, the tears beginning anew, "your mother would be so happy! I wish she were here."

He clasped Panna's elbow. "I do too."

Thirty

MRS. BROWNLOW SCURRIED AROUND THE ROOM AS IF she were running on double shots of espresso. The deadline of one hour had sent her into overdrive. It had sent Panna into something akin to shock.

With the taste of him still on her tongue, Panna bounced between sizzling desire and the certainty she was making a terrible mistake.

Jamie had been banned from the room while Mrs. Brownlow worked. Panna's gown had been declared "not right at all for a bride," and the muscles in her legs were jittering inside her skin as if she were a rabbit about to bolt.

"I need a drink," Panna declared.

Mrs. Brownlow, who was busy brushing Panna's hair into something that looked less like the communal scratching post at a cat shelter, peered at her. "Aye, I think that's a good idea."

Panna expected her to call for a servant, but instead Mrs. Brownlow lifted her skirt and withdrew a flask from the top of her stocking. Panna clearly needed to explore this area of undergarment subterfuge in more detail.

Panna took the flask, popped the cork, and took a long swallow.

"You can rest assured," Mrs. Brownlow said, "the second time will be better than the first."

Panna coughed, sending a fine spray of sweet sherry through her fist. Mrs. Brownlow was *not* talking about marriages.

"And if Master Jamie is the man I think he is, the third time'll be even better."

Panna thought the first time would be crackin' fantastic—that is, if she and Jamie ever got to it.

"He's a good man," Mrs. Brownlow said. "You must tell him it's like a wriggling fish."

"I beg your pardon?"

"The place between your legs," she said under her breath. "And he must hook it with his finger. My Bobby went at it like he was trying to cudgel a weasel with a fence picket. That dinna work, lass. Oh, it works fine for them, but then again, what doesn't? A tiny fish. And it must be his finger. Though, in a pinch, yours will work as well."

Panna considered this advice, downed another gulp of sherry and said, "Do you suppose Jamie is much of a fisherman?"

Mrs. Brownlow's eyes twinkled. "Oh, I should think so, don't you? And if not, I'm sure he has it in him to learn. I can see it in the way he looks at you."

Panna flushed. "I hope."

"There are *other* things a man will want to do." The approbation with which Mrs. Brownlow said this made it seem these other things would not be cured with something as simple as a hook and a wiggle.

"Oh?"

"You have to understand, they hold their cocks in very high regard."

Uh-huh.

"I think if they could do so without damage," Mrs. Brownlow added, "they would happily wear it as a feather in their cap."

Panna thought of Sunday strolls along the waterfront. "I see."

"There's no place too grand to hold it. So you must not take offense."

"Too grand?"

Mrs. Brownlow surreptitiously passed a hand across her mouth.

Panna bit her lip. "Oh dear."

"'Tis not as bad as you think. And if you are in no mood to linger—for sometimes you will not be—'tis the fastest way home. I have three sisters, and we've had eight husbands between us. Not a one could last longer than a sheep's shearing."

Eight husbands. "So Bobby...he was your first husband?"

"No, my second. The first was Davey. A good man he was, though he drank more than he should've. Took to his bed with a fever one Hogmanay. Never got up."

Mrs. Brownlow had returned Panna's hair to a glossy shine and was now weaving it into a series of braids. Panna played with the pins in her hand. "Was it hard for you to remarry? Did you feel like you were abandoning Davey?"

"I mourned him for a year, lass. But a woman's

heart is large. A man can only love one wife. But a woman can love many husbands. I haven't abandoned Davey. I've locked him away. He's in his own place there, safe and secure."

"Like a chamber of a nautilus shell."

Mrs. Brownlow smiled. "Aye, I suppose."

The safe spaces in one's memory. Where we preserve those we've lost. But unlike a nautilus shell, the spaces aren't separated by walls. They are connected by doors that one can reopen whenever one needs to.

Mrs. Brownlow ran to fetch an aged hand mirror from the dresser and gave it to Panna. Panna's hair had been pinned into a loose French roll and decorated with ropes of tiny braids. "Oh, it's beautiful. Truly. Thank you." She turned the mirror over and saw that a loopy *S* had been engraved on the back of it. "Do you think Sorcha would be pleased with the way Jamie has turned out?"

"Oh, aye. Handsome, brave, smart. Of course, he's always been handsome. Even as a tiny bairn."

"You knew him as an infant, too?"

"*Shh*," the woman said, glancing toward the door. "You mustn't tell Hector. I visited Sorcha once when he was but a fat baby. I gave him a turkey bone. Sorcha said it was the first food he held for himself. He sat in front of the fire and gnawed on it for an hour, happy as a pup."

"But Sorcha died right after Jamie was born."

"Oh, no. That was later. I sent Annan's best surgeon. The one Hector himself used. Paid with my own coin. Not that it did much good." Mrs. Brownlow sat down next to Panna on the bed. "I also gathered her things when she passed. There wasn't much. A gown or two I gave to the poor-house. A trinket box from the earl," she added disapprovingly. "Three or four books. They're on the shelf in the wardrobe."

Panna turned to look but the wardrobe's doors were closed. "Could I give them to Jamie? I have no other present for him."

"Aye, and give him the little ark too. You should have it for your bairns."

The morning sun was high in the sky now. The Cumbrian hills looked like emerald cabochons, and Bridgewater's castle sat like a carved piece of ivory in their midst, the peaked roof of the chapel rising from the design.

"Do you think Jamie's grandfather regrets what he did?"

"Aye," Mrs. Brownlow said. "Though I think it's taken him many years to come to that. And he would not want anyone to know."

"But people know he built the chapel for her. Or is Jamie the only one?"

"Built the chapel for her?" Mrs. Brownlow laughed. "Oh, no, lass. When that chapel went up, Hector was furious. 'Who dares to touch my castle?' Of course, the lands had been taken by the Crown, so he had no basis for the complaint. He thinks the priest sold Sorcha's jewelry and built it to rub the MacIverses' noses in his wickedness."

"The priest who cared for Jamie and his mother?"

"Aye."

"I know Jamie finds great comfort in that chapel."

"Maybe he's the one who built it, lass. He's made a good bit of money on water pumps."

If Bridgewater had built it, he certainly had tried to hide that fact. He'd railed against what he perceived to be his grandfather's attempt to assuage his guilt by building it.

"Are you ready, lass?" Mrs. Brownlow gestured toward the door.

Panna's heart leaped in her chest. Had an hour passed already? She lifted the flask and drank.

"Careful, now," Mrs. Brownlow said. "A little is good. A lot...well, let's just say a lot can be as bad as none. I saw a bride once drink so much whiskey she fell asleep in the carriage of one of the wedding guests. She slept all the way to the man's estate in Glasgow. Awoke with the cock's crow. And that reminds me: if Jamie tells you the only way to get rid of a cockstand is for you to tend to it, you look him in the eye and tell him you know better."

Panna wondered which eye she meant.

Thirty-one

BRIDGEWATER SWALLOWED AND TRIED TO CLEAR HIS throat. He found his mouth drier than he'd ever known it. He wished he had his uniform. It didn't seem right to ask Panna to stand beside him while he wore a dusty, shot-riddled coat. He rubbed his sweating palms on his breeks.

"You look fine," Hector said. "A groom shouldna outshine the bride."

"No chance of that, I'm afraid." Bridgewater wondered where Hector had drummed up a priest on such short notice and if banns would have to be posted, but then he remembered Scotland's lax marriage laws and realized one of the castle's blacksmiths could probably perform the ceremony as well as anyone here.

"Was the girl relieved?"

Bridgewater felt the blood rise once again on his cheeks. Exactly how much censure was he going to have to endure for a fornication that had not taken place? Had she been relieved? Hardly. She'd agreed, but he'd seen the hesitation in her eyes. And her words had made it clear that whatever they shared, it was not love.

And you say this vow will mean no more to you than it does to me?

"Aye," Bridgewater said, "I believe she was quite beside herself with joy."

"As I'd expect. You have done quite well financially for a bastard whose father has given you nothing."

Not to mention a man whose grandfather has denied me what might also be considered mine.

MacIver saw the unspoken sentiment in Bridgewater's eyes. "Aye, well, the time has come for you to claim what is yours."

"I have no need of your money."

"Nor do I offer it."

Bridgewater swallowed his pride. "But if my grandmother had a ring that should have been passed to my mother, I'd like to have it."

The Scot stared, his rheumy eyes appraising the man before him. "Your mother was disinherited. There is nothing of mine or my wife's that belongs to her—or to you."

Bridgewater tried to keep the disappointment from his face. He'd hoped for something to give to Panna.

"However," MacIver said wearily, "I know your grandmother would've wanted you to have something. Let me see what I can find."

He made his way stiffly to the door and said a few words to the guard in the hall. When he turned, Bridgewater said, "When are you planning to speak to the clan chiefs?"

"Lower your voice. No one commands me, especially not an English army officer." MacIver closed the door. "The council begins after our breakfast. You and your bride will join us for that."

An unpleasant tingle went up Bridgewater's spine. "I can't be seen here."

MacIver held up a bony hand. "Dinna fash yourself. A wedding answers nicely. Your superior officers can hardly complain about a man running off to Scotland with his sweetheart to marry. If only that had been the reason you'd brought her," he added under his breath.

"Even I could've managed an excuse for being found in *Scotland*," Bridgewater said with irritation. "'Tis being *here*, in Nunquam, that will get me hanged."

"Is it a crime for a man to enjoy a wedding breakfast thrown by his grandfather?"

"Where the only guests are the heads of the Lowland clans?"

MacIver shook his head. "You inherited your father's lack of imagination. 'The guests, General? My grandfather's closest friends.'"

Bridgewater rolled his eyes at the suggested explanation. "I think you should tell the clan chiefs that the army has taken some actions that concern you."

"I don't need advice from a man who was still in a clout when I'd led my thirtieth charge. I'll keep my own counsel, thank you. I have little enough reason to trust you."

"I am marrying the girl," Bridgewater said with steel in his voice. "As you asked."

"That was not all I asked. Come." MacIver waved him to his side.

Bridgewater joined him reluctantly.

"Hold out your hand." MacIver withdrew a blade from his belt.

Bridgewater felt a sickening chill. "Why?"

"'Tis time to take your rightful name."

"I have a name."

"The name isn't yours. Sorcha couldn't remove the stain of bastardy with a pen and a prayer any more than she could put the earl's ring on her finger." He laid his cane against the table and took Bridgewater by the wrist. "Open your hand."

Bridgewater unclasped his fist, and MacIver said, "Your blood spilt in fire or battle. That is how you become a MacIver."

The old man raised his blade, its edge sharpened to a gleam.

The door opened, and Panna entered. "What are you doing?" she cried.

"Panna," Bridgewater said, "you've not been formally introduced. This is Hector MacIver. My grandfather."

Thirty-two

THE ENTRANCE OF THE PRIEST AND MRS. BROWNLOW immediately after Bridgewater's introduction precluded any further activities involving the knife, a turn of events for which Panna was quite grateful. MacIver sheathed his blade, though the look he gave Jamie made it clear their tête-à-tête had been halted only temporarily.

"Is this the couple?" asked the priest, a slight man with glasses and a black cassock.

MacIver grunted.

The priest eyed Panna with a businesslike interest. "Did the groom rape her?"

"I certainly hope you don't think I'd marry a man who raped me," Panna said.

Jamie bit back a smile, but the priest, whose attention hadn't wavered from MacIver's face, waited.

"Apparently not," MacIver said.

"*Apparently* not,'" Jamie repeated under his breath and shook his head.

"Was she a virgin?"

"Aye," Jamie said firmly, and a pained look came over the priest's face.

Panna, who knew enough to follow Jamie's lead, tried to look appropriately deflowered.

"Where are your people, lass?"

"Penn's Woods. My parents are dead."

"She's under my protection," Jamie said, giving her a gentle look.

The priest *tsked*. "And this is what you consider protection?"

Jamie's cheeks colored, and he lowered his eyes.

Panna gave his elbow a reassuring touch.

"Do you understand the sanctity of the vows you're about to take?"

The priest had directed this at Jamie, perhaps assuming a woman wouldn't have the mental capacity to comprehend such a thing or that Jamie would be answering for the both of them.

"Aye," Jamie said.

"Are you able to promise your fidelity to her, in body and in spirit? Provide her with a home and such protection as you are able to offer?"

The priest imbued the word "protection" with the tiniest note of irony.

"Aye." Jamie's voice had grown softer. He looked as if he didn't quite believe what he was saying—and why should he, after all? He didn't believe in marriage and had made it clear this performance was for the sake of peace.

"The promises you're about to make, sir, last until the end of time, not a day or two, or until you tire of her and long for another."

Jamie grimaced. "Aye."

The poor man was enduring quite a lot of

humiliation on behalf of the people of the borderlands, Panna thought. She suspected the beating at Adderly's hands had been easier.

"*Forever*, sir," the man repeated. "Not a day or two."

"I *understand*," Jamie said sharply, which did little to endear him to the priest.

"This is your grandson?"

MacIver nodded.

"In your opinion, is he fit to enter into the bonds of marriage?"

MacIver gave Jamie a long look, running his tongue along the inside of his cheek. "As you know, Father, his mother was banished from the family. I've not had the pleasure of making his acquaintance until recently, though I have observed him from afar. He is an able soldier—"

"English?"

"Unfortunately, aye. And a canny investor."

"He rebuilt Bridgewater Castle," Panna said.

"He did." MacIver settled back against the table. Panna could tell his body ached. "With a fine chapel for his beloved mother."

Jamie twitched with anger, and Panna squeezed his arm.

"He's no more bullheaded than most Englishmen," MacIver added, "and I've seen one or two glimpses of an almost Scottish sensibility. I'm comfortable he'll make a decent husband for the girl. In any case, he's clearly besotted."

It was Panna's turn to flush. She stole a glance at Jamie, who kept his eyes fixed ahead.

The priest nodded, though his face made it clear he

was short of satisfied. He adjusted his glasses, opened the book in his hand, and peered at Panna. "I trust you know the man well enough to be sure of your heart?"

"I—" Her tongue seemed to have turned to a wad of cotton in her mouth, and all she could do was tighten her grip.

"'Tis an ignoble sign, you see, that he could not forestall his desires. A man like that could easily abandon you."

But it'll be I who'll leave him. "Yes, I'm sure of my heart." She was careful not to look to Jamie, who evidently was not as sure of his own.

"Then you're ready to begin?"

They were the same words her minister at home had said before her wedding to Charlie, and Panna felt a tide of emotion rise in her throat and an uncomfortable prickling in her eyes. "Yes."

The priest found the page and reluctantly began the vows. But his words were lost in the din of the blood rushing in her ears. She felt light-headed and wondered if she was about to faint. Despite her promise to Jamie as well as her own belief, the vow she'd spoken seemed to carry enormous power—more than she'd even suspected—and she felt as if she'd collapse underneath the weight.

Perhaps sensing her unsteadiness, Jamie wrapped his arm around her waist.

She didn't remember responding to anything, though evidently she had, for the priest turned to Jamie and said, "Do you have a ring?"

Jamie shook his head.

The priest sighed and gave Jamie a look that suggested this didn't surprise him. He was just turning the page when MacIver hobbled up and thrust something into Jamie's palm.

Jamie reached for Panna's hand and threaded a ring onto her fourth finger. "With this ring, I thee wed and pledge my troth."

His hand was shaking, and so was hers.

"May God bless you," the priest said, and then, just as fast as it had begun, it was over. The priest closed his book and everyone began to move. Mrs. Brownlow, who, unsurprisingly, had been crying, threw her arms around Jamie. The priest offered his handkerchief to Panna, who was stunned to discover she, too, had tears on her cheeks. And MacIver, face softened, offered Jamie his hand in congratulations. Jamie took it and nodded. He looked a bit like a man who had just won an elephant and didn't quite know what to do with it.

A bell began to peal somewhere in the depths of the castle, and MacIver sent Mrs. Brownlow to have a cask of his finest French wine opened so that his breakfast guests could toast the newlyweds.

When Panna looked for Jamie, she found him enduring a lecture from the priest on the advantages of the *agápe* over *éros*.

MacIver interrupted. "Leave us," he said to the priest.

"I was just—"

"Leave us. And take the girl."

Panna shook her head. "I'm not leaving."

The priest met MacIver's eye. MacIver made a motion with his hand. The priest scurried out, and MacIver closed the door.

"I take it you wish to see the price your husband paid for my cooperation," he said to her.

Jamie said, "Leave her out of this."

"What are you going to do to him?" Panna said.

"Listen to that," MacIver said, drawing his blade again. "She's as besotted as you."

"It's all right, Panna," Jamie said.

"'Panna,'" MacIver said. "'Tis not a name I've heard before."

"'Tis short for Pandora," Jamie said, and his grandfather chuckled.

"You're are a devotee of mythology, I see."

"My mother was," Panna said.

"Best take care not to open any boxes of trouble in my house. Your husband can tell you what that will get you."

He grabbed Jamie's hand and, in a flash of steel, drew the blade across his palm. Jamie jerked, and Panna muffled a cry of horror. A bright-red line appeared, and MacIver pulled Jamie toward the candle. He held Jamie's hand high above the flame and let the blood drip into the flickering orange, sending hot wax sputtering in every direction. He murmured something in Latin, eyes closed.

The blood overflowed the wick's base, falling in narrow streams of red down the side of the candle. Panna felt nauseous, but Jamie only stared into the face of his grandfather, eyes burning with a fire as bright as the flame's.

"Swear your oath to the clan," MacIver commanded.

"I swear my oath."

MacIver said something more in Latin, then said, "*Nunquam obliviscar.* Say it. 'Tis the MacIver motto."

Jamie pulled his hand away. "I don't need to say it. I'll never forget."

MacIver smirked. "Then welcome to the family."

Thirty-three

"HONORED LADIES AND GENTLEMEN," MacIver boomed as he ushered the wedding party into the dining hall, "'tis not every day I would welcome an English soldier to our midst."

The guests quieted instantly, and more than a few made growls of complaint. Panna, who was still in a daze, felt all eyes turn toward her and Jamie.

"For the occasion of my grandson's wedding, however, I'm willing to make an accommodation, and I hope you will be too. He and his bride eloped yesterday to Scotland"—a gasp went up—"and I was given word he wished for my blessing."

Jamie managed a stoic smile.

"They'll be joining us for breakfast only. I'm afraid his obligations preclude him from staying after for our, er, meeting."

A number of the men chuckled.

"Please give them your congratulations—Captain and Mrs. James MacIver Bridgewater."

The table managed a smattering of applause, more polite than enthusiastic, and Jamie and Panna were directed to a pair of open seats.

"MacIver is your middle name?" she whispered to Jamie.

"Edward, if I'm not mistaken."

The wine was poured, and MacIver toasted Panna and his "long-absent" grandson. Panna had never in her life been so happy to be offered a drink at eight in the morning, and she downed half the goblet's contents in a single swallow.

As the serving of the courses began, Panna's other tablemate, a woman she assumed to be the wife of one of the chiefs, said, "Many congratulations, Mrs. Bridgewater. Have you known the captain long?"

"No," Panna admitted. "This was quite sudden."

The woman, slim and in her early twenties, with fine, high cheekbones, chestnut hair, and eyes the color of a spring sky, smiled. "If I'm honest, I am surprised to hear that Captain Bridgewater married at all. I didna think anything would divert him from his career. You must be very special."

"You know him?"

"I know *of* him, of course. The exploits of the English army are tracked quite closely, even in a village as small as Annan." She waved off the servant offering slices of ham, just as she had the servant offering beef and fish pie a moment earlier. She touched Panna's hand. "May I?"

It took a moment for Panna to realize what the woman meant. Then she saw the ring Jamie had placed on her finger. In the confusion of the ceremony and oath taking, Panna had forgotten all about it. It was a gleaming cabochon emerald surrounded by white pearls and set in gold dark with age. The cabochon was as big as her thumbnail and glowed with sparks the color of Jamie's eyes.

Panna gave the woman her hand and turned, alarmed, to Jamie, who had been watching her.

"My grandmother's," he said simply. "I wanted something for you."

Rattled as much by the sentiment as by the stone, Panna returned her attention to the woman, who examined the ring and nodded appreciatively.

"It's stunning," she said. "I wish you great happiness."

"Thank you."

"Captain," she said to Jamie, "I was just wishing your bride joy. Perhaps you'd be kind enough to introduce me."

Jamie shifted awkwardly. "I beg your pardon. Of course. This is my wife, Panna Kennedy Bridgewater, lately of Penn's Woods."

"And I am Abigail Kerr—of Langholm." The woman bowed her head in greeting.

Panna bowed in return. "I'm very pleased to meet you." It was her husband whom Jamie had climbed the vines to consult.

"Your grandfather says you eloped last night," she said. "Were you married here in Annan?"

The question had been directed to Jamie, who stared at his roast beef, obviously uncomfortable.

"Aye," he said at last. "We were able to convince the priest to unlock the church with a handful of coins."

"A story you will tell your grandchildren, I'm sure."

Panna tried the ham. It was succulent and slightly smoky. "This is marvelous," she said, but neither of her companions was eating. "It must be a great source of pride to you to know how well respected your husband is among the clan chiefs," Panna said, cutting another large hunk.

Abigail blinked. "I dinna have a husband, Mrs. Bridgewater."

Jamie took a quick sip of wine. "Lady Kerr is the chief of Clan Kerr, Panna."

"Chieftess," Lady Kerr correctly softly.

The second piece of ham seemed to turn to dust in Panna's mouth. Abigail was the chief Jamie had been visiting.

An uncomfortable silence fell over their corner of the table.

"I think I need to take a walk," Panna said, standing. "The excitement has been a bit overwhelming. So glad to have met you." She bowed.

"Panna—" Jamie said.

She ran to the door.

❧

Jamie leaped to his feet and gave Abigail a quick, helpless bow. He owed her an explanation, but he owed Panna one first. Besides, what could he say to Abby? He certainly hadn't known when he'd crawled through her window a few hours ago that he was going to be forced to marry before he saw her again.

MacIver caught his sleeve. "Let her go."

"I need to—"

"Sit. Do you recall the scouts I told you I was sending out?"

"Aye, but—"

"Sit down, Jamie."

The chair nearest MacIver was occupied, but the man, hearing MacIver's words, dropped his fork and offered Jamie his place.

Jamie sank into the seat as Panna disappeared.

"One of the men has returned," MacIver said so quietly that Jamie had to lean forward to hear amid the buzz of conversation at the table. "He tells me that half the bloody English army is amassing five miles from where we sit. And you advised me to send the clans home? You're a damned spy sent by your father, and the moment my visitors leave the castle, I'll have you cut to pieces and fed to the dogs."

Jamie said, "I couldn't tell you."

"And you shall pay the price for your foolish game."

"If it weren't for me, you wouldn't have found out. Why do you think I came to you?"

"Because I can destroy England's efforts in the borderlands."

"I stand by my words," Jamie said. "You must not attack. But even you should see why now. You'll be outmanned five to one. You don't want to see a thousand of your men die."

"Who says I don't? A thousand dead could mean ten thousand raise arms in response."

Jamie shoved the plate away and brought his mouth to his grandfather's ear. "I don't believe you. A thousand dead is a thousand dead, that's all. You'll never overcome the English army. Not today. Not on this battlefield. And you'll be remembered as the man at the beginning of the end for the Scots. Listen to me: Do *not* do it. Convince your fellow chiefs to put down their arms."

MacIver laid a hand on Jamie's wrist as if he were giving him an affectionate squeeze, but his grip was as hard as forged iron. He gazed into his grandson's eyes. "You're walking a fine, fine line, Captain. Two of my men will follow you when you leave this room. You'd better pray that I'm in a happier mood at the end of this morning's council session than I am right now."

He released Bridgewater's arm and thumped him affably on the back. "Many happy returns."

Thirty-four

Bridgewater knocked tentatively on Panna's door.

"What?" she called.

"May I see you?"

With a grudging sigh, she opened it. The look on her face, neither friendly nor angry, made him wary.

"I think…I may have hurt you."

She returned to the wardrobe, which stood open, and gazed at the shelves as if she were intent on rearranging them.

"You haven't hurt me. Are things settled now with your grandfather and the clans?"

"He found out the army is gathering in Cumbria."

She didn't turn. "Good. That should convince him to call off the attack, shouldn't it?"

"I'm afraid it only made him more suspicious of my motives. It took all I possessed to convince him again that a call to put down arms would be in Scotland's best interest. In fact, I'm not sure I did convince him."

"So now the clan chiefs meet?"

"Aye, the chiefs meet." The clan chiefs and

Abigail Kerr. He lowered his head. "I'm sorry, Panna. I owe you—"

"You don't owe me anything, Bridgewater."

She'd abandoned the use of his Christian name, and he felt the loss sorely.

"I owe you the truth."

"You owed me the truth when you woke me after you were shot, not now. We're not a couple. This marriage is for show. Let's not let our game here get in the way of remembering that."

"I went to see Abigail because she's often served as my eyes and ears into the goings-on of the clans. We've been friends for many years." He saw the look on Panna's face and amended his statement. "More than friends."

"Oh God, what a position you've put me in," she said, anger turning to distress. "She seems like a nice woman. I don't want to be the person who comes between the two of you."

"Our friendship isn't like that. There is no 'between' between us—or rather, there is, but the space is open to anyone." He met Panna's eyes. "Her stipulation."

"I saw her face, Jamie."

He chewed the inside of his mouth. He hadn't thought Abby capable of anything deeper than a shared regard and pleasure—not with him at least, not when her attention was consumed with retaining the respect of her clan and keeping control of it. But he was hardly an expert at understanding women, and he would never dare doubt the look of certainty in Panna's clear, blue eyes.

"If what you say is true, I owe her an apology as well."

"As do I."

"No," he said firmly. "No, I cannot have"—he almost said "my wife"—"you apologizing to her. It would suggest a position of inferiority. I cannot have her thinking that she…" He searched for the right phrase but realized there wasn't one.

"That she what, Jamie?"

"That she takes precedence, I suppose. I'm a married man now, even if our marriage was an expedient. I won't be going to Langholm anymore. 'Twould dishonor you."

"Though our vows mean nothing?"

He hoped she hadn't seen him flinch. "I have no high opinion of my moral stature, Panna, but I'm not the sort of man who wants to be known as a husband who strays."

"And yet we'll be saying good-bye very soon, Jamie. What then?"

What was behind her question? Did she want him to ask her to stay? Or was she merely looking for reassurance that she'd be able to return to her own time? He searched her face but didn't have enough experience untangling the emotion behind those eyes to know.

"I…don't know."

She returned to the wardrobe, and he damned himself for his inability to get anything right.

"Panna?"

She stood tiptoe and grabbed three books from the wardrobe's uppermost shelf. She smiled and handed them to him.

"They were your mother's," she said. "Mrs. Brownlow said I could give them to you. It's not much, but I think it might make a nice addition to your library."

His heart swelled. He had a few letters his mother had received from her friends after she'd been banished, as well as the notes the earl had written to her, but the priest had sold or given away most of her belongings.

Bridgewater sank onto the bed and opened the first book. It was a history of Scotland, which made him chuckle. The pages most worn were the sections on William Wallace and the history of the MacIver family. The book had been inscribed by Hector MacIver: "To my beloved daughter. 'Tis time for you to learn your place in the world."

"I suppose this was given to her before she was sent away." Panna had seated herself beside him and was reading over his shoulder.

"And I have no doubt studying this was as important as studying the Bible."

"That's heresy," Panna said with a slight smile.

"Not in this place."

Bridgewater could smell the scent of lilac wafting from a sprig that Mrs. Brownlow had put in Panna's hair. He ached with a longing like hunger. How he wanted to fill himself with her.

She lifted her head, and he was too slow to hide the look in his eyes.

He reached for her cheek and brought her mouth to his. The books clattered onto the floor, but he didn't care. He had no interest in the past, only in the moment he was living now.

She made a small noise, which undid him. A storm flew across his flesh, as if a thousand tiny mortars were exploding, and his heart raced to stay ahead of it.

"I don't care about Abby," he whispered. "If banishing her to the far shores of the Shetland Islands would restore a smile to your face, I'd do it in an instant."

Panna put two fingers to his lips and drew him slowly back onto the bed.

Thirty-five

THE BED FRAME GROANED UNDER THEIR WEIGHT, BUT Panna felt as light as air. Jamie fumbled as he drew the ribbons from her laces, and she wondered if he was as affected as she. The touch of his hand on her breast sent a lurch through her belly. She pressed her mouth to his, reveling in the tang of wine there.

He explored her shoulder with his mouth, and she saw him wince.

"Are you all right?" she asked softly.

"There isn't an inch of me that doesn't hurt, but I'm determined to bed you."

She laughed, and the giddiness filled her like helium. She let her eyes trail over his body and then drew her hand along the span of his back that probably hurt him least.

"If you think that's soothing, lass," he said, "I can assure you it is not."

She laughed again.

"Come," he said. "Let's get you undressed."

They stood and he helped her out of her gown. Her heart beat against the linen of her shift as he gazed at her.

"God, you're lovely. But before we go further, there's something I need to take care of." He stepped into the hall, and she could hear the murmur of voices outside. A moment later he returned with a smile and closed the door firmly.

"What?" she demanded.

"There are guards outside, you know."

"Your grandfather is not exactly a trusting man, is he?"

"No. But I have purchased an hour of uninterrupted privacy. The guards were reluctant to make such a promise, concerned as they were about us using the windows for an escape—"

"And Lord knows you have a taste for climbing walls."

"The fact of which I am grateful they are, as yet, unaware. However, they were not immune to the appeal of a new and clearly desperate groom."

His eyes met hers, and her breath caught in her throat.

"There was a price, though," he said.

"One you paid, I hope."

"I have made a down payment, to be sure."

She looked at him, confused, before it dawned on her that her gown was nowhere to be seen.

"You gave them my *dress*?"

"They were quite satisfied a lady would not mount an escape without one."

"Then they're fools." She thought with satisfaction of her recent escape from Adderly's room.

"Not everyone knows what it means to be up against Panna Kennedy," he said, adding, "lucky for them" as an afterthought.

He skinned off his shirt, and she was again amazed at the muscularity of his chest as well as the signs, past and present, of the violence he'd endured.

She went to him, blissful, and he pulled the shift over her head, drawing her against him.

"At last I can hold you," he said.

She shivered, not from cold but from the knowledge of the journey on which they were embarking. It had been a long time since she had taken a man into her arms.

He picked her up and laid her on the bed, lights twinkling in those clear eyes. He undressed then lowered himself over her. He entered her without preliminaries, sighing as he brought his entire length inside.

"I just had to feel you," he said.

She'd been more than ready for him. He held his hips still and brought his mouth back and forth across the tight flesh of her nipple. Then he took it gently between his teeth.

"*Ooh.*"

He tugged at the other nipple, watching her from beneath his long lashes as she stretched and moaned.

"'Tis torture to be inside you," he said.

He slipped free and turned her to her side. With a single movement, he reburied his cock and brought himself against her back. "Let your hair down."

She pulled out the pins, arching for a moment as he made a few deep thrusts, and allowed her hair to fall over her back and on his chest. He brought a handful of tresses to his cheek and rubbed it there. "'Tis like rays of silken sunshine."

The mirror on the wardrobe captured them in full,

and the blood pounded in her chest as she saw herself stretched out with him behind her. He had found a thin braid and was unraveling the strands, thrusting his hips slowly as he worked. Her body responded to each movement, breasts swaying, hips moving to meet his, fingers stretching.

He caught their reflection in the mirror and chuckled, drawing a thumb from the pale curls of her pubic hair to the white mounds of her breasts.

"Oh, aye," he whispered. "I shall like to watch this."

Slowly he plucked her nipples, pulling just enough to send shock waves through her. She writhed against him, bringing his thickness tighter against her swelling bud.

She could feel him watching her, and she rubbed against him like a cat. Her nipples, always rosy, had become dark-red blossoms.

He gathered her chin in his fist and turned her head to kiss him. She wove her fingers into his hair, enjoying the prickly stubble of his face on her cheek.

His breath was more labored now, though he barely moved inside her. The loneliness she'd felt for so long seemed to be falling away. She prayed for time to stop. In the mirror, his fingers played in the curls between her legs. Then he let a thick finger dance over the tender flesh where their bodies met.

"Oh, yes."

He brought a second hand to meet the first and slipped both forefingers into her slit.

"Oh, Jamie."

He thrust his hips as his fingers plucked and tugged. Every movement drew her deeper and deeper into the rising storm of pleasure. She clasped her hands behind his neck, spread her legs, and let him ravish her.

"I'll never forget this," he said into her ear, "or you."

She felt the wave of pleasure begin to break and rode it hard, crying out shamelessly. When she relaxed, he uncoupled from her and lowered his head to her thighs.

"The pain from my wounds may kill me, but I'll be damned if I'll miss the opportunity to know the taste of you." He brought his mouth to her bud, and the wave rose again, slowly at first, and then harder and higher, until it hit the shore so fiercely and relentlessly that she buried her mouth in the sheets to drown out the choking cry.

When she relaxed, he flopped onto his back and curled an arm around her thigh. She was too limp to move, but their fingers met and laced, and he made a deep groan followed by a long, happy sigh.

"That was nice," she said.

He squeezed her hand. "There's more to come. If I can get these old bones moving, that is."

"Your bones seem perfectly fine." She traced the sturdy rib cage and iron-tight forearms. "Aching they might be. Old they are not. And as far as moving…"

Her eyes strayed to the blunt instrument swaying ever so slightly between his legs.

"Oh, that," he said.

She had been right: any familial resemblance between Jamie and his half brother ended here. Jamie was long and thick with a carpet of golden-brown fur. She wondered what it might be like to take his length in her hand and feel his desire strain against her.

Their eyes met, and his dared her to do what he knew she was thinking.

With a flush, she took hold of him, amazed as always at the silk in which such a steely surface was wrapped. She caressed him and he thickened.

"I want you like a whore," he said breathlessly, "riding me shamelessly, your breasts bouncing as I watch."

A torrent of heat scorched her belly.

"And I want you on your knees, showing me the tricks that mouth has learned. But for now," he said, "I want you just like this."

He pulled himself on top of her, his body a shield from the cares of the world, and entered her slowly. The green in his eyes sparked like lakes in the summer sun. How she would welcome mornings if each one began like this, she thought. He held her gingerly, moving as if she might break, which made her smile, for she knew he was the one in pain.

She laid a hand on his cheek, lost in a joy so deep the chirps of the sparrows outside seemed as if they might be from another time. His hips, ropey with muscle, moved hesitantly, finding the rhythm at which he might labor unpained. The lush warmth he stirred in her made her sigh. She ran a hand over the wounds in his back, hoping her touch might comfort him. He smiled.

"Do you want to finish now?" she asked. "There are things I could do…"

"I shall finish soon in any case. God help me, I am nearly undone by the look on your face and the sounds of your pleasure."

She provided more of the latter, groaning happily, and a few moments later he pulled himself free, spilling his seed with a husky sigh.

He gathered her in his arms and closed his eyes. "That," he said simply, "is an argument for heaven."

She laughed, taking in the light, soapy scent of his hair and the fragrant musk of his skin. That *had* been different from the trysts she remembered. Perhaps it was because she was older now—or perhaps the knowledge that their time together was limited had made her conscious of the emotion beneath the physicality—but her heart told her it was something else.

When she lifted her hand and gazed at the ring on her finger, the certainty suffused through her.

Admit it, Panna: the lovemaking was different because of the vow you made.

Her more pragmatic self was quick to disagree. *You know that's ridiculous. Even if you were foolish enough to have meant it, a vow like that means nothing unless each person has pledged it from the heart.*

And yet even her more pragmatic self could not deny the singular magic that had just transpired. While her experience with lovers was far from extensive, she'd bedded enough men to know the difference between bone-rattling sex and soul-quenching love.

Seeing her hand extended, he lifted his as well, and she brought her palm to his, enjoying the way his fingers dwarfed hers. The gash left by his grandfather's knife was a dark, crusty red.

"Do you still long for your husband?"

The question startled her from her thoughts but she smiled. "Charlie? I'll always miss him. He was a good man. Does it hurt?" She ducked her head toward Jamie's hand.

"I hurt in so many places I can hardly feel it. Should

I assume by your changing of the subject you don't wish to speak of him?"

"No, it's all right. He died two years ago after a long illness. We'd been married eight years."

"Do you have children?"

"No. I guess it was something we thought we'd always have time for. And then suddenly the time was gone." She realized that in Jamie's world, there was no reliable way to plan when to have children, and that even the act of pulling out prior to ejaculation was like some sort of casino game in which every player eventually loses.

"What was he like?"

"Strong. Funny. Smart. And so determined to help other people. He really taught me a lot about generosity of spirit."

Jamie stroked her hair. "Were you in love?"

A marriage based on love would be an exception in this age.

"In my time, people almost always marry for love."

He lifted his head. "In truth?"

"Yes."

He leaned back on the pillow, making a noise of surprise. "Marriage must be joyous there."

She chuckled. "You'd be surprised. While people marry for love, the same willingness to let emotion rule means marriages end in bitter fights, infidelity, and even boredom."

"But not yours?"

He'd asked without judgment, only curiosity.

"No. We loved each other till the end." She choked on the last words, reliving the terrible despair.

He squeezed her shoulders. "'Tis a cruel thing that

a marriage born of love would end so unhappily. I'm very sorry."

"I never thought I'd love another man—" She froze. Good God, what had she said? Had he caught it? His arms hadn't moved, but she was certain his breathing had changed.

He rose to an elbow and lifted her chin. "What do you mean?"

"Nothing. I'm sorry."

"If you love me—or think you might—I need to know."

She dared not say it, but he saw the truth in her eyes.

He rolled on his back and ran a hand wildly through his hair, exhaling with surprise. She felt as if she'd been kicked and struggled for a breath.

He caught her hand and tugged the ring free.

"Sit up," he commanded, jumping to his feet.

She got up blindly, hardly aware of anything but the roar of embarrassment in her head.

"Did you make your vow to me?"

"What are you saying?"

"I'm saying that before we stood in front of the priest, we agreed that our words carried no weight. Did your words carry weight?" he said, face flushed with emotion.

"Not in the way you mean."

"You didn't pledge your body to me? You didn't pledge your heart?"

"*No.*"

"Do you pledge them now? To me? Forever?"

She wasn't sure what he was asking, and his agitation was upsetting her. "'Forever' has no meaning to us, Jamie. You're sending me back to my world, and you'll stay in yours."

"Take this ring," he said, "and make your pledge. I swear I'll keep you at my side. If I have to burn down what's left of MacIver Castle to put a cork in that execrable hole, I'll do it. Pledge your troth, and I swear to you we'll never be parted."

"Jamie—"

"I know my mind, lass. Do you know yours?"

"If you know your mind," she said sharply, "speak it. You haven't shared it with me."

A crimson stain spread across his cheeks, and he dropped to one knee. Given that he was naked and half-erect, this made for a very fascinating picture.

"My heart yearns for your heart, just as my body yearns for your body. And if you can't see both plainly, then I've failed you. I can't say I loved you from the moment I saw you. I'm afraid I had other designs on you then. Despite my words, I admit my appetite was most carnal at our first meeting. And then when you spoke... God, what a wicked tongue you possess! All I could think about was getting myself between those thighs and hammering the insolence out of you."

Her heart thumped, but Jamie's excitement had stirred something more than passion in her. She felt as if she were standing at the edge of a cliff, her back to the abyss, and Jamie was telling her to let go and jump. She so wanted to believe. Her heart rose in her throat.

"You've professed your lust," she said, fighting to keep her voice steady, "but that I could have apprehended without a word. I've heard nothing from you that suggests your feeling for me rises any higher than that absurd signal flag between your legs."

He stood, and Panna saw the absurdity being replaced by something more dangerous. He looked her in the eye.

"I love you, Panna. I thought I'd die when I believed Adderly had hurt you. I've no family and few friends. You've made me feel whole, as if I'd been given a reason to live and a reason to die, both at the same time. And that terrifies me. But now that I've had it, I can't let go. Please, Panna, please, do not break the man you have made."

She touched his cheek. "I won't. Oh, Jamie, I won't."

He swept her into his arms and kissed her, a long, lingering kiss that tasted of ancient hurt and new beginnings. She didn't know what her declaration meant for them beyond this hour, but she didn't care. She knew it was right.

He took her left hand and held the ring beyond her finger. "Make your vow to me, Panna."

"I make my vow."

"And I to you."

He slid the ring on her finger and threw his arms around her. Then he lowered her onto the pillows.

"Absurd, is it?" she said.

With a casual thrust, he entered her again, and she gasped.

"I shall make you eat your words," he said. "Or worse."

This time his lovemaking was not so gentle, and Panna's flesh, already tender, burned with his fervor. His own moans made his choice of desire over comfort plain, and in a minute or two, through sheer force of flint on steel, the mound of tinder in her belly exploded a second time.

With a deep grunt, he spilled his desire between her scorched thighs in grinding thrusts that fed the fireball between her legs like blasts of oxygen. She cried out as he drew her closer, jerking her hips, until the only sound she could form was a hoarse moan. Her arms fell limp to her sides.

"God help me."

Eyes gleaming, he said, "I like the flavor marriage imparts to this." Then he flicked the tip of his tongue over his finger. "And this as well."

He stretched out beside her and for a long moment neither said anything. Panna felt as if she were being borne along on the warm waves of a tropical sea, sun on her back, buoyed by happiness that lifted her like a life preserver. For the first time in years, everything seemed effortless.

"You make love like a twenty-first-century man," she said, smiling.

One eye slitted open. "Is that a compliment?"

"Of course."

The eye closed.

"Though I didn't exactly mean it that way."

Both eyes opened. "Oh?"

"You make love very well," she added quickly. "I mean, I hope you could tell I liked it."

The color rose on his cheeks. "I liked it too."

"But I guess I expected it to be...different." She met his eyes shyly. "I wasn't sure if people of the eighteenth century...knew as much."

He snorted.

"What?"

"You're under the impression the people of your time have gotten a leg up on things, are you?"

She threw him a look regarding the double entendre, which he ignored. "Yes. I mean, obviously."

"*Obviously?*"

"You don't think an extra three hundred years makes a difference?"

"In something that's been going on between men and women since Adam and Eve. No, I do not."

"Seriously?" She sat up, tucking the sheet under her arms. "With all due respect, I think you're wrong. I know for a fact that the people of the twenty-first century have a much wider, er, range of tastes. I think mores have loosened up enough so that people don't worry so much about what's right or wrong anymore—as if there was ever anything one could do wrong in bed."

"Oh, there are quite a few things one can do wrong in bed," he said. "It took me several years and a number of very disappointed faces before I began to fully understand what they were."

Panna grinned. "That's not what I meant."

"I know what you meant, but I don't think it's true. Like you, I think the pleasures of a bed are limitless. However, I believe people have understood that for quite a long time."

She considered the shocking things she had seen on TV or read in books and shook her head. "That's simply not possible. I mean, c'mon. What's the most outrageous thing you've ever done?"

"Is this a contest?"

Panna thought of the Cleopatra costume that had

turned a drive home from Charlie's sister's Halloween party into a long and very public game of Riding Caesar's Charger. "Um…"

"Uh-huh," he said smugly. "That's what I expected."

"No, no. I'm game. Go."

"And to the winner?" he asked.

"To the winner goes the satisfaction of…" The gleam in his eyes disconcerted her. "…the satisfaction of…"

"Choosing the next game?"

She felt a slightly terrifying frisson go through her. "Sure," she said, licking her suddenly dry lips.

"My tale involves three."

Panna covered her face with her hands and collapsed on the pillow.

"You'll tell me if you wish me to stop, aye?"

The trouble was she didn't.

"An acquaintance of mine—let's call her Maria— was a woman of curiosity and varied tastes. 'Twas her express wish I witness her and her cousin explore, shall we say, the limits of their family bond."

"She *slept* with her cousin?"

"I'm afraid there was to be very little sleeping involved."

"And he agreed?"

"'He'? Maria's cousin would be offended."

Two women? *Oh God, I'm hosed.*

"These limits, it seemed, were ones they'd tested before with great success. However, they'd come to hear a rumor that gentlemen, whom they heretofore assumed would be put off by their friendly experiments, would in fact find them of the utmost interest, an idea they could hardly believe."

"And you were willing to help them settle the issue?"

"'Twas a matter of some import to Maria."

"You are too kind."

"Thank you."

"Maria's cousin—Louise, I believe her name was—was unwilling, however, to accept my word for it, either before or after. As she said, 'One might be willing to lie in order to preserve the fragile feelings of one's companions.' And so they imagined a situation in which my words would play no part."

Oh. My. God.

"Instead," he continued, "Maria rigged a rather elaborate, mmm...perhaps 'maypole' is the best way to describe it. 'Twas a full yard of pink ribbon wrapped carefully and may I say rather tightly around—"

"I get the picture."

"But their triumph was a small bell—I do believe it came off one of Maria's cats—which hung to the side, rather like a bloom on a lady's cap. Without any words on my part, the bell would either ring or not, and Maria and Louise would have their answer."

Panna pressed her lips into a line. "Ingenious."

He laughed. "So I thought as well."

She sighed with comic weariness and snuggled close to him. "So you're actually going to make me ask?"

"Ask what?" he said innocently.

"If the bell sounded."

"I believe 'a peal of St. Stephen's' was the phrase Louise used."

"Are you sure it wasn't 'appeal of St. Stephen'? I understand he was rather tall and plain looking."

Jamie began to tickle her.

"Stop, stop! I give up."

He freed her and stretched out again.

"Though it certainly explains your fascination with ribbons," she said. He extended a hand to tickle her again, but she rolled out of reach.

"Come, lass," he said, pulling her toward him. "'Tis your turn."

"How could I top that?"

"Well, there is one way."

"Hmmm."

"Shall we consider the issue settled, then?"

"I still think—"

He gave her a dangerous look.

"—that you're right. Very little has changed."

"Good girl." He clasped her hand and lifted it slightly to admire the ring.

Tiny flashes of green fire danced in the center of the stone. "I have to admit, your grandfather has excellent taste."

"It helps to be as rich as Croesus."

"To me it looks like the hill your castle sits on."

"Your castle now too, Panna." He got up on an elbow and brought her hand to his lips. His eyes were almost the color of the sky now, filled with the light from the windows. "Will you stay with me, lass? Here in my time?"

This was not the first time the thought had crossed her mind. There was a gravitas to the place that had drawn her in even before she had found herself falling in love with him. The daily life-or-death struggles were a far cry from her world of books and library administration. Poor, sweet Steve. He hadn't known when he dropped her off at the library Friday night after the disastrous blind date at Marie's that she'd be disappearing forever.

Oh God, disappearing forever.

"What is it?" Jamie released her hand.

"I'd like to stay with you, Jamie, I would—"

"But?"

"No. No 'but.' It's just that the last person to see me was this really sweet guy named Steve—"

"Ah."

"No, it's not like that…though I suppose it might have been. He was very good to me. Do you have blind dates here?"

Jamie frowned. "Blind? Like Tiresias? Or the Cyclops after Odysseus put the flaming stake in his eye?"

"It's not quite that bad, but it's close. A blind date is when a friend sets you up with a person you haven't met but who the friend thinks would be a good match for you."

"Oh, that. Aye, it happens."

"Well, that's what Steve was. The trouble is, if I don't show up again, he may be in trouble, since he was the last person to see me. But I suppose we don't need to worry. I mean, it isn't like I'd never return. The passageway is there. I'd just have to think of a reason for going away for long stretches—you know, maybe marrying a man from England, which *is* true, after all. And in any case, I'd want to see my brothers and their families occasionally, and—What? What is it?"

Jamie had draped his legs over the side of the bed and was staring, shoulders sagging, at the floor. He shook his head. "You can't go back. Or, rather, you can, but if you do, you can't return."

"What? No. I've already come back twice."

"Aye, and three times is the limit. 'Tis what Undine says."

"Your friend?"

"She's a naiad, or so she says. And sometimes I believe her. But she knows the ways of the unseen world. If she's right, you may stay here or return to your time, but if you return, the portal will be closed to you and you'll never be able to return."

Panna had seen a naiad sculpture in a fountain once in Rome—a lithe, sensuous woman curled temptingly across a giant fish—and Panna had some idea they were fairies who made their homes in water—but to find a self-professed one living in northern England…

"*If* she's right," Panna said. "You said it yourself. She may not be."

A light knock sounded, followed by a barely audible "I'm here to make the bed."

"One moment," Jamie called out. "Indeed, she may not be right," he said to Panna. Then he gave her a mournful look and reached for his breeks. "But is that really something we wish to test?"

Thirty-six

JAMIE REACHED FOR THE KNOB. THE LAST HOUR HAD been the happiest of his life, and now he might lose it all. He couldn't deny Panna her chance to return. He, more than anyone, knew what it meant to be torn from the people you loved and left alone in the world. But to have felt this elation and then have it torn away? It was too cruel to bear.

The servant on the other side of the door held an armload of linens. Jamie had gotten Panna into her shift, and he hoped the woman could help Panna with the gown. The men in whose care he had left it stood eyeing him from the far end of the hall. He signaled, and one lumbered over with the garment balled up in his arms.

"Did you enjoy your honeymoon, laddie?"

Jamie cringed. He was sorry to have had to expose Panna to such prurient remarks. On the other hand, he wouldn't have chosen to forgo the hour, not for all the tin in Cornwall—and he didn't think Panna would have, either.

"The privacy was much appreciated," Jamie said, taking the dress. "Thank you."

"What's she doing here?" the man demanded, pointing at the servant, who looked over her shoulder at Jamie.

"She's making our bed." Had they not seen the woman go by?

"You're allowed no visitors."

"She's hardly a visitor." Jamie dug in his pocket for a coin. He did not usually tip servants, but there was something about the way the woman had met his eyes...

She finished tucking the coverlet around the mattress and wiped her hands on her apron.

"Thank you," Jamie said, extending his hand.

The woman reached for the coin and curtsied. The guard escorted her out, and Jamie hurried to the door to watch them go. The woman followed the man to the end of the hall, pausing only briefly to glance at a narrow door Jamie had assumed was a closet.

He closed the bedroom door and looked at the folded note in his hand.

"What's that?" Panna said.

"I don't know." He opened it and read.

I'm waiting a mile down the Edinburgh road with a horse. Adderly knows you're at Nunquam. A warrant has been issued for your arrest. Advise.

                                                                    —*C*

Bridgewater sank onto the bed. Everything was forfeit—his wealth, his home, his commission, Panna. And perhaps his life.

"Jamie, what?"

He handed her the note. His only duty now was to protect her.

She scanned the paper. "Does this mean you're in trouble?"

"Put on your gown. We must go."

"Who was she?" Panna asked, handing back the note.

"Clare's cousin's husband's sister. The one who got word to Clare that the clans had been called. At least, I presume she is. If she was able to get to us without the guards seeing her, it must be possible for us to get out the same way." He stuffed the note in his pocket.

The door swung open and the guards entered.

Jamie leaped to his feet, putting his body between Panna and their visitors. "I paid for my privacy," he said sharply.

"English money means very little here," the shorter man said. "Not when your grandfather has sent for you."

"My grandfather can go hang," Jamie said, reaching for a boot. "And so can you."

He heard Panna's gasp but didn't see the swing. The man's blow caught him on the jaw, knocking him onto the bed.

"'Tis impolite to speak ill of your host," the man said. "Or did your father not teach you that?"

Jamie rubbed his chin and stared at the blood on his palm. He flew to his feet in a cold rage, delivering a brutal blow to the man's stomach. But when he turned, he was looking into the barrel of the other man's pistol.

"Come," the taller man said with a leering smile. "We'll see who shall hang."

The guard who'd been punched, now on all fours, vomited. "Bastard." He staggered to his feet and caught Panna by the hair. "You have such a pretty mouth. I wonder if your husband knows what to do with it." He grabbed her hair and forced her onto the bed, then reached for his breek buttons.

Panna shoved him away. "I'll bite your cock off, you bloody half-wit."

Jamie dove for the man, knocking him to the floor. With a yowl, he grabbed the man's throat.

"Let him go!" the man with the pistol yelled. His companion dug at Jamie's hands, but Jamie had thirty pounds on him and his hold was too strong.

"Promise me her safety," Jamie said, "or I'll crush your friend's throat." The man's mouth stretched open in a useless attempt to draw a breath. His face was as red as the blood on Jamie's chin.

The standing man looked from his companion to Jamie.

"If you were going to shoot me, you would have," Jamie said. "Promise me her safety or I'll crush it now."

"I promise."

Jamie released the other guard. The man rolled to his side, gasping for air, and climbed to his feet. "Let's hope your word means something this time. Step outside. My wife needs to dress."

The man gave him an impatient look. "The door stays open."

Jamie grabbed the collar of the man on the floor and dragged him into the hall, dumping him there and then returning.

"Dress quickly," he said to Panna as he pulled on

his boots. "No one will hurt you." He stood and helped Panna into her dress and shoes.

"I don't know what will happen next." He reached for his coat. "Follow my lead—and be prepared to run."

"Hurry!" the man in the hall called.

Jamie took Panna's hand.

"Wait!" she cried and ran to the ark. She grabbed the animals and stuffed them in her pockets. Then she dropped to her knees and picked up the books as well as some papers that had fallen from them. She slipped the papers in her bodice. "I don't know if we'll be back."

"We won't. Not if I have anything to say about it." Jamie leaned toward her as if to tighten her laces and whispered. "If anything happens to me, tell MacIver you carry his heir. It'll guarantee your safety."

Thirty-seven

PANNA HURRIED ALONGSIDE JAMIE, WHO MOVED AS IF he were planning to take his grandfather by the neck and throttle him when he found him.

They were led by the guards to the same high-ceilinged hall in which they'd breakfasted, only the plates had been cleared and the twenty or so clan chiefs sat ominously silent, glaring at them as they entered. MacIver no longer occupied the seat at the head of the table. He'd been moved to a chair in the middle. Robbed of his rightful place, the man looked frail and hunched. He didn't meet his grandson's eyes, which turned Panna's gut to jelly. She clutched Jamie's hand.

Another chief stood near the now-empty seat reserved for the leader of the clans. He held up a hand and pointed to a place next to the hearth. One of the guards poked Jamie with his pistol. With a look of anger, Jamie shook his way free and parked himself where the chief had pointed, inserting himself in front of Panna.

"I am Cathal," the chief said, "chief of Clan Bruce."

"I know who you are." Jamie stood straighter.

"I've taken your grandfather's place as questioner to ensure fairness."

Panna thought she heard a faint snort from Hector.

"Why have you chosen to betray your country-men?" Cathal asked.

She felt Jamie flinch, as if he'd been hit by another shot, and she willed him the fortitude to answer.

"I don't think of my visit here as a betrayal."

Several clan chiefs leaned forward, and one, a lanky young man with a pock-marked face, muttered, "English filth."

"That, I'm afraid, is what has us concerned," Cathal said. "Your grandfather has said he wants us to heed your exhortation to hold our arms. He says he relies on his intuition. Hector MacIver's intuition has led us through many a difficult time in the borderlands. But it's not enough for every man here. And Hector has agreed to abide by the will of the group, have you not?"

Hector pressed his lips together and nodded.

"You tell us to stand down, yet you didn't tell your grandfather that English troops were gathering over the border. There are many here who consider that an egregious omission."

Jamie held his tongue, though Panna could tell he was vibrating with the effort to do so.

"And you say you were in Scotland to marry, though the marriage was sudden and there is at least one here who questions your avowed ardor."

A flush came over Abby Kerr's face, and she gave Panna a regretful look.

"They consummated their vows," the guard said, "and had a lively time of it."

It was Panna's turn to redden, and Jamie gave her hand a reassuring squeeze.

"Your army has taken great satisfaction in slaughtering our countrymen. You yourself have captained regiments that have inflicted mortal harm on many of our people. In short," Cathal said, "your behavior doesna paint a picture of a man particularly worthy of our trust. However, the council has agreed to give you time to speak."

Jamie cleared his throat. "I hold the ties to my mother's countrymen as highly as I hold the ties to my own."

"Liar," someone said.

"Quiet," Abby said. "Let him talk."

"I came with a turbulent heart," Jamie said. "What I want more than anything else is peace for the people who live in the borderlands."

"That and a father's name," someone said.

"*Silence!*" Cathal ordered.

"Through an accident, I became the possessor of information which made it clear now is not the time for the Scots to do battle."

"What information?" Cathal said. "You ask us to trust you, but you dinna give us reason to. We need more than your word."

"Please, I've risked everything to come here. In fact..." Jamie paused, and Panna felt him teetering on the verge of saying something more, but he licked his lips and shook his head. "In fact, some of the risks will be quite painful to bear. I know you to be honorable men and women—honorable men and women I have met on the fields of battle. You know the meaning of fealty. The details of what I've learned or how I learned it I cannot share. In truth, there will be many who say I shouldn't have shared as much as I have, but I make my own choices and will live with the consequences."

"Hear, hear."

Panna searched the sea of faces for signs of sympathy but found little to give her comfort.

"And if I've betrayed anyone's trust here," Jamie added, "all I can say is you didn't deserve it, and I most humbly beg your forgiveness."

Abby Kerr stared, tight-lipped, into her goblet.

"The price for raising arms right now is too high," Jamie said. "You have to believe me. Stand down. Send your men home—"

"With a thousand English soldiers an hour from our door?" a chief at the far end of the table cried.

"Aye. I know it looks discouraging, but—"

"Discouraging? We'll be slaughtered by the same bloody-minded Englishmen who've burned our villages and raped our women."

"I lost thirty men at Dunkeld," another chief said.

"Don't believe the Englishman!"

"He's his father's bastard son!"

"The men of Clan Turnbull stay in the borderlands!"

The table was growing more agitated. A few men stood. Panna clung to Jamie's side.

Cathal raised his hands. "Enough!" The chiefs quieted, though the ones standing made no motion to sit. "We've heard Captain Bridgewater speak. Are there any here who would believe him? Show me your hands."

The man who said "Hear, hear," raised his hand, as did two chiefs who had sat stonily silent near the head of the table. A fourth raised his hand despite the hiss of his tablemate. Slowly, Abby's hand rose, and Panna gave her a grateful smile. But no other hands went up, not even Hector MacIver's.

Cathal gave the table another long moment to see if any more of the clan chiefs would offer their support. He needn't have bothered.

"Six for," Cathal said, "fourteen against. Hector, do you have anything to say on behalf of your grandson?"

Hector shook his head, a black look upon his face. "No."

Cathal hesitated. "This may be your only chance to affect his fate."

"He's the son of a lying English blackguard. He's chosen his fate."

The bile in his words made Panna's breath catch. Jamie swayed.

Cathal said, "The punishment for spying is hanging. 'Twill be carried out within the hour. Take them back to their room."

Jamie squared his shoulders. "What of my wife?"

"She'll be held until the close of the battle, then escorted to the Solway ferry," Cathal said. "If you have any gold upon you, I suggest you give it to her now. 'Twill be the only money she'll have."

"No," Panna said, "I won't leave."

Jamie held up a hand. "May I have your word she'll be safe?"

Before Cathal could answer, Abby said, "You have my word and the word of the council."

A balloon of panic filled Panna's chest, nearly choking her. "No, wait! You need to listen. Jamie can't tell you, but I've taken no such oath—"

"Panna, no."

"The English army won't attack unless you do. The queen's commands don't allow it. All you need to do is wait three days, and the army will return south. That's all the time they've been given."

A silence so complete fell over the room, Panna could hear the breathing of the hounds that lay under the table.

"She lies to save her husband's skin," someone whispered.

One of the chiefs said, "I canna allow the safety of my clan to depend on the word of the wife of an English officer."

"We should hang her too."

A fevered commotion broke out at the table, stopped only by Hector's clear voice. "She's as guilty as he is. She shall share his fate."

"No!" Jamie cried, and the guards immediately pinned his arms.

Hector rose from his seat and made his way to Jamie. "'Tis the worst sort of by-blow who shames both sides of his blood. You're a disgrace." Then he spit on Jamie's boots.

"And you're a liar."

Hector grabbed his shirtfront and shoved his grandson hard against the wall. "Take this piece of English offal to the pig house," he said to his guards, his eyes blazing into Jamie's. "They may await their fate in the shite. And as for the wench," he added to Panna, "do you see the box of trouble you have opened here? See if you can do the same there."

She wished she still had her box cutter. She would gladly have shoved it into his neck.

Another guard took her arm, and she kicked his shin.

"Cunt," the man said, and cracked her across the face.

With water running from her burning eye, Panna was led with Jamie through the bowels of the castle into the blinding daylight of the courtyard and down a rise to the animal pens. There, they were shoved past pigs voicing irritated squeals into a small, wooden structure stacked high with stinking piles of straw.

One of the guards searched Jamie while another grabbed the books from her arms. "A lot of good they'll do you here." He tucked the books under his arm. "What do you have in your pockets?" He reached for her again, taking a generous feel of her ass. "Wait, what's this?" He pulled out the handful of animals from Noah's ark and laughed. "And you two will be the pair of pigs." He tossed the animals onto the floor and crushed them with his boot. Then the guards left, and the lock was fastened behind them.

Jamie pulled her into his arms. "Did he hurt you?" He lifted her chin and winced at the sight of her throbbing eye. "Oh God, I've failed you. I can bear everything else but not that."

"No," she said. "If it weren't for me, you wouldn't be in this mess."

"Satisfying as it may be, 'twill do us no good to sit here excusing each other's guilt. We've got to look for a way to escape." He walked the tiny perimeter, quietly pressing his shoulder against the wall as he moved. "As sturdy as a fort," he said.

Panna crouched, the crushed animals bringing her inexplicably to tears. Only a fox remained unbroken. She picked it up. "Oh, Jamie."

"Come." He helped her up and guided her to a large, wooden box with a lock, then sat down and pulled her onto his lap.

"Your grandfather surprised me," she said. "I'd thought perhaps…"

"I know." He tucked her head into the curve of his neck.

"He even joked with me about my name."

"He sways with the wind. Today's wind was a strong gust away from compromise."

She ran her hand along his cheek. "Everyone's abandoned you. And you don't deserve it."

"*You* haven't abandoned me, Panna. You came back for me twice."

"What sort of a box *have* I opened? Your grandfather was right: I'm like my namesake. I should—Oh my God! My namesake!" She jumped up. "Get up! Get up!"

When he stood, she tried to lift the lid, but it was locked. "Why would a box in a pig house be locked?"

"I don't know." Jamie gave the lock a calculated kick and it dropped into the mud.

Panna pulled open the lid and found…nothing.

"There's nothing in here."

"What did you expect?" Jamie asked.

"I don't know. 'Do you see the box of trouble

you've opened here? See if you can do the same thing there.' There was just something about the way Hector looked at me when he said that."

Jamie's brows went up and he got on a knee, feeling along the bottom of the box. "There's a finger hole at each end."

"A what?"

He didn't bother to explain. Instead, he pulled the bottom up and handed it to her. She looked in. "There's a ladder!" she whispered. "It goes to a tunnel!"

He picked up the lock. "Go! As quickly as you can."

She slipped the fox in her pocket and stepped into the box. It was barely wide enough for her shoulders, but she was able to find a foothold and descend into the darkness below. Jamie followed, closing the lid and replacing the floor as he went.

The passageway smelled of rotten food and dirt, and was so narrow that Panna had to turn sideways to move forward.

"Where does it go, do you think?"

"If I know a Scot, and I do, to a store of whiskey and, I hope, a door to the outside."

Jamie was right on both counts. After at least a hundred feet of pitch darkness and cobwebs, they found themselves in a tiny storeroom filled with barrels and lit only by the light seeping in from a trapdoor in the ceiling. A ladder leaned against the wall below the trapdoor.

"Lord," Jamie said, taking a deep sniff. "This is *fine* whiskey. 'Tis a shame we can't take some."

"Perhaps you and your grandfather will be able to share a glass someday. He saved you, Jamie."

He nodded. "Saved *us*."

"It was you. He has no other family."

"And that's the reason he didn't speak for me. If he had spoken up—"

"They wouldn't have trusted him," she said. "He was able to send us to the pig house because they thought he was on their side."

Jamie grinned. "Damned canny Scot."

Panna began up the ladder.

"Ah, ah, ah." He caught her arm. "I go first. We don't know what's out there."

She let him lead. He removed the door in the ceiling, just as he had on the other end, and a load of dirt tumbled onto her head. He gave her a sheepish look. "Apologies. But the news is good. We seem to be in the middle of a stand of oaks."

He helped her out. Nunquam was visible through the trees. They were within shouting distance of the gates, which sent fingers of fear walking down her spine.

"Where's Clare?" she whispered.

"A mile down the Edinburgh road, which luckily"—he gave the shadows a quick look—"is in the opposite direction, right over that hill."

They stole through the trees, and every crack of twig underneath their feet made Panna start. At one point, a distant dog barked, and she expected a pack of hounds to come bounding into view, followed by several hundred clansmen with swords. Jamie insisted on keeping off the road—wisely, she had no doubt—but the path through the trees was hard on her kitten-heeled mules. This *Three Musketeers* stuff was definitely losing its shine.

Yet that would be what she was choosing if she decided to remain here with Jamie. For the first time since he'd told her she couldn't come back if she returned to the twenty-first century, she had a chance to think about what that might mean.

Her parents were dead, but her brothers were still alive and would be for many years. Could she go without seeing them and cheering their children from the sidelines?

The sidelines.

That's what it would be. She wouldn't remarry. She knew that in the core of her being. Whatever she'd been thinking when she agreed to marry Jamie, her feelings were very different now. That was his ring on her finger, and she would hold their vows sacred, even if three hundred years separated them. And that would mean she'd never have a child if she returned, or make a family as her mother had done, or die surrounded by her children and grandchildren. She'd work at the library and be the good aunt and live at the margins of other people's lives. Could she deny herself the profound joy of intimate love and a family she might enjoy if she stayed here, in the past? Perhaps more important, could she deny that to Jamie?

"You're quiet," Jamie said.

"I've been thinking about you."

He squeezed her hand and smiled.

"I don't want to leave you," she said.

"I know it, lass. I know it."

❧

And know it he did. Which made every moment they shared infinitely precious to him. He'd taken a vow to protect her, and until she was safely out of Scotland, he wouldn't be able to rest. Out of Scotland and, if she'd agree to it, out of England as well.

He'd lose everything. Once the idea would have destroyed him, but he'd won something more important than money or glory or even the acknowledgment of his father. He'd won the love of a remarkable woman. And he loved her in return. For the first time in his life, he belonged to someone, which made everything else seem inconsequential.

The call of a nightingale split the morning air.

He paused, and Panna frowned.

"What?" she asked.

He shook his head and whistled the call in return.

The sound of footsteps came through the forest, and in a moment, Clare came into view with two horses on a lead. He bounded toward Jamie. "There isn't much time, sir. Adderly's issued a warrant for your arrest. Men are gathering at the ferry crossing."

Jamie snorted. "Did they think they could take me by storming Nunquam?"

"Perhaps they were counting on your grandfather to hand you over obligingly." Clare smiled. "I myself would have placed money on it."

Jamie looked at Panna. Hector had surprised them all.

"How did your plea to the council go?" Clare asked.

"Poorly. You'd have thought an English spy had stolen into their midst."

Clare didn't laugh. He'd heard the kernel of truth in Jamie's words. "What happened?"

Jamie sighed. "A sentence of hanging. Though it wasn't much of a trial."

Clare's eyes widened. "How did you—"

"We found an escape tunnel, courtesy of my grandfather."

Clare nodded approvingly. "Blood is thick."

"And surprising," Jamie said. "I'm glad to know I still have a few allies left." He thumped Clare on the back. "I have friends in Savoy, near Turin. Whatever the state of my reputation here, I know I can always find work as a soldier there."

"How can I help? Can I deliver Miss Kennedy somewhere for you?"

"No, Clare, you can't," she said. "Jamie and I are married now."

She held up her hand to show off the ring, and Clare's face broke into a lopsided grin. He gave her a courtly bow. "Best wishes for your happiness, milady."

"She'll need them," Jamie said with a sigh. "'Tis a rather unlucky alliance at this point."

Panna scoffed, and he luxuriated in the feel of her arm around his waist.

"You got married, Captain Bridgewater?"

Jamie turned. He hadn't seen Clare's companion, who had been standing quietly behind one of the trees.

"Thomas!" he exclaimed. "How are you?" The boy's arm was in a sling, and he stepped toward Panna, eager to get a look at the ring.

"Better, sir, thank you. The surgeon says I shall have the use of it again within a month or so."

"Though he is not to play hoops or climb any trees until then," Clare said sternly, and Thomas, who had evidently not been as attentive to the surgeon's wishes as he should've, kept his eyes averted.

"'Tis as big as a beetle," the boy exclaimed, admiring the emerald.

"I told him I thought it looked like one of the hills of Cumbria," Panna said.

"Oh, I beg your pardon," Jamie said. "This is Thomas Heatherton. He's one of the rebels."

Panna smiled. "I believe I recall you speaking to the earl about him." She shook Thomas's hand.

Thomas scratched his nose. "The surgeon also told me to tell you he's glad for a broken bone now and then—that he can do without the pistol and knife wounds that make up your usual custom."

"That's what he said, is it?" Jamie said, chuckling. He pulled several coins from his pocket and put them in Thomas's hand. "Be sure he gets these, will you?"

The boy nodded.

"I'm glad to see you in one piece. The rebels need you." He tousled the boy's hair.

"Thank you, sir. 'Twas kind of you to come for me."

"Thomas was the one who found out about the warrant," Clare said.

"Oh? How?"

"'Twasn't me exactly," Thomas said. "Clare says I must keep my distance from Lord Adderly and his men for a bit. 'Twas my sister, Rose. I had her run behind the line of children following the laundry maids from the castle to the river. Nancy, the head maid, was telling the other maids what she'd overheard. Lord

Adderly is very particular about his shirts, you see, and the one he'd taken off when he arrived this morning was bloody. Nancy was telling Jane, the newest maid, how to get the stains out when Nancy overheard his lordship telling his secretary to draft a warrant for your arrest. Nancy pretended not to hear, of course—the best way to keep hearing more, she said to the other maids—and hurried out with Jane."

"I see. Well, remind me to speak to Nancy about her impertinence the next time I see her."

"He called you a bloody bastard," Thomas said matter-of-factly then looked at the ground and reddened. "I probably shouldn't repeat what he said about Mrs. Bridgewater."

Jamie cleared his throat. "No. Probably not. Well, please thank Rose for me. How old is she now?"

"Six."

"And please give her this one, aye??" He slipped another coin into the boy's hand. He turned to the horses. "Where did you get this one, Clare?"

"Well, the one is mine, of course. As to the other… well, let us just say I hope the army doesn't do a close count of its beasts anytime soon."

Jamie laughed. The horse was a beautiful chestnut-brown mare with lively eyes. She'd be an excellent ride.

"What will you do?" Clare asked.

"We'll buy ourselves onto a boat near Gretna and cross the firth," Jamie said. "That way we avoid the ferry as well as the troops stationed in the town. From there we'll go to Whitehaven for a ship to Dublin, and from there to Amsterdam and on to Savoy."

Clare pursed his lips, considering.

"You'll go through Cumbria? You don't want to try Edinburgh?"

Bridgewater looked at Panna. Clare was right. Though Whitehaven was the nearest port of sufficient size to offer a ship on which they could book passage, they'd have to travel within a few miles of Bowness to get there. How much risk was he willing to take?

"Whitehaven is closer," Jamie said at last. "And there are ways to avoid the soldiers. I think we'll do all right."

Clare shrugged.

"Can you get to the rebels?" Jamie said. "I don't know what Adderly has planned nor whether he intends to follow the warrant for my arrest with additional warrants for them. They need to be prepared, especially if the clans are going to attack the army."

"The clans are going to attack?" Clare paled. "They'll be slaughtered."

"Aye." Bridgewater felt his own helplessness. "I've done all I can do. All we wanted was peace. We might as well have been trying to harvest the stars."

"You did your best, Jamie. We all did." He thrust out his hand.

Bridgewater wavered slightly. He'd be saying goodbye to the one man he could call his friend. And they would likely never see each other again.

The handshake turned into a rough hug.

"If you are in want of money," Clare said when they broke apart, "I have a wee bit—"

"You're kind. I put some money aside in Whitehaven for just this sort of thing. Not a lot, but enough to get us to Savoy."

Clare climbed onto his horse, and Bridgewater turned to Thomas.

"You're a brave lad. You do the rebels honor. I want you to find your sister and take her back to your father's house in St. Cadoc. For the next few days, the borderlands will be no place for children."

"But, sir—"

"My orders. You are too valuable a spy to lose in a foolhardy battle. Promise me."

The boy looked down, petulant. "I promise."

"I'll never be able to thank you enough for what you've done for Jamie and me," Panna said to the boy. "You've helped save our lives. I'm honored to have made your acquaintance." She shook his hand solemnly, and his eyes lit with pride. "I must thank you, too, Clare."

Clare nodded and took the lad's good arm. He pulled him into the saddle behind him.

Bridgewater met Panna's gaze. It was time to leave.

He helped her into the saddle and got on behind her. This would do until he could he could get them to Whitehaven.

"Good luck." Clare geed his horse to a trot. "And congratulations on winning your lady's hand."

I have won *it*, Bridgewater thought proudly. She'd come to him, against all odds. She'd agreed to marry him, against all odds. And then she'd told him she loved him, against all odds. He'd never be as happy as he was this very moment, and if this was all he was ever given, it would be far more than he deserved.

Clare and Thomas disappeared into the woods, and Bridgewater brought his arms around Panna's waist and flicked the reins. "I hope you don't mind a little rough travel. The way we'll be going, there aren't any roads."

"I like anything with you."

❧

Within an hour, they had reached Gretna, near the eastern tip of the Solway Firth. An hour after that, they were back in England, angling west again, although Jaime was taking care to stay off the roads. Perhaps it would have been safer to avoid Cumbria altogether and catch a ship at Tynemouth on the North Sea, but his stash of money was in Whitehaven, and unfortunately they couldn't survive on love alone.

Panna had been unusually quiet for the last quarter of an hour, though he could hardly blame her. He'd been putting this off, but he knew he couldn't delay further. He pulled the horse to a stop and climbed down to look at her directly.

"I don't take your accompaniment for granted," he said, reaching for her hand. "Despite what I said back there to Clare, I don't assume that the voyage I'm embarking on includes you." She opened her mouth to speak and he stopped her. "Please," he said. "Let me finish. I've asked you to give up your family and friends, your library, and everything you know about the world. No one should have to do that. I've lived without a family, without anyone, for so long. I'd never wish it on someone else. I love you, Panna, but I'll get you to that chapel if that's what you choose."

Her face was brimming with emotion, and she

clasped his hand tightly. "Would you come to the future with me?" she asked.

He blinked. The thought hadn't crossed his mind, perhaps because he had an obscure fear of finding out what the future held or perhaps because there was a part of him that still didn't quite believe such travel was possible.

"I-I-"

Her eyes clouded. "If you don't want to—"

"No!" he cried. "No. I would happily accompany you. Do you think I... What I mean to say is, do you think there's a place for a soldier like me in your time?"

She broke into a tender smile. "Unfortunately, there is. Oh, Jamie! You'd come to my time? There are so many things I want to show you!"

He chuckled. "I hope I'm prepared for it. If the rest of your world is anything like you, I shall require a sizable anchor just to keep from being swept away. I'm still reeling from the notion of tofu turkey. Is it perhaps East Indian?"

She laughed, but then the joy left her face so quickly he felt as if a storm *had* blown over him.

"I just remembered not everyone can go through the passage," she said. "My friend Marie tried. For her, it was like trying to go through a wall."

"Oh." The happiness that seemed so certain only a moment ago was gone, replaced again by dark uncertainty.

Panna stroked his cheek. "I'll never leave you, Jamie. Never. If you can't be with me in my world, I'll stay with you in yours. I promise."

He leaned his head against her hip, and she caressed his hair. The comfort of her touch was overwhelming.

"You're worse than a Siren," he said, groaning happily. "We need to be on our way. Together."

"Yes."

He climbed into the saddle again. "Let's make our last journey, then, whatever it is."

Thirty-eight

THEY'D AGREED THAT THE CASTLE COULD NOT reasonably be approached until nightfall—not with a warrant out for Jamie's arrest and every soldier between there and Newcastle as well as half the clansmen in Scotland looking for him. Jamie had led them to a safe house on the outskirts of Bowness, a small cottage owned by the elderly parents of one of the rebels, people known to provide medical care to people in need. Their hosts had laid out a generous spread for dinner, but Panna had been too nervous to eat more than a roll and a few bites of sausage.

Now, they sat on stools in front the house, watching the foot and horse traffic on the main road in the distance. Jamie and the man, whose name was William Hillier, shared pleasantries about the coming harvest, and Panna considered how different her life would soon be. She gazed at the distant towers of MacIver Castle and the peaked roof of the chapel. Whether Jamie could make it through the passageway in the chapel or not, every day from here forward would be nothing like her life had been for the past three years. The thought made her both nervous and very happy.

William's wife, Sarah, emerged from the house carrying two tattered red coats, a relatively clean shirt, breeks, and a pair of boots. Jamie caught Panna's eye.

"Have you ever wanted to play soldier?" he asked.

While she might have wanted to once, what she'd seen so far in the borderlands had certainly made that desire disappear. Nonetheless, she followed Jamie inside the house and into a back room. Their plan was to wait until the change of watch at ten and, with hats pulled down low, march through the ruins at the rear of the castle like two soldiers on duty, and reenter through the door near the ruins Jamie had exited a few nights earlier.

Panna looked at the uniform skeptically but lifted her arms so that Jamie might undo the ties on her gown.

"Seems a shame to waste such a fine undressing by putting you right back into another set of clothes," he said.

"Do you keep such things all over Cumbria?"

"By 'such things,' do you mean houses, uniforms, or kindly parents?"

She laughed and her gown fell free. "All three, I guess."

"The rebels dare not have a base camp for fear of being attacked. As such, it is most convenient to have a few dozen lairs tucked around the countryside. There's a cave with pistols and gunpowder in Tarraby, a barn in Longtown with bandages, splints, and blankets, and even a brothel in Carlisle with a set of clothes so fine it could get a man in to see the queen herself."

Panna pursed her lips. "Not in your size, I hope."

He cleared his throat. "Er, no."

"Hm." She pulled on the breeks and buttoned them. Jamie gathered the dress while she pulled on the boots.

"Wait!" she cried. She dug in the pocket of the gown. "The fox," she said, pulling the figurine out triumphantly.

"God, I love the look of you." He gave her a frankly desirous glance. "Like a modern Diana, ready to ride into battle."

She pulled him into her arms and kissed him.

He said, "How I should like to lay you on this bed and take those breeks off again."

"Do you often feel that way about your fellow officers' breeks?"

"If they filled them out like that, I would."

She grinned, lifted her arms, and, with a tug, he removed her shift. Something hit the floor.

"What's this?" She stared at a folded piece of paper until she remembered. "Oh, that's right. This was on the floor under the bed in your mother's old room. I think it fell out of one of the books." She pulled the clean shirt over her head and donned the coat. "Oh, Jamie, I'm so sorry we lost her books and the rest of the animals from the ark."

"The fox is enough," he said, taking it from her hand. "Thank you for saving it for me."

She opened the paper and discovered it was a handwritten note. She read the first few lines. "It's from the earl to your mother. Oh, *Jamie*."

He took it from her outstretched hand and read it himself. When he finished, he sank onto the bed. "He's my father."

"Did you doubt it?" She sat beside him and patted

his arm. "'I look forward to meeting our son.' He wrote it, Jamie. He wrote that to Sorcha. Is this the year of your birth?" She pointed to the date written in clear script at the top.

He frowned. "No, it's two years after. I don't understand. She died a few weeks after I was born."

"Not according to what Mrs. Brownlow told me. She said she visited your mother and you when you were just old enough to hold a turkey bone on your own. You had to be at least six months old."

"I can hardly believe it." He clutched the letter as if it might disappear.

"Your father wrote the letter to her while Sorcha was in the care of Father Giles. It was after she left your father to have her baby. Your father said he loved her. Did you know they'd seen one another after he'd married Adderly's mother—Wait. Was it after he'd married Adderly's mother?" Panna had only the barest grasp of the timeline.

"Aye," Jamie said automatically, still staring at the note. "My father married a week after I was born."

"Oh, your poor mother. You can show him this. It's in his hand. He signed it. You can say—"

"I can, Panna, but 'twill make no difference. He doesn't acknowledge me."

"This will *force* him."

"You mistake a legal acknowledgment for one of the heart," he said gently. "I have no use for the first."

"Oh." Of course, that would be the only thing that mattered. She put her arm around him and squeezed. "Well, at least you know now. If you had even an inkling of doubt, it should be gone."

"Why can't he acknowledge me?" he said sadly. "Other men have bastard sons."

"I know it's hard to hear, but the only thing you can do is to let go of your desire for him. I ached for Charlie for two years. Some of it I had to do. But there comes a time when it's time to let go. I can't believe I'm saying it, but it's true."

Jamie laced his fingers into hers. "Thank you. Come. Let us see if we pass muster."

Their hosts were enchanted with Panna as a soldier, though Sarah did offer her the whispered advice to "keep her arms crossed as much as possible."

Jamie had declined to ride with her on the grounds that "two soldiers sitting that close would certainly catch *someone's* attention," and Panna was just about to mount the horse when there was a commotion in the distance involving a wagon and several soldiers. One of the soldiers was walking toward the cottage.

Jamie and Panna exchanged a wordless glance and slipped inside. When the door was closed, Jamie armed himself with a sword hanging over the fire. He took a position just out of sight near the open window and Panna waited near the back door.

The soldier told Hillier there was a woman in the wagon who was out of her head, repeating the name "Jamie" over and over: Would the gentleman and his wife be willing to look after her?

William said he would check with his wife and went to the door.

"Is this woman not your wife?" the soldier said, evidently referring to Sarah.

"Sister!" Sarah cried in great distaste. "Please. I have my standards."

"Damn your mouth, wench," William said, and went inside. When the door closed, he mouthed, "A trick?"

Jamie pondered for a moment then shrugged. "Say aye," he mouthed back.

"Are you willing to let her stay?" William said more loudly to Panna. "Perhaps she'll have a coin or two to spare us."

Panna realized she had a part to play. "I suppose. A night or two. No more." It had been her best approximation of a northern English accent, though she had seen Jamie wince when she'd spoken. "Perhaps his wife was born in Penn's Woods," she whispered after William had slipped back out.

"Doubtful," Jamie said with a grin. "Cumbria men aim a bit higher."

By the time the soldiers carried the woman into the house, Jamie and Panna were hidden in the trees behind the barn. When Sarah gave the all-clear sign, they returned.

The woman was covered in dirt and dried blood. She had two black eyes, and both were swollen shut. Her clothes were torn. She'd obviously been brutally attacked. Panna was so shocked at her appearance she didn't see the look on Jamie's face.

"*Undine.*" He looked as if he'd seen a ghost.

The woman struggled to open her eyes. "Jamie? Is that you?"

"Who did this to you?"

"Your brother."

Jamie's face went rigid. "He'll never do this to another, I promise you."

"Jamie, he knows."

"Knows what?"

"About her." Undine looked at Panna, and Panna felt an uneasy shiver.

Jamie turned to William and Sarah. "Can we have a moment alone?"

They ducked out and closed the door.

"Undine," he said, taking her hand, "this is my wife, Panna. We married this morning. What does Adderly know?"

"That she's from the future."

If Adderly truly possessed this knowledge, Panna knew she was in great danger. The flash of worry in Jamie's eyes confirmed it.

"How?" Jamie demanded. "How could he know this?"

"He's been to the future," Undine said. "To a library in the colonies."

Panna gasped. "There's a statue of him in my library," she said. "I thought it was you. I mean, it looks just like you. I thought you were him when we met."

"Adderly went to Panna's library?" he said to Undine. "In Panna's time?"

"No—" Panna said firmly at the same time that Undine said, "I don't think—"

They both stopped, and Panna gestured to Undine to speak first.

"I don't know which library he visited," Undine said, "but I know he bedded the library keeper there."

Jamie turned to Panna.

"Not me, I can assure you," she said.

"The woman's name was Clementina," Undine said.

Panna's mind raced as she tried to work the story out. "The statue's been there since the library was built. I assumed it was given by one of his descendants. The librarian he bedded was the founding librarian, a hundred years before me. He presented himself as a descendant of John Bridgewater, and he gave the library a lot of money."

Undine shifted on the mattress, and Panna saw the bruises on her legs. What sort of brute would do that to a woman?

"He visited three times. When he returned here the third time, the passageway was closed to him forever. That's how I knew. I'm sorry I didn't tell you when you came to me," Undine said softly. "I try to keep men's secrets. If I had known you were in love with her..." She looked at Panna.

"Don't worry yourself. Adderly came to you?"

"Aye. This morning. He wanted to know what you knew. I didn't want to tell him."

"And he beat you?"

"Aye. He thought I was dead."

She tried to lick her cracked lip, but the swelling was so large her tongue couldn't reach it. Panna poured a cup of water and held it to Undine's mouth so she could drink.

"That's the only thing that saved me," Undine said, giving Panna a faint smile. "After he left, I made it as far as Drumburgh, looking for you, but I must have fainted. The next thing I knew, I was lying in a wagon on the road to Bowness."

Jamie patted her arm.

"I'm sorry," Undine said. "I didn't want to tell him that you were asking about time travel, but he made me."

"William and Sarah will see to it you're cared for," he said. "You'll stay here until you're well. Everything will be taken care of."

"Jamie, he's so jealous of you. In the end, you both lack the same thing: the acknowledgment of a father."

Jamie hung his head. "How much I would've liked to have a brother."

He unfolded himself from the bed and led Panna out. Sarah was stacking the dishes from dinner.

"Will you and William—"

"Of course," Sarah said. "We'd be happy to. Don't worry about your friend. We'll take care of her."

Jamie put a handful of coins on the table. "It's all I have."

"It's more than enough. I haven't forgotten what you did for Robert."

William was nearby, gathering apples in his small orchard, when Jamie and Panna emerged. The warm violet of twilight was quickly being replaced by the blue-black of night. "I fear every moment we stay now in this time," he said under his breath. "Adderly will stop at nothing till he possesses you."

"But I know so little about this time—or what comes after."

"A little will be all it takes. A man like Adderly measures himself only by the power he possesses. The possibility of knowing even a bit of what the future holds would be more alluring than gold."

"You're scaring me."

"I mean to scare you. Adderly's a dangerous man. We must get you out of Cumbria."

"I can't believe he was a war hero."

"A war hero?"

"At the Battle of Ramillies."

Jamie gazed at her blankly.

"There's a statue of him in my library that says, 'Hero of the Battle of Ramillies.'"

"The statue you thought was of me?"

"Yes. And I had...well, developed a certain level of interest in finding out more about him."

He narrowed his eyes. "I see."

"When I looked him up, it said he really was the hero of the Battle of Ramillies—that the French called him 'Le Fantôme Rouge' because he'd managed to carry so many wounded men on the front lines to safety without being hit."

Jamie chuckled. "I'll be damned. I suspected he'd started the stories. I had no idea history would have gotten her grip on them and held on."

"You're saying it didn't happen? There were no wounded men?"

"Oh, it happened. Only Adderly wasn't Le Fantôme Rouge."

She saw the truth in his eyes. "You were."

William walked up, lugging a basket of crab apples. "First of the season," he said, and offered one to the horse, who took it happily. "How's the lassie?"

"Her name is Undine," Jamie said. "Sarah said she would take care of her."

"Aye, I thought she might. The mother in her, you know. You needn't worry, lad. Sarah checked her when she came in. Several of her fingers are broken and a rib or two, but she'll recover."

"Thank you, William. 'Tis time for us to take our leave."

The man put down the basket and picked up the sword and sword belt he had set against the door frame. "Take this. Please."

Jamie lifted the weapon from the scabbard and balanced it in his hand. Panna could see the name "Robert Hillier" engraved on the hilt. Jamie bowed deeply. "You do me a great honor."

Sarah appeared in the doorway with the red coats in her arms, and a stillness came over her as she watched Jamie swing the sword in a gentle arc.

He returned the sword to the scabbard and undid the belt, buckling it around his waist. He shrugged on one of the coats and helped Panna into the other. Then he lifted Panna onto the horse.

"Take care of yourselves," William said.

"We will." He shook William's outstretched hand. "Thank you."

Jamie was silent as they made their way toward the main road, Panna on the horse, Jamie walking beside her.

"Robert is their son?" Panna said at last.

"Aye."

"What did you do for him?"

He sighed. "I buried him."

Thirty-nine

EVEN IN THE DARKNESS AND DRESSED AS SOLDIERS, THE fear of being discovered put Panna on edge. Jamie walked a good distance in front of her horse, as if she and he were strangers.

"There are enough new soldiers in Cumbria from the south that an unrecognizable one shouldn't cause any concern," he'd said. "Just keep your hair tucked into your hat and your coat buttoned. If you're stopped, grunt an answer and keep on going."

But she was more worried about him. He *was* recognizable, not to mention wanted, which was why he'd insisted that they walk to the castle separately.

Jamie gave the signal to leave the road, and she followed him to the bank of the river, where the horse waded in far enough to drink. The firepots were burning, giving the castle a menacing look, and she could see the silhouettes of soldiers along the ramparts and clustered at the front gate. She couldn't imagine how they would manage to get past them all.

"Are you all right?" he said. He was crouching by

the water a dozen feet from her and making a show of washing his hands.

"Yes."

He chuckled. "Every soldier says that before a battle. I know you're scared. You should be. 'Twill help keep you safe. Do you know the ruins?"

"Yes."

"There's a door there behind a pile of rubble upon which three almost perfect cubes of rock sit."

"That's the door I went out on my way to Clare's house."

"Aye. However, there is no handle on the outside. On either side of the door are stones carved to look like friars. The one to the left of the door can be removed. You'll have to work it with your nails. Try catching the man's nose. Once out, you can reach the inner latch and let yourself in. Just remember to return the friar to his proper place."

"Won't you be ahead of me?"

He hesitated. "That's the plan."

But plans do not always work as they're supposed to, and he wanted her to be able to escape if something happened to him.

"Once you're inside, throw the bar across the door. It will keep anyone and anything out for a good ten minutes."

She understood, but whether she'd actually do it if Jamie was on the other side was another matter.

"We'll leave the horse tied here. We may need him again. Otherwise, the army will find him in the morning."

"Got it." She slid out of the saddle and tied the lead

around a nearby branch. She knew she couldn't give Jamie a kiss. And she understood quite well this might be the last moment they'd have to speak freely before they went through the passageway in the chapel.

He stood and gazed at her, as always completely attuned to her thoughts.

"In a quarter of an hour, all of this will be behind us," he said.

"I know."

"We'll never be separated. I won't let it happen."

"Nor I."

"Look." He pointed to the sky. "Do you see the Butcher's Cleaver?"

The heavens were a swirling sea of sparkling stars, and the double star he had shown her that night seemed to sparkle when she found it. "Yes."

"That's us, lass. We shall dance as they do, be as close as they are, and someday we will collapse upon one another, our eternities melded just as our lives once were."

She didn't have the heart to tell him that the stars were six trillion miles apart and would never, ever get any closer. "I love you, Jamie."

"And I you."

She held her open hand out to him and slowly squeezed it closed—as close to a hug as she could give. He did the same.

"I've never met a woman like you, Panna. You've certainly lived up to your name."

She laughed. "My mother would be pleased to hear you say it."

"Are you ready?"

She nodded. "Let's do it."

Jamie went first, walking purposefully down the road, around the castle, then up the rise to the ruins. She followed, taking care to walk as much like a man as possible. An actress friend of hers once told her that all she had to do was walk as if she owned the world and was sporting a pair of mangoes between her legs.

Jamie disappeared among the ruins. She could hear the buzz of distant conversations, laughter, and footfalls. The troops were out in force everywhere around them.

She passed the half-wrecked walls of a room still standing amid the rubble, fifty or sixty feet from the door.

"You there."

She froze. Two soldiers were lumbering up the hill toward her. She lowered her tricorne to hide as much of her face as possible.

"Are you from around here?" said the heavier of the two, eyeing her more closely.

"Mm-mm." She nodded. They stank of alcohol.

"We're new in town," the other said. "Where do you find the whores?"

"In Bowness," she said gruffly. "Down the road a bit."

"Who's the cheapest?"

"Ask for Clare. You'll get a workout." *Of course, you might be dead when it's over, but you'll get a workout.*

"Can she take us both at once? We've only got three shillings between us."

"Clare can definitely take you both at once."

He elbowed his companion happily. "Head or tail?"

The other laughed. "Toss a coin, my friend."

The first bowed to Panna. "Many thanks. Oh, and you'd better hurry if you're on duty. The colonel was just about to call the roster."

She nodded her thanks.

Jamie was probably already through the door. She walked quickly through the scorched stones then remembered the mangoes. With a hitch at the pocket of her breeks, she slowed to a stroll and made her way past the mound with the three cube-shaped stones, her hands clasped in lord-like fashion behind her back. As soon as she was out of sight, she ran to the door. It was locked, and the friar was in place. Where was Jamie? She prayed he was waiting for her on the other side.

With effort, she wiggled the little man free, clutching his nose for the final pull, and reached into the hole revealed behind him, every hair on her body standing on end.

She found the latch and opened it. Slowly she pushed the door open, holding it ajar with her foot while she slipped the stone back in place.

Panna stepped cautiously into the darkness. Someone slammed the door behind her, and she leaped a foot in the air.

"It's me." Jamie slid the bar across to hold it fast.

"Oh, thank God."

"Let's go."

He led her up the circular stairs, and though her eyes had long adjusted to the night, the only thing she could see was the edge of the center wall and the outline of Jamie's coat.

They emerged in Jamie's hidden room and waited

until their eyes adjusted to the dark. Jamie dug briefly in the sacks and pulled out a pouch. He shook it. "More gold," he said, before slipping it into his pocket. "I wish I had another pistol here. I left the two I carried at Nunquam."

From the window, she could see inside the bow window containing the surveying seat one floor below. No one was there and the space was dark, but that didn't mean no one was in the library.

He led her back down the stairs, down the passageway under the library, and up to the door opening into the hallway in front of the chapel. "I'll go first. Count to twenty, then follow. If you hear a noise, throw the bar and go to Clare."

He lifted the bar, opened the door, and slipped out.

She began to count. At ten, she followed. The hallway was empty. The door to the chapel was open. She ran inside.

A hand went over her mouth, and the room brightened with a whoosh. Adderly put the torch he'd lit into its holder and lowered his pistol.

"You see, Captain? I told you if you kept quiet, I wouldn't shoot her."

Panna spun around. Two guards held Jamie's arms. The look of despair on his face broke her heart.

"What do you want?" she demanded.

"The captain, for one," he said. "He's a traitor, and I suspect you may be, too."

"You're pathetic," Panna said. "He outshines you in everything, and you can't bear it."

Adderly brought the back of his hand across her cheek. Jamie roared. "You bastard!"

"You and I will be spending quite a bit of time together, Mrs. Carnegie. You'll want to watch your tongue."

"I won't tell you anything."

"Oh, you'll speak. You will *beg* to speak. Tell me, Captain, did your sweetheart tell you that she came to me drunk and offered me her wares?"

"*Liar!*" Panna cried.

"She is a most accommodating lover. She sucked my cock like a courtesan. Would you care to watch her do it again?" He reached for his breek buttons.

Jamie ripped himself free of the guards and charged. Adderly lifted the pistol to shoot, but Panna threw herself at his arm, knocked the gun out of his grasp, and sent it flying into a corner.

One of the guards caught Jamie's arm. Jamie swung his free fist into the man's chin. The man fell backward with a groan, and his eyes flickered closed.

The other guard drew his sword.

Panna ran toward the dropped pistol, but Adderly grabbed her arm. He'd had the same idea.

Jamie unsheathed Robert Hillier's sword and met the guard's swing with a ferocious clang.

Adderly had both of Panna's arms now. He flung her out of his way. She managed to get a hold of his breeks and used her body as a deadweight to hinder him.

The guard thrust his sword, catching Jamie's side. Panna's heart jumped into her throat, but only his coat had been pierced, and the sword became tangled long enough for Jamie to ram his sword into the man's thigh. The guard fell to the ground with a choked scream.

Adderly broke free of Panna, and he and Jamie raced for the gun. Adderly reached it first, but Jamie managed to kick it under the pews. The corner made maneuvering hard, and Adderly managed to unsheathe his sword before Jamie could get his into position.

Jamie leaped backward, just missing Adderly's thrust. In an instant, they were in a furious battle, the ringing of clashing blades filling the room. Adderly swung and hit the corner of the crypt, sending a sliver of marble flying.

"Panna, go!" Jamie cried.

But she wasn't going to leave him. She ran toward the pews to find the gun, but Adderly held her off with a slash of his blade that brushed her coat.

The guard with the wounded thigh grabbed Panna's ankle, pulling her to the floor. She kicked the man's nose, and he yelped in pain but held his grip.

Jamie fought furiously, but Adderly forced him to back slowly toward the kneeler in front of the crypt.

"Jamie, behind you!"

It was too late. He fell backward, and in an instant, Adderly had his sword point on Jamie's throat.

"How good it will be to see the noose tied 'round your neck."

"Let her go," Jamie said hoarsely. "I'll confess to whatever you want."

Adderly laughed. "You'll confess and she'll watch." He pressed the blade a degree harder and a rivulet of blood ran down Jamie's neck. "Do you know where my men are heading in an hour? What's the name of the town where your little urchin lives? St. Cadoc? By morning St. Cadoc will be burnt to the ground, and every man, woman, and child will be dead. The only witness will report it to the clans."

Jamie spat and Adderly kicked him.

"My war will be on," Adderly said, the fire of lunacy in his eyes, "the war I've longed to fight. And we won't stop until the only Scots left will be on their knees, begging for mercy."

Panna struggled to free herself. She could see the pistol three pews away.

"My father will never allow it," Jamie said. "You're an embarrassment to your uniform."

Adderly's face turned beet red. "You know, I thought I wanted to see you hang, but I think I prefer to kill you myself." He gripped the hilt with both hands and lifted the sword.

"Stop it!" the earl roared as he burst through the door. "That's your brother!"

Panna froze, as did Adderly—just long enough for Jamie to roll free.

"He's your brother, Adderly!" the earl cried. "My flesh and blood! Sorcha was mother to you both!"

Aghast, Jamie looked at Adderly. Adderly chewed his lip furiously, then swung the sword with all his might.

Jamie flung himself out of the way. Adderly's swing hit the wall instead, sending the flaming torch onto a pew cushion.

Jamie sprang to his feet and charged. Adderly ran down the aisle.

The earl caught Jamie's arm and shoved him hard against the wall. Jamie's sword crashed to the floor. "He's your brother!" he said. "Stop it!"

Jamie caught his father by the shoulders and shook him. "Why wouldn't you admit it?" he said, furious. "Why did I have to wait until now to hear the words?"

Just as the earl shoved him away, a thunderous explosion filled the room.

Panna turned in the direction of the noise. Adderly held a smoking pistol.

"Oh, Jamie. No. *No!*" she cried, kicking free of the guard.

Jamie stood staring at his father, stunned.

"What have you done?" The earl gazed sorrowfully at Adderly. A small black hole had appeared in the middle of the earl's chest.

"*No!*" Adderly cried, horrified. "*No!* I meant to shoot *him!*"

"Brothers…" the earl said softly and crumpled.

The torch's flames had engulfed the pew cushion and were now beginning to lick the walls and nearby curtains.

"Get help!" Jamie shouted to Adderly.

Adderly looked at the pistol as if he didn't recognize it as his own.

"Get *help!*"

Adderly dropped the pistol and ran.

Jamie pulled Panna to her feet. "Go through the passageway."

"Not yet. Not without you."

He grabbed the wounded guard and dragged him into the hallway, away from the fire.

Panna took the earl's hand. He was breathing sporadically, his eyes wide and glassy. "I loved her."

"I know. You built this chapel for her, didn't you?"

"Aye. Adderly was born two years after Jamie." He coughed and blood drained from his mouth. "My wife had already miscarried twice. She was told she'd never be able to have any children. I had to have an heir."

"And you only took one of them?" Panna said, horrified.

"Adderly was an infant. Sorcha was dying."

Jamie returned, waving away the smoke. He grabbed the second guard and pulled him out.

"But why didn't you take Jamie too?" Panna asked.

"My wife would accept a bastard infant she could call her own. Not a two-year-old. We never told anyone."

"Adderly's not your heir. He wasn't born to a legal wife."

"I love them both, but Adderly *is* my heir. I've claimed him as my own, and no one can change it."

Jamie returned, coughing. He knelt by his father. "Come."

"Leave me. I'm dying." He clasped Jamie's forearm. "You're a good man. I'm very proud. I wish...I wish things had been different."

His eyes closed and his arm fell to his side.

Jamie clasped his father's hand and kissed it. Then he pulled Panna toward the small door by the altar. "Is this the one?"

"Yes."

He drew her into his arms and looked into her eyes. She knew what he was going to say.

"I can't go."

"I know." She began to cry. "St. Cadoc."

"I'll come. I swear it. I swear on my mother's honor I'll come to you."

"But how, Jamie? The chapel is burning."

"If the door isn't here, the passageway will be. It has to be. You must go."

"Oh, Jamie. Your father was weak, but he loved you. He told me so. And he loved your mother. He was the one who built the chapel."

Jamie's eyes widened. "He said that?"

"Yes."

Flames were pouring into the chapel now, streaming thick orange fingers up the ceiling.

"I have to go, Panna. I'm sorry."

"Wait." She grabbed his hand and pulled it into the void. Like hers, it disappeared into the darkness. "I had to be sure."

He pulled her into his arms and kissed her. Tears ran down her cheeks.

"I'll be waiting, Jamie."

"I will come."

Forty

"ARE YOU SURE YOU'RE ALL RIGHT?" MARIE HAD turned off every light but the one over the circulation desk and was watching Panna from the entry hall, tote bag in hand.

"Yes." Panna gave her friend a smile. "You worry too much about me. I like that."

Marie smiled back. "Well, when you didn't show up yesterday…"

"I know, I know. I should have called. But, man, I felt lousy."

Marie shifted. "It wasn't Charlie, was it?"

Panna shook her head. "No. Believe it or not, this time it wasn't Charlie. Charlie and I have come to a little understanding."

"You have?"

"Yep. He thinks it's time I moved on. I think he's right."

"Oh, Panna, I'm glad."

"Yeah." She nodded. "Me too."

"So, Steve?"

"Well, let's give that a little time, shall we?" It shouldn't take more than a few days for Jamie to arrive. Panna was determined to remain hopeful. Jamie had never failed to keep any promise he'd made to her.

"Are you staying long?" Marie asked. "I feel bad. This wasn't even your day to work."

"You know me. I can't stay away."

Marie hesitated. "And you're sure you're all right?"

"Positive."

"All right. See you tomorrow."

"Love you, Marie."

Marie turned, surprised, and smiled. "I love you too."

Panna waited until Marie was gone, then laid her head and her arms on the desk and stared at the tiny fox before her.

Forty-one

PANNA WAS GLAD MARIE HAD STOPPED ASKING HER why she was the first person in the library every morning and the last person to leave every evening.

Tonight she was wrestling with herself over how to let go. One would think she'd be an expert, having already let go of one husband. But somehow that didn't make it any easier.

Jamie had been like a wonderful, exciting dream. But dreams end, and life goes on. Jamie had lived—or died—and she would never know what happened. There was nothing in Google or Wikipedia that gave her any clue—nothing in any of the books in this or any library that said anything more than that the Earl of Bridgewater had died in 1706 and the earldom had passed to his son, John Bridgewater. Nowhere was one word written about James Bridgewater.

Panna gazed at the statue, wondering if she'd been foolish to have once wanted to unlock its secrets.

She would believe that Jamie had tried to come to her but wasn't able. She would believe he'd always love her. She would believe that in the end he'd find happiness, just as he'd want her to do.

She looked at the ring on her finger, the ring she would never take off. The emerald sparked in the overhead lights like the firepots on the ramparts of MacIver Castle.

With a gentle tug, she slipped it off the fourth finger of her left hand and placed it on the fourth finger of her right. It sat on top of the plain gold band Charlie had given her.

A noise in the entryway made her look up. The main doors swung open. Steve entered with a bag in his hand.

"Hey," she said, surprised.

"I hope you don't mind. I just got off my shift. Marie gave me the key."

"Heck no. I was just finishing up."

"I brought tacos from Mendoza's. Pork and beef. They're fantastic. I thought maybe you'd be hungry." He shrugged his shoulders.

"God, they smell great. I'd love some. Thanks."

He came around the circulation desk and took a seat beside her.

"I know this hasn't been a great time for you," he said, unwrapping the tacos. "I just wanted to say, if you need a friend...well, I'm here."

"Thank you, Steve. I could use a friend."

He handed her a taco and a napkin. "Say, that is quite a statue you have there. Is he some kind of hero or something?"

She put her head on his shoulder and started to cry.

Forty-two

Andrew Carnegie Library, Carnegie, Pennsylvania
Eight months later: May 1, 8:03 p.m.

PANNA CLICKED SHUT DOWN ON HER COMPUTER AND turned off the monitor. "Done!"

Marie, who had already put on her coat, said, "I am so ready to hit the bar."

"You and me both, sister, even though I am relegated to club soda."

Marie looked toward the entryway. "Do you ever miss sitting in the shadow of a really great eighteenth-century package?"

The statue had fetched nearly two hundred grand at auction. It turned out Adderly had commissioned the statue from Lorado Taft, a famous sculptor at the turn of the century, though nobody had known it. Panna hoped visitors to the Art Institute of Chicago would enjoy spending their days staring in awe at the future Earl of Bridgewater. She'd had enough of it.

"Remember, you can't always believe what you see," Panna said, smiling. "Statues lie."

"Well, let me tell you, that was a pretty big lie." Marie grabbed her umbrella. The sky was clear now, but it had been raining on and off all day. "Are you ready?"

"You go ahead. I'll lock up here. Steve's picking me up. Save us seats."

"All right. See you at PaPa J's." Marie lifted the barrier and headed out.

Panna reached for her bag—not as easy as it used to be, with her belly resembling a bowling ball—and changed from her flats to her rain boots. When she sat up, Jamie Bridgewater was standing in front of the entryway stairs, looking at her.

She felt as if she'd turned to glass. No part of her would move. She could scarcely breathe.

He took a halting step toward her, and a boundless joy billowed in her chest like the sails of great ship. He was *alive.*

In half a dozen steps, he was standing at the circulation desk, his face a canvas of gratitude and disbelief. He took the hand she held out toward him, choked back the moan of one who has evaded utter devastation, and began to cry.

So did she.

For Panna, the only thing in the universe that existed in that moment was the warmth of his hand and the realization that they were finally together.

"I tried, Panna. I tried."

"I know."

"This was my third trip. If I hadn't found you…" He couldn't finish.

"But you did. I'm here, and you're here. That's all that matters."

"Twice I found myself in Clementina's time, and twice I returned, devastated."

He looked thinner, his face more drawn, and her heart trembled. "Have you been well?"

"Well enough, if you can call a life without you even living. I left the army, was living with the rebels. The castle is gone. Collapsed."

"How did you…"

"The passageway survived. I dug through the rubble for days to find it. Undine wanted to take me to Paris, to show me a passageway there, but I would only trust this one to take me to you." He shook his head, trying to find the words. "I was so afraid I'd never find you. After the second time I returned from the future, I walked from Bowness to Newcastle and back, praying in every church along the way. I was terrified to try again, knowing it would be my last attempt. Undine said I must wait until Beltane to try."

"Beltane?"

"The first of May. 'Tis the time when the earth's magic is most potent."

"And it worked." Panna said a quiet prayer of thanks to Undine. "How is she?"

"Undine? She's well…quite well." He smiled. "She's joined the rebels, too."

"I'm not surprised. And St. Cadoc?" Panna asked, almost afraid.

"Saved," he said. "Thomas helped. The rebels were magnificent."

She squeezed his hand. "I'm so glad."

"Losing you and them in the same night would have been too much to bear. As it was, I damned myself many nights for my foolish determination to save them."

"And I praised it."

There was a knock at the front door. Steve waved. Then he saw Jamie and stopped.

Jamie had seen her eyes. "Who's that?"

"Steve." She said the word as softly as she could. She knew Jamie would receive it as a blow.

"Oh." His hand fell free.

"I have to unlock it." She wiped her eyes and, with a pounding heart, opened the barrier and came around the desk.

Jamie's face twitched, first in happiness, then in pain.

"You're...with *child*?" Considering her size, the question was clearly rhetorical.

"It's yours," she said, smiling through the tears.

He pulled her into his arms, hugging her so tightly that she could barely breathe. She clutched his neck and held him fast.

"Oh, Panna," he whispered, "what if I had missed this?"

She pulled away. "Please. Let me say something to Steve."

Jamie caught her hand. "Did he... Have you... married him?"

"No." She shook her head. "He wanted to. I told him I couldn't. We're just friends. He's been very good to me. But, Jamie, I told him about you. He knows."

She went through the entryway and Jamie straightened, hoping to present himself as well as he could to someone who meant so much to Panna.

When she opened the outside door, Steve met her eyes. "That's him, isn't it?"

"Yes."

He gazed at Jamie. "I'm Steve. Steve Trexler."

Jamie gave him a courtly bow, the deepest she had ever seen him make. "I owe you a great debt for taking care of my wife."

"It was my pleasure. Are you really from 1706?"

Jamie looked at Panna. "Aye. I am."

The look in Steve's eyes was one of amazement and disappointment. "She wasn't sure you were coming. I wasn't, either."

"He tried, Steve," Panna said. "Twice."

"It took me a good deal longer than I was expecting. I'm most grateful to have found her."

"I would have married her," Steve said, the faintest hint of challenge in his voice, "and made her happy, I think."

Jamie nodded solemnly. "I can see that you would have. Panna is lucky to have a friend like you."

Steve's jaw muscle flexed for a moment. After a long pause, he stuck out his hand. Jamie shook it.

"I'm going to just head out, okay?" Steve pointed to his car.

"Yeah, okay," Panna said. "I think we'll... I mean—"

"I'll tell Marie you're not coming."

"Thank you." She stood on her toes and kissed Steve's cheek. Then she hugged him. "Really. Thank you."

Steve paused at the door and looked back at Jamie. "You take care of her."

Jamie said, "I give you my word."

Steve nodded. He took a step then stopped. "I'm a big fan of *Highlander*. We need to talk."

Jamie bowed his head, clearly uncertain what he was agreeing to, then he and Panna were alone. Her life had stopped and started so many times, she could hardly believe her happiness. She leaned against the stair railing, smiling at him.

He extended a hand toward her stomach. "May I?"

He laid his palm on top of her wriggling flesh and shook his head, amazed. "I can't believe my good fortune."

"There's more—though I'm almost afraid to tell you."

"What is it?" He took her hand.

"Part of my reluctance comes from fear of hurting you. But the other, Jamie, comes from fear of hurting *me*."

"Don't fear, Panna. I'll never let anything hurt you again."

She bit her lip. "Your father told me he took Adderly from your mother as she lay dying. He wanted an infant whom he and his wife could raise as their own. But he left you with the priest."

Jamie rocked on his feet, hurt apparent on his face. "I came to the same conclusion myself, though I couldn't be certain. Father Giles told me what I didn't know. He had begged my father to take us both, but my father's wife wouldn't allow it."

"I'm sorry."

"Our child will never know a want of affection or constancy."

"No."

"The irony in all this is that Adderly finds himself a

bastard too," Jamie said. "And though he is my father's heir, I have seen the sorrow in his eyes. It pains me."

"He's not a bastard, Jamie—and neither are you."

A cloud of confusion rose in his eyes.

"I sold the statue of Adderly," she said. "I couldn't bear to look at it, and the sale provided the library with the funds we needed to operate. But the movers discovered a box in the base. Adderly had hidden it there when he had the statue built. When I opened it, I found your parents' signed wedding license. The earl and Sorcha were married in Gretna, a year before you were born."

"But how…"

"I don't know. Maybe your father convinced her that the marriage wasn't legal. Maybe when she heard the Bridgewater family was having money troubles, she agreed to step aside and let him marry another. Maybe she was angry at him and wouldn't acknowledge the marriage herself. We may never know the reason your mother chose not to go public with the license. All I know is I called the church in Gretna when I found it, and the record is there—has been there since the day they married. It's still there, Jamie."

He shook his head as if trying to remove cobwebs from it. Everything he'd known had just been swept away—well, almost everything.

She let go of his hand and looked him in the eye. "Jamie, *you* are the heir of the Bridgewater title. Your father's marriage to his other wife wasn't binding. It couldn't be, since he'd married Sorcha first. Even if they claimed Adderly as their son, it doesn't matter. You are the eldest son of your father's only legal marriage. You are the earl."

He sank onto a step. "My God."

She wrapped her arms around her waist, trying to keep herself from shaking. She knew she wouldn't be done until she'd told him everything.

"You can go back," she said. "You can go to the church in Gretna, find the record, and claim your rightful place."

Though if he did return, the trip back to 1706 would be his last.

The idea of a future of wealth and position swam for an instant across his face; then he looked at her, aghast. "My *rightful* place? Do you think for one moment I'd give up what I've struggled so hard for the past year to find?" He swept her into his arms. "You could offer me the kingdom of Genghis Khan and I'd turn it down. Indeed, you offer me more. You offer your hand, your bed, and your child. Could any man be richer?"

Epilogue

"IT'S *ASTONISHING*," JAMIE SAID WHEN THEY'D REACHED the top of the stairs.

"Forty-seven glorious feet."

He gave her a look and she giggled.

"C'mon," she said. "You have to admit it does have a certain...look to it."

The telescope, angled majestically skyward, stretched from the wooden floor to the domed ceiling high over their heads. The night sky was visible through a narrow opening in the dome.

"Certainly reminds a man that majesty is in the eye of the beholder. Tell me, are all library keepers like you?"

"We have a reputation of being prim—"

Jamie snorted.

"—but the truth is, it's a handy disguise. We're pretty wild about anything that goes on between the covers."

Jamie caught the gleam in her eye and laughed. His gaze returned to the telescope. "The workmanship is amazing. Could the lens really be that large? It's beyond belief."

Poor Jamie. So much had been beyond belief for him in the last three months, but nothing more than their perfect miracle of a daughter, Marie Clare. Panna found herself pretty much in awe, too.

"My friend Alan is one of the astronomers here. He watches the place on the weekends. He's lecturing to some academics downstairs. He says the place is ours for the next hour. There's something I wanted to show you."

Jamie raised a roguish brow and she poked him. "You can look at that anytime," she said.

"Not as a loyal subject in the kingdom of Marie Clare. 'Twas good of Marie to take her for the evening. I take it Marie's gotten over the surprise of me?"

"You she could handle. The fact that the little pouch of gems you brought with you meant I could quit my job—*that* she's still getting over."

"But you didn't quit."

"Old librarians don't retire. They just turn the page."

He pulled his gaze from the telescope long enough to rake her from gladiator sandals to the top of her halter dress. "You're not old. Not by a long shot."

She grinned. "Now you're getting the lingo."

A clock rang the hour.

"Ooh, it's time," she said.

"Time for what?"

"Would you like to take a look? Alan set it up for us."

Jamie broke into a grin. "I wondered when you'd ask."

He put his eye to the telescope's eyepiece. "My God!" He looked at her, amazed, and looked back. "The stars from the Butcher's Cleaver."

She bumped him with her hip. "The Big Dipper. You're a twenty-first-century man now, remember?"

"'Twill take more than a pair of jeans and"—he grabbed the fabric at his neck and looked down—"a Paolo shirt to make me a twenty-first-century man."

"Polo. It's a process." But that part of the process he was nailing. He looked like a god in those Levi's. She gazed at him fondly. "Jamie, does it bother you that after all you've been through, you're still an outlander?"

He gave her an amused look. "No one with a family could ever be an outlander."

She smiled, and he returned to the eyepiece. "To be able see the stars like this... Oh, Panna, it's beyond anything I could have dreamed. Truly."

"I'm glad. Will it matter to you," she said carefully, "that the two stars are six trillion miles apart and never get any closer?"

He'd heard the note of sadness in her voice and looked at her. "If you think for a moment that I give a whit about two lumps of burning coal and how far apart they are, you are quite mistaken. I have my own partner for the dance. And we join together *every* night."

He took her by the waist and brought his mouth to hers.

She tasted that same warm fire that lit her body every time they touched. He backed her into an empty desk and gently pressed her onto the surface.

"I am reminded of a surveying seat in Cumbria," she said, grinning.

"I don't need to survey my possessions," he said. "I own the bloody world."

Acknowledgments

This book owes its existence to so many! Karl O'Janpa, for his design excellence; David Chesanow, for his impeccable copyediting; fans and first readers, especially Susan Aitel and Karin Tillotson, for their sharp eyes and undaunted support; Marie Guerra, for her friendship and editorial prowess; Megan McKeever, for her sage and thoughtful feedback; Manuel Erviti and Donna Neiport, for revealing the hidden secrets of libraries and librarians; Meredith Mileti, Teri Coyne, Mitchell James Kaplan, Vince Rause, M. A. Jackson, and Todd De-Pastino, writers extraordinaire, for sharing the adventure with me; Mary Irwin-Scott, Kim Koslowski, Wileen Dragovan, Diane Pyle, Mary Nell Cummings, Dawn Kosanovich, Karen Schade, Valli Ellis, and Judy Hulick for reviving me with lunch or a drink or a text whenever I most needed it; Andrew Carnegie, for changing the world with his 2,509 gifts and reminding us that the man who dies rich dies disgraced; the folks at Allegheny Observatory, for a fascinating look at stargazing. I am in debt to the Andrew Carnegie Library in Carnegie, Pennsylvania, for possessing enough magical details to inspire this story and to the amazing Morgan Library and Museum in New York for giving me a pretty darned good idea what the library of a wealthy, book-obsessed man might look like. Claudia, even a book wouldn't be enough to dedicate to you. It would have to be a library or a planet or something equally epic. Thank you for always pulling me through. Cameron, Wyatt, Jean, and Lester, you fill my days with joy and laughter.

About the Author

Gwyn Cready is a writer of contemporary, Scottish, and time travel romance. She's been called "the master of time travel romance" and is the winner of the RITA Award, the most prestigious award given in romance writing. She has been profiled in *Real Simple* and *USA Today*, among others. Before becoming a novelist, she spent twenty-five years in brand management. She has two grown children and lives with her husband on a hill overlooking the magical kingdom of Pittsburgh.